# THE POPE OF
## Palm Beach

# TIM DORSEY

# THE POPE OF Palm Beach

*wm*

WILLIAM MORROW

*An Imprint of* HarperCollins*Publishers*

THE POPE OF PALM BEACH. Copyright © 2018 by Tim Dorsey. All rights reserved. Printed in the United States of America. No part of this book may be used or reproduced in any manner whatsoever without written permission except in the case of brief quotations embodied in critical articles and reviews. For information, address HarperCollins Publishers, 195 Broadway, New York, NY 10007.

HarperCollins books may be purchased for educational, business, or sales promotional use. For information, please email the Special Markets Department at SPsales@harpercollins.com.

FIRST EDITION

*Map by Virginia Norey*

Library of Congress Cataloging-in-Publication Data

Names: Dorsey, Tim, author.
Title: The pope of Palm Beach : a novel / Tim Dorsey.
Description: First edition. | New York, NY : William Morrow, [2018]
Identifiers: LCCN 2017031747| ISBN 9780062429254 (hardback) | ISBN
    9780062429261 (tp) | ISBN 9780062791733 (lp) | ISBN 9780062429278 (el)
Subjects: LCSH: Storms, Serge (Fictitious character)--Fiction. |
  Florida--Fiction. | BISAC: FICTION / Humorous. | FICTION / General. |
  GSAFD: Humorous fiction.
Classification: LCC PS3554.O719 P67 2018 | DDC 813/.54--dc23 LC record
available at https://lccn.loc.gov/2017031747

ISBN 978-0-06-242925-4 (Hardcover)
ISBN 978-0-06-285116-1 (BAM Signed Edition)

18  19  20  21  22   LSC   10  9  8  7  6  5  4  3  2  1

*For Rusty and Cynthia Dades*

Serge's Hometown Treasure Map

Loxahatchee River
(10 miles)

Northlake Blvd

Lake Park

U.S. Highway 1

Park Ave

Ocean Dr

A1A

Silver Beach Rd

Singer
Island

Grounding
of the
Amaryllis

Phil Foster
Park

Riviera Beach

Blue Heron Blvd

Lake Dr

Darby's
Place

The Pump
House

Broadway

Peanut Island

N

Port of
Palm Beach

Palm Beach

# THE POPE OF
## Palm Beach

# Prologue

The sun was going down behind the Big Burger when the alligator came flying in the drive-through window.

It scampered past a milkshake machine and scattered teenagers working the french-fry baskets. The manager hung his head. "Not again."

The driver of a fourteen-year-old Honda Civic sped away from the restaurant and traveled south on U.S. Highway 1. He wasn't mad at Big Burger. In fact he had never even eaten there, although now he wanted to someday. It was just another aimless afternoon that started when he spotted the three-foot gator sunning itself next to a golf course and threw a surf-casting net over it without understanding his motivation. The driver had previously used the net for fishing, but he recently began carrying it around in his car at other times for the broader possibilities. After the golf course, the driver stopped at a convenience store and stared at Slim Jims for a while before buying gum. He got back in the car with the captive reptile on the passenger seat and saw the Big Burger across the highway. And he thought to himself, *Sure, why not?*

Thus continued the Florida epoch of fuck-it lifestyle decisions.

The story of the alligator would make news across the country and overseas, but in Florida it wouldn't even top the wildlife report because a body had just turned up in a nearby motel room with two live spider monkeys dancing on it. The chattering alerted police.

The Honda continued south, past a man on a riding lawn mower twirling Philippine fighting sticks, then a strip club called the Church of the New Burning Bush that would soon lose its tax-exempt status.

Back at Big Burger, customers finished clearing out of the dining area with free food and apologies. Employees loitered in the parking lot. A small gator with its mouth taped shut emerged under the arm of a state game official. Police got the Honda's license off the surveillance tape, and two officers headed south with discussions of sports and alimony.

A sea-green Chevy Nova drove by the fast-food joint, stereo on the Delfonics.

"*...Ready or not, here I come...*"

"Serge." Coleman pointed out the passenger window. "What's all the craziness at Big Burger?"

Serge glanced over. "Gator. Next question?"

Coleman cracked open a sweaty Schlitz, forgetting the already open one between his legs. "Where are we going again?"

"The next stop on our literary pilgrimage of Florida."

"Oh right," said Coleman. "Books. Reading. *Ewwww.*"

*Flick.*

"Ouch, you flicked my ear again!"

"Cultural reinforcement," said Serge. "Everyone comes to Florida touring beaches and bars, but few realize the rich literary heritage all around that people just drive right by every day. Their awareness begins and ends with Hemingway."

"Sloppy Joe's Bar!" said Coleman.

*Flick.*

"Stop!"

"It drives me batty that our most famous author won the Nobel Prize, yet we've reduced him to a logo on a line of tank tops, shot glasses and refrigerator magnets. What profound quote would Papa utter if he suddenly came back to life and saw what was going on?"

"Uh . . ." Coleman strained in thought. "'These new phones are the shit!'"

*Flick.*

The Nova rolled up to a red light between a police car and a lawn mower. Coleman lowered his joint below window level. "So what's our next stop on this reading trip of yours?"

Serge checked his watch. "We'll have to hurry if we're going to make it to the library on time . . ."

C ars streamed into the parking lot from all directions. The lighted information sign in front of the Palm Beach Gardens Library: BOOK SIGNING 7 P.M.

A green Nova found a spot near the back of the lot, and Serge and Coleman joined the rest of the patrons heading for the doors.

Inside the community room, a grid of chairs filled fast. A long table stood along the back wall with a punch bowl and bags of Keebler cookies that produced low-range joy.

When the time came, the library's director made the intro-duction, and the audience broke into the kind of applause you'd hear at a ribbon cutting for a minor historical marker.

The author took up a position behind the podium, greeted the crowd with a smile and cleared his throat. He opened a hardcover book and began reading:

CHAPTER ONE

My day had been exceedingly normal—which extended the streak to 9,632 normal days in a row—when the shotgun blast sent my life in an entirely new direction.

That's what shotgun blasts do quite well.

Don't ask me who I am right now, or if I'm dead. Even I don't have the answer to that last one yet.

It was 1989, just after midnight, down by the docks at the port. There was no moon, only the red and green running lights of vessels big and small navigating the narrow channels around Peanut Island.

I remember riding my bike down there as a kid and watching the boats. Some came in from the ocean through the jetties of the Lake Worth Inlet, others up the Intracoastal, still more from the canals behind homes on Singer Island. It had always been a busy waterway, even at night.

These were the days long before Homeland Security or DEA radar aircraft, and the Port of Palm Beach was still more than a bit lawless. Later some officials would go to jail for taking bribes.

I heard a small Evinrude outboard approaching the docks, but saw no beacons. The growl of the motor grew louder. There was a yellow light—one of those lamps over the fuel pumps at the end of the soggy wooden pier—and it glinted off the barrel of a twelve-gauge.

A shout: "Too late! Run!"

*Blam!*

The audience at the library formed a signing line that wrapped around the room. Books cradled in arms, anticipation.

One by one they got their autographs.

*"You're the greatest."*

*"Love the writing style."*

*"I'm you're number one fan."*

*"Remember the time you tied a guy to the bridge in the Keys?"*

The author looked up. "That was actually Hiaasen."

*"I'm so embarrassed."*

"Don't worry about it." The author handed the book back, and the reader ran away.

The event wound down. The lights went off, doors were locked, and the last of the library staff drove out of the deserted parking lot.

Hours later, a lone vehicle rolled quietly up to the curb by the front door. Guilty fingers reached from the driver's window. They grabbed the handle of the library's night deposit box, seeking to return a shopping bag of overdue titles under cloak of night.

The driver fed volumes through the slot two and three at a time, until his shopping bag was half-empty. Then the door on the box wouldn't budge. He rattled the handle again and again.

"Damn, it's full. Why don't they empty these things?" He drove off like a thief.

The library was dark and lifeless again, a syrupy red pool of blood spreading out from under the dripping book-deposit box.

# PART
## One

# Chapter 1

SEPTEMBER 5, 1965

A lifeguard in short blue swim trunks slouched atop an old wooden stand. A silver whistle hung from his lips as he scanned the shore of the Atlantic Ocean. There was a teeming, splashing crowd in the water. Par for Labor Day weekend.

The Chamber of Commerce was relieved. Hurricane Betsy had threatened to ruin the holiday, but now the Miami tracking station plotted it swirling well out to sea north of the Bahamas and, as they say, the coast was clear. It was one of the beaches that in earlier times always flew a storm-advisory flag, and today's color was white. Let the money roll in.

Beach umbrellas covered the sand like toadstools, and the breeze carried tinny-sounding music from dozens of newfangled radios called transistor.

"... *What's new pussycat? Whoa-ooo-whoa-ooo-whoa-ooo* ..."

"... *Hang on Sloopy! Sloopy, hang on!* ..."

"... *Wooly bully!* ..."

The lifeguard suddenly stood in alarm and blew his whistle

three sharp times, aiming a stern arm. A group of children involved in horseplay knocked it off. This was back when authority meant something, and lifeguards got laid a little more. He sat back down in a suave slouch.

Behind the lifeguard and the sand was Ocean Avenue. *Avenue*. Barely a street. A row of boxy cars sat in angled spaces at steel parking meters. A Rambler, a Skylark, a Fairlane, a Bel Air, a different Rambler. Across the road stood a modest line of short, flat-roofed buildings. One named the Beach Shop had a coin-operated scale out front that told your fortune, another was simply called Sundries, the next sold hot dogs that people ate outside on the kind of concrete benches and tables supplied by a company that also sold birdbaths. Advertising signs for Coca-Cola, Coppertone, the *Palm Beach Post*. A burnt-red panel truck for Wise potato chips arrived at the curb. Some of the people eating hot dogs wore dresses and dress shirts.

The adults didn't pay it much attention, but there was a small item along the avenue that fascinated all the kids. Rising up from one of the flat roofs was a tall pole and a contraption at the top consisting of three spinning, rounded metal cups. In meteorologic terms, an anemometer. Currently the sun sparkled off the cups as they rotated in lazy circles.

A Mercury Montclair pulled up to a parking meter. The doors opened. Little Serge pointed skyward. "What's that?"

"A wind thing," said his mother.

"What's it do?"

"Measures wind."

"Why?"

"People want to know."

"Why?"

"Just keep up."

"Why do potato chips come in trucks?"

"I don't know."

"They're not heavy."

"Will you keep up?"

Little Serge took off sprinting.

"Slow down! Come back here!"

Soon the family settled onto the beach with blankets and an umbrella. Little Serge's face appeared giant and distorted in the device he was holding to his eye.

His mother looked down. "Where'd you get that big magnifying glass?"

"From the house."

"Are you going through all our drawers again?"

"Not now."

It was a small, middle-class town on the north side of West Palm called Riviera Beach. Residents reached the water by crossing a short drawbridge to Singer Island, named after a sewing machine heir. The shoreline ran south from the public beach, past the regal Colonnades Hotel, where the stars hid out in the working-class surroundings. Bob Hope, Jackie Gleason, the Stones. Anyone could stroll through the hotel, and most wouldn't notice an unassuming local billionaire named John D. MacArthur, who conducted business daily from a table in the coffee shop.

Finally the island came to an abrupt halt at the jetty. The jetty marked the edge of the Lake Worth Inlet and the entrance to the port. Just a golf-ball shot across the inlet, but an economic galaxy away, was another jetty guarding the north end of Palm Beach. The Breakers, the Kennedys, Worth Avenue, Gucci, Rolls-Royce, Swiss bank accounts.

They were always dredging the narrow inlet between the two islands because of the deep-drafting cargo ships making their way into the Port of Palm Beach. This required a rusty sand-transfer station. But there was no way that eyesore would be placed anywhere near all that old money on Palm Beach. So back on Singer Island, just behind the jetty, stood a giant, two-story-tall metal drum with a crane-arm extending out over the water. It didn't have an official name. But the surfers called it the Pump House.

The surfers.

What a pain. At least to the establishment. The Pump House was the favorite word-of-mouth spot to catch waves along Florida's east coast, and the water was always full of boards. Which also meant surfing riffraff illegally climbing the Pump House's crane-arm to dive into the water. Or surfing the inlet through heavy ship traffic. Or paddling all the way across to make landfall behind a Palm Beach mansion, triggering a law enforcement response like the invasion of Normandy.

But this day nobody was on the crane-arm because a police car was parked nearby to prevent nonsense. Then the cop left and the crane filled up again with kids. Jump, jump, *splash, splash*. The jumping stopped. Everyone silently turned from the Pump House to gaze out at the end of the jetty.

Shafts of light from heaven appeared—actually just a cloud break, but there might as well have been angel harps. A faded yellow board turned around, and a leathery man stood up. The next wave lifted him leaning forward, focused and fearless, toward the beach.

The kids along the beach barely blinked as the surfer executed cut after cut, each swish shudderingly close to the waves crashing and spraying off the jetty's jagged boulders that nobody else dared near. But that's what it took for the maximum ride and, unlike the youth watching from shore, the veteran surfer had the instincts of years in these waves that averted peril. Then he hung ten—that would be toes—off the front of the wooden longboard before the waves tamed near the beach and he gently eased up into the sand.

The kids gathered around as the surfer nonchalantly picked up his board, a coveted Yater Spoon. They peppered him with questions, praise. *"That was incredible." "You're the greatest." "Can you teach me your cutback?" "Should I ride goofy foot?"*

The surfer stopped and held court. He always had time for the kids. His skin was bronzed and prematurely aged, but his eyes were clear and hazelnut. He wasn't muscular, because nobody worked out with weights back then, though his stomach was marble. They said he almost looked like Sandy Koufax, but not quite. On his left shoulder, a tattoo of an anchor and a ribbon indicated service on the USS *Iowa*. Gunner's mate, Pacific theater, shelling the Japanese on the Eniwetok Atoll. He never talked about the war. The vintage of the tattoo meant he was now long in the tooth as surfers go, almost forty-three. To the kids, that was practically, well, dead. If the man had been any other adult, he would have been irrelevant. But this guy was the legend.

Word of his conquests leaked down into every local schoolyard, and the teens now surrounding him had been hearing the stories long before picking up their first board.

The surfer had been riding this coast since he was their age, often the only one in the water. And that was cool. The wartime experience had turned him into a spiritualist and a reader. Hermann Hesse, Aldous Huxley, *The Dharma Bums*. He developed a worldview that people complained too much.

*"Are you going back out?"* asked one kid.

*"What wax do you use?"*

*"What's the tattoo mean?"*

"Nothing important," said the surfer. "And don't you go getting one."

Then he noticed a smaller boy behind the others, not talking, arms clutched into himself. Alone in the crowd.

"You back there," said the surfer. "What's your name?"

"Me?" Quickly looking behind himself to find nobody. "Uh, Kenny."

"Kenny, how's your surfing?"

"Getting better."

The bigger boys began laughing, and they weren't laughing *with* him.

"Kenny," said the surfer, "how 'bout you and me go out and ride the next one together?"

The laughter stopped.

"Really?" said Kenny.

"Sure, come on."

It was another of the surfer's life philosophies: always look for those not being included, and include them.

The gang on the beach quieted again as the asymmetrical pair began paddling back out along the jetty.

*"Wow, Kenny gets to ride the Pump House with the legend."*

*"How cool is that?"*

*"Someday I want to be just like the Pope."*

Most of the kids didn't know the surfer's first name, which was Darby. But his last name really was Pope. They all simply called him by his nickname.

The Pope of Palm Beach.

A black Dodge Dart left the Pump House and headed north on Singer Island. The car's roof rack held two surfboards. The Pope approached the public swimming area, then hung a left onto Beach Court, the shortcut back to the Blue Heron Bridge and the mainland.

A police car sat on the shoulder near a stop sign, watching for kids patching out. "Hey, Darby," the officer called out his open window. "How's it going?"

"Same old. How's the family, Frank?"

"Can't complain. By the way, thanks for coming to talk to my kid's class. You made my son a hero . . ."

Beach Court was a block over from the shore and the shops. It had its own short row of buildings—the south end anchored by the uncommonly tall Sands Hotel, formerly the Beaumont, before they added the fourth story. It was the singular 1940s hold-over that clashed with all the new low-slung, ranch-style roadside motels popping up along A1A and U.S. 1 with the now-required swimming pools that every station wagon full of tykes demanded.

Attached to the hotel was a series of connected single-floor businesses, some retail, some office, always changing depending on the leaseholder. Like the people inside the address at 2441.

The enterprise had started in the fifties as a fancy international magazine headquartered in Manhattan. That changed in the 1960s. Whether it was the rent or a need for new scenery, they decided to up and move to Florida because—hey, they were a magazine, they could plant their stakes anywhere—and of all places they ended up here.

Inside, keys pounded a manual Underwood typewriter. Even though it was the holiday weekend, there was always a deadline. A young editor yanked a page from the roller and fed another. The editor was starting at the bottom but had ambition. He would reach fame in twenty years, but right now it was just another Sunday, and he had the office to himself. The perfect time to finish polishing one of his first short stories and see his own name in print between the magazine's covers.

He took a break to fetch notes from his car. A Dodge Dart spotted him and rolled into the parking lot.

"Charles!" yelled the Pope, a ruddy arm hanging out the driver's window to shake hands.

"Hey, Darby."

"What are you doing here today?"

"Writing. It's quiet," said the editor. "I'd ask what you're doing, but I already know."

Darby got out, and they shook hands again, redundantly. The Pope knew everyone in town. Made it a point.

Everyone.

"Oh, I got that book you wanted." The editor quickly ran inside and returned with the title.

"Thanks. I'll get it back to you."

"No rush. But I know it'll only be a couple days. You read like crazy."

"You mean for a surfer?"

"You know what I mean. Still welding at the port?"

"Going on fifteen years. Hard habit."

The two friends stopped and stared east at the water a block away.

"Charles, how come you never go to the beach?"

"I have to write . . ."


. . . A block east on the public beach, a skinny little boy lay on his stomach in the sand, digging industriously. He was bent over at the waist ninety degrees, and the top half of his body hung straight down into the hole. Handfuls of sand flew into the air and onto his mother's legs.

She lowered her copy of *Look* magazine. "Serge! What on earth are you doing?"

"Digging." Serge pulled himself up out of the hole and stared at the ocean again, gauging the incline to the shore. Then back down he went, clawing some more until he hit the water table, and it filled the bottom of his tiny pit. Theory confirmed. Check that off the list. He picked up a sand flea and examined it with his magnifying glass, counting legs.

A short distance up the beach, a plumper child about the same age ran in giddy circles until he got dizzy and fell facedown. He would eventually pick up the nickname "Coleman," for which he'd ever be known, but right now his parents still called him Seymour.

"Seymour, what are you doing?" asked his mother.

Seymour stood and took off along the shoreline. Some stuff had washed up on the beach. They looked like funny little balloons. Clear and thin with a tint of blue. Seymour gleefully giggled as he ran around popping them all with his bare feet . . .

. . . Little Serge looked up from his magnifying glass when the lifeguard blew his whistle three long times.

"Mommy, why is that boy screaming like that?"

"Blessed Mary!" She sat up. "Why *is* he screaming like that? It's like he's being murdered!"

Up the beach, lifeguards from three different stands converged on the hysterical crying from a child who had just stomped on a whole school of man o' wars. Seymour had complicated matters by flopping around and rolling in the stinging tentacles.

"Somebody grab him!"

"I'm trying to, but he's got them all over."

"Be an adult!"

"Shit. Ouch." The lifeguard grabbed a nearby beach blanket for insulation.

"Hey!" yelled a sixty-eight-year-old retiree from Utica. "I was lying on that!"

"Sorry, emergency," said the lifeguard. "City will reimburse."

"What's going on?"

"Portuguese man o' war."

"The Portuguese? Jesus!"

The rescuers eventually applied soothing first-aid balms, and Seymour's cries dissipated into sobs.

One of the lifeguards capped a tube of ointment and turned to a colleague. "Put up the jellyfish warning signs."

"Man o' wars technically aren't jellyfish, but colonies of zooids."

"What's wrong with you? Just put up the signs already!"

A shrug. A stick was hammered into the sand.

Tranquillity returned.

Back up the shoreline, Little Serge sat on the front of a beach blanket, eating Cheetos and examining his orange fingerprints with the magnifying glass. He looked at the water's edge and noticed something. He put the glass down and reached into his mother's beach bag, pulling out a children's book of sea creatures. It had big pictures and few words. He flipped pages—hermit crabs, mollusks, fire coral—until he finally came to a picture he remembered. He looked up again at the shore and nodded to himself. He put the book away.

Little Serge walked down to the surf and got on his knees. The magnifying glass scanned over his find. From his children's book, he knew not to touch. He found a washed-up stick and slid it under the discovery.

"Mom!" he yelled, running back to his family's blankets and umbrella.

She lowered her magazine. "Serge, what do you have dangling from that stick?"

"It's a Portuguese man o' war . . . Oops."

It fell off the stick and onto her feet. Her head snapped up straight with wide eyes.

# Chapter 2

The noon sun hung high and unfettered over the Florida Keys. Two navy jets out of the air station on Boca Chica roared low over the Gulf Stream. Fly fishermen silently cast lures on the backwood flats. A seafoam-green 1969 Chevy Nova raced east.

The Overseas Highway was a straight, two-lane shot through the Saddlebunch Keys. A thin ribbon of land surrounded by a canvas of emerald and turquoise water, so shallow and intoxicating in spots that it made travelers want to stop and walk out there, but they kept going.

*Screech* . . .

. . . Serge and Coleman stood thigh-deep far out in the water, nothing around, looking back at their tiny Chevy coupe parked on the side of the highway. The body of water was ringed by mangroves and dotted with little saplings reaching up for life.

Serge wore a tarpon hat and nodded from behind polarized sunglasses. "Dig it."

Coleman raised a can of beer. "Whatever happened to your literary tour of Florida?"

"This is it." Serge studied a motionless great blue heron, which in turn studied the shallows before firing its long, sharp beak down into the water like a spear and coming up with a fish.

Coleman stuck the empty can in a fanny pack and pulled out another. "What's this got to do with books?"

"Florida is all about water, and the authors knew this. Think about it: *River of Grass, Cross Creek, Islands in the Stream*—the last actually refers to the Bahamas, but the titular Gulf *Stream* is right over there."

"Here's what *I* know." Burp. "Your reading tour blows serious chunks."

"Coming from you, that means it's the *perfect* tour," said Serge. "The Keys have ignited several literary flash points over the years, and all the greats saw this water. That's why the tour started in Key West, with perfunctory stops for Hemingway and Tennessee Williams. But that's low-hanging fruit I've seen a million times, which is why we just sped by taking photos. So now we're drilling deeper into the 1970s movement of Harrison, McGuane, Thompson, and artists in different media like the painter Chatham, not to mention Jimmy Buffett, the fierce workaholic who marketed his unemployed-beach-bum persona into the economic might of a small nation. And it all started right around here, where he and the others reverently fished off skiffs as if this were a cathedral."

"Even more *boring* . . ."

"It will become exceptionally *non*boring this afternoon. An unavoidable errand to correct a moral misunderstanding." Serge sighed. "Another working vacation."

"Let's jump to that part now."

"Coleman, can't you just stand still in a location of visual bliss and drink in the serenity? Please, join me." Serge clasped his hands in front of his stomach and stared across the rippling water. "That's enough serenity." He took off running and splashing.

"Wait for me!"

The green Nova cruised onto Sugarloaf Key and made a right turn near Mile Marker 17. Serge placed a hand on his buddy's shoulder. "Lucky for you, this next literary stop comes with a theme park ride to penetrate the marijuana tar pit of your brain-pan."

"Really? What kind of ride?"

"A natural one, so it's also free."

The Chevy reached the southern end of the island, where Sugarloaf Boulevard meets old State Road 4A. To the left, a permanent barricade blocking off an abandoned stretch of the road.

Coleman gestured with the last beer in the six-pack. "What's the deal with all the no-parking signs? There's like a hundred of 'em with nothing else around."

"That had me curious, too," said Serge, parking a quarter mile away with an inexplicable number of other vehicles in the middle of the boondocks. "The first time I came here, I was the only person seeking it out for my own particular reasons. Little did I know that many young locals regularly visit the same location with completely different intentions."

They walked back to the corner and climbed around the barricade. Coleman stumbled and caught his balance. "So we're trespassing?"

"One would think, but no," said Serge. "The barricade is to stop vehicle traffic, but it's still a public road as far as pedestrians go. And believe it or not, this used to be U.S. 1 until they relocated the section a couple miles north."

They hiked down the lonely, bright gravel road. Silence except for rocks under their shoes. The air was still from overhanging branches blocking the sea breeze. Coleman wiped his forehead. "It's damn hot."

Serge pulled down the flap of his tarpon hat to cover his neck. "There's a great place to cool off up ahead."

"But you still haven't explained any of this, and my eyes are stinging."

Serge swept a hand to the left. "Decades ago, people in boats on Upper Sugarloaf Sound were forced to navigate all the way around the island to get to the ocean, so they quarried a channel through the limestone to save time. And up ahead is the bridge over it."

"I'm starting to hear something," said Coleman. "Voices."

"The locals," said Serge. "The pass under the bridge has these flat limestone shelves along the edge of the water, creating the perfect spot to sun yourself, picnic, party or just hang out. And since there are no homes around, and the road is closed, it's the perfect out-of-the-way place not to be hassled. The police know all about this and look the other way because it lets the kids blow off steam away from the rich residents and free-spending tourists."

Voices grew louder. The western end of the small span came into view.

"Does this place have a name?" asked Coleman.

Serge pointed at a sign.

Coleman read it: "No jumping from bridge."

"So the locals call it the Jumping Bridge."

Up ahead, two teens climbed onto the concrete railing.

Down below: *"Jump! Jump! Jump! . . ."*

They jumped, knifing into the deep, cool water with a pair of splashes. Heads bobbed to the surface. "Did you get it?"

Someone on a limestone shelf raised a cell phone and nodded.

The next youth approached the railing. *"Jump! Jump! Jump! . . ."* Splash. And so on.

"This place totally rocks!" said Coleman.

"I knew you'd come around."

"Absolutely!" He stuck his head inside his T-shirt to light a joint. "No cops to mess with you for weed!"

"Coleman, there's more to it." Serge spun around. "All the nature . . ."

*"Jump! Jump! Jump! . . ."*

Coleman took a long hit. "And you just tripped over this place?"

*"Jump! Jump! Jump! . . ."*

"A coincidence of the cosmos," said Serge. "I had no idea any of this was going on out here. My whole reason for seeking this spot—"

*"Will you jump already! . . ."*

Serge and Coleman stopped talking. They realized they had reached the crest of the bridge. A line of kids waited impatiently behind them.

"Serge, I think they're yelling at us." Toke, toke, toke. "They want us to jump."

Serge leaned over the railing and stuck two fingers in his mouth for a shrill whistle. "Everyone, listen up! May I have your attention!" He spread his arms down toward the crowds on the limestone lounge areas. "The celebrated jumping will soon resume, but first, some news that's sure to jazz up your day! In 1973, a young author named Thomas McGuane published a groundbreaking novel and one of the finest books ever on the Florida Keys called *92 in the Shade.* He knew all about this place you have here long before it was a thing. And when they made the movie in 1975, he had them shoot a crucial scene here where Peter Fonda, playing the lead role of Thomas Skelton, and Margot Kidder, as Miranda, catch fish off this bridge. Isn't that swell?"

*"Boring! . . . Jump! Jump! Jump! . . ."*

"Hey, you idiots!" yelled Coleman, joint clenched in his teeth. "You need to listen to this man! He's like really smart and shit like that! . . . *Whoa! Aaauuu! . . .*"

Serge lunged to snatch the back of Coleman's shirt but just came up with a handful of air. His friend was already over the side.

Coleman executed one of those dives that gets a zero from the judges, like someone accidentally falling backward out a window. All arms and legs flailing before a belly flop.

He popped to the surface with the buoyancy of beer fat. "I'm good." Then dog-paddled to a limestone shelf, where teens hoisted him out of the water.

*"Dude, that was insane! Have a beer!"*

"Thanks," said Coleman.

*"Man, I've never seen a belly that red! Have another beer!"*

"Righteous."

Someone held up a cell phone. *"You're already on the Internet! You're getting hits! Have a joint . . ."*

Serge scrambled down the embankment. "Good Lord! Are you okay?"

"I never want to leave this place!"

"Unfortunately we have that other thing I need to tend to."

*"Let him stay! . . ." "Let him jump again! . . ."*

"Guys, he's in jumping retirement," said Serge. "Reflect fondly on all he's given you."

Coleman drained the longneck Bud in his left hand, then the one in his right. "I'm jumping again!"

*"Hooray!"*

Everyone else was able to walk up the embankment, but Coleman needed the help of his hands and knees.

*"Jump! Jump! Jump! . . ."*

Coleman stuck an index finger in the air to gauge the wind. "A cannonball!" He climbed up on the railing but tripped, and it was another deranged cartwheel before an even worse belly flop.

They pulled him out. *"Here are your beers."*

"Right!" Guzzle, guzzle, guzzle. "Jumping again!"

*"You da man! . . ."*

Dive after dive. Bigger splashes, larger red marks covering his body, until finally . . . well, let's put it this way: If you're a fan of classic rock, imagine Joe Cocker in the Olympics going off the ten-meter platform.

"Coleman! Coleman! Can you hear me?"

"Is that you, Serge? What happened?"

"Professional exhaustion. We have to get you back to the car." He grabbed his pal under the pits. "Hey, kids, can you give me a hand with your hero?"

## SEPTEMBER 7, 1965

Three rounded metal cups spun like a propeller above a roof on Ocean Avenue. The beach was empty and so were all the spaces at the parking meters. The sky churned purple-gray.

A steel pole stood out on the sand. The storm-advisory pole. Today it flew two flags. Both red squares with smaller black squares in the middle.

Hurricane warning.

A lone city truck with a revolving amber light rolled slowly down the street. A worker got out and took down the flags before they ripped apart.

Everyone had been so busy with Labor Day that they never saw it coming. And why would they? Because nobody had ever seen a storm-tracking chart like this one.

Hurricane Betsy had indeed been chugging straight out to sea in a steady northeast direction until the storm was so far away that it was but a memory. Then, of all things, it simply stopped. Didn't even make a U-turn, just went in reverse, backtracking its course and taking dead aim at South Florida.

Crazy time.

All Floridians knew the drill. Batteries, water, food, candles, radios, plywood. But there had always been a few days' notice instead of a few hours. Store shelves emptied in a frenzy. Some of the plywood went up, but the rest—to hell with it. Stuff was already going airborne. An empty inflatable backyard pool took to the sky like a flying saucer. Anything else left outside was written off. Time to shelter in place and roll the dice.

Darkness fell, but it wasn't night. Little Serge's grandfather remained outside, lugging a sheet of plywood.

"Dad!" Little Serge's mom yelled out the front door. "Will you get in here!"

"Just a minute."

"No! Look what's going on out there!"

He looked. So did Little Serge, standing on his tiptoes at the window. He'd been told not to go near the windows, but he was Little Serge.

Earlier in the day, his grandfather had pulled the floor mats out of their car and was hosing them off when the news broke. The mats had been forgotten. Now they fluttered on the front lawn before lifting off like Arabian carpets and sailing toward the horizon until the two little dots disappeared.

"Wowwwwww!" said Serge.

His grandfather ran inside and slammed the door.

"Where's Little Serge?" shouted his mother. "Serge! Get away from that window! What did I tell you?"

He scampered back to his designated spot in the hallway, the central-most location in the house.

Hunkering began.

It was the era of feckless optimism. Seat belts were optional, people smoked everywhere, and television hailed the miracle of DDT. Also, no evacuation-route signs. Hurricanes were just something you rode out. The hallway was tight quarters for the extended family: the little boy, parents and grandparents.

One thing his folks were good at was not letting Serge worry. They got out the board games. "Little Serge, what do you want to play? Trouble? Chinese checkers? How about Candy Land? Candy Land's your favorite."

"Monopoly," said the child, sitting with a metal drum of Charles Chips in his lap that was almost as big as he was.

"Really? Why would you rather play Monopoly than Candy Land?"

"Money!"

Serge rolled the dice and moved his tiny metal race car onto Baltic Avenue. "I want to buy a house."

They intentionally let Serge win.

"Look at all my money!"

Serge stuffed his mouth with potato chips. He stopped and looked around. Nobody else was talking. All paying attention to a transistor radio and the storm update from WJNO. Serge slowly packed more chips into his mouth. Something was wrong. They never let him eat so many potato chips. Then he looked toward his bedroom door. They weren't making him go to sleep. *Hurricanes are cool!*

Suddenly the power went out.

"What's going on?" asked the boy.

"Nothing."

They lit candles. With the electricity gone, the wind outside howled even louder. Rain hammered the roof and small debris pelted the windows. One of the panes shattered.

"What was that?" asked the boy.

"Nothing."

Little Serge watched his dad and grandfather drag mattresses out of the bedrooms.

"What are they doing?"

"Hey!" said his mom. "Let's get out the Ouija board!"

His family was devoutly Catholic, but some loophole let them believe in the power of the Ouija. Serge and his mother used fingertips to move the plastic triangle and contact late uncle Homer, who reported back that everything was A-OK.

*Smash!*

A tree broke loose and hit the edge of the roof. His dad got up again.

Potato chips filled a mouth. "What's going on now?"

"Just some noise."

And so on into the wee hours, radio reports, melting candles, yawns.

Serge finished constructing a glorious stomachache. His young mind processed all the new info: nonstop games, bottomless chips, no bedtime, a bunch of stuff breaking outside, talking to dead relatives. This was the best day of his entire life.

"Mom, when can we have another hurricane?"

# *Chapter 3*

**P**redawn workers in cherry-pickers repaired downed power lines, and city trucks cleared the roads of uprooted palms.

Hurricane Betsy made official landfall in the early hours of the eighth before departing into the Gulf of Mexico. Its strength and surprise attack registered it as the first Atlantic storm to top a billion dollars in damage. That was 1965 dollars.

A gloomy morning saw residents circling their homes to assess the havoc. Then they got busy with rakes and garbage cans.

Others went down to the beach. It was standard procedure after a hurricane. Storms tended to change things. Chunks of shore might be missing. Other chunks were suddenly there. Hotel signs ended up on top of other hotels. You never knew.

But the silent crowd that had lined up on the shore of Singer Island never expected this. They all just stared upward in open-mouthed awe.

During the early days of September, a 441-foot Greek freighter called the *Amaryllis* had sailed from Manchester, England, bound for Baton Rouge. During the height of the storm, the ship found itself literally fighting for its life down the coast of Florida. But safe harbor was just ahead. The crew reset their course for the Port of Palm Beach. Which meant reaching the Lake Worth Inlet and entering the jetties by the Pump House. The crew began breathing easier. Only a mile to go.

A mile too far.

If one ever needed to comprehend the power of a hurricane, the only requirement was to see how insanely far into the beach Betsy had driven the bow of the massive cargo ship. Which is what all the residents were now doing, loitering behind the old Rutledge Motel, staring up at this ten-story metal monstrosity that had freakishly altered their skyline.

And while they were paralyzed in amazement, the weirdness intensified. They heard strange twanging sounds. Coming from the ship.

"Look!" Someone in the crowd pointed up at the deck.

Someone from the deck waved back. Then someone else, and another, until the whole railing was full of sailors and smiles. The crew was still on board. And playing Greek instruments. They might not have been so festive if they had known that international red tape would strand them on the ship another two months—except for a couple of sailors who secretly hopped ashore and ended up in Memphis. Go figure.

But for now, it was a celebration of meeting new friends after not having sunk in a hurricane. An interpreter from the Coast Guard arrived. The bonding continued.

So did the surprises.

The ship's enormity and placement produced more head-scratching consequences. It completely altered ocean currents and the angles of the frothing waves now breaking offshore. And while the crowd's attention was focused on the deck, a teenager pointed in another direction.

"Look!"

What the hell?

Nobody realized it at the time, but the youth culture all up and down the coast was about to experience a tectonic shift.

At the rear end of the vessel, behind the giant exposed propeller, something new appeared.

Actually some*one*.

The tiny person stood up on a wooden surfboard and expertly rode the crashing waves down the ship's waterline.

"It's the Pope!"

## BACK TO THE PRESENT

"And here's another sign of the End Times," said Serge. "The ultra-rich now have something called a social media butler."

"How does that work?" asked Coleman. "A guy walks around with a cell phone on a silver platter?"

"Who knows?" Serge hit the gas as they climbed another bridge in the Florida Keys. "But this whole plugged-in, scalable, wider-coverage-area, texting, sexting, Twitter-verse, twenty-four/seven lifestyle has gotten completely out of hand. The country is now brainlessly hurtling toward the day when our entire existence is spent lying in an alkaline-neutral sarcophagus bath capsule wearing a virtual helmet that uses eye movements to buy stuff on the hologram Amazon planet."

"What if you accidentally get something in your eye?" asked Coleman.

"Then it's another shopping spree where drones and hovercraft forklifts descend on your home with pallets of wind chimes, tube socks, badminton rackets, orthopedic neck pillows, turkey thermometers, ceramic Siamese cats, and you've just downloaded the complete works of Shakespeare and Kool and the Gang."

"I hate it when that happens."

"And I'm sure they have automatic locks on your bath capsule until you pay, the fuckers."

"Screw the rich."

"Except it's unfair to lump all wealth together because it's the American way. But I'm making the call right now: The ones with social media butlers are on the asshole side of the ledger. And what are they posting? 'Messed over some of the little people,' 'Ignored the plight of others,' 'Gave lobster to my dog in front of the help and giggled,' 'Life is so hard looking at color swatches,' 'Traded a lobster for sex with the undocumented maid,' 'Fired my disgruntled social media butler for posting all the previous stuff.'"

Coleman had his head out the window like a beagle.

Serge looked over and compressed his eyebrows. "What, pray tell, are you doing now?"

"The Seven Mile Bridge totally rocks."

"That's a given, but you're acting really weird, even for you."

"*Yooop, yooop, yooop, blaba, blaba, kareeeeee-nuck-nuck-nuck . . .*" Coleman windmilled his arm out the passenger window. "Hey, Serge, I'm making the car go faster."

Serge gave another quick glance. "Did you take some kind of hallucinogen again?"

"You don't notice air until you're going this speed. Then it feels like if Jell-O was a gas."

"Coleman!"

"I only took half a dose . . . I think . . ."

"You *think*?"

"One of the side effects of good psychedelics is you can't remember how much you took."

"What's a side effect of bad psychedelics?"

"You wake up in another time zone."

Communication broke down until they reached the Long Key Viaduct. Coleman pulled his head back inside. "Whew, glad that awful shit finally wore off."

"So you're not going to take it again?"

Coleman gave him an odd look. "You don't know anything about drugs, do you?"

"A blind spot that I have made peace with." The Nova headed out over the water again. "And your trip recovery has perfect timing. We're almost to my next order of business."

"Almost where?" Coleman cracked a beer to smooth out the transition like 120-grit sandpaper.

"Remember that story in the news about this snotty little thirty-two-year-old brat who became president of a pharmaceutical company?"

"Not yet."

"Well, his corporation bought another small pharmaceutical firm, which is no big deal. And they inherited the patents, including one for an anonymous drug that was taken for granted for half a century."

"Still no bells ringing."

"This jerk figures out that in rare situations, it's a drug of last resort with no available alternatives. It fights a protozoa infection that is normally harmless in adults. But when a mother passes it to a newborn, the drug is a game-changer. This new young president correctly figured that parents of dying children are the most desperate customers of all, so he held their babies for ransom, raising the price of the medicine from twelve dollars a pill to seven hundred."

"Whoa!" said Coleman. "I remember that. I've got his face in my head right now. He's mean."

"An understatement," said Serge. "He even appeared on talk shows with stupid cowlick bangs, still smirking like he was proud and enjoying his celebrity, glibly asserting it was a brilliant business decision that he had no intention of reversing."

"What's your next order of business?"

"Reversing it."

"But how? We're in the Keys."

"After going on TV, the backlash became too much in New York. He leased a place down here to lay low."

"If he's in hiding, how do you know about it?"

"*Everyone* knows about it," said Serge. "Unlike other places, hiding out in the Keys depends not on secrecy, but the nature of Keys people. Protesters picketed the first day, but being Keys people, the tenacity to protest has the life span of a margarita."

Serge crossed the bridge to Upper Matecumbe and pulled over. "There it is."

"I don't see it."

"That abomination of a beach mansion barely visible through all the vegetation." Serge started the car again. "Luckily, I've already scoped it out."

"When?"

"On the way down," said Serge. "Remember me dropping you off at that bar?"

"The Lorelei!" said Coleman. "Big Dick and the Extenders used to play there."

"So then I found my way down to the shore and flanked around behind his pad."

"Weren't you worried he might call the police?"

"He *did* call the police." Serge pulled over again as the sun went down with fanfare. "The hyper-rich constantly try to run you off their beaches and deny Florida to the masses. But there's a little-known Florida law: You can walk all the way around the state—even behind private resorts and mansions—as long as you stay below the line of the mean high tide."

"What's that?"

"It involves math, so let me do the talking if it comes up." Serge walked back to the trunk. "Anyway, I was strolling along the sand at dusk and stopped behind his place to stare in the back windows."

"Why?"

"Because I don't like him. And I wanted him to see *me*." Serge removed a gym bag and slammed the lid. "It had the desired effect. He finally notices, and I wave happily. He makes these angry motions for me to get off his property. I shake my head and continue staring, now with binoculars. So he comes storming down his back porch, screaming he'll have me arrested. I explain the whole mean-high-tide thing, and he says, 'We'll see about that!' He pulls out a cell phone and calls the cops. I watch the changing expression on his face as he listens to a second rendition of the high-tide rule, and his head is about to explode. He storms back inside yelling it's 'unfair,' and I watch with my binoculars as he closes all the curtains in such a fury that he tears one of them down, and then he's thrashing around with the curtain rod and the fabric, getting tangled and falling through a glass coffee table."

"But why did you want him to spot you in the first place?"

"Calibrating his reaction dynamic to negative stimuli for my project. Assholes like him think they can always outsmart you, but in reality their arrogance is their weakness, and if you play it with finesse, they'll follow the bait right into your hands. It's an intricate project, with several compartmentalized steps, each requiring sequential timing. Luckily, this douche-canoe is bait-sensitive."

"Why do you need so many steps?"

"I don't, but each one has so many cool trivia facts that I just had to string them together for a domino effect." Serge began hiking down a sandy path next to a hotel. "They've made such life-saving strides in the field of biochemistry since I was in school."

The pair finally reached the shore and turned west. "Stay behind me," said Serge. "Closer to the water the better."

"It's kind of peaceful out tonight," said Coleman.

"And the stars!" Serge dropped his gym bag and unzipped it. "Can't buy this slice of heaven. Here are your binoculars."

"Thanks." Coleman turned toward the giant glass windows on the back of a mansion. "He's walking around in a bathrobe at night. What's that about?"

"Panache."

"I'm calling him Panache Boy," said Coleman, following the

young man with his binoculars. "Panache sounds cool if you're high. *Panache, panache, panache...*"

"Okay, try not to ruin this."

"What's he doing now?"

"Noticing us." Serge adjusted focus as the executive burst out the back door. "And here he comes now, right on bait-cue."

The young CEO marched down the dark beach. "You again! What did I tell you about staying off my property?"

"I remember," said Serge, still using his binoculars even though the resident was only a few feet away. "And what did I tell you about the mean high tide? You should trim your nose hairs."

"I'll destroy you! Your whole families!" yelled the young chief executive. "Do you have any idea who I am?"

"Yes, why?" said Serge. "Forgot your own name?"

"I'm Sterling Hanover, president of Medaxo Pharmaceuticals!"

"Panache Boy," said Coleman.

"Get out of here! Both of you!"

Serge and Coleman interlocked arms and square-danced at the edge of the surf, singing off-key: "*The mean high tide, the mean high tide, everyone loves the mean high tide...*"

"Stop it! Stop it right now!"

The pair switched arms and spun in the opposite direction. "*...The mean high tide, the mean high tide, you'd kick us out if you could, but the law ain't on your side...Why? Ohhh-hhhhhh, the mean high tide, the mean high tide...*"

Sterling's face became a deep red as he pursed his lips tight. "You're going to get it now!" He turned and ran toward the mansion. "You don't fuck with Sterling Hanover!"

The pair picked up their binoculars.

"What's happening?" asked Coleman.

"Looks like he's trying to find something in a desk drawer." A door slammed. "He's coming back. We'll soon find out."

Square dancing resumed. "*...The mean high tide, the mean high tide...*"

Sterling returned to the shore, and the dancing abruptly ceased. The young man grinned wickedly. "What's the matter? Not so chipper anymore?"

"What's with the Tasers?" said Serge.

"One for each of you!" said Sterling, aiming with both hands like a cowboy movie. "I am *so* going to enjoy this!"

"Serge," said Coleman. "Part of your plan, right?"

"I didn't see this coming."

"What are we going to do?"

"Don't worry. He's too much of a pussy to use them."

"Oh, I am?" Sterling's grin curled up into a prep school sneer.

"We're not trespassing," said Serge. "You'll go to jail."

"Look around!" Sterling briefly pointed the Tasers in opposite directions up and down the shore. "There are no witnesses on the whole beach! I'll just say you fell back across the mean-high-tide line after I Tased you. Who do you think they're going to believe? I'm rich!"

# Chapter 4

Thirty tiny children sat in thirty tiny school desks. All crying inconsolably.

Except one.

Little Serge rolled his eyes.

A large, stern nun shaped like a water heater stood yelling at the front of the classroom. Her name was Sister Imogen. She bore down on the students, and crying intensified. Her nun hat had those fins.

Sister Imogen once again was threatening to keep the entire class after school. But it was a double threat: She also wouldn't tell their parents.

In second grade, being kept after school without telling parents was the death penalty. Their folks would show up to take them home, wonder where the kids were and eventually leave. Then Sister Imogen would turn the class out on the street after dark and of course they'd all die. They'd discussed it at length on the playground.

The children glanced nervously out the window. Parents began to arrive. The survival clock was ticking. Suddenly one of the seven-year-olds, a kid named Jimmy Scarpotto, suffered a breakdown. He ran to the front of the room and bent over. "Spank me! Do anything you want! Just let me go!"

"Sit back down!"

"But my mom doesn't know I'm being kept after school!" Racking sobs. "Spank me!"

"I said, sit down!"

Halfway back in the room, Little Serge covered his face with his hands. "The shame."

Then, to everyone's amazement, Jimmy kicked Sister Imogen in the shin and ran out the door.

"Come back here!" The nun chased after him.

Serge used the opportunity to dash to the front of the room. "Everyone, listen to me! Don't show fear! They can smell it. It's what she wants!"

There were many such days at Saint Francis Elementary in Riviera Beach. Besides facing death after school, Serge's other big memory was being sent to the office.

He brought a baking-soda-and-vinegar rocket to class, and it somehow went off, shattering against the blackboard.

"Go to the principal's office!"

Out of the blue he decided it would be an interesting experiment to start repeating everything the nun said.

"Get out your pencils."

*"Get out your pencils."*

"Who said that?"

*"Who said that?"*

"Go to the office!"

*"Go to the office!"*

The next day he chose not to speak at all, rigidly gripping his desk until three nuns pried him loose.

Another time his desk was simply on fire.

"The office!"

Then the big one. He started taking Communion, but on the way back to his pew, he'd furtively remove the little white circle from his mouth and stick it in his pocket. "This is way too important to just eat." And one morning Sister Imogen happened to look inside Serge's open cardboard pencil box to see all these Communion wafers stacked like poker chips. She gasped and grabbed her heart. "What?" said Serge. "I'm collecting them. See? I've written the dates on each one."

A trip to the office *and* confession.

"I want to kill Sister Imogen."

"What!" said the priest.

"Of course I'm not going to *do* it," said Little Serge. "I'm just hoping for some kind of car accident."

Another powerful memory was all the scuttlebutt on the playground. The scarier the story, the better. Like the kid at Saint Clair's in the next town who was kept after school and never seen again. But the most frightening tale making the rounds was *Trapper*. And not just at the playground, but in nearly every household in the county. All the parents talked about Trapper. Which was quite a phenomenon because Trapper wasn't in the news, and almost nobody could even remember ever seeing him. It only made the rumors all the more mysterious, and adults referred to him in ominous, hushed tones. That's how it filtered down to the schoolyards. Every child who grew up in that time and place knew the story of Trapper.

The maximum bogeyman of Palm Beach County.

Trapper was short for Trapper Nelson. A wild and crazy hermit who lived in the remote woods way up the equally wild Loxahatchee River, where almost nobody dared venture. He was said to live off the land, skinning alligators and anything else he could catch. And he'd shoot on sight anyone who came near his camp. Maybe skin them, too. The few people who'd gotten close enough by canoe reported glimpses of a shadowy figure dart-ing among the trees onshore. Then hearing warning shots. He was known as the "Tarzan of the Loxahatchee." The kids in the schoolyards loved that.

The actual facts were less mythical and more fascinating. Vincent Nostokovich was born in New Jersey around 1909. He hopped freight trains, was jailed in Mexico, and gambled his way to Florida, ending up on the beach near the Jupiter Lighthouse. He made money selling animal furs during the Depression and bought cheap land as far up the Loxahatchee as was navigable. Which meant no neighbors or anything else for miles. Trapper was tall and rugged, and by hand he cleared part of the land, built a makeshift dock and used slash pine and mortar to construct cabins and shelters so sturdy that they easily weathered every hurricane. He built pens for some of the animals he captured alive, and opened Trapper Nelson's Zoo and Jungle Gardens in the 1930s, where visitors on boat tours often stopped for lunch.

Then it started unraveling. His health declined, the state ordered his zoo closed due to poor conditions, and he fell behind on property taxes. It all combined to usher in the hermit era. Bitterness, paranoia, warning everyone to keep away or else.

"He always carries a shotgun," said one of Serge's friends on the playground.

"And there's buried treasure," said another.

"Wow."


**THE PRESENT**

On a peaceful night in the Florida Keys, pharmaceutical president Sterling Hanover aimed a pair of Tasers and fired. Serge anticipated the shot and dove to the side like a soccer goalie on a penalty kick. The dart and wire flew harmlessly into the water.

Coleman, not so agile.

*"Aaaaauuuuu! Aaaaaaauuuuuu!"* Flopping in the sand like a stranded fish.

"You bastard!" yelled Serge, tackling Sterling and turning off the voltage to the weapon that had harpooned his pal.

( . . . We now move forward with your regularly scheduled program, already in progress . . . )

Sterling Hanover sat tied to a post-modern chair in the rear of the house. "What are you going to do to me?"

"Hold still." Serge flicked a droplet off the end of a hypodermic needle.

"*Aaauu!* You stabbed me!"

"Don't be such a baby." Serge showed him the syringe. "Only a prick."

"You poisoned me?"

"No, this is medicine. You of all people should recognize that."

"You drugged me! I'll sue!"

"Just a little insulin," said Serge. "You have that one-too-many-doughnuts look."

"I'm starting to feel weird," said Sterling, his eyes sweeping around the feng shui interior. "Getting thirsty. Now I'm hungry . . ."

Serge examined the remaining level on the syringe. "When I said a little, actually a lot. I'm all about transparency."

"I'm hungrier than I've ever been in my entire life!" said Sterling. "I have to eat something right now!"

Coleman stumbled over after helping himself at the wet bar. "What happened?"

"He's going into insulin shock, insane thirst and appetite. Step One is complete."

"No, I don't mean that." Coleman looked out the glass doors facing the ocean. "Down on the beach. What happened to me?"

"You were Tased, bro." Serge began undoing the knots around Sterling's wrists. "He got you with that space-age gun over on the coffee table."

Sterling broke free.

Coleman picked up the Taser. "He's going to escape!"

Serge grabbed his friend's arm. "Don't shoot. He's not going anywhere except the refrigerator."

Sterling was stuffing his face with stuffed crab when Serge seized him around the neck. "Our whole culture eats way too much comfort food . . ."

"*Aaauuu!* I'm still hungry! Where are you taking me?"

"To nature's harvest." Serge twisted an arm behind Sterling's back and led him across the room.

From another direction: "*Aaauuu!*"

Coleman twitched and flopped on the snow-white tile floor. Serge grabbed the Taser again and switched the power off. Coleman sat up and slapped the sides of his own face.

"You moron," said Serge. "You accidentally Tased yourself."

"No, that was deliberate," said Coleman. "I like it."

"You what—?"

Crash, smash, glass breaking. Sterling was back at the open refrigerator, arms inside, scooping the entire contents of a shelf toward his chest. Serge captured him again and led him outside toward the shore. "Why eat that genetically altered crap in a suspended-animation preservative stew when you possess some of the freshest food our state has to offer right in your own backyard?"

"Where?"

"Over by those mangroves. A couple of magnificent beach apple trees. See the succulent, glistening fruit?"

Sterling took off at a sprint.

Coleman waddled over with a Romanian crystal rocks glass topped off with vintage Rémy Martin Louis XIII. "What's going on now?"

"Step Two," said Serge. "You've got about three hundred dollars of liquor in that glass."

Gulp. "Not anymore."

Over in the mangroves. *"Ahhh! Ahhh! Ahhh!"* Sterling spit out the first bite of fruit and ran back screaming. "My mouth is on fire! My hands! My eyes!"

Serge pulled a bottle of spring water from his gym bag. "Here you go. Don't swallow because you'll wash the bad stuff down and then your esophagus and GI tract will give you air-raid sirens. Just gargle and spit, repeat . . ."

Coleman reached way back and flung the rocks glass high in the air toward the house.

"That's a four-hundred-dollar piece of crystal," said Serge.

*Crash.*

"Not anymore." Coleman looked down at a gagging, drooling young man. "I get it. You put something in the bottled water."

"Nope." Serge grabbed another of the bottles and sipped it himself.

Sterling continued flushing his mouth. Between rinses: "My eyes, my throat, my whole face and neck." Gargle, spit. "Why is everything burning?"

"I'm all about transparency." Serge pointed at the tree. "Now, *that* was poison."

Cough, cough. "Those beach apples?"

"A big no-no. All residents down here learn not to eat them."

"Then why'd you let me?"

"To polish your Sunshine State survival skill set." Serge poured more water on a washcloth and handed it to Sterling. "The early Floridians four thousand years ago went through the same trial and error. A guy on the edge of the tribe screaming and clawing his eyes, and the chief: 'Make a note. Don't eat that one.'"

Sterling wiped his burning face with the moist towel. "But you said it was a beach apple."

"It is," said Serge. "Sounds delicious and inviting, doesn't it? From the manchineel tree, found in the mangrove lowlands of

Florida, particularly in the Flamingo area on the southern tip of the mainland and along the Keys. Spanish call it 'little apple of death.'"

"I'm going to die?"

"Not likely, but the experience is a bitch on tractor tires." Serge pulled a field guide from the gym bag. "Says here that it's one of the most highly irritant trees on earth. Don't eat the fruit, don't touch it, don't brush against it, don't even breathe near it. Wow, you picked the wrong plant."

"I'm starting to feel better," said Sterling. "Except my nose . . . my whole sinus cavity is still burning up."

"Got just the panacea," said Serge, pulling out a small bottle of nasal spray and tossing it. "Non-medicated saline solution, so there's no problem if you use too much."

Sterling sprayed and sprayed until water poured out both nostrils. "It's starting to work."

Coleman fired up a joint. "It's starting to get boring."

"Actually it's just about to get ridiculously interesting," said Serge. "Step Three."

"I get it," said Coleman. "*This* time you put something in the nasal spray. It's not water."

"No, it's really water," said Serge. "Just not what originally came in the bottle. It's Florida river water. It's got a kicker."

"River water?"

"I could have just filled it from a river, but then I wouldn't be sure about Step Three, so to be on the safe side I stole this sample from a wetlands lab in Gainesville," said Serge. "The security was next to nothing because other than me, who bothers?"

"Why'd you have to steal water from a lab?"

"Because they were studying what I needed for my project," said Serge. "It's pretty rare, but worldwide more than half the cases that have been diagnosed come from Texas and Florida. *Naegleria fowleri.*"

"What's that?"

Serge grabbed Sterling's left arm and steadied him on the walk back to the house. "As usual, I was boning up on my Florida ecology, and when I first saw it on the Internet I thought it was click-bait—the freakiest, most nightmarish thing I've ever heard of that exists in our state—but it's definitely real, and more than lives up to its name: brain-eating amoeba."

"Good God!" said Coleman. "And I thought flesh-eating bacteria was bad."

"You'd *pray* for those critters if you had the brain-eaters in your head," said Serge.

"And that's what this rich dude has right now?"

"Afraid so."

Sterling staggered on. "You do realize I can hear everything you're saying. You're just trying to scare me. That's bullshit."

"Of course it is," said Serge. "Just like your pill pricing. Anyway, the amoeba can only infect you through the nose, where it travels to the brain. Normally this cantankerous bugger feasts on bacteria, but it's somehow attracted by neurochemicals and will switch its value menu to your gray matter."

They returned to the house though the glass doors.

"Back in the chair for you!" said Serge, looping and knotting rope again.

"Haven't you done enough to me?" Sterling began to tremble. "I swear not to tell anyone. Why don't you just let me go?"

"I *am* going to let you go." Serge pulled hard on a sailor's hitch. "But we'll wait till morning."

"Why?"

"Party!" yelled Coleman, drinking hundred-dollar slugs straight from the Rémy decanter.

"He's right," said Serge. "We always celebrate at the end of the semester. And you're just about to graduate."

"Serge! Come here! He has excellent taste in music!"

Serge trotted over to the built-in media shelves. "So he does . . .

And I've got the perfect tunes for the occasion, in honor of our host over there."

He selected a Floyd CD and stuck it in the stereo.

"Crank it!" said Coleman.

Serge turned the volume up to eleven.

"... *Money!* ... *It's a hit!* ..."

## *Chapter 5*

Station wagons brimmed with Cub Scouts, heading north on U.S. 1 from Jupiter toward Hobe Sound. They turned into the entrance of Jonathan Dickinson State Park and paid at the ranger station. A million field trips from every school and organization ended up at the park, because it was inexpensive, outdoors and the kids burned themselves out running around.

Little Serge thought his Cub Scout uniform was stupid, but he liked his compass and flashlight and mess kit, and especially the snake-bite kit. He saw the wooden observation tower in the distance, the one he'd now climbed like ten times from all his other field trips. It stood on a natural sand dune that rose an entire eighty-six feet above sea level and was called Hobe *Mountain*. Because it was Florida.

A troop of little blue caps bounced up to the top of the tower, looked at the ocean, bounced back down. The cars drove through the park to the landing by the water. Everyone changed into swimsuits and began splashing. Except Little Serge. He had another agenda. This might be his only chance. He strayed from the group to the rental canoes. He didn't have any money but figured: *I'm just a kid. What are they going to do?*

The adults were so busy making sure nobody drowned that they never noticed Serge slip the boat into the water and paddle out of sight around the mangroves and cabbage palms.

The boy kicked off his shoes and paddled along in quiet solitude, bend after narrow bend, in childhood heaven. Branches overhead, osprey nests, herons, manatees, rows of turtles sunning on rotted logs sticking out of the brackish water. And alligators. Some became curious and neared the boat, and Serge simply clapped his paddle down flat on the surface to disperse them. The canoe disappeared around another ancient hairpin turn.

The Loxahatchee River.

Serge wiped his forehead and looked up as a hawk circled the sun. He checked his compass. The paddle went back in the water. It was taking longer than he thought. The river twisted and bent and forked as the sun tacked across the sky with more birds. It began to taper and still. Water bugs danced. Trees formed a canopy. He ducked under a cabbage palm that grew horizontally out from the shore before yearning upward. That's when Serge saw it.

He paddled to a fallen-down dock and tied off his boat. Bare feet climbed ashore. Small arms clawed their way through branches.

A click from a rifle. "Stop! Who goes there!"

He stepped into a clearing. "I'm Serge."

The rifle lowered and eyebrows went up. "You're just a little kid."

"Correct."

The man suddenly jumped up and down. "*Yah! Yah! Yah!* Get out of here!"

Serge covered his mouth and giggled.

"Why are you laughing?" asked Trapper Nelson.

"You're funny."

"You're not scared?"

"Why?"

Trapper scratched his forehead. "Where are your parents?"

"I don't know."

"What are you doing here?"

"Looking for you."

Trapper examined Serge. Another scratch of his forehead, thinking, *This is the strangest kid I've ever met. And they call* me *weird.* "Well, you must be hungry after all that paddling. You like possum?"

"We'll find out."

They headed to an outdoor fire pit.

"What's that tall thing over there?" asked Serge, pointing at a rusty pyramid of corrugated metal sheets.

"My personal water tower made out of recycled scrap."

"Cool."

They passed one of the cabins. Something painted on the side: HURRICANE LOG, 1947, 1948, 1949 . . . with different numbers of stars next to each year. Then the empty pens where the animals had once been. Trapper handed Serge a plate and fork, and the stories began. ". . . Celebrities used to come to my zoo. The Hollywood actor Gary Cooper, and Gene Tunney, the boxer . . ."

A half hour later, the boy's plate was licked clean.

Trapper leaned back. "Then came World War Two, and I was in the army at Camp Murphy right near here. It's part of the park now, but in those days it was an ultra-secret radar installation with five thousand soldiers . . ."

"Cool . . ."

## THE PRESENT

Arms splashed in the dark water.

Someone doing the backstroke a hundred yards offshore as the rising sun peeked over the Gulf Stream. A shrimp trawler sailed by. Pelicans and gulls looked for breakfast.

Serge finished his ocean laps and removed swim goggles as he trudged onto the beach. He beat his chest like a gorilla. "Yes! Another day of living!"

He went back inside, wet feet across the marble, stepping over a body. "Coleman, rise and shine!"

"*Grrrr,* the mean high tide . . ."

"Come on, buddy, get up! . . . Our new friend is already wide-awake."

And how. Sterling Hanover's head snapped side to side. "Spots!" He looked down. "And I'm trying to make my fingers move, but my toes move instead."

"No," said Serge. "Those *are* your fingers."

"Man," said Coleman. "He must really be hallucinating."

"One of the symptoms. A *gentler* one. The sledding only gets rougher, and you know what that means?" Serge hopped up and down in childlike excitement. "Time for Step Four."

That was Coleman's call to action. He strained and pushed himself up. "I've got to see Step Four!"

Serge circled behind the captive and cut the ropes with a pocketknife.

Sterling massaged his free wrists. "You're letting me go now?"

"Unless you want a different Step Four."

"No, no, no. I like this one."

"Good, but first I'm curious about something," said Serge. "You've caught every break in life. Yet instead of giving back, you choose to inflict misery and hardship on the least fortunate. Is money that important?"

"I get it now," said Sterling. "You're one of *those* people."

"What people?"

"The ones who don't know anything about business." Sterling stood up and put his arms out for balance like he was on a high wire. "Do you have any idea what it takes out of me to run a company? Talk about a burden! When you have a monopoly in a desperate-customer situation, it's your responsibility to gouge prices, but lazy people just expect handouts."

"Twelve dollars to seven hundred a pill sounds like the mother of all handouts," said Serge.

"Just the opposite," said Sterling. "Few have ever achieved such a profit margin. But do I get any credit? No, the press is so unfair, like I'm supposed to just ignore the shareholders. Since when is infant mortality my fault?"

"That's enough," said Serge. "Just checking to make certain Step Four fit the crime . . . You're free to go."

Sterling sat back down.

"You don't want to go?"

"I'm a little shaky, for some reason."

"Oh, the amoebas," said Serge. "It's their breakfast time."

"You really were serious about them?" Panic arrived on the scene. "What am I going to do?"

"You're in luck!" Serge pulled a copy of a scientific article out of his pocket. "It's fascinating reading, and I have you to thank! Your company's drug fights parasitic infection by inhibiting key metabolism that the protozoa need to thrive in infants. Likewise the amoebas currently doing the conga between your ears are also parasites, but much more aggressive, and only early treatment with a top-shelf anti-fungal drug will work. Guess what? Your anti-parasite pills work on amoebas, too, and they're some of the best money can buy!"

"I didn't know that."

"It's because there aren't enough amoeba cases to justify phar-maceutical TV ads like, 'Find yourself having to pee too much during golf matches and bar mitzvahs? Ask your doctor if Urinex is right for you!' . . . So my advice is that you get to the nearest drugstore toot-sweet."

"Of course!" Sterling wove across the marble floor to a cell phone sitting on a cabinet. "I've got a doctor on call and he'll phone in the scrip."

"Good thinking," said Serge. "But not a word about us or it's the chair again and more steps."

"Don't worry... Hello? Doctor Spiel? I need a prescription..."

Sterling finally hung up and felt his pants pockets. "Where's my wallet?"

Serge held out an Italian billfold. "Right here."

"What are you doing with it?"

"Stealing it," said Serge. "We're criminals. It's our responsibility to take wallets, and you want to talk about bad press?"

"But I need it."

"I need it, too. Credit cards. People always wonder how I pay for my research trips. And I wouldn't report them stolen if I were you, unless you'd like us to come back for another fun-filled-yet-always-educational visit."

"But how am I supposed to pay for my medication?"

"I don't know why, but I took pity and put some of your cash on that counter." Serge tapped his wrist. "Tick-tock."

Sterling grabbed his keys, and Serge snatched them away. "You're in no shape to drive. Amoebas are worse than texting. We'll take my car."

The green Nova cruised a half mile, and Serge dropped Sterling off at a shopping center. "Don't forget to write."

Sterling staggered in a circuitous course across the parking lot before reaching the drugstore entrance.

Coleman placed a cool can of beer against his forehead. "What was Step Four anyway?"

"Wait and see," said Serge. "In the meantime, I have a confession to make, and you're the only person I can trust. Promise not to tell anyone?"

"Pinkie swear." They interlocked fingers.

"Okay, here goes," said Serge. "And promise to be understanding because this is as personal as it gets . . ." A deep breath. "I've come to accept that I have an alternate sexual orientation."

"Wow, that *is* a big confession," said Coleman. "But you've been my best friend forever, so I'll support your lifestyle. What is it?"

"This is kind of embarrassing," said Serge. "Uh . . . I'm turned on by women in plaid."

"Plaid? That's your big secret?"

"Coleman, I'm baring my soul here."

"Sorry. Go on."

"I wasn't aware of it for the longest time, but I finally put two and two together." Serge averted his gaze out the window. "Just about every woman I've ever fallen for has had a plaid shirt or two. And many a relationship ended just because they had to do the laundry."

Snicker. Coleman quickly covered his mouth.

"This isn't funny!"

"I know." Another suppressed giggle. "It's just that it's so weird."

"That's why we have to keep this quiet until it gains acceptance," said Serge. "I dream of the day when I'll be leading a parade with a banner of a plaid rainbow, but until then . . ."

"I watch a lot of TV," said Coleman. "The country's changing."

"Not fast enough. Who would have thought that the last social barrier would be the politics of sexual arousal?" said Serge. "There's no accounting for what wakes up a stiffy. It's on autopilot, doing whatever it wants without clearance from the tower. That's why they're so personal and private, yet the bongo-beaters of hate want to know all about mine. I don't think about *theirs*. You tell me who's the sick one."

"Plaid." Coleman whistled.

"I have a theory: The United States is over-sexed and under-laid. Way too much suggestive media and not enough follow-through. The pressure builds until there's bound to be a problem."

"Two words," said Coleman. "Shower soap."

"Anyone with a quality love life has neither the time nor inclination to blame national woes on marriage certificates," said Serge. "And if you *are* doing that nonsense, you're unwittingly advertising to the entire world that the people you want to fuck don't dig you. Those are cards you should definitely play a little closer to the vest."

"A plaid vest."

"Shut up."

# Chapter 6

**1968**

Surfboards. Everywhere.

Wood and fiberglass, long and short, single and twin fin.

The kids came in a variety of ages and heights, but all their hair was bleached from the sun and salt. All fit and strong and, if you saw a photo of the scene today, it might take a few minutes to notice, but then: Hey, none of them are overweight. Oh, right, no cell phones or video games yet.

The *Amaryllis* had been aground at Riviera Beach for almost three years now, and word had swept the surfing culture that this was The Spot on the east coast of Florida. They paddled and splashed and waited on their stomachs for the next big one to ride in. A good number of curious adults were also showing up along the shore, taking in the sights and sounds of their changing world.

It was a glorious time.

"... *Sittin' on the dock of the bay* ..."

"... *Mony, Mony!* ..."

*". . . Here's to you, Mrs. Robinson . . ."*

And it was all about to end. The ship was so heavy and the bow so far into the sand that for the longest time nobody could figure out what to do, at least not with the small local budget. But the Army Corps of Engineers had gotten involved, and in less than a month, the accidental landmark would be dismantled and sunk offshore as an artificial reef, ushering in a new era of scuba diving, but that's another story.

Darby Pope paddled his board out past the propeller again. Kenny was right beside him. He was fifteen now, not as scrawny, but he still tagged along behind the Pope everywhere he could.

The next wave approached. "Kenny," said the Pope. "Just stay outside of me from the ship."

"Okay."

After a brief run, they neared the shore, the Pope gracefully, Kenny not so much. They grabbed their boards out of the shallow water.

"See you still got it," said a sweaty man in street clothes.

Darby looked up. "Oh, Councilman Finch. How's the family?"

"Better than the campaign." A laugh.

"You've got my vote."

"That makes you, me and my wife." Another laugh. "By the way, thanks for helping my son the other day with those bullies."

"Anyone would have done it . . ."

Kenny grabbed his board and caught up with Darby. "Who was that?"

"Just a friend on the city council."

"You know everyone." Kenny stopped and looked south down the beach to the end of the island. "Nobody's at the Pump House anymore."

"Waves are better here," said the Pope. "And less dangerous." He sat down in the sand near their stuff and opened a novel.

"You're always reading."

"I like books." Darby turned a page.

Kenny got out his board wax. "Did you see the new surfing book that just came out called *The Pump House Gang*?"

"By Tom Wolfe," said Darby. "Read it the day it went on sale."

"Naturally," said Kenny. "Is it about us?"

Darby shook his head. "Another group of surfers in La Jolla, California, that hung out on the beach near a sewage pumping plant. The name's a coincidence."

Kenny looked out at the ocean. "Want to go again?"

"Got another idea," said Darby. "Want to see something you've never seen before?"

"What is it?"

Darby told Kenny his plan.

"You actually know him?"

The Pope knew everyone.

L ittle Serge got on his tiptoes to touch a giant beached alligator skull mounted on the wall of a cabin.

"Why is that here?"

"Why not?" said Trapper.

"Why do you leave your doors open?"

"Because it doesn't matter."

"Can I hold your gun?"

"No."

Serge ran outside. "Why do you have animal pens?"

"Slow up." Trapper chased after him. "You sure are a curious little sumbitch."

"What's a sumbitch?"

"If you settle down, I'll teach you some stuff about dangerous animals. Deal?"

Serge sat on the ground and closed an invisible zipper across his mouth.

"Okay, that big rack yonder is where I stretch my pelts. Right now I'm drying a big snakeskin. Lots of constrictor around here.

Grab 'em fast behind the head, and the other hand a few feet back before they coil." He pointed toward trees. "On the south side are several families of wild boar. People think: pigs, cute, harmless. But these are several hundred pounds with tusks and can easily run down and kill a large man. That's why I always carry a sidearm over there. Follow me . . ." They crawled on their bellies through underbrush. "See where it's been pushed down? This here's a rabbit trail. You take a piece of vine like this and fashion a snare like that and hang it on twigs in a narrow spot, and by morning you got a rabbit."

"You kill bunnies?" asked Serge.

"Ya gotta eat. Or use 'em for snake bait." He gestured at a spot on the small trail. "That's scat. You probably know it as poop. It's also great bait. All the animals out here use scent. That's how I catch stuff. Remember, it's all about scent, and I baited this trail earlier." Trapper suddenly dove into the brush and disappeared, then came out with a modest-sized python by the neck.

"Wow!" said Serge. "That's how you catch snakes?"

"And bobcats and—" Trapper's head suddenly jerked. "What's that sound?"

"What sound?" asked Serge.

"Shit, somebody's coming . . . Stay here." Trapper crept from the brush and silently dashed through the trees on a secret route he used when he wanted to get the drop.

Serge bumped into him from behind.

"I thought I told you to stay back there!"

"Are you going to shoot someone?"

"Don't be so inquisitive."

"What's 'inquisitive' mean?"

"Just pipe down!"

Trapper clicked his rifle and burst through the last branches protecting the bank of the river. He fired a shot in the air. "Get the hell off my property!"

"Trapper, relax. It's just me."

Trapper lowered the gun. "Darby, what are you doing here?"

"Been a while." Tying the canoe to the dock. "Thought I'd pay a visit. I brought a friend. His name's Kenny."

Just then, a small head poked out around Trapper's legs.

"Who's the little fella?" asked Darby.

Trapper shrugged. "Damnedest thing. Just showed up like the world's his oyster."

"All alone?" asked Pope. "How'd he get this far up the Loxahatchee?"

"Was wondering the same thing till I saw all the energy he had running around." Trapper grabbed the sides of his head. "And the questions! This is definitely the weirdest kid I've ever met."

Darby bent down and smiled. "What's your name."

"Serge. What's yours?"

"Darby."

"Why do you have a tattoo?"

The Pope reached in his canoe for the walkie-talkie he always carried when he went upriver. He got ahold of the ranger station back at Jonathan Dickinson.

"*Oh, hey, Darby. We were just talking about you. Haven't seen your face in a while.*"

"Was just here three weeks ago."

"*For you, that's a while.*"

"Listen, you wouldn't happen to be missing a kid back there, would you?"

"*As a matter of fact, frantically so. And one of our canoes is gone.*"

"I think I found both."

"*Where?*"

"Trapper's."

"*Trapper's? How on earth did he get all the way up there?*"

"Hold on. He's loose."

"*Loose?*"

Darby dropped the walkie-talkie, and they all took off into the woods.

Inside an unassuming drugstore in the Florida Keys, Sterling Hanover leaned maniacally over the counter at the pickup window. "Please hurry!"

"One second," said a graying pharmacist with bifocals. He twisted the childproof cap shut. "Just have to ring you up."

"*Eeeeeee.*" Sterling slapped himself in the head to throw the parasites off balance.

The pharmacist punched a few buttons and bent closer to the computer screen. His name tag said IRV. "That can't be right."

"What's the problem?"

"Says here this bottle of thirty pills costs twenty-one thousand dollars."

Sterling twitched as his hands burrowed deep in his pockets, pulling out crumpled currency that he tossed on the counter. "But I only have a couple hundred. And I really need that medicine. It's a matter of life and death."

"Let me see what I can do." Irv's fingers pressed more buttons. "Probably just a glitch. I'll run it through again."

Sterling began gyrating in a combination of the chicken dance and someone who'd been leg-whipped over a gambling debt.

"Nope, still twenty-one thousand," said the pharmacist. "Which I know is wrong because we'd never keep drugs that expensive in a little branch store like this. They send a courier down from Miami when needed . . . Let me look at something else . . . Yeah, that's weird. Shows here we originally had them priced for twelve dollars, so it does make sense we'd stock them in this branch . . . But why would it say they're now seven hundred each?"

Sterling's gaze followed a swarm of imaginary butterflies across the ceiling of the store. "Can I have them?"

The pharmacist abruptly looked up. "I remember now. It was in the news. That greedy company jacked prices through the roof! I hate that kind of exploitation that gives us all a bad name! . . . Well, since we bought them cheap before the price hike and they were originally twelve bucks, I can override the computer." Tap, tap, tap.

Sterling swatted the air in front of him because the butterflies were attacking him with blowguns. "Sound business decision."

"What?" said the pharmacist. Tap, tap, tap.

"The media had a vendetta."

The pharmacist stopped and squinted. "Do I know you?"

Swat, swat. "Never been in here before." Swat.

"Yes, I've definitely seen your face before. Just can't place it."

Sterling decided his hair was trying to escape. He grabbed the top of his head. "I'm really, really rich."

"That's it!" Irv took a step back and stretched an arm out firmly. "You're the obnoxious little pipsqueak who victimized all those parents."

Swat, swat. "You don't know how hard my job is. Heavy lies the crown." Swat.

Irv angrily pressed buttons. "The price is back to twenty-one thousand."

"But I need them! How about one pill?"

"Okay." The pharmacist extracted a tablet and offered it in his palm. "That'll be seven hundred dollars, please."

"But I already told you, I don't have that much."

"That's not what I hear."

Sterling's eyes locked on the pill, and he lunged. The pharmacist closed his fist around the tablet and jerked his arm back.

"Criminals took my wallet! Have mercy!"

"Get out of my store, you bastard!"

The air was now thick with gummy worms swirling around Sterling's head. He plucked them and filled his mouth. "Can you at least print out the prescription my doctor called in so I can take it somewhere else?"

Irv smiled in sweet irony at the near future. "I would be more than happy to do that."

A not-so-silent printer clattered to life and a document chugged onto the tray. "Here you go."

Sterling snatched it. "Ha! You're not the only business in town!" A final gummy worm in his mouth, and he was out the door.

The pharmacist picked up the phone . . .

. . . Outside, Coleman pointed. "She's over there."

Serge raised binoculars. "Where?"

"By the news boxes. Cutoff shorts and an untucked plaid shirt."

"Heart be still."

Something large and blurry suddenly blocked Serge's view. "What the—" He lowered binoculars. "Sterling, what are you doing lying on my windshield?"

"You've got to help!" He plastered the prescription printout against the glass. "Take me to another pharmacy!"

"Don't you know anything about Florida?" said Serge. "There are only two major drugstore chains. And whenever you see one, the other is always on the next corner. It's like a zoning law down here." Serge aimed an index finger.

Sterling turned. "I see it!" He jumped off the car.

"What's he doing?" asked Coleman.

"Only the amoebas know."

Sterling high-stepped across the parking lot to avoid the radioactive porcupines. He dashed through honking traffic and into the drugstore on the opposite corner. The entire staff was already waiting, thanks to the phone call from Irv.

They formed a riot line. *"Booooooooooo!"*

"But I need my pills!"

"Seven hundred dollars," said the chief pharmacist.

"I don't have it! I'm pleading with you!"

*"Booooooooo!"*

Sterling stood and whined with pursed lips. "I'll drop the price! I'm in charge! They're back to twelve dollars!"

"Okay," said the pharmacist.

"Okay." Sterling fished his money out again. "Give them to me."

"When we get word from the national office," said the store manager. "Sorry, it's just good business."

Sterling whimpered the whimper of terminal desperation. He ran back onto the street, glancing east and west. His world began spinning to the soundtrack from *2001: A Space Odyssey*. A meteor shower fell in the middle of the day. The road sparkled like it was encrusted with diamonds. He plucked polka-dot hexagons off his arms.

"Somebody! Please help me!"

Sterling fell to the ground and began slithering across U.S. 1. Cars screeched to a halt. Someone called 911. Bystanders assembled curiously along the shoulders of the road.

An ambulance arrived, and the paramedics flipped him over to test vitals and check his pockets. One of the EMTs noticed the pharmacy staff emerging from the store. "He doesn't have any ID on him. Anyone know who he is?"

"That's Sterling Hanover."

News of his identity ran through the increasingly incensed crowd of onlookers.

Sterling fought as the paramedics struggled with the oxygen mask. "What's wrong with him?"

"Apparently he needs these pills," said the pharmacist, holding up a small plastic bottle.

"Give them to me," said the EMT, reattaching the oxygen.

"They're seven hundred a pill."

The other paramedic looked up. "Seven hundred! . . . Wait, Sterling Hanover? That's the prick from the pharmaceutical company?" He looked at the other EMT. "On second thought, the guy just looks drunk to me."

"This is a job for the police," said the first paramedic, packing up his gear. "Lunch break."

The ambulance drove off as the roadside crowd clapped and cheered.

Sterling ran up to them and grabbed someone by the shirt. "Compassion! I'm begging!"

"Get the fuck off me, you spoiled brat!" A hard shove.

Someone else: "You better start running!"

"Why?" asked Sterling.

Punch.

"Ow, you hit me."

"Run!"

He ran.

The crowd began following, slowly at first, because the dense formation of the mob needed time to space out and find the groove, but then quickly picking up rhythm and speed as a single unit: residents, tourists, pharmacists, sunburned bums who wove hats out of palm fronds.

Sterling glanced over his shoulder. "Stop chasing me!"

*"Keep chasing him!"*

*"And let's hit him with rocks!"*

*"Good idea!"*

Fling, fling, fling.

"Ow, rocks."

A green Nova rolled slowly down U.S. 1, keeping pace with the jogging vigilantes.

"There she is," said Coleman.

Serge leaned out his window. "You! In the plaid shirt! Dinner and a movie?"

She jogged and threw a rock. "I'm busy."

"How often do you do laundry?"

Sterling was certifiably delirious and low on steam, but escape was soon at hand. He saw the waterway ahead cutting between the islands.

"Look!" yelled someone in the crowd. "He's going for the drawbridge!"

"Don't let him get away!"

Sterling approached the paved apron to the bridge. Red lights flashed, and the orange-and-white crossing arm was down. He ran around it.

Drawbridges are particularly dangerous for pedestrians, and each year in Florida several are seriously hurt or killed because people on sidewalks pay less attention to traffic signals. Then a few find themselves dangling high in the air with a great view but a tenuous grip on the railing. If they're lucky, it's a splash in the water. If not, a bruising tumble down the steep metal grating.

But virtually all those mishaps occurred when the spans were rising, and now that these were more than halfway down, the bridge tender had turned his back on the action and opened a magazine on hot-air ballooning.

Sterling stumbled up the lowering span and prepared to jump to the other side, but his depth perception was shot. He leaped and hit the edge of the other span with his chest, slipping until his fingers clung to the grate.

A motorist on the far side of the bridge—who didn't know what was going on—jumped from his car in alarm and ran up to the crossing gate, yelling to Sterling: "Just fall in the water! Just let go!"

The gang on the other side: *"Don't let go!" "Hang on!"*

The bridge tender continued reading about "Five Must-Have Cheeses" for ballooning over the turning-of-the-leaves in New Hampshire.

The green Nova stopped behind the flashing lights, next to the crowd of onlookers.

"There she is again," said Coleman. "What are you going to do?"

"The key is not to act creepy," said Serge. "It's all about finding the perfect romantic moment."

Coleman gestured ahead with a Pabst. "If he doesn't let go, his hands will be hurt bad."

"Actually, the ends of the bridge that mesh together are a bit thicker." Serge patted his abdomen. "He's roughly looking all the way down to belt level."

*"Let go of the bridge!"*

*"Don't let go!"*

The two spans enmeshed.

Silence and a collective wince. A blood slick poured from the bridge, and an epidemic of vomiting chain-reacted through the crowd.

Serge stuck his head out the window. "You free now?"

# Chapter 7

1976

The water at the public beach was inviting and empty. No surfboards, no swimmers. The wooden lifeguard stands were long gone.

Families didn't come to Singer Island anymore. Just some teenagers. And they didn't come to the beach. They loitered. None of them had even heard of the *Amaryllis*.

*"Hey, man."*

*"Whatcha got?"*

*"Half O-Z, a dime."*

Money and pot changed hands. Police increased patrols.

All the quaint old beach shops had met the wrecking ball, and the little spinning wind gauge was in a landfill. Instead there was now the Ocean Mall. A strip mall. It was supposed to modernize the beach and bring the people back, but it just made off with the soul. Businesses conducted an industry of going out of business. The dress-up restaurant next to the Sands Hotel was now the Island Room titty bar.

The stores on life support tried to lure customers with stereos blaring out the doors.

"... *Dream weaver* ..."

"... *Turn the beat around* ..."

"... *Philadelphia freedom* ..."

It was an orphaned time. Mom-and-pop motels came down and condos went up. The only people still tending the flame had moved back down the beach to surf at the Pump House, but it never felt the same. The only constant was the Colonnades Hotel. It was old-school. Heyday gone; dignity intact. Which meant it would have to be demolished.

Darby Pope and Kenny strolled through the hotel with their surfboards. They passed the coffee shop, where an old man read a newspaper and made notes on a legal pad.

"Hi, Mr. MacArthur."

"What? Oh, hi, Darby." A sip of coffee. "Still surfing, I see."

"Yes, but everything's ... different."

The billionaire nodded in resignation. "It's all new."

The pair headed out the back of the hotel toward the beach and a short hike to the Pump House. It was ugly weather for tourists, which meant a great day for surfing. Kenny had reached the age of twenty-three, and all the younger board riders now looked up to *him*. He was generally considered the second best surfer on the coast. A distant second. The Pope was still out there on the waves, defying age, which was early fifties.

The cloud ceiling became lower and grayer. The waves aggressively sucked back out at the shore. It was an incoming low tide, the best time to hit the Pump House, at least according to the surfing press (*surfing press?*). The peaks formed over a triangular sandbar, right side producing mild tubes, the left a nightmare. On a strong day like this, the spot was well known for snapped boards, sprained wrists and bloody scrapes on the bottom. Lose a board altogether on the wrong series of the breaks, and sport became survival, like trying to swim in a cross fire of riptides.

That's why they loved it.

The younger surfers had been tearing it up for hours, some of the best action in months. Then came the wipeouts. That always happened at the Pump House, but today they were becoming viciously frequent.

And spectacular.

Boards and their thrown riders experienced serious airtime in opposite directions. Half the kids were soon watching from the beach; the more daring still hanging tough. Then the biggest wave yet crested and broke early, tossing them like bathtub toys. They decided to cut their losses, but still took a beating as they paddled in.

Now all the kids were staring out from the shore at empty water.

*"It's just too hairy."*

Two men walked past them and into the water.

*"The Pope and Kenny are going out? In this!"*

*"Wow."*

They paddled in a wide circle to the north, where the edge of the receding breaks didn't pull back as much. The boards reached a perfect spot off the end of the jetty, waves doming in front of them toward the beach. They instinctively stood up at the same time, and their tandem ride began as it had a thousand times before.

Onshore. *"I knew they could do it!"*

*"This is like history."*

On the break, everything smooth. Kenny smiled to himself. He had been waiting for just the right moment for months. Time to dispel this *second* best surfer label. It wasn't envy or bitterness, just the constructive competitive spirit that his mentor had instilled in him. Ready to challenge the master.

He suddenly dipped and cut across the nose of the Darby's board.

"Kenny, what the hell are you doing?"

Kenny was doing something he'd been instructed not to do ever since the day they met back 1965. He was riding *inside* the Pope along the jetty. The rule probably had a purpose back when he was a skinny kid, but now Kenny was an adult and could arguably surf as well as anyone.

What he'd never be able to match was how the Pope could read the water. It was a simple equation of years, and the Pope intuitively saw everything in a three-dimensional geometric model, from the topography of the sand on the bottom, all the way up to the tips of the peaks. And right now what the Pope saw was a swell on the lean side of the sandbar, pushing water into a trough and about to form an A-frame peak with a wicked backwash just in front of Kenny, pushing him to the south.

To the jetty.

*"Noooooo!"*

The Pope shifted his weight forward, nosing the board down the wave in nothing that remotely resembled traditional technique. From here, he was making it up as he went.

Kenny remained confident as he executed his flawless run. He never saw it coming. Competing waves met, and the water changed all at once. Instead of sweeping triumphantly into the beach, he was now fighting for balance, heading the other way toward where the waves were now pounding the eight-foot boulders so hard that they sprayed clear over the jetty and into Lake Worth Inlet on the other side.

The Pope swooped his board down fast next to the rocks and began a northern curl up the trough. If he were surfing alone, it would have been a thing of beauty. But Kenny was coming in at a stronger angle, and the physics of two opposing objects in motion had already made its decision.

The Pope jumped off his board and tackled Kenny around the waist, and they both went into the water.

The kids onshore couldn't see anything except a wooden Yater Spoon longboard splintering on the rocks and ending up on both sides of the jetty.

# Chapter 8

Serge dashed from a house in the Florida Keys and jumped in a car at the curb.

A woman wearing only a plaid shirt stood back in the doorway. "When will I see you again?"

"Maybe next laundry."

A seafoam-green Chevy Nova barreled north up the coast of Florida. The stereo blared road-trip music courtesy of Queen, Deep Purple and War.

"*. . . I'm in love with my car . . .*"

The windows were down, and a salty sea breeze whipped the occupants' hair into bedlam as they cruised Highway A1A.

Serge glanced over. "Coleman, what in God's name are you doing?"

"*Hmm, mumhh, mooshum . . .*"

"Take the sweat sock out of your mouth."

Coleman did. "What's the question?"

"I know I will regret asking, but why are you chewing on your own sock?"

"Because it's not a sock right now." Coleman opened the end to show Serge the leafy green contents.

"You're chewing pot now?"

Coleman shook his head. "I made my own catnip toy. See? I drew a smiley face with whiskers on the side."

"I guess this is a two-part question. Why are you chewing a catnip toy?"

Coleman rubbed it on his face, then curled up in the passenger seat and pawed at it. "I couldn't find a weed guy, so this was my backup plan. I think it's working."

"Coleman, catnip only works on cats."

Coleman faced Serge with sagging eyelids and a string of drool from his mouth. "Huh?"

Two hours later, they passed a burnt-red lighthouse standing on a high point overlooking the Jupiter Inlet. The driver had a bottle of spring water, and the passenger a Colt malt.

"I found a joint! Why am I always losing these?"

"Where was it?" asked Serge.

"In the sweat sock." Coleman lit up. "Look at the size of those sand dunes!"

"That means we're in Hobe Sound," said Serge. "Home of sugar-white drifts and sea-turtle nests."

"Remember your earliest road trips?" Coleman flicked ash over the edge of his door, and the wind took the whole joint out the window, then blew it back in.

"Better get that." Serge snapped open a bracket on the dashboard and passed a small fire extinguisher.

"I'm on it." Coleman knelt backward and blasted the backseat. White contrails of fire-retardant mist streamed out both sides of the car. "Another close one." He returned the extinguisher to Serge, who snapped it back in the bracket. It was a seamless procedure from heavy practice.

"Where were we?" asked Coleman.

"Early road trips."

"Right," said Coleman, upending the can of malt liquor. "When we were kids riding with our parents."

"Utter nightmares," said Serge. "Because your parents were in charge of the itinerary."

"I remember they had to pull over because I swallowed a penny."

"You swallowed a penny?"

"A few times. These were long trips for a kid."

*". . . I'm a highway star . . ."*

"My most painful childhood memory was going to Disney World," said Serge. "Right after they opened Space Mountain."

"I remember that." Coleman popped another can. "It was like the only thing the kids in the schoolyard could talk about. 'It's incredible! You're flying around in the dark in your rocket ship, through all these galaxies! You can't see where you're going and suddenly this bar appears, and you think you're going to get your head chopped off, but then the rocket dives under the bar!'"

"Almost getting your head chopped off was the best part," said Serge. "Everyone at my school knew about it. Kids took weekend trips with their parents and came back on Monday to file their reports: 'Yep, almost chopped off.' So when my family finally went to Disney, it was number one on my list. Then things immediately flew off the rails."

"What happened?"

"My folks saved up a bunch of money and stayed at the Contemporary Hotel."

"The one with the monorail running through the lobby?" said Coleman. "That seriously rocked!"

"It was the first Disney hotel designed light-years ahead of its time. Now it's an ancient homage to an obsolete vision of the future, which is even cooler," said Serge. "I know I'm supposed to hate Disney, but you have to tip your hat to certain things, like Space Mountain, which, in another believe-it-or-not, future-becomes-the-past factoid, is currently the oldest operating roller coaster in Florida."

"Righteous," said Coleman. "So what went wrong when you came with your folks?"

"The monorail was right outside our room, which meant you were supposed to get in it and zip over to the Magic Kingdom. But no, my folks had this stupid thing they always liked to do called *visiting*."

"Visiting?"

Serge nodded with gritted teeth. "It involved prolonged sitting in a room with relatives and friends."

"What did they do?"

Serge threw up his hands in aggravation. "Visit! Sometimes it involved a cheese ball. And you know me. Sitting still like that is the ultimate torture, but normally I could just run outside our house and escape the horror show. Except this time *The Visit* was at a hotel on the road and I got sucked into that bastard. Even worse, there was something tantalizingly close that I really needed to get to. I'm in that room crying and stomping my feet and pointing out the window: 'Look! Space Mountain is *right there*! We can catch the next monorail!' . . . 'No, no, no, we're visiting.' . . . 'We've been visiting for an hour! I hear the monorail!' I started waving my arms frantically like a baseball coach. 'Come on! Let's get moving!' . . . 'No, we haven't finished visiting.' . . . I started running in a circle: 'Are you kidding? Who are we visiting? The only people in this room are the same motherfuckers that live in the house we just came from!'—of course I cleaned up the language because that would have been a non-starter . . . Then my mom got out her camera . . . 'Great!' I cheered. 'We're finally going!' . . . 'No, I want to take some pictures first.' . . . 'In the *room*? Just kill me now!' And they pulled me away from the window because I was banging my forehead on the glass. I still have those photos they took of me with the saddest expression like some refugee in *Life* magazine on crutches with a bucket of brown drinking water."

"That bad?"

"Gets worse. We finally made it to the Magic Kingdom and we were there all of two hours when they start heading back to the entrance. 'Wait, where are you going?' 'Back to the room.' I said, 'Why? Did you forget something?' My mom said, 'No, we're going to visit.' They told me I was screaming at this point. You know how I occasionally get carried away and lock on to something? Especially when it involves space?"

"It's come up."

"'Mom! I haven't been on Space Mountain yet!' Well, she was really overprotective and said, 'You're not going on Space Mountain anyway. It's too dangerous.' . . . I'm like, 'Mom, I can see your lips moving, but you're just babbling.' She repeated that I wasn't going on Space Mountain, and that's when I froze in a concrete position, folded my arms tight and said, 'I am not leaving this park until I go on Space Mountain!' They said, 'Yes, you are!' And tried to grab me, but I jumped back. 'Come here, Serge!' They reached again and I jumped back again, and this went on like nine or ten times, but I was a quick little squirt and there was no way they were going to catch me. A large crowd began staring and giving us room, and the next part is actually funny now: My family fanned out to circle me and effect the capture, but I saw it unfolding and just fucking bolted. Now it's a chase. I swear to God this really happened, running all over the park, but see, I screwed myself. Today when you enter Disney, you hand them a pile of cash the size of a car payment, and all the rides are free. But back then, you got a book of tickets, A through E, depending on the quality of the ride, and Space Mountain was an E, or ninety cents, except I didn't have any tickets or money, so I had to stop running and negotiate with my folks at a distance. 'I need an E ticket!' 'Come with us right now!' 'I'm not leaving!' So my mom eventually held out an E ticket, but I thought it might be a trick and was skittish about the exchange. And then *that* went on over and over, like she was trying to hand-feed a potato chip to a wild squirrel. Finally I yelled, 'Put the E ticket on the ground and back away!'"

"What were the other people at the park doing?" asked Coleman.

"Oh, it was a big scene, but what did I care? My folks were the ones acting embarrassing. Anyway, they all eventually huddled and came to the consensus that they would never get to leave the park unless I went on the ride, so they set the ticket on the ground, and I snatched it and ran off to Space Mountain."

"Was it worth it?"

"Definitely," said Serge. "Almost got my head chopped off."

The Nova continued north and made a left turn in the middle of nothing. They cruised slowly up to a guard shack, stereo blaring.

"... *The low . . . ri-der . . .*"

"Two tickets, please," said Serge.

He was handed the stubs and a map. "Keep up the excellent work!"

The Nova rolled several miles down a winding road through the hot, hostile scrubland of saw palmettos and wire grass.

"What is this place?" asked Coleman.

"Jonathan Dickinson State Park," said Serge. "The legend of Trapper Nelson."

# Chapter 9

Eyes blinked. *Where am I?* The Pope felt the back of his head in sand. He looked up into the ashen faces of the paramedics leaning over him.

"It's me, Peter. You had a surfing accident at the jetty." He pinched one of the Pope's legs. "Do you feel that?"

"Feel what?"

He pinched the Pope's arms. "How about that?"

"What are you talking about?"

The paramedics gave each other a silent look. "Okay, let's get him stabilized on a board and to the hospital."

Kenny stood nearby with the kids. Tears rolling down his cheeks, shaking with fear and guilt. "Is he going to be okay?"

"It's best you talk to the doctors."

"I want to ride with him."

They let Kenny into the back of the ambulance, and the lights and sirens came on.

Pennies and nickels splashed into the water at the base of the fountain. Kids had been doing it for years. Rising from the fountain was a cone-shaped array of clear plastic strings that reached the ceiling and were brought to life by a circle of multicolored spotlights embedded in the roof.

The centerpiece of the Palm Beach Mall.

Everyone who grew up back then remembers that fountain.

The Palm Beach Mall was the first in the area. One of the first anywhere, for that matter, touted as the largest covered shopping center in the southeastern United States. The concept of a mall was so new and futuristic that long before the stores were even open for business, residents made special family trips on the weekend just to look at it. It opened October 26, 1967. Governor Claude Kirk and Miss USA cut the ribbon.

Now malls were everywhere. Newer, bigger. Shoppers went to them instead. And the original one on Palm Beach Lakes Boulevard was viewed like a fancy suburb that had gone downhill until cars were on blocks in the yard.

Kenny worked at the mall. He ran a register in the Paperback Booksmith. It was corporate America's idea of a hip place, with ads for concerts and the latest piped-in music.

"*. . . Girls just want to have fun . . .*"

"*. . . Dance hall days . . .*"

"*. . . Ghostbusters! . . .*"

Kenny continued ringing up the occasional customer. One of the books on display near the counter was written by sixties radical Abbie Hoffman, entitled *Steal This Book*. When Kenny wasn't looking, someone stole it.

The mall's employees were idle the last hour before they turned off the fountain's lights. Kenny made the final sale of the day—to himself—and locked up. Then he got in his '73 Beetle and drove where he always did each night, toward the Port of Palm Beach and a short residential street just south of the Blue Heron Bridge.

The VW pulled up the driveway of a two-bedroom wooden bungalow that was out of place among the overgrown ranch houses. Kenny grabbed a brown paper bag of groceries off the passenger seat and went inside:

"I'm making spaghetti!"

"I'm not hard of hearing!"

Kenny came into the living room. "Got you a book."

Darby Pope raised his La-Z-Boy lounge chair as the hardcover landed in his lap. "It's the new Willeford. *Miami Blues.*" He looked up. "How'd you know?"

Kenny smirked. "How do you think?" He disappeared into the kitchen.

Darby reached onto the tray next to his chair and opened a prescription bottle for another pill. Darby had never taken pills, not even aspirin. And when pot swept the surfing culture, well, he considered it essentially benign and he didn't judge, but it wasn't for him. Now he found himself swallowing pill after pill just to get through the day, and spent days just getting through the pills. He never came close to complaining. Could have been worse. Much worse.

The eight intervening years had passed in a blink. They'd barely gotten Darby to the hospital in time. All the way over in the ambulance, a paramedic silently watching the monitors. Blood pressure dropping and dropping. He was facing death by a thousand cuts. He lost consciousness.

They triaged his wounds, ignoring the shallow slash marks to his back and finally washing away enough blood to locate the big puncture where he slammed a pointy boulder with the fleshy side of a thigh.

The ambulance guys crashed through the emergency room doors with the stretcher. "It's Darby!"

A nurse standing with a clipboard relayed the word back: "It's Darby!"

They came running and got him to the OR. You would have thought the president had been shot. They spared nothing, and by sunset he was out of the woods.

In the following week, attention turned to the long-term picture. The spinal injury. All the doctors with all their training could only come up with this: Wait and see. These were the helpless days. The Pope never let on, cheering up all the moping visitors who came to see him. And did they visit. Dozens a day, the surfers, the lifeguards, the shop owners, former schoolmates, park rangers, cops, bankers, politicians.

The Pope knew everybody.

Then one day Kenny sat bedside and thought Darby was sleeping and gently placed a hand on his right arm.

Darby turned his head. "I must have dozed off."

Kenny sprang to his feet. "You could feel that?"

Darby's eyebrows jumped. "I could feel that!"

Doctors and nurses jammed the room. Tests. From there, the breakthroughs came fast. In seventy-two hours, all sensation, followed by movement and a full regimen of physical rehab.

After a month, a crowd of doctors and nurses gathered in the lobby. They applauded and cheered as Darby waved good-bye with his cane, then limped out the doors into the sunshine.

Once away from their view, his smile dissolved.

His surfing days were over.

I'm browning the meatballs," Kenny yelled from the kitchen. "I know you like them brown."

"I can smell 'em," said Darby, washing another pill down with half a glass of room-temperature tap water. He opened a book.

Kenny had arrived outside the hospital the day that Darby was released. He was in worse emotional shape than the Pope. "Sorry I'm late. Let me help you."

"I can walk fine." He struggled slowly toward the car.

"Let me get the door."

"I can get it myself." Another ordeal.

The VW arrived back at Darby's bungalow near Blue Heron. He had always wanted to live on the beach, but the prices were not in line with a ship welder's pay. So in '52 he'd found a place on the mainland as close to the bridge as possible. One of the few remaining wood frames, because the Pope wasn't ranch-style.

Darby was still young then and went to work on the joint. He tore out the plaster and nailed up planks of unfinished cypress. He ripped out the ceiling, exposing the trusses and beams, and hung his surfboards. He built in a tongue-and-groove bookcase. He found a taxidermied marlin at a yard sale. He saw a guy selling oil paintings on the side of the road and bought a picture of a fiery-red royal poinciana in a distressed white frame. He knocked down walls, leaving the load-bearing piers, to open everything up. He was done. He stopped in the middle of the sunlit floor and turned all the way around with a smile.

A magnificent space for his head.

When he first got home from the hospital, the visitors kept coming like they had in Darby's recovery room. One day, they stopped coming. Only Kenny remained.

The Pope always made Kenny feel at home when he visited. A few months after the hospital, Kenny got a brainstorm. "Why don't I move in? I could help."

*I don't need help,* thought the Pope. But he was worried about Kenny. Great moral character, though not the most focused guy in the world, bouncing between low-paying jobs and living in a crime-prone apartment complex on U.S. 1 that Darby shuddered to think about. The Pope saved well over the years, and had good insurance from his shipyard job at the Port of Palm Beach. If Kenny believed he was being useful, it wouldn't seem like charity.

"That's a great idea," said Darby. "I really could use the help. And since I paid off this place years ago, don't worry about any rent."

What Darby hadn't realized yet was that he indeed needed Kenny. Darby was a social creature. That's how he got to be the Pope. But with restricted mobility and that damn cane, he got out less and less. It just became too much. He stopped knowing everyone, and they stopped thinking about him.

The seventies became the eighties. "Hey, I have an idea," said Darby. "Let's go down to the Pump House. I haven't seen it in years."

"Can you make it?" asked Kenny.

"For the Pump House, definitely."

They drove over in the vintage VW. Kenny knew the walk would be difficult, but he hadn't realized the degree. It took almost a half hour with that cane to limp down the jetty to the beach. Joints throbbed in revolt, but Darby was determined. When he reached sight of the shore, it was all worth it. A wave of nostalgic joy, and a smile so big it hurt.

Kenny ran ahead to the new crop of surfers. He pointed back at Darby.

"Guys, check it out. It's the Pope!"

"Who?"

"You know, the legend."

"That old man with the cane?"

"You've never heard of the Pope of Palm Beach?" said Kenny. "Only the best surfer in the entire history of the Pump House."

"Yeah, whatever . . ."

Darby wasn't so far away as to be out of earshot. He still had that big smile when Kenny returned, but now it was a fraud.

"Man, were they impressed!" said Kenny. "Everyone still talks about you!"

"Really appreciate you bringing me down here."

"Anytime."

As he limped back toward the car, Darby vowed never to return to the Pump House, and he never would.

# Chapter 10

The Nova stopped to let a snake cross the road. Coleman unscrewed a flask. "I remember this state park now. We were always taking field trips here as a kid."

"*Everyone* took field trips to Jonathan Dickinson," said Serge, slowing the Nova at the train tracks. "Named after some dude who shipwrecked nearby in 1696. Normally being immortalized by a park is great tidings, but if Johnny were here today, I'm sure he'd say, 'What is this bullshit? All the positive things I did in life, but no, I get in *one* little shipwreck.'"

"I remember the swimming area down by the docks where they made all us kids go in," said Coleman. "And there were alligators!"

"Of course there were alligators. It's a brackish stretch of a Florida river!" Serge parked near the picnic pavilions. "I remember looking at my parents: 'What? Get in *that* water? And you were giving me static about Space Mountain?'"

Serge led the way down toward the shore. "Right on time. Here she comes now."

A covered pontoon boat pulled up to the pier. Departing sightseers got out and Serge and Coleman got on.

Soon they were quietly sailing up the remote, tea-colored Loxahatchee with all kinds of lush vegetation thriving from the banks. Three turtles perfectly lined up to sun themselves on an exposed log. An osprey circled before landing in a nest with a mullet.

"Off to your left is a manatee," the captain said in his tour-guide microphone. The boat listed to port as the tourists stampeded over.

A woman shaped like a yam and wearing a too-tight Bon Jovi shirt raised her hand. "We live in Crystal River and we have lots of manatees."

"That's nice," said the captain, thinking, *We're out in undiluted nature and it's still all about you.* Coleman wasn't thinking anything, clandestinely hanging over the starboard side to suck down half a flask of $1.99 vodka with a red-eyed scorpion on the label.

"And if you look to your right," said the captain as he pulled back on the throttle, "there's an alligator up in those mangrove roots."

The boat tilted the other way. Cell phones snapped photos. Serge and Coleman glanced at each other and shrugged.

After that, all the tourists were silent, transfixed by the water as the boat slowly pushed on. Bend after ever-narrowing bend, deeper into the jungle and a primordial sensation that nature was in total control.

Out of the quiet came a prolonged, reverberating croaking noise.

"Is that some kind of giant poisonous swamp frog?" asked a woman from Bismarck.

"No," said Serge. "A liquid lunch."

Coleman patted his stomach and covered his mouth. "Sorry."

The pontoons split the water as salinity fell and gator population rose.

Coleman leaned sideways to pull a wedgie out of his underwear. "This reminds me of *Apocalypse Now*."

"Good analogy," said Serge. "Based on Joseph Conrad's *Heart of Darkness*. 'The river wound through the park like a main circuit cable that plugged me straight into Trapper.'"

"Trapper!" said Coleman. "Man, when I was in school, all the kids whispered about that crazy hermit who lived way upriver, and we were all scared shitless. But I don't think anyone actually ever saw him."

"I did," said Serge.

"What? Really?"

Serge nodded. "I stole a canoe when I was too young to get a penalty, because I wanted to meet him and see what the fuss was about."

"Jesus! What happened?"

"He couldn't understand why I wasn't afraid. Then the people in charge of the park retrieved me because I was a missing kid. But first they had to catch me."

"Space Mountain."

"Trapper was better at it than my parents."

"Trapper *trapped* you?"

"Poetic, isn't it?"

Coleman examined his fingernails and decided that their whole concept was freaky. "By the way, whatever happened to that literature-tour-of-Florida thing you were doing?"

"We're on it right now."

"We are?"

"Trapper."

"Nelson again?" said Coleman. "But he didn't write."

"No, but one of my all-time favorite Florida authors penned an excellent novel about him."

"Who was that?"

"Guy named Reese," said Serge. "Published three of the state's finest books in the 1980s. He followed up his fictional account of Trapper with a pair of similar books on the Bahamian Conchs who founded my hometown, and a murder mystery set amid the east coast beach culture. Then inexplicably he just stopped. Nothing. Crickets. When the Internet came along, I figured there had to be some bread crumbs, but zero again, like he vanished off the face of the planet."

"Probably killed by a moose," said Coleman. "That's my bet. It could really happen, too, you know, if you made a false move on the moose. Man, am I high! He must have made a false move. But how can a move be false? It's still a move. 'Moose' is another one of those words when you're stoned. *Moose, moose, moooooose.*"

"You're starting to fuck this up again. Remember our long talk?"

"No, really." Coleman flapped hands erratically inches from Serge's nose. "How can you tell me that's false?" He took a swig from the flask and tapped the side of his head. "I'm always thinking." Burp. "Moose."

Serge hung his face in his hands.

The pontoon boat navigated a final bend and reached a lonely location so far upriver it became a creek filled with clumps of brush that prevented further passage. On the left bank, thin, cut-down trees stood upright in the muck to support the rusty metal roof of a primitive dock. The dock itself was nearly submerged at high tide. The boat nosed up and the passengers climbed out.

A park ranger narrated as he led the herd in hiking shorts and straw hats and sneakers, first to the empty cages of the defunct personal zoo: rickety, nailed-together pieces of hewn wood gathered from the land and enclosed across the front with scraps of chain link. A few of the cages still had hand-printed signs for raccoons, wildcats, and alligators.

"Hang back," Serge told Coleman, tucking a coffee thermos under his arm and aiming a camera. *Click, click, click.* "I love people, but I hate tour groups. The guide will be trying to explain priceless history, and there's always one or two who keep raising their hands to volunteer how it relates to their lives. Ruins the experience for everyone. 'We had our own hermit back in Wichita, except he lived in an apartment. And he wasn't technically a hermit, just dirty.' Or worse, they try to top the tour guide: 'Did you know I can bench-press three hundred?'"

"Like the manatee woman back on the boat," said Coleman. "Screw that noise."

"Amen." Serge rotated in place. *Click, click, click.* He lowered his camera. "This place relates to my life. That thatched hut and lean-to are just like I remember when I took my canoe trip. But I really remember the spanking later. Isn't it weird how the most vivid childhood memories are when the adults got excited over nothing?"

"I remember all my spankings," said Coleman.

"Me too," said Serge. "Like when my dad had to mow the lawn and went in the carport. Then he calls my mom out. 'What is it, dear?' 'Look! Someone stole the lawn-mower engine!' 'That's odd. Why didn't they just steal the whole thing?' 'I can't figure it out.' And they're still staring down at the empty chassis when a roar comes up the street, and I go zipping by in my new homemade go-kart. That was my go-kart spanking."

"I remember one," said Coleman. "I didn't really get spanked, but there was definitely a lot of excitement. It was when I was really little and got abducted."

"Stop right there!" said Serge. "Good God, you never told me you were abducted."

"I was so young, what did I know?" said Coleman. "The only reason I remember now is because I was playing in the kitchen while my mom was making dinner, and I mentioned something about a playground, and she asks, 'What playground?' And I say the one that the nice man gave me a ride to. She grabs me hard by the shoulders: 'What nice man?' I say, 'The one who pulled up in his car when I was playing in the yard and opened the door and told me to get in, so I did. And then later he dropped me back off at the house and left.'"

"Jesus!" said Serge. "Anything could have happened to you!"

"That's what my mom said. More like yelled. She completely lost her shit and called the police, and then there were a bunch of cops in our living room, and they're all asking me to describe the man and anything that might have happened. And then my dad comes in the front door, and I point and say, 'There he is now.' My mom says, 'No, that's your father.' I said, 'Right, that's the nice man who told me to get in the car and took me to the playground.' Now she's shaking the daylights out of me. 'You scared us half to death! Why on earth did you say a nice man took you to the playground?' I said, 'What? You mean Dad isn't a nice man?'"

Serge just stared with an open mouth.

*"Excuse me?"* the ranger called out. *"Could you catch up with the group?"*

"Better get moving," said Serge. "This is a mandatory tour because they don't want anyone stealing souvenirs."

"Everything you see here was made by hand," said the ranger. "Trapper cleared the land by cutting down all these trees by himself with an ax. The slash pines have a large natural amount of turpentine, making them rot-free and bug-resistant. He used the logs to construct those two cabins and the other structures so sturdy that they've weathered countless hurricanes—"

"Bang!" yelled Serge, collapsing to the ground and lying still with his eyes closed.

Everyone ran over. Serge remained motionless.

"Did he have a heart attack?"

"Is he dead?"

"Make room!" said the ranger.

Serge hopped back up with an irrepressible grin. "That was just a re-enactment. This relates to my life. Did Trapper kill himself? Or was it murder? You make the call!"

The ranger glared.

"What?" said Serge. He picked his thermos up off the ground. "Time for coffee! I was saving it for The Special Place!" Brown fluid tricked down his chest as he chugged.

The ranger just shook his head and led the gang into one of the cabins, stopping at a fireplace. "In April of 1984 some rangers were restoring these grounds and found a loose brick in this chimney that they were going to mortar back in position. Except the brick was loose on purpose. It was Trapper's hiding place, where they learned that the legend of his secret treasure was true. Almost two thousand dollars in old coins were discovered and are now housed in a museum in Tallahassee."

Serge bounced on the balls of his feet. "Ooo! Ooo! Pick me! Pick me!"

The ranger sighed. "Yes, you in back."

"I've been to Tallahassee! A lot of those coins are more than a hundred years old with rare dates and mint marks, pushing their true value into six figures. And when the park announced the discovery three decades ago, they put out a press release saying that Trapper's homestead was thoroughly searched and no more treasure turned up. You had to say that whether you were thorough or not because waves of treasure hunters would come out and dig up the place until it looked like a bombing range. Were you really thorough or just farting around? This relates to my life because I used to collect pennies. I can bench-press three hundred."

A pregnant pause. "We were thorough . . . Now, if all of you will follow me to the next building . . ."

Tourists dutifully filed out the door.

"Coleman, come here!"

"What?"

"Give me a hand with this brick. I think it's loose."

The ranger stuck his head back in the cabin. "What are you doing?"

Serge spun around. "Nuthin'."

"Please keep up with the group."

The tourists left the last building and reassembled in front of the pens. The ranger placed his hand on the chain link. "And this is where Trapper kept the menagerie that he caught himself. Before his health declined and he became paranoid, tour boats often came here for picnic breaks, and Trapper charged a small admission to see his tiny zoo. He also entertained the northerners by wrestling alligators—"

"Serge, stop! You're hurting me!"

"Hold still! I have to get my chin over the top of your head so I can stick my arms out."

The ranger stood at a loss. "What are you doing?"

Coleman was on his stomach with Serge straddling his back. "Just alligator wrestling."

"We don't actually have a rule," said the ranger, "because nobody remotely envisioned the need. But please, no alligator wrestling with other people in the tour group."

"That kind of destroys the mood, don't you think?"

The ride back in the pontoon boat was universally quiet.

"I don't think he likes you," whispered Coleman.

"This is embarrassing," said Serge. "Assigned mandatory seats next to the ranger so he can watch us. Is this what nature trips have come to?"

The Nova pulled away from Jonathan Dickinson after its occupants were firmly requested to visit other parks.

"What do we do now?" asked Coleman.

"Visit other parks."

It was a brief drive to the sea spray of the blowing rocks at Hobe Sound. Serge leaped out of the car. "Let's go watch the turtles!"

They traversed the boardwalk over beach vegetation and hit pristine sands.

"I don't see any turtles," said Coleman.

"We have to wait until dark." Serge plopped down on the shore. "Turtles are the best!"

# Chapter 11

1984

Florida grapefruit!
Indian River grapefruit, to be exact. No other way to start the day.

That had been Darby's thinking since the early fifties. He always hurled himself into each new morning. Up before dawn to watch the sky unfold. Then newspaper and grapefruit. Later would come eggs and toast and the morning TV news with the fishing report.

But first the grapefruit. And not poured from some container, but just off the tree, sliced in half. They delivered Indian River grapefruit to the long packing house with all the big windows sitting right up to the sidewalk on U.S. 1 near the Dairy Belle and Riviera Theatre. You could actually watch through those windows as the old-style citrus crates were packed and shipped every day. The stretch of U.S. 1 was called Broadway, making kids think the street in New York was named after theirs.

Slicing the grapefruit in half was just the beginning. The only way for Darby to truly enjoy the ritual was to work for it—carving each anticipated bite from the rind with a special serrated spoon.

"I've got your grapefruit!" Kenny came into the living room with a bamboo tray. "Already sliced it away from the peel with a knife and cut the bites to make it easier."

"Thanks."

Darby sighed, popped a pill and stared at his bookcase with a framed packing-crate label that people now collected. The Riviera Beach packing house was long since closed, along with the Dairy Belle, and the theater had gone X-rated before being leveled for a Walgreens.

Darby's evolution after the hospital stay was like a pro athlete at the end of a long and storied career. The perfunctory tearful press conference, well-wishes from everyone in the front office, camera flashes. Then: *Now what?*

Instead of springing up from bed each morning, he lay there listlessly with the heart tugs from the missing piece.

Surfing.

Aging athletes handle retirement two different ways. Some passively wait for the missing piece to just go away, but it never does. The successful ones replace the piece. That's what Darby did, and those early waking moments of regret became fond memories. He even relented and allowed Kenny to hang a large black-and-white photo of Darby riding a wave in his prime.

Darby found his replacement piece accidentally, and in a most unlikely place. Here's what happened:

The longer he lived with Darby, the more Kenny became fascinated with his hero's . . . *stuff*. That's the way guys are. Drink lots of beer and look under the hoods of muscle cars, look at tools in the woodshop, look at signed baseballs. Kenny started with the old surfing trophies stored in cardboard boxes—"Why don't you put these out?"—his old ribbons and yellowed newspaper clippings— "You should do something with these"—then the closet—"I didn't know you had guns."

"A few."

"You don't seem like the hunting type."

"I'm not." Darby read the sports section. "I could never shoot anything, I mean that's alive. I just enjoy target practice. Something about it relaxes me."

"What's this one?" asked Kenny, walking back over to a lounger in full recline.

"Whoa!" Darby popped the chair upright. "Don't move!"

Kenny froze. "What's the matter?"

"First, never let the line of the barrel cross anything that you'd be sorry putting a bullet in. Point it at the floor."

"Okay." He lowered it.

"Next, every gun is loaded."

"This thing's loaded?"

"No, I never leave a loaded gun in the house," said Darby. "But you don't know that. So you always check the chamber. Even *I* check the chamber whenever I pick up one of my own rifles that I know I've unloaded."

Kenny looked at the alien mechanism. "I don't know how to check it. I don't know anything about guns."

"Bring it here."

Darby worked the bolt on the Remington. All clear. He handed it back. "Why don't you put that away for now. Having a gun out without purpose is an unnecessary variable."

Kenny headed back to the closet. "You have ammo?"

"Sure, what good's a gun without bullets?"

"Will you take me shooting?"

"Maybe."

Kenny closed the closet and ambled over to Darby's last and largest collection of stuff: the handmade bookcase that took up the entire back wall of the living room, floor to ceiling. "Anything good here?"

"It's all good."

Kenny started with the first photo-filled surfing book and

ended a few weeks later with the last photo-filled history book. Everything else—all the novels—was considered filler and skipped. To Kenny, books that were just entire gray pages of words were like high noon to a vampire. Not his fault. When he was in school, publishers weren't targeting his age group the way they are now. And as for the curriculum, *Beowulf* and *Wuthering Heights*. No disrespect intended, but young boys are the highest-risk group of becoming non-readers, and the Brontë sisters weren't helping the cause. He learned to hate books before he could learn to love them.

One evening he stood staring at the bookshelf. And staring. He finally walked away.

"What's the matter?" asked Darby. "Couldn't find something you liked?"

"I've read them all," said Kenny.

"You haven't read any."

"Yes, I have."

"You've just been looking at pictures."

"The others aren't for me," said Kenny, grabbing the dinner tray off Darby's chair-side table and heading for the kitchen.

*Not for me?* Darby gazed incredulously at a wall of titles that constituted an entire curriculum on twentieth-century American lit. He heard dishes and utensils clanging in the kitchen sink. This was a serious problem.

Kenny came back into the living room. "Want some of these chips?"

"Sit down," said Darby. "You don't read books?"

"I did in school." Kenny shrugged. "Didn't like it."

Darby rested his head back in thought. "Did they make you read *Beowulf*?"

"Don't remind me."

"*Wuthering Heights*?"

"Gag."

"That explains everything." He pointed at the back wall. "Middle shelf, fourth book from the end."

Kenny grabbed it. "Here you go."

"No, it's for you."

"What for?"

"I want you to read it."

"Why?"

"*Why* read a book?" said Darby. "If you read books, you'd understand that question is like 'Why breathe?'"

"But I don't want—"

Darby held up a hand. "The schools back then got it all wrong. Watch any kids eat: They never start with the vegetables."

Kenny looked at the orange-and-yellow dust jacket. "*Breakfast of Champions?*"

"For my money, *Slaughterhouse-Five* was his masterwork, but this one is a better gateway drug."

The next morning, Kenny stuck the book back on the shelf.

"What?" said a surprised Darby. "You didn't like it?"

"I finished it."

"Finished? But I just gave it to you last night."

"Couldn't put it down," said Kenny. "I never knew there was a book like that."

"There's a whole *world* of books like that," said Darby. "When did you have time to sleep?"

"I didn't." Yawn. "I have to go to sleep."

When Kenny awoke, he went straight for the bookcase. "What else you got?"

"Third shelf, book eight."

"*Catcher in the Rye?*"

"Its appeal is a bit younger," said Darby. "But since you're just getting started . . ."

"I know. Vegetables, gateway."

The next day.

"Bottom row, second from the last."

"Better give me another while I'm here."

Darby hid his amazement. "Same row, number six."

"Heller, Thompson," said Kenny, disappearing into his bedroom.

And so on. "... Top shelf ... fourth shelf ... ninth book ... the one on the end ..."

On a Friday night, Kenny sat next to Darby in the living room. He turned the last page of his current book and closed it. He realized Darby was staring at him. "What?"

Darby just blinked a couple times. "I don't know what to say."

"Neither do I," said Kenny. "Why on earth didn't they teach these in school?"

"Did you notice that most are a bit anti-authority?"

"So?"

"So they teach you how to think," said Darby. "So that's why they don't teach them in school."

Then on to the Florida authors. MacDonald, McGuane. Darby pointed. "Try the Willeford you bought me."

One morning, Darby was on his second grapefruit, reading the *Post*. He heard a clattering sound from the kitchen. He raised his eyes and stared blankly at a point on the wall. "This I've got to see."

Darby grabbed his cane and hobbled into the next room. "Where'd you get the typewriter?"

*Clack, clack, clack.* "Pawnshop."

"Why?"

"To write."

"What are you writing for?"

"That's like, 'Why breathe?'"

"Don't be smart," said Darby. "I meant, is that a résumé or a letter to the editor?"

"I'm just writing because I like it."

"Since when do you write?"

"Three minutes ago." *Clack, clack, clack.* "I really like it."

"What are you writing?"

"A novel."

Darby rubbed a hand over his eyes. *What have I done?* He pulled out a chair at the kitchen table and struggled into it. "Don't take this the wrong way, but I just don't want you to get frustrated."

*Clack, clack, clack.* "What are you trying to tell me?"

"You've never written before," said Darby. "You never *read* before a few months ago."

"I always got A's when we had to do reports in school." Kenny stopped typing and turned with the happiest face that Darby had ever seen. "Remember when you were a little kid and watched a big football game on TV? And after it was over, you were so jacked up that you just had to run outside with the other kids and play football and fantasize you were in the game you just saw? Remember?"

Darby nodded.

"That's the effect these authors have on me." He squeezed his hands together. "I've never had bigger idols in my life. I don't know how they can possibly do what they do with just black-and-white words on a page. They make me feel and laugh and suck me into another world until I forget they're just words. They're doing the impossible."

Darby chuckled. "I had a mild inkling that you might *like* reading."

"I love it!" Kenny turned back to the typewriter. "And I want to know what this feels like, even if it's just fantasizing. I don't care if it's bad."

*Clack, clack, clack.*

Darby had found his replacement piece.

*Chapter 12*

The brown wooden boat was a close cousin of a Chinese junk, the kind you might see packed shoulder to shoulder with Haitian refugees. The kind that sank.

Many such vessels were scuttled and abandoned, half sticking out of the water, littering the mangrove coastline of South Florida from Fort Lauderdale to Biscayne Bay. And those derelicts were in better shape than this one, riding unnaturally low in the water, somehow still able to negotiate a truce with buoyancy.

But the boat didn't attract attention docking in the Miami River, where questionable maritime was the norm. Pickup trucks and men waited. A dozen had jumped aboard before the mooring lines were secure. And by the time those ropes were tied, the men were off again. They swiftly packed cocaine bricks under tarps and bungees. Someone slapped the side of a truck, and the pickups were off.

It was a loose convoy of six. They preferred Fords. Only two had the drugs, the middle trucks. The rest were for eventualities.

The leading trucks beat the bushes for police. They had special switches installed so they could feign broken taillights if needed to draw the heat. And if, somehow, the cops tried to pull over one of the middle trucks, then there were the trailing drivers, who would promptly crash into the police cars and apologize.

They arrived at the warehouse between Hialeah Gardens and the Glades on Okeechobee Road. The black predawn sky had just begun to yield as a string of high beams hit unpainted metal, and other men on the ground quickly slid open the twin galvanized doors.

It was a profitable little business that was compartmentalized in a much larger octopus. Everyone knew they were part of something bigger, but nobody knew what. Except the leader of the crew, Greco.

Greco got his start as many had, unloading those boats on the river. Lean, ambitious and uneducated. Both his strength and weakness was a wholesale lack of sophistication. His business sense remained basic, but more essential, so did his relationship with violence. Casual, no hesitation or self-reflection. He would go far.

The lines of secrecy about the chain of command might have been strict, but everyone knew the top bosses. One Saturday at dusk, the seven-year-old grandson of one of these kingpins hopped on a new shiny bicycle and zoomed down the driveway without looking.

The mangled bike still lay in the street when the ambulance took the child away unconscious. Police tried to console the shaken driver, who lived four doors down. The boy would make a full recovery, but right now all that anyone knew: He lay in a coma with broken legs. The neighborhood whispered that the driver should get out of town. But it was an accident, he thought. Surely that counted for something.

They found the driver a week later, piece by piece, in a road-fill quarry circled by vultures. The next night, Greco was down at the river about to unload a Jamaican trawler. A tap on his shoulder. Someone pointed toward the open back door of a Lexus.

"But I'm supposed to unload," said Greco.

"You have the night off."

They frisked Greco, and he got in.

It was an anonymous three-bedroom Mediterranean house. The screen door featured the original wire sculpture of a sailfish. The den had discount wood paneling and paintings of saints. An older man relaxed in his favorite chair. A tray sat in front of him with a TV dinner, and in front of that, a TV. The man used the remote to switch the set off. He turned to the four people who had just entered the room.

"Are you the one they call Greco?"

"Yes."

"I have heard an interesting rumor about you concerning a certain one of my neighbors." The old man scooped up a final fork of corn niblets from his tray. Then he silently pointed around the room with the utensil, meaning there had been recent problems with listening devices. "From now on, I only want a yes or no. Leave out any details. Is it true what they say you did?"

"Yes."

"Did anyone tell you to?"

"No."

"You just decided to do this thing without any authorization?"

"Yes."

The old man faced the blank TV. A pause. The trio who had escorted Greco were on call for whatever they were asked next. The remote control clicked the TV back on and turned the volume up extra loud. "If you haven't heard, I am a man who likes to show his appreciation. I have some work that requires someone with your talents. I've already assumed you will accept."

The old man raised a palm slightly, meaning he would now watch TV, and they would now leave.

Greco got to work, which was what they call wet work, and he received high marks. People began disappearing, then turning up. In metal drums, in the river, in burning cars. The disappearances were perfect vanishing acts, and the discoveries high drama. Messages received loud and clear.

From there, Greco was given his own crew and assigned the leg of the smuggling operation from the Miami River to the Georgia state line on I-95. The simple, unambiguous assignment was an exact fit for his business instincts.

One night a tiny rat hole was found in one of the cocaine bricks. A shot was heard outside the warehouse. Greco walked back in. The crew was down one unloader. But no more rat holes. Another time, a member of the group got picked up on a Saturday night for a concealed gun in a nightclub. Sunday morning, guards found him shivved in the county lockup. No margin for plea bargains. Everyone else began behaving on the weekend. The bosses liked Greco's tight ship and left him alone.

The old millennium became the new. Greco's crew had tripled. So had business complexity, technology and banking laws. They assigned him an accountant. Greco didn't understand why, but didn't say so.

The accountant was gnomish and seemed bent over even when he wasn't. He wore glasses with unfashionable round lenses that lent the impression of a scurrying little creature with tiny claws. He always smelled like cucumbers from the sandwiches he ate every day. Greco thought he was funny. His name was Salenca.

Salenca kept coming to his boss with his latest ideas.

"No, no, no," said Greco. "Just the cocaine."

"But identity theft is the future," said Salenca. "Do the math. The difference in prison sentences alone makes it a no-brainer."

"*You* do the math," said Greco. "That what you're paid for. Not ideas."

Salenca was undeterred. "We steal the information from the magnetic strips and sell it to Russia and China. We bundle them and make a killing."

"Steal how?"

"Just walk by a person," said Salenca. "They have these new electronic receivers that you hide in a briefcase or handbag. I can go out at lunch in downtown Miami and come back with a hundred cards."

"No, no, no, cocaine. Leave me alone!"

"Can you at least ask your bosses? Maybe I could have a tiny crew of my own and try it out as an experiment."

"You? With a crew?" Greco cracked up. "I like you. But seriously, leave me alone."

Salenca went back to work, keeping his ideas to himself. He kept records in code, and then those codes were encrypted on special flash drives used by military contractors with security clearance. It was tedious and lucrative. Salenca wanted it to be more lucrative. He began using a different accounting method. Without permission. He wasn't worried; it would all be Greek to Greco.

A month later, a black Mercedes arrived at the warehouse. They called for Greco and Salenca. This type of meeting was more than rare.

All the top bosses.

It was held at a mothballed safe house in Tamarac, where there was a certainty of no FBI bugs. The three kingpins were all sitting, and there were no more chairs. The row of bosses gave the general appearance of the logo from Pep Boys automotive repair.

"We noticed that you've started using a new accounting method," said boss number one.

"We have?" said Greco.

"Yes, one that allows someone to skim from us," said boss two.

"What?" said Greco.

"Frankly, we're surprised," said number three. "You have a reputation for running a tight ship."

"I don't know . . . what you're talking about," said Greco.

"No need to explain," said the first boss. "Perhaps we were expecting too much. You came to us with a certain skill level that has worked out quite nicely. We know you don't have a degree in accounting."

Greco went to speak, but boss number two held up a hand. "We've had our people look into the books, into certain bank accounts we weren't expecting to find. And we located an interesting one that was recently opened by your ledger man, Salenca here."

"Salenca!" said Greco, spinning toward his accountant with the shock of underestimation.

"Me?" Salenca shouted as two goons seized him by the arms. "There must be some explanation!"

"There is," said boss three. "Small amounts have been regularly deposited and quietly withdrawn from a money market fund in your name."

"What fund?" said Salenca.

"You son of a bitch!" Greco yelled. "Let me kill him myself!"

"That won't be necessary," said the second boss. "But you can help us."

"I'm so sorry for all of this," said Greco. "It won't happen again. Anything you want. Name it."

"Who do you think should be your successor?"

"Wait . . . What?"

"Who should take over your crew?"

"Can't we talk about this?" said Greco. "I'm going to lose my crew just because this weasel tricked me with some numbers?"

Boss three shook his head. "That's not why."

"Then what is it?" said Greco.

"Apparently you understand far more about accounting than we could have ever imagined," said boss one.

"Uh, no, I don't."

"I didn't finish explaining the results of our investigation," said boss two. "After the money left Salenca's account, it was wired directly to the Caymans."

"So it's about the money." Greco began nodding. "I understand now. But I'm sure we can get it back. I'll see to it personally."

"We've already gotten it back," said boss two. "That's not the problem."

"Then what is it?" asked Greco.

"The Caymans are an interesting place. We do most of our banking there, too, and with much bigger assets, so we draw a lot of water in those islands. They take bribes."

"The account the money went into had your name on it," said boss three.

"You're looking at me?" Greco pointed. "You mean Salenca."

Boss one shook his head. "No, we're positive. We took the liberty of going through your cell phone. And we discovered something else interesting: the account number and access PIN of Salenca's money market. Any explanation what those were doing in there?"

"I barely know how to use that damn phone!"

"At first we thought the two of you were in it together," said boss three. "But we found no connection between Salenca and his account. All the information was solely in your possession. And all the transfers were made electronically from your phone. In case the skim was ever detected, you had framed your own accountant to take the fall. Tragically, we almost fell for it."

The goons released Salenca and grabbed Greco.

"This is a huge mistake," said the thrashing crew captain. "It's the first I've heard of any of this. Please give me time to figure it out!"

The boss on the end looked at the goons and tilted his head. Time to take Greco for a ride.

Shoe heels struggled for traction on the floor as they dragged Greco from the room.

"Excuse me?"

The three bosses turned toward Salenca. "Yes?"

"May I?"

There was a brass lamp on the desk. Before they could answer, Salenca had ripped off the shade and gripped it around the neck. He charged Greco, bringing its base down hard on Greco's nose, dropping him to the ground. Salenca pounced, ferociously swinging the lamp over and over, knocking him out, then killing him, then still going until the skull opened.

Other heads in the room recoiled. They all had pretty hard shells, but even for them, this was a bit much. And they definitely hadn't seen it coming from such a milquetoast.

"I think you can stop now."

"What?" said Salenca. "Oh." He dropped the lamp and stood up with red flecks across his face. "I hear you're looking for someone to take over his crew. I have some ideas . . ."

# Chapter 13

Swish. *Crack!*

The three-wood met the dimpled Titleist golf ball, and the tee shot sailed down the dogleg fairway. An electric cart followed it along a winding path. A cane sat in the back of the cart where a bag of clubs would normally go.

"I love golf," said Darby.

"I didn't know you played golf," said Kenny, turning the steering wheel.

"I don't, but I love golf courses," said Darby. "Florida courses. Look around. What's *not* to love?"

Kenny looked around. The sun, a shatteringly clear sky, red and yellow tropical flowers, scattered old-growth coconut palms bending along a fairway that was so manicured it looked like someone had used tweezers. Then clusters of sabal palms in the distance toward the twin towers of the landmark Breakers Hotel, originally built by railroad magnate Henry Flagler.

"Construction began in 1896," added Darby. "Oldest eighteen-hole course in the entire state, and considering all the golf down here, that's saying something."

They came to a stop at a sugar-white sand trap. A tall young man addressed his ball with a six-iron and sent it over a water hazard, landing with a backspin on the sixth green. The cart started again.

Kenny held a clipboard against the steering wheel. "I don't know anything about golf."

"That's what the coaches are for," said Darby. "Did you call them?"

Kenny nodded. "I don't know why I can't just be a writer. What does watching people hit balls have to do with it?"

"Fundamentals."

The day that Darby had first found his roommate typing in the kitchen, he'd laid down a firm rule: If you're going to attempt something, give it your very best shot, nothing less. He picked up the phone. "I'll call Lardner."

"Who's that?"

"One of the sports guys I know at the *Post*."

A few minutes later, Darby hung up. "It's all set. You're now officially a stringer for a daily city paper."

"You got me hired at the *Post*?"

"No, you don't exactly have a job." Darby eased himself back into a chair at the table. "You'll go to high school sports events, write something up and phone it in to the desk. That's a stringer. Pays ten bucks."

"But I don't know how to write."

"Precisely," said the Pope. "Trying to develop a new skill—writing, surfing, whatever—is a lot like learning a foreign language. You can take a bunch of courses in a classroom, or you can move to that foreign country. The latter demands survival."

"But I don't want to write about sports."

"Even better." Darby yanked the page out of the typewriter. "You need to do something where you're forced to write on a regular basis whether you like it or not. A stringer."

"But what if I suck?"

Darby finished reading the page Kenny had just written. "Oh, you're definitely going to suck. That's what the rewrite desk is for. You'll see what you've written and learn from what they had to change."

"What about my novel?"

"I'll be your editor."

"You know how to edit?"

"No, but I know how to read." Darby gestured at his bookshelf. "I'll be your test audience and point out what successful authors do that you should try . . ."

. . . And now they were riding down a golf-cart path on Kenny's first assignment, a tournament where the Breakers had donated the course for a few hours. "I'm getting nervous," said Kenny. "They're already on the twelfth hole and I haven't written anything yet. I don't even know what's going on."

"Doesn't matter," said Darby. "Just talk to the coaches at the end. They'll give you all the results and pithy quotes. They know the routine."

"Sounds like they're doing all the work for me."

"Except the writing . . ."

They reached a hole that ran along the Atlantic Ocean. A player tossed a few blades of grass in the air to gauge the onshore breeze.

"I really appreciate you getting me this stringer thing," said Kenny. "But is it okay in the meantime if I write other stuff that I'd enjoy?"

"Sure, just as long as you keep up your job at the *Post*. What do you want to write?"

"A story, except I can't think of one."

"I can think of a million."

"Because you know everybody," said Kenny. "I don't."

"I'll give you my stories," said Darby. "And you write them up. How about Trapper?"

"Trapper Nelson? The hermit you took me out to meet that day?"

"Make it a mystery," said Darby. "Historical fiction. It's got all the elements. Remember the day back in 1968 when they found Trapper dead from a gunshot?"

"Every school kid in this county does." The electric cart continued up the path to a putting green of Bermuda grass. "We were riveted. As if the Trapper myth wasn't big enough already, now this spooky tale of unsolved murder on the Loxahatchee. Except the police officially ruled it a suicide, so I'm sure it was just imaginations running wild on the playground."

"Not quite," said Darby. "The adults had questions, too. I mean, who kills themselves with a shotgun blast to the *stomach*? Respectable people around here still debate to this day. That's where you should start. Of course, it will be badly written."

"Is that supposed to be encouraging?"

"All first drafts are bad. Then you keep polishing as you develop your craft from working at the *Post*."

The cart rolled on as Kenny began jotting on his clipboard. "Tell me what you remember about him."

"Where do I even begin?" said Darby. "Before he became a hermit, he was strong as an ox and dashingly handsome. Romanced numerous society women, entertained tourists, plus a legendary appetite. I once saw him eat eighteen eggs for breakfast. Then there was the secret treasure. Trapper intensely distrusted financial institutions . . ."

An hour later, the golf cart sat idle next to the eighteenth green. The last high school coach had walked away from Kenny as he finished taking quotes and scribbling his handwritten story. He gave it to Darby with hopeful eyes. "What do you think?"

The Pope read down the page. *Yikes! I thought it might be a little bad* . . . He concealed his thoughts and smiled. "This is your big break. Phone it in."

*Team America.*

That's the title of history's most underrated political-satire musical comedy film starring puppets that have sex. And one of the film's best stage production songs: "We Need a Montage!"

A tennis ball cleared a net in Riviera Beach. A player threw his racket in the air. Kenny wrote feverishly about the high school victory.

A baseball cleared the left field wall in Boynton. Kenny grilled the coach.

Fingers furiously hit the keys of a manual typewriter.

A diver jumped off a springboard in North Palm. Kenny barked to an editor.

"... *We need a montage!* ..."

Lacrosse game, football game, soccer. A pen scrawled notes. Volleyball, track and field. Coaches peppered with questions.

A hand smacked the return carriage of a manual typewriter.

Cross-country, wrestling. Dimes jammed into pay phones.

"... *We need a montage!* ..."

Chess club, math bowl. Spectators going wild. Kenny sprinted from the door on deadline.

*Music fades out* ...

Kenny pulled a completed page from the typewriter. He set it on top of a stack of similar pages, then picked up the whole pile and tapped it into alignment on the kitchen table.

Darby was in his lounge chair finishing a bowl of chili when Kenny handed him the stack. "Finished the first few chapters."

"Let me see that." Darby put on glasses and began reading. He took the glasses off and looked up. "It's kind of hard to read with you hovering over me staring like that."

"Sorry." Kenny took the seat next to him, straining to stare in the opposite direction as hard as he could.

"That's even more distracting."

"I'll go in the bedroom." He left.

Darby made notes on the pages with a ballpoint pen. An hour later. "Kenny!"

The younger man materialized in front of the Pope like a hyper puppy. "Well?"

"It's bad."

Kenny frowned.

"And that's good," said Darby. "You're starting. Now just keep going. You'll build up the muscles."

"Any suggestions?"

"Relax," said Darby.

"Okay." Kenny sat down and slouched.

"No, I mean relax at the typewriter. You're pushing too hard and overwriting."

"I don't understand."

"When I read this . . ." Darby held up the pages. "I feel like I'm reading *writing*. Just have a conversation with the reader."

"You got it," said Kenny. "Listen, I have a few more questions about Trapper. Did he really put up signs that land mines were buried on his property? . . ."


. . . One year later.

*Clack, clack, clack.*

Darby was amazed at his roommate's newly discovered work ethic. The clattering of typing keys never seemed to stop, all hours, every second Kenny could cram in while not out covering sports. When Kenny had first expressed interest, the Pope thought there was a good chance it was just a phase—initial exuberance at discovering what reading was all about. Darby understood the right books could have that effect.

But Kenny's focus and output never waned. He spent so much time at the kitchen table he was losing his surfer tan. He looked down in thought. The plastic tablecloth had starfish and seashells. *Clack, clack, clack.*

Darby sat in his lounge chair turning the last page of a first draft. He set his editing pen down. "It's all here except the writing." Handing the manuscript back. "Do it again."

Another year passed. *Clack, clack, clack.* Pages ripped from the spool. Darby put on his glasses and grabbed his ballpoint pen to mark up the manuscript. Kenny went surfing.

A few days later, Kenny came in the front door with his surfboard and a sunburn. The Pope was staring at him. Kenny set the board against a wall. "What?"

"How many drafts is this?" asked Darby.

"Five."

"I'm amazed."

"You're kidding." Kenny took a seat. "It's that good?"

"No, it's still totally amateur hour."

"I don't get it. Then why are you amazed?"

"Because how far you've come. You didn't just stick with it. You strangled it. You had a talent you didn't realize, and you worked like a dog to get it out." He patted the top of the manuscript on the table next to his chair. "Be very proud of this. It's something nobody can ever take away from you."

"What about getting published?"

"I have something to confess," said Darby. "I knew all along that publishing was a one-in-a-million shot. I figured you'd lose interest or not have talent. I was just excited by *your* excitement and wanted to encourage you to see how far it went. I didn't remotely anticipate you'd have this level of commitment, or that you'd sustain it for two solid years."

"So you're saying it's not good enough to get published?"

"What I'm trying to say is I feel a little bad that I might have led you on in that area." Darby held up the manuscript. "You shouldn't let it detract the least bit from how great you should feel about this."

"Give me that." Kenny grabbed the stack of pages and went in the kitchen. *Clack, clack, clack.*

Another year passed.

The sun had just set. Kenny came in the door with his surfboard. The eleventh draft of his manuscript sat on the table beside Darby. Next to a bottle.

Kenny was puzzled as he propped his board against the bookcase. "What's the champagne for?"

"I'm speechless." A cork popped and ricocheted up in the roof beams. "You did it."

"Did what?"

"Wrote a book. A *good* book," said Darby, pouring a pair of glasses. "They're fools if they don't publish this."

"How do you know?"

"Because I read a lot of books, and at times I forgot I was reading yours." Darby offered one of the drinks. "The prose just flowed like anything I'd buy in a store or check out of the library. I never picked up my pen to make any edits, and I couldn't stop turning pages. Cheers!"

They drank the cheap stuff.

"I'm making you co-author," said Kenny.

"Not a chance."

"But they're *your* stories," said Kenny. "You fed me all the material—I just wrote it up."

"Everyone has stories," said Darby. "But few follow their dream. This is all yours."

"Okay, then I'm using your real name for the character based on you."

"That's your decision."

They began drinking straight from the bottle.

"So what now?" asked Kenny.

"I know some people I can call."

# Chapter 14

THE PRESENT

Juno Beach.

A full moon rose over the Atlantic Ocean, sending shimmers of light across the waves. The moon was low on the horizon, large and yellow, then whiter and brighter as it climbed.

"For a boring literary tour, Trapper's place was actually pretty cool," said Coleman.

"Kicked out of a state park." Serge shook his head. "Because I care too much."

The pair sat alone on the quiet, dark beach, far up the sand against the sea oats.

"So where are the fantastic turtles I'm supposed to see?" asked Coleman.

"Keep your voice down," Serge whispered. "There's the first one."

"Damn!" said Coleman. "That's the biggest freaking turtle I've ever seen!"

"Loggerhead," said Serge. "And there's another. Now three. Stay still."

The large sea creatures did what millions of years of genetic memory told them: Find this specific shore on specific nights. They were patient old animals, slowly ascending the beach and leaving unmistakable trails of uniform flipper tracks that looked like small army tanks were invading. Then the flippers went to work digging and flinging sand.

Coleman furtively toked a joint in his cupped palm. "When you first mentioned turtles, I was thinking about the little bitty ones I had for pets as a kid."

"Turtles are the perfect first pets for children," said Serge. "Because it's hard to fuck up that program. Little plastic pond from the pet store, add water, and the turtles say, 'We got it from here.' Hamsters on the other hand, totally different story, like they're having meetings to work at cross-purposes."

"I remember my turtle pond." Coleman took a double-clutch final hit off the roach and flicked it. "Had a plastic palm tree you snapped into the middle of the island. All day long, turtle goes up the island, back in the water, up the island, looks at the palm tree, back in water. I can dig it."

"I used Legos to go condo with my turtle pond. I think I may have overstimulated them." Serge pointed. "The sand flinging has stopped. Here come the eggs."

"Check it out," said Coleman. "We're not alone. Other people are into the turtles."

A hundred yards away, couples strolled the upper edge of the beach, giving the creatures a wide berth. Some sat down like Serge and Coleman and kept their voices low.

"This is a good sign," said Serge. "Certain segments of society are now placing a premium on simply enjoying the wonders of our wild creatures without making them play bicycle horns. Notice the respect they're showing, taking care not to disturb this miracle of life. Some volunteers even come out to place protective netting around completed nests so beachgoers the following days don't accidentally crush the eggs. And possibly most important of all, they know to cut their headlights before pulling up. Likewise, all the homeowners around here kill their backyard lights during nesting season because turtles use the moon to navigate back to the sea."

"It is pretty dark," said Coleman, about to fire up a joint.

"Coleman! No light!"

"Sorry." He stowed the doobage in his pocket. "Happy to take one for the turtles."

"You are achieving nobleness, round-headed one." Serge placed an approving hand on his pal's shoulder. "After eons of nature's harmonic rhythms, the sprawl of mankind has introduced artificial light to the beach. This strange new illumination discourages the females and results in a phenomenon called 'false crawls,' often prompting them to tragically dump their eggs at sea. Likewise, these lights also disorient the little hatchlings, causing them to head the wrong way and end up in parking lots and miniature-golf courses, which is less than ideal no matter how the lightbulb industry tries to spin it. Luckily, scientists sounded the alarm before the artificial-light deniers could gain footing. And look around! Everyone's down with it! Everyone's joining hands to follow the rules of tranquillity and respect for these majestic animals..."

"*Woo-hoo!*"

"*Holy shit!*"

"*Look at all these big fuckin' turtles!*"

Coleman squinted up the beach. "What's that?"

"Every denier movement has a few holdovers." Serge watched as a gaggle of drunken young men staggered along the shore, erratically waving powerful flashlights.

They formed a circle around one of the larger loggerheads, giggling, swaying off balance, chugging beer and shining their flashlights down in its eyes.

"Frat boys again," said Coleman. "I *hate* frat boys."

"Actually that's an unfair judgment," said Serge.

"It is?"

Serge nodded. "There's no arguing that frat boys have had their share of miscues, but it's become a lazy stereotype, and now every time a bunch of young white dickheads do something obnoxious, it gets blamed on frats. But when you break it down, the vast majority of the fraternity brethren aren't into this kind of baloney because they're too busy back at the universities' laboratories perfecting the ultimate strain of grain-alcohol party punch for date rapes."

"When you put it that way . . ." Coleman stopped and pointed. "I think the guy on the end is peeing on the turtle's shell. That's really wrong when she's laying eggs."

"I'm throwing it out there that it's probably wrong in general." Serge stood and dusted sand off his legs. "I can even understand those poor guys who steal the eggs for money, but this is off the meter."

"What are they doing now?" asked Coleman.

The wind carried a slurring voice. *"Lift up her ass! I want to see the eggs dropping."*

Serge glanced left and right along the shore. It was growing late, and the last of the well-behaved nature lovers were leaving. He took a deep breath. "And I was planning a quiet evening."

He strolled down the sand to the raucous group. "Excuse me, gentlemen. I thought I would live my entire life without having to utter this sentence, but could you please put the turtle's ass down."

"What are you, a cop?"

"No, but I am in law enforcement," said Serge.

"If you're not a cop, then what laws are you enforcing?"

"The laws of nature." Serge grinned. "Consider me one of Darwin's elves."

"Fuck off, old man!"

"In your culture I'm sure that's the same as 'glad to see you,' because I'm glad to see you, too!" said Serge. "Now, if I could just borrow a couple minutes, because your frontal lobes aren't fully developed yet, and I need to explain a few things."

One of the young men killed the rest of his beer and threw the can down with extra force, clanging it off the turtle's shell. Then he shoved Serge hard in the chest, knocking him to the ground.

"I wanted to sit anyway," said Serge. "Long day. So I'll keep it sweet. No peeing on the turtles, either . . . make that all wildlife collectively so it's easier to remember. And the next is a subjective call, but someone has to make it: I'm eighty-sixing you from this beach."

"You're banning us?"

"Just for nesting season," said Serge. "Don't take it too hard. I got tossed from Jonathan Dickinson this afternoon, and that was for *positive* behavior."

"You son of a bitch!" Another, larger member of the group dove on top of Serge, twisting his arm behind his back. Several years ago the young man had been a wrestler in high school, and now he was the guy who talked about having wrestled in high school. He pinned Serge with a knee, then turned his head so it was facing the turtle. Coleman ran off and hid.

The wrestler pushed Serge's face hard into the beach and leaned close to his ear. "This is what you get for fucking with people like us." He called over to his friends. "Go ahead and do that thing we were talking about."

They did.

Serge screamed. "No, not that!"

The others continued their activity as Serge wept in the sand. The wrestler leaned again. "See? See! This is what you get!"

"I promise I'll go away right now and leave you alone," Serge pleaded. "Just stop, for the love of God! Clouds are covering the moon!"

They didn't stop. After the first turtle, the gang moved on to the next nest, and the next, working as a team to lift the massive turtles—mid-egg-laying—and turning them around so they'd be disoriented in the clouded night and unable to find their way back to the ocean.

"Stop it!" cried Serge. "Anything you want . . ."

. . . Up the beach near the sea oats, Coleman hid under cover of darkness. He took a purposeful step forward, then a hesitant step back, then forward, back, forward, back. Giving himself a pep talk: "Your best friend needs your help. I'm definitely running down there this time . . . Okay, definitely right now . . . Okay, this time on three. One! Two! . . . I'm really going to do it this next time . . ."

Meanwhile, the drunken gang had moved far up the beach, leaving the wrestler alone to do as he pleased with Serge. He sneered sadistically. "Bet you didn't expect this when you came down here to give us shit!"

"Just one question," said Serge, turning his face in the sand. "Do you have a favorite ball?"

"What?"

"Your balls," said Serge. "You must have a favorite. I know you shouldn't have favorites, like your children, but I secretly prefer my left. I call him Sparky. You should name your balls."

"Are you trying to be funny?"

"I couldn't be more serious. Which is your favorite?"

The wrestler's eyes snapped wide as he suddenly understood the question, feeling the barrel of a pistol up the leg of his shorts. He slowly rose off his victim.

"That's much better," said Serge. "I used to wrestle, too. And you broke a fundamental rule: Always be aware of *both* your opponent's arms."

". . . *Cowabungaaaaaaaaa!!!* . . ."

Coleman charged down the beach, tripped over the turtle, and took a header in the sand.

"Right on schedule." Serge poked the wrestler in the ribs with the gun. "I need your help."

"That's why I came."

"Get the shovel," said Serge.

"What shovel?"

"The shovel I now keep permanently in the trunk," said Serge. "I'm weary of having to buy a new one every time."

It grew even later. The beach was all theirs. The rest of the drunken confederation had dissipated into the sleepy, wandering remnants for which they are known.

"I'm getting tired." Coleman stopped to pull from a flask of bourbon.

"I can't do this alone." Serge heaved. "They're depending on us. Now come on."

The pair grunted as they shuffled and rotated slowly in a circle before setting the loggerhead back down, now aimed once again the correct way toward the ocean. Serge wiped his brow and looked behind, where the three turtles they'd previously assisted were now crawling back to safety.

"There's the next one," said Coleman.

They arrived to find flippers vainly flapping, and a turtle thinking, *Where did all these sea oats come from?*

More grunting and shuffling before they waved good-bye to the departing turtle. The process repeated a half-dozen more times until all the molested animals were on their way home. The only ones that remained were those who arrived after the foolishness and were now at some stage of digging nests and depositing eggs.

Serge and Coleman returned to where they had begun the night. "Our work here is almost done," said Serge.

"Great!" Coleman pulled a sticky shirt away from his chest. "Party time!"

"I said *almost.*"

"What's left?"

"Hand me the shovel."

## Chapter 15

1987

The dogs sounded the alarm.

Barking up a storm, all down the street. Big ones, little ones, in windows, behind fences.

Darby and Kenny were playing poker in the kitchen when they heard the racket. A hand of cards fanned out, aces high. "Sounds like mail's here."

Kenny got up.

Darby absentmindedly fiddled with his chips and discarded the jack of diamonds. He realized the house had been suspiciously quiet for longer than it took to get to the door and back. "Kenny! What's taking so long? I got a hot hand here!"

Kenny slowly turned the corner into the kitchen.

"Jesus! You're white as a sheet!"

Kenny just handed Darby a padded envelope. He pulled out a new hardcover book with a glossy dust jacket depicting the Loxahatchee River.

FLORIDA TARZAN. Then Kenny's name. A NOVEL.

"They sent you an early copy," said Darby.

Kenny stood in a trance, speaking monotone. "I can't believe this is actually happening."

Darby laughed. "Maybe you should sit down before you faint."

A few minutes later, Kenny opened his eyes and felt an ice pack on his forehead. "What happened?"

"You fainted."

Six months earlier, Darby had made a few phone calls, as promised. He knew someone, who knew someone else, who knew a writer, who knew an agent. Darby initially was able to get the book read as a favor. Then it wasn't a favor. The writing stood on its own.

So Kenny now remained frozen with the book in his hands, still in disbelief at the sight of his name on the cover. The phone rang.

"Darby here. . . . Sure, hold on." He covered the receiver. "It's your publisher."

"Hello? . . . What? When? I guess, I mean I don't know anything about that. Okay, just send me the information."

Darby studied the back of the dust jacket. "This is a good photo of you, fishing off the seawall in a little baseball hat. How old were you, nine?"

"They want me to do a book tour," said Kenny.

"Well, look at you, Mr. Big Shot."

"They said it would just be a small one to start, but I don't even know what a tour is."

"You sign your name a lot."

The book first came out as most firsts do—to a general yawn because he had no name recognition. Then the *Palm Beach Post* liked the angle of local history, and Kenny's book review received especially large placement because of all the historical file photos that the newspaper used.

The initial signings along the Gold Coast were unusually packed for a debut. Nobody anticipated how many people had grown up in the area and recalled the stories from their childhood. They wanted to know more.

Kenny sat demurely at a table near the back of the bookstore. He blushed more and more as the line of customers came through.

A real estate agent handed him a book. "I remember hearing all about Trapper on the playground . . ."

Then a mother with two tots. "The rumors scared the heck out of me . . ."

A grocery clerk. "My parents were suspicious about his shooting . . ."

Auto mechanic. "I remember taking like ten field trips to that state park. I threw up ice cream once . . ."

Bartender. "I love that character the Pope of Palm Beach. Is he based on anyone real? . . ."

School nurse. "Are you married? . . ."

Hours later the event wrapped up, and Darby patted his friend on the back.

Kenny stuck pens in his pocket. "Are they all like this?"

"You'll find out."


Florida didn't have an identity back then. No established regional culture or roots. Other states inflated with pride. Hoosiers, Yankees, Rebels, Cornhuskers, the Lone Star State, Live Free or Die, Great Potatoes. Florida was a food with little taste or smell, like iceberg lettuce or rice cakes, and its many residents subconsciously felt an emptiness of not belonging to something.

Kenny had unknowingly struck a vein. He'd wrapped his mystery in a tapestry of universal childhood memories that only his state could have produced. Tropical storms, early rockets at Canaveral, cracking open coconuts, going barefoot in winter, water skiers at Cypress Gardens, dolphins at aquariums, seeing an alligator and not thinking it was special, going to the beach and it was no big deal, all those national game-show hosts bellowing: "You've won an all-expense-paid trip to Florida!" And kids watching the shows at home: "Why?"

Other newspapers got wind of the fun little nostalgic book with real native tidbits. More reviews. The publisher expanded Kenny's appearance schedule up and down the coast, from Jacksonville to Miami, then the other coast, Tampa to Naples.

Then another accidental stroke. Publishers hadn't yet begun producing "young adult" books, which meant young teens. No *Harry Potter* or *Twilight* or *Hunger Games*. Kenny's simple, conversational style of prose bridged age groups before anyone was trying. Add in the elements of a mysterious bogeyman and secret treasure, and he soon had a hit with both parents and children.

A landscaper with his daughter handed Kenny a novel to sign. "It's the first book we've read together. We had a blast."

A mother and her son. "It's the first book he's read on his own. I can't thank you enough."

A librarian. "Are you married?"

Back at the bungalow, the phone rang. Kenny grabbed it. ". . . I see. I see . . ."

Darby was arranging fly-casting lures in a shadow box when Kenny came into the room. "Who was it?"

"My publisher wants a bigger tour."

"Where?"

"It involves airplanes."

Two weeks later, Kenny returned from a regional tour of the Southeast. He tossed his suitcase in the corner.

Darby rearranged an album of old surfing photos. "How'd it go?"

Kenny just stood. "Weird. My biggest dream was just being able to hold a book and see my name on the cover."

"What was so weird?"

"Guys offered me joints, and women offered sex."

"Casual or committal?"

"Both."

"Welcome to your new life."

The phone rang. "Hello? . . . I see, I see . . . *When? . . .*"

Darby smiled at a photo of a much younger Kenny on the beach. "Who was it?"

"My publisher. They want another book."

"So write one."

"They want it in six months. How am I going to do that? You saw how long the first took."

"You better get crackin'."

"I think I'm in over my head," said Kenny. "I don't even have a story."

"I've got a million," said Darby. "Go over to the bookshelf. Fourth row . . ."

Kenny returned with an antiquarian history volume. "*WPA Guide to Florida*?"

"Published 1939, with a nice frozen-in-time section on Riviera Beach," said Darby. "We used to be nicknamed Conchtown, because this was first settled by families of Bahamian fishermen known as Conchs who squatted on the south end of Singer Island at the beginning of the century, then settled proper in the 1920s from Fifteenth to Twenty-First Streets in a community called Inlet Grove. The cool thing is it was all documented by a trio from the WPA including eminent Florida writer and historian Stetson Kennedy, except the WPA chose not to publish it."

"What a shame."

"Except I have a bootleg copy."

"No surprise there."

"Second shelf . . ."

Kenny flipped through a stack of xeroxed pages beginning with a poor photo reproduction of two small children walking toward a five-and-dime along a hot, empty gravel road that would become Dixie Highway. "This is so cool! . . . But how is this my next book?"

"It was pretty lawless back then. Make up a mystery, and I'll supply the heritage." He got up with his cane.

"Where are you going?"

"To show you where they used to live a few streets over in primitive wood frames like this one. Are you coming? . . ."

*Conched Out* hit the shelves. Parents and kids read together. Another book tour.

Kenny covered the phone. "They want another book."

"Write what you know," said Darby. "Make it a surfing book."

"Why would they be interested in that?"

"They will if it's a murder mystery. Have some young surfing kids figure it out."

*Hang Ten* was released, complete with histories of the Pump House and the *Amaryllis,* where they found the dead body in the first chapter.

More autographs. More readers.

*"I remember when that ship went aground . . ."*

*"I got fined for surfing the inlet . . ."*

*"Are you dating anyone? . . ."*

Fame did what fame does. Feeds on itself. Kenny made the rounds of book festivals, spoke in schools, commanded a fee as a keynote speaker on the rubber-chicken circuit. He did drive-time radio shows by phone from his motel, and appeared on spunky morning-TV programs between dieting tips and fashion no-no's. His publisher was now flying him all the way to California.

*"Do you want to go out for drinks with us afterward? . . ."*

*"Do you need a research assistant? . . ."*

*"Can you write my biography? Everyone always tells me my life would make a great book . . ."*

Kenny arrived back from the airport and immediately plopped down on a couch in the bungalow. "I'm exhausted. I never knew it would be like this."

"Be careful what you wish for," said Darby.

## THE PRESENT

A shovel flung sand high into the night.

A solitary endeavor. Coleman was too stoned and Serge too impatient. "Fine, I'll dig it myself. Just wait back by the sea oats and make sure our friend doesn't try anything funny."

"But what if someone comes along and spots us, like a cop?"

"They do occasionally patrol at night, but it depends on the beach. The ones with reputations for partying, public intercourse and drug deals get heavy coverage, but this is a calm one with only spot checks."

"But what if we're unlucky and there *is* a spot check?"

"First, *you* split. All they'll find is that tied-up dude in the sea oats a hundred yards away from me. How am I responsible for that?"

"But don't you think you'll look a little suspicious?"

"I'll look *outrageously* suspicious," said Serge. "Digging a giant hole on the beach in the middle of the night. So what? I'll explain that children dig holes in the beach all the time, and there's no law against that. I'm just taking it to the next level because I have a sexual need to move sand."

"Stiffy," said Coleman.

"It's a free country," said Serge. "They'll be totally off balance, looking at me like I have a second head growing out of my shoulder, but there's little more they can do besides ask me to stop digging and find another outlet."

The pair walked in opposite directions. Serge launched a shovel of sand as Coleman plopped down in the darkness. Coleman smiled at their captive, quite still with all the rope and duct tape. He extracted a joint from his pocket. "Oops, almost forgot." He stuck it away and smiled at the wrestler again. "I was going to share that fatty with you." The captive tried to scream under the tape. Coleman nodded: "I know, I know, but the turtles have to come first." He pulled out his flask and looked back at the beach.

Sand continued flying like there was a sand version of a water sprinkler, and Serge became shorter and shorter in the hole.

Coleman sipped his bourbon and squinted into the night, seeing double now, except where Serge had been. Serge was gone— just sand flinging up from the deepening hole. The sand stopped, and the shovel ejected high into the air, landing in the oats. Serge crawled out . . .

. . . And now here they all were at the end of the night. Serge lay on his stomach. He planted elbows in the beach, propping his chin on his hands. He looked into the hole with a wild face.

"How are you doing down there?"

*"Mmm! Mmm!"*

"Great! Glad you like it!"

The wrestler was vertical in the hole, sand packed down around him to his neck. The top of his head stood a half foot below ground level, with a sufficient radius of free room to twist and jerk his face back and forth in the crater to assess his predicament.

Serge's knuckles knocked on the head. "Up here. Look at me . . . That's better. Only polite when someone's talking to you . . . I heard you say earlier that you had an interest in sea turtles. And have I got a *National Geographic* moment in store for you!"

*"Mmm! Mmm!"*

"Glad you asked! Of course there's risk involved! Nature lovers have known that for years. Just ask Marlin Perkins from Mutual of Omaha. Actually, it would be better to ask his assistant, Jim, because Marlin was always back in the air-conditioned tent wearing an ascot and sipping mimosas while Jim wrestled anacondas in quicksand. Lucky for you, no quicksand here. In fact you are about to experience something I'd like to coin *slow*sand. And now for your bonus round. I always like to give my contestants a chance to win. I think you've already figured out the grand prize, as well as the parting gifts for losing contestants. So here's your bonus . . ."

Serge leaned over the edge of the hole and whispered. Then he sprang to his feet and slapped his hands together. "Well, that about does it . . . Coleman, come on! Give me a hand!"

A late-arriving loggerhead finished her crawl at a desired spot and began flinging sand with flippers.

"Grab that side," said Serge.

"But I thought you told me it was wrong to disturb the turtles, unless we were turning them back around after assholes messed with them."

"That's correct," said Serge. "I'm in the wrong here. But you're a witness: I'm not thinking straight. On the other hand, I'm saving her the work of digging, so it's really a wash. I should be a rationalization coach . . . Ready? Lift! . . ."

The pair strained and shuffled sideways.

"This one's heavier than the others," said Coleman.

"Only a few more feet."

The captive looked up in terror as a moon shadow fell over his face.

*"Mmm! Mmm!"*

Serge and Coleman stood up and panted.

"Her back flippers are flapping in the air," said Coleman.

"Give it a minute. She'll soon figure out the digging requirement is complete."

"You're right," said Coleman. "Here comes the first egg."

"They're in groups called 'clutches,' with more than a hundred eggs laid at a time."

"Wow," said Coleman. "That's amazing."

"It's the wonderment of life on earth. Did you know that the eggs aren't gender specific? The sex of the hatchlings is determined by the temperature of the sand in the underground nest. Lower, males. Higher, females."

"That's a trip." Coleman bent down and peeked behind the turtle. "His head's getting pretty covered up in there."

"And he'll be providing heat, which means more females,

which means more eggs in the future," said Serge. "In an ironic twist, he's contributing to restocking the population."

"You planned that all along, didn't you?"

"Looks like she dropped the last egg," said Serge. "Now she's using her flippers to cover them up with sand."

*"Mmm! Mmm!"*

They watched until the turtle finished up at the hole and began her journey back to the shimmering sea.

Coleman upended his flask. "By the way, what was your bonus round?"

"The eggs are spherical, so they create a natural honeycomb air pocket, and the sand isn't packed very tight or deep." Serge knelt and pulled a bunch of drinking straws from his pocket, jamming them down through the sand into the egg chamber. He blew hard on them to clear the clogs and provide air. "I told him if he kept his cool, the eggs would hatch, and the little turtles would bust through the surface and save his life. He was a major jackass, but I hate to ever write anyone off, and this is the best way to teach him that all us creatures, big and small, are in this thing together."

"So how long does it take the eggs to hatch?"

"Shouldn't be long, but I haven't gotten that far in my marine biology book." He pulled out his smartphone and tapped on the screen. An Internet page came up. "What? Eighty days! Oops! I think I owe someone an apology."

Suddenly there was a thrashing in the sea oats, accompanied by a weaving flashlight beam.

Coleman aimed his flask. "I think one of the others came back."

Fifty yards away, an inebriated young man stumbled onto the beach, in limbo between buzz and hangover. Cursing, punching the air. He found a turtle. He got down on his knees.

Serge smacked himself in the forehead. "I really want to go to bed."

The man struggled to rotate the turtle.

Serge strolled over. "I thought we had a productive talk earlier. Was I stuttering?"

He looked up. "You again! Get lost!" Then more slow rotating.

Coleman arrived. "What's going on?"

"Another one straying from the herd."

"Should I get the shovel?"

Serge shook his head. "I might be able to reason with him . . . Excuse me? Please stop rotating the turtle."

"Bite me." The turtle continued turning.

"Want the shovel now?"

"No, I can't ever play that contest again," said Serge. "I didn't know the eighty-day hatching time with the other guy, so that one's really not my fault. But now that I'm aware, it would be wrong. You have to have principles."

"Then what are you going to do?"

"As I said before, the punishment has to fit the offense. He's just being a dick, so if I overreact, that would be wrong, too. He has to become a bigger dick."

The young man was losing patience and strength with his task. "Fucking turtle!" He pounded the top of the shell with his fist.

"Getting warmer . . ." said Serge.

His fist became sore, and he picked up his baton flashlight, trying to bash the shell open. An errant swing broke a chip off the edge.

"Ding, ding, ding!" said Serge. "We have a winner! . . ."

. . . A half hour later, Serge and Coleman sat cross-legged under the edge of the sea oats. They watched calm waves roll in, creating a foamy shoreline in the moonlight. The waves had a rhythmic, tranquilizing sound that relieves stress and can be purchased in an electronic box from the Sharper Image for $199.

"The key to life is all about relaxation," said Serge.

"Ain't that the truth." Coleman gestured ahead. "That guy's way too tense."

"*Aaaaauuuu! . . .*"

"He's fixating," said Serge. "I can always spot the type."

"You even explained the extra-easy bonus round," said Coleman. "Because of all the rope."

"And the kind of duct tape I used will eventually come loose in water." Serge nodded happily. "I've never done a double-header contest before, and this half is even better! If all goes according to plan, and he happens to win, he'll be a celebrated pioneer like an astronaut, able to report key turtle data to advance their preservation. I'm actually envious of him now."

The pair lay back on the sandy incline and interlaced fingers behind their heads.

"What a pretty night."

"You said it."

Two giant sea turtles that had just deposited eggs were halfway back to the ocean. The crawl was slower this time. Heavily duct-taped to their backs: knotted ends of thick rope. The ropes trailed behind them some distance and were tied respectively to each ankle of a turtle menace. His hands remained free, but the ankle knots and his inebriation posed a problem.

"He keeps trying to sit up and reach his feet, then falling back down."

"People need to go with the flow," said Serge. "I told him to enjoy the nice nature ride down the beach that few will ever experience, but he has too much negative energy."

"Maybe he's afraid of the water?"

"Why? I made sure the ropes were long enough so that even if the turtles dive under, he can still paddle on the surface and become famous as history's first human tracking buoy."

The turtles reached the waves and began swimming.

"What if the turtles swim in opposite directions?"

"Hmm." Serge pinched his lip. "Maybe I should have told him to do stretching exercises first."

The captive's toes hit the water.

*"Aaaaaauuuuu!..."*

The turtles swam farther, and the man began to paddle.

"I told him it would work," said Serge.

"He's really being pulled out fast," said Coleman. "I always thought turtles were slow."

"Don't judge by their speed on land," said Serge. "Now the screams are heading north. I would have sworn they'd swim south. The contributions to science on this guy."

"He just went under," said Coleman. "Now he's up again screaming. Now he's under . . ."

They waited in silence.

Serge finally stood. "They dive deeper than anyone thought. Another research breakthrough."

Coleman joined him on the walk back to the car. "Two sea turtles dragging some guy across the beach and out to sea. How cool is that?"

"It's the beauty of creation," said Serge. "Keep watching nature, and you'll always see something new."

# Chapter 16

**T**ypewriter keys sat silent.

"I'm all out of gas," said Kenny. "I don't know what to write next."

Darby reclined in his lounger and stared up at the open rafters holding his retired surfboards. "This town's always had a crusty history. I remember when Burt Reynolds's dad was chief of police. A tough guy's tough guy. Single-handedly disarmed two dudes waving knives in this dive on Blue Heron and snapped the blades off in the top of the bar."

"You want me to write about Burt's dad?"

"Just tuck it in for historic atmosphere. What I'm trying to say is there's always something funky going on in this town. Like turtle eggs."

"Eggs?"

"You need to tap into all the invisible worlds surrounding us every day that most people never imagine," said Darby. "Riviera Beach has these subcultures believing the eggs of endangered sea turtles have mystical powers. There's high demand to use them for religious ceremonies or aphrodisiacs or both, so they fetch ten bucks a dozen, and during nesting season the eggs are poached all up the coast to Juno Beach. For years, the cops had been scratching their heads: Who's digging up eggs?"

"That's terrible," said Kenny.

"At least it makes business sense," said Darby. "Not like drunken jerks who think it's a hoot to pick the giant turtles up and turn them around so they head the wrong way trying to return to the ocean."

"Someone should kill them."

"Maybe you can in your next book." Darby grabbed his cane and strained to stand. "Let's go for a ride."

They pulled into a parking lot with a view of cargo containers and a dry dock.

Kenny got out and looked up at an industrial crane. "The Port of Palm Beach?"

"Some of the turtle eggs are smuggled out of here because they're worth far more in certain Caribbean markets."

"That's not economically logical for a few eggs."

"Few? Police caught one raggedy guy who harvested thirteen hundred eggs in a single night. And *he* was disorganized. You do the math."

They began a walking tour of the piers. Darby took a break and waved his cane toward a row of massive petroleum storage tanks. "If you know anything about history, ports are the nexus to the entire culture. And the source of the wildest stories. I used to work here."

"I know, arc welding."

"Twenty-six years. Didn't pay the best, but financed a surfing lifestyle," said Darby. "If you work anywhere that long, you tune into the daily cycles and notice all the little out-of-place stuff others miss. You've got a totally overlooked wealth of material out here for your next book."

"How so?"

"When people think of ports in Florida, they picture Miami, Port Everglades in Fort Lauderdale, Port Canaveral, Jacksonville." They reached a boardwalk, and Darby took a careful step onto a board painted caution orange. "Few realize that the tiny town of Riviera Beach is home to one of the biggest ports on the eastern seaboard—and the eighteenth largest cargo destination in the entire country."

"You're kidding." Kenny looked around to recalibrate his impression: railroad spurs, semi-truck platforms, a busy swarm of forklifts. "I've lived here my whole life and just drive by."

"That's because all the other ports are surrounded by metropolitan madness. But what's around here?"

"Just a tiny town." Kenny watched a crane lift a steel container of pre-formed fiberglass motel bathtubs. "And this stretch of U.S. 1 is so empty it's almost toxic."

Darby stopped to rest. "That's why it's so attractive to people who are doing everything they shouldn't be doing."

"How do you know?"

"Like I said, you work long enough in a place, you pick up vibes." His cane navigated another treacherous step near the new cruise-ship terminal with tinted green glass. "I want to introduce you to some people."

They arrived in a covered portion of a shipyard. Hard hats, echoes of clanging metal, acetylene torches and showers of sparks.

"Brady."

No answer.

Darby wrapped his hands around his mouth. "Brady!"

A welding helmet looked around. Then a hand in a thick glove raised the visor. "Darby!" The welder turned around: "Hey, everyone! Look who's here! It's Darby!"

All work came to an abrupt halt as a crowd of fireproof aprons circled the former co-worker. Smiles and slaps on his back.

*"How's it been hangin'?..."*

*"You still look great..."*

*"Been meaning to visit..."*

*"Would have called, but with the kids in school..."*

They migrated over to a picnic table next to the Igloo ice-water dispensers.

"What brings you here?" asked Brady.

"I want you to meet my friend," said Darby. "This is Kenny Reese... Kenny, the gang."

"The famous author?"

Kenny blushed.

"Still a little bashful," said Darby. "He's started a new book, and it might be about the port..."

The pleasantries petered out as the workers had to get back to their torches. It was down to just Brady, Darby's closest friend from the old job. The sun began to set, and they grabbed plastic chairs, moving out on the concrete deck overlooking the municipal marina next door.

"Man, it's great to see your face," said Brady, rubbing arthritic knuckles. "Without you around, I'm the last of the old guard, and I'm getting too old for this shit."

"So take your pension," said Darby.

"And do what?" Brady flicked a wrist at a pleasure craft navigating the channel between Peanut Island. "Go sailing?" He turned to Kenny. "What do you think?"

"I'm a neutral observer."

Darby watched a large yacht with a radar dome swing around in the turning basin. "I was starting to tell Kenny here about the glory days. Remember turtle eggs?"

"And just when you think you've seen everything." Brady faced Kenny again. "These eggs were headed for Port-au-Prince or some damn place. Customs did a routine sweep, and they were about to let the boat go when they heard this strange racket in some boxes. These were rookie smugglers who didn't know about refrigeration. The eggs hatched! All hell broke loose, people screaming and diving overboard, knocking over boxes, little turtles flapping around everywhere."

"That's messed up," said Kenny. "But I don't know if anyone can write a whole novel on turtle eggs."

"That's just a for-instance," said Darby.

"Crazy stuff like that was happening all the time," said Brady. "Like the guys who brought these parrots up from Panama that sell for more than two grand. Things got fucked up again. Naturally, they all flew away."

"Don't forget the monkeys," said Darby.

"Monkeys?" said Kenny, getting out a pen and notebook.

"These cute little gibbons," said Brady. "They got loose, too, running through the welding shop and tearing up our break area. When people hear that you work at the port, they think, 'Ooo, you must be worried about drug smugglers.' I say, 'No, monkeys that can open your lunch box.'"

"See, here's the thing about people breaking the law out here..." Darby watched a small Zodiac boat speed up the channel in growing darkness. "They think they're so clever, and if they act cool and nonchalant, nobody will notice them. But the eyes that work on the docks see all."

A pen scribbled. "So it's mainly exotic-animal smuggling?"

Brady shook his head and pointed at the cargo containers on the deck of a Liberian-flagged freighter. "Dollars to doughnuts there's more than a few stolen cars in there. They love the Mercedes in South America. Even more popular are spare parts from chopped vehicles that can't be traced."

"Bicycles," said Darby.

"Oh, you wouldn't believe what they pay in the islands for a ten-speed," said Brady. "A used bicycle goes for twice the price of a new one in the States."

A small fish splashed next to the seawall, which meant a larger fish was behind it. Darby stretched weak legs under the table. "Changed much since I was here?"

"Starting to," said Brady. "And it's bad."

"How?" asked Kenny.

"There's always been contraband around here." Brady nodded across the water to the nearby shore of tony Palm Beach. A squadron of pelicans glided on the breeze. "Rum came in here like nobody's business during Prohibition because all that old money wanted to get their drink on. And one of the biggest smugglers lived over there. Probably heard of him, Joseph Kennedy, the president's dad. Of course he never got his hands dirty, and all the law around here was on the take."

"Then came the sixties," said Darby. "We started seeing drugs, but it was mainly pot. Some stoned clowns trying to make a few bucks. Half the time they could barely steer the boat and did more damage hitting the pylons than what they made off weed."

"Right after Darby left, the worm turned," said Brady. "It wasn't obvious at first, but then it couldn't be ignored. A much scarier breed of cat started showing up at the docks. Scars, prison tats—and not American prisons."

"Cocaine?" said Darby.

"We don't ask, but yeah," said Brady. "It really got edgy when the police started showing up."

"To make arrests?" asked Kenny.

"To get paid." Brady watched the fin of a small hammerhead slice across the channel. "Then the DEA came around, which was more frightening because they were on the level. Nobody wanted to be seen at the port talking to the feds. We all played dumb, which made them think that maybe we were in on it, so they planted one of their undercover agents in the shop."

"If he was undercover," said Kenny, "then how did you know he was DEA?"

"Couldn't weld and kept asking about cocaine. Call *us* suspicious," said Brady. "Finally burned himself with the torches so many times that he was almost on permanent disability leave, and they pulled him off the assignment because what was the point if he was home in bed?"

Kenny flipped a page in his notebook. "I had no idea. Right in my own backyard."

"Darby," Brady said uneventfully. "Did you see that Zodiac boat?"

Darby nodded. "Right out the corner of my eye. Been watching since it made the channel."

Kenny turned around. "What boat?"

Brady and Darby in unison: "Don't look!"

"Why not? What's going on?"

"Nothing you want to witness," said Brady. "Zodiac boats are fast, but more importantly, they ride as shallow as anything out there. And definitely draft higher than whatever the Coast Guard or Marine Patrol has."

Darby made a circular gesture with his right arm. "Probably met a sailboat offshore, then made the inlet."

Brady pretended to look in the direction of a cargo container marked TROPICALA. "Notice how the cooler is about ten gallons too big for a Zodiac?"

"Picked up on that," said Darby. "And how he's now straining too hard to lift it for anything legitimate to be inside."

"Mm-hmm," said Brady.

Kenny's gaze ping-ponged between the two old friends. "Wow, I never would have noticed little things like that."

"The eyes of the dock see all."

The welders kept tabs with peripheral vision as the man carried the cooler and slid it into the bed of a nearby pickup truck. He grabbed a piece of paper from the vehicle, then got back in the Zodiac, undid a rope from a cleat and sped away from the marina.

"I have no idea what just happened," said Kenny. "If there's something valuable like drugs in the cooler, why did he just leave it like that?"

"Dead drop," said Brady. "Apparently the arrangement involves the links in the chain not meeting face-to-face."

"But the stuff's just sitting out in the open in the back of that truck where anyone can steal it, especially in Riviera Beach," said Kenny. "Or it could be discovered by the authorities, who'll arrest the pickup's owner."

"A couple of things," said Darby. "First, it's unsecured, so any decent defense attorney can argue that whoever owns the pickup isn't responsible for whatever someone might toss in the back when he isn't around."

"You said a couple of things?"

"Don't turn around and look obvious like you did before," said Darby. "But there's a police car by the gate. Nothing will happen to that cooler."

Kenny jotted notes nonstop, head down, until he realized nobody at the table was talking. He raised his head and saw the men staring across the channel. "What are you looking at?"

"*Now* you can watch the Zodiac boat," said Brady.

He did. The inflatable vessel quickly traversed the channel and made landfall on the sandy shore of Peanut Island. The man got out and walked toward a coconut palm that looked different from all the others, angling out crooked over the water. He reached the base of the tree and got down on his knees.

"Why is he digging?" asked Kenny.

"Payment," said Darby. "Another dead drop. Got the location from the map in the back of the pickup when he delivered the load."

The man retrieved a small, waterproof nautical box from the sand and threw it in the Zodiac. He pushed the boat off and sped out of sight around the south end of the island toward the inlet.

Moments later, another Zodiac came around the opposite end

of the island and docked at the marina. A different man got out and walked over to the pickup. The truck started up, he drove off, and the police car followed.

Darby turned with a sly grin toward the young writer. "Getting enough material?"

# *Chapter 17*

**A** moody espresso machine hissed a bitter liquid into a tiny cup that was promptly knocked back. The coffee aficionado wore a lime-green guayabera with two vertical rows of iguanas. He had a slight paunch, not unreasonable for his fifty years. But his toupee broke the cardinal rule of toupees by looking like one. Even across the street or looking down from a building: Yep, that's a toupee. His skin was mocha, and his name was Salenca. Nobody ever brought up the hairpiece, and Salenca thought it was the perfect crime.

It was the industrial side of western Miami between the airport and the Everglades. An area where office buildings looked like warehouses and vice versa. This particular building wore both hats. Rooms stored drugs, guns and stolen art. Others housed rows of employees on phones and computers. The drugs were being phased out. It was the new era of techno-crime, and ID theft was the future.

Salenca had the only personal office, sitting up on steel beams near the ceiling at the end of the building and looking out over what used to be the shipping department of a T-shirt printing company.

Months had passed since Salenca's big promotion. Nobody ever figured out that he had framed his boss for framing *him*. All they knew was that Salenca possessed the Midas touch. The credit-card racket had money pouring in from thirty-seven countries and counting. And who would ever have guessed they'd need to hire a tech staff?

Salenca asked for another meeting with the bosses.

"What's this new idea of yours?"

"Garbage."

"Garbage?"

Salenca nodded. "It's the future."

The bosses glanced at each other. "I thought it was the *past,*" said boss one. "The families up in New York and Jersey were neck-deep in garbage, until we showed them how much more could be made from cocaine."

Boss two nodded. "That's when they began switching from the waste business to drugs. And now you want us to go from drugs *back* to garbage?"

"No," said Salenca. "That's old garbage. I'm talking batteries."

"Batteries?"

"It used to be just car batteries," said Salenca. "But technology has so radically evolved over the last two decades that it's created a sea change. Everyone's got a cell phone and a laptop, and they all have batteries that eventually need to be thrown away."

"So throw them away already."

"Not that simple." Salenca popped the battery out of his own phone and held it up as a visual aid. "It's about heavy metals. Cadmium, mercury, lead. You got your manganese, your lithium ion . . ."

"We'll take your word," said boss three. "Skip to the money part."

"There are all kinds of new federal regulations requiring businesses to dispose of certain types of garbage in specific ways. *Expensive* ways," said Salenca. "And not just batteries, but medical waste, construction materials like asbestos, the list goes on and on."

"How does that concern us?" asked boss one.

"It's often too costly for companies to get rid of the stuff themselves," said the accountant. "So now all these new businesses have cropped up that specialize in regulated disposal. They're hired by the other companies. That's where we come in, underbidding the competition and making a fortune."

"Do we know how to dispose of this stuff?" asked boss three.

"Not remotely. That's why we'll dump it at night. That's our profit margin."

"What if these other companies don't want to sign contracts with us?" asked boss one.

"Our best sales pitch: muscle and arson."

"Forgive me," said boss two, "but this sounds like a lot of work. Is it more profitable than drugs or ID theft?"

"No, but the cost–benefit ratio is better." Salenca could see their eyes glazing over. "Remember when I explained the disparity of prison sentences between cocaine and credit cards? The less harsh the penalties, the lower the chance that someone will flip on us for the prosecution? And the risk is even less for disposal violations. We incorporate a legitimate company, and if they hit us with EPA fines, we just bankrupt it. And if they go after corporate officers, they're all overseas associates of ours in places without extradition. It's about diversification. We'll basically be getting paid a killing for creating a lot of confusing paperwork."

"Confusing is a good way to put it," said boss one. "I don't understand any of this, and I love it. What will you need?"

"More guys and a bulldozer."

The bosses took a vote, consisting of nodding at each other. They set the accountant loose.

**S**alenca sat in a posh chair on the nineteenth floor of a gleaming office building in downtown Miami.

A vice president sat on the other side of a mahogany desk. He had a view of the causeways to the beaches. He closed a leather-bound prospectus. "I'm sorry, but we already have a company we're very happy with."

"We cost less," said Salenca.

"It's not worth the unknown," said the VP. "They have a proven track record."

"So do we, but not in disposal."

"How do you mean?"

Salenca turned east toward the floor-to-ceiling windows, looking down at a seaplane skimming across the bay before taking off to the Bahamas. "You like your view?"

"Uh, yeah."

Salenca pointed up at the two serious men standing behind him with clasped hands. No necks. Linebackers in shiny suits.

The VP quickly opened the leather binder again. "Come to think of it, we have had some reliability issues lately with the current company . . ."

And so it went, downtown tower after tower, collecting contracts. Salenca assembled his reinforced crew back at the warehouse the next morning at dawn. He distributed pages with their collection routes.

"Don't we need garbage trucks?"

Salenca shook his head. "This kind of waste doesn't take up as much room. Your pickups will do."

"Is any of this stuff dangerous?" asked another driver.

Salenca handed him a page. "Just watch out for syringes in the biomedical containers."

They read down their assignments as Salenca stepped back. "Okay, everybody, look alive. The collection is child's play. And you all know the rallying point, but you must arrive at the precise ten-minute intervals on your sheets. We don't need a million pickups there at the same time attracting attention. And don't go anywhere near the place before midnight . . ."

The western sprawl of South Florida was like a military campaign: aggressive, coordinated and ruthless. All along Highway 27 and the Sawgrass Expressway, charging right up against the boundary of the Everglades.

It was a fortified wall of sorts: tight rows of identical two-story stucco homes, all designed for maximum floor space on minimum lot size. Swimming pools, barbecue pits, Jacuzzis. On the other side of the wall, alligators.

Each subdivision opened with tours of the model home. And before the first deed was inked, bulldozers were already plowing the next subdivision.

One such bulldozer arrived at midnight on a flatbed truck. It was not sent by the developers.

In all directions, empty land, cleared and packed flat with little orange ribbons flapping from surveyors' stakes. In coming weeks, the acreage would be a compelling subject for time-lapse photography. All at once, an entire platted community would rise: plumbing, slabs, concrete blocks, roof trusses, plywood, shingles, paint, sod and cheerful nuclear families whose key to happiness was lack of imagination. But right now, there weren't even streetlights.

Workers backed the bulldozer off the flatbed.

"Why'd you pick this particular lot?" asked the man behind the controls of the big Tonka truck.

Salenca waved a clipboard. "They just poured the footer, so the foundation isn't far off."

The bulldozer rolled onto the land as the first pickup truck arrived. Men quickly pulled the tarp off the bed and unloaded the contents. They carried it to the middle of the lot, where a kitchen with an island sink would soon stand. The bulldozer finished digging the hole, and they threw it all in.

Salenca checked his watch. The departing pickup passed the incoming one on the dark street, and the process repeated. And repeated, every ten minutes until the last truck arrived. "Hold it," said Salenca. "Don't dump. I've got other plans for your load."

The next day before lunch, the driver of the last pickup arrived at the warehouse with hazardous cargo still under its tarp.

"Follow us," Salenca said out the passenger side of a Mercedes.

"Hope you don't mind me asking," said the driver, "but why are we taking the last load to the disposal company whose contracts we just stole?"

"To create a paper trail that we disposed of some of it according to regulations," said Salenca. "Then if any of what we're doing turns up, we point the finger at them."

"Sounds like a lot of effort for just a paper trail," said the driver. "Won't they just deny it?"

"They won't be in a position to be believed."

"I get it. You're planning something else."

"This is a two-birds-with-one-stone kind of thing..."

Minutes later, another high-rise executive office.

"I can't believe you're sitting there!"

"Why?" asked Salenca.

"You stole a bunch of our clients with underhanded tactics, and you have the balls to come into my office?" said the exec.

"You don't want our business?"

"Get the hell out of here!"

"You can always file a complaint," said Salenca. He pointed up at the linebackers in suits. "And there's the complaint department..."

... A pickup truck backed into the receiving bay and unloaded.

Salenca removed a document from his clipboard and handed it to the dispatcher. "Here's a manifest of the contents."

T hat night:
The pickup trucks arrived at the rallying point in staggered sequence. The bulldozer and freshly dug pit were waiting. Everything proceeded exactly as it had the night before.

Salenca stepped into the headlights of the last incoming pickup and put up his hands. "Stop."

"You don't want me to dump?" asked the driver.

"Not here." Salenca headed back to his Benz. "Follow us."

Shortly before dawn, they all arrived behind the legitimate disposal company that Salenca had visited the day before. He got out of the Benz and walked back to the pickup driver's window. "Cut your headlights. See those Dumpsters behind the building? . . ."

The driver nodded.

Salenca stood with his associates from the Benz, watching the pickup swing around back and unload the cargo into the trash bins.

"Now I'm totally confused," said the accountant's driver.

"We didn't get as many contracts as I had hoped," said Salenca. "I only intended to use the *threat* of violence, because roughing up civilians is bad business. Some of the companies called my bluff. So it's time to thin the competition."

"Would I be correct to assume that what's being tossed in those Dumpsters right now is similar to the manifest of what we dropped off here yesterday?"

"Identical."

Salenca waited until banking hours before calling in the anonymous tip on a burner phone.

The feds did what they do best. Be feds. Hazmat teams collected the illegal waste from the Dumpsters. Padlocks snapped shut on the receiving bay's roll-down doors. TV cameras filmed agents escorting executives from the building.

Salenca's regular cell phone began ringing nonstop. All the holdout companies had garbage stacking up, and they were now calling *him*.

Salenca was happy, and his bosses even happier.

Collections multiplied. They added more trucks. Dumps at the rallying points became logistical operations. Offshore accounts bulged. Everything going like silk.

Until the police car showed up.

Future subdivisions were not on the officer's routine patrol because they were just empty lots. But the officer was on the nearby expressway when he caught a glimpse of the bulldozer chugging away in the middle of the night. And a Mercedes.

Luckily, the last load had been dropped, and the dozer was pushing soil back into the hole.

The cop exited his patrol car with a flashlight. Salenca smiled and met him halfway. "How can I help you, Officer?"

"Why are you here at this hour?"

"Wish I wasn't," Salenca said with an air of disgust. "We're pouring twenty foundations in the morning. I was spot-checking and found improperly prepped footprints. That's how you end up with cracked slabs and lawsuits. And now I have to be back out here in four hours."

All the officer saw were people working. Strange hour, but no potential crime except maybe vandalizing dirt. "Okay, take care."

"You, too, Officer."

Later that day, an emergency meeting in the warehouse. Salenca walked down a line of men at attention, handing them pages.

"I'm sure you've all heard about our close brush last night," said Salenca. "From now on, we're using a new disposal technique."

"What kind?"

"One that eliminates the cost of a bulldozer."

# *Chapter 18*

The sound of typewriter keys in the bungalow was something that always made Darby smile. "How's it coming in there, kid?"

"Half and half."

"What's that mean?"

"Well, I've got lots of great action for the first part of the book with all the crazy exotic animals and stolen cars, but I don't have an ending, and I always start at the ending. Hell, I don't even have the middle bridge."

"That can be fixed," said Darby. "I'll give you all the bridges and endings you need."

"Plus I personally knew my subject matter in the other ones, but I really don't know anything about the Port of Palm Beach. I'm running low on details to paint it in the reader's mind."

"That's an even easier fix." Darby grabbed his cane. "Let's go."

"Now? It's really late."

"Best time."

They arrived at the port, and Kenny drove toward where they had parked the other day when he met Brady and the rest of the old welding gang. Darby surveyed the nightscape, which he could read like the waves. "Let me out," said the Pope. "Then park on the other side of the dock, by the rail yard, and walk back."

"Why?"

"The late hour. In certain situations it's helpful to create separation from your vehicle," said the Pope. "There are many reasons, and if one ever comes up, you'll understand the value."

Kenny shrugged but did as he was told. After parking, he began the hike back along the desolate industrial waterfront. Nobody around to ask any nosy questions. This would be impossible today, with all the Homeland Security after 9/11. But it was still the 1980s, when few could envision the day that the port would need to start inspecting cargo containers with Geiger counters.

The young writer completed his trek and rejoined Darby at their regular spot on the docks behind the welding shop. They dragged over plastic chairs, and Kenny got out his notebook.

"Don't take notes," said Darby. "Just sit and absorb."

Kenny absorbed. The twinkling lights on the waterfront mansions across Lake Worth. Running lights on motorboats. Headlights crossing the tall arch of the new Blue Heron Bridge. Security lights blazing in the rail yard. The moon was just bright enough to make out the pines and palms on Peanut Island.

Over at the adjacent marina, it was dark in a particular spot where it usually wasn't. Only someone who knew the port like Darby would have noticed.

"What are you looking at?" asked Kenny.

"Shhh." He kept his eyes on a boat ramp where the security lamp was out. This time it wasn't a Zodiac. It was a scuba diver. He had just swum under a nearby cargo ship and unfastened a load of cocaine from a giant magnet, which another scuba diver had attached to the hull in South America.

The diver left his fins and tank on the pier and delivered the load to the open bed of a waiting pickup truck. Then he went back to the ramp and swam away toward Peanut Island.

Darby turned to Kenny and raised his eyebrows.

K enny continued typing during the day, and hanging out at the port at night. It wasn't eventful like the first two times. In fact it was boring.

"This is boring," said Kenny.

"Boring is when you notice stuff."

Kenny noticed inbound planes from Europe. Some kind of party going on behind a mansion. The police cruiser that had just pulled up. Then footsteps. Kenny's hands reflexively covered his face when the flashlight beam hit them.

"What the hell are you doing here!"

"Roger."

"Oh, it's you, Darby." The officer clicked the flashlight off. "Listen, you really shouldn't be out here this late."

"Why not?"

The cop exhaled. *Darby, don't bust my balls. You know what's going on.*

Darby moved in and out of all circles in town, including some he couldn't exactly tell Kenny about. He wasn't involved in anything himself, but he was trusted.

The officer headed back to his car. "Just be careful . . ."

. . . The typing in the bungalow accelerated with each new trip to the port. "I need some of that plot help you were talking about."

"I'm there." Darby hobbled into the kitchen. "I wrote down a few ideas."

"Thanks." *Clack, clack, clack.* "I can actually see the rest of book in my head now . . ."

Darby was asleep in his chair, dreaming about a bygone time

when his body was whole, on top of a wave beside a rusty, grounded ship. Something roused him.

Kenny shook his shoulder. "Sorry to wake you, but I'm at an important part in the second draft. Remember how you said that if I couldn't vividly visualize something myself, there's no way I could get the reader to?"

A groggy Darby tried to clear the fog. "I remember what I told you. What do you need?"

"Go back to the port to get my head in the right place to see everything with new eyes. The slow-motion climax needs more details."

"Give me a minute to get my bearings." Darby rubbed his face. "What time is it?"

"Almost two."

They were soon back on the dock in their usual plastic chairs.

"I love the ending you gave me," said Kenny. "They'll never see that coming."

"Glad you liked it. And you might even get some more material tonight."

"Why do you say that?"

"Don't be obvious," said Darby. "Just act like you're talking to me and peek over my left shoulder."

"A police car? But we see them all the time."

"Except there are two officers in the car tonight. That means something's on."

"You notice everything."

The black-and-white cruiser sat fifty yards back, officers facing the water with their lights off. Eating egg-salad sandwiches and drinking coffee from Styrofoam. Killing time.

Darby and Kenny were enjoying the uncomplicated pleasure of a balmy breeze off the water. Most of the mansions' lights were out across Lake Worth. Traffic on the giant arch bridge to Singer Island was down to nothing. Darby felt a subconscious tug from the days of the old low drawbridge. Some of the best bridge fishing in Florida, practically deep-sea with the huge stuff that swam in that inlet.

Kenny was having his own throwback moment. Aroma memories of fresh fried catfish, hush puppies and slaw from the Crab Pot under the end of the bridge.

"Ever camped on Peanut Island?" asked Darby.

"Many times," said Kenny. "Scouts, Little League, skinny kids lining up for that rope swing from the giant tree near the edge of the shore."

"Every kid around here remembers that rope swing."

"But remember how you had to swing way out to clear all the land and roots before letting go and diving in the water? We could have broken our necks."

"Wouldn't have been worth doing otherwise."

Kenny turned around. "What was that?"

"Be still."

They listened. A deep motorized sound out in the water. They looked in that direction, but no running lights. "This is a big one, diesel," said Darby. "Running slow."

Kenny glanced to his left. "Someone unscrewed the lightbulbs on the pier again."

They sat back to enjoy the show. From the darkness appeared the fiasco of an old shrimp boat pumping way too much smoke and laboring as it chugged toward the docks like something important was about to snap in the engine.

A few curt shouts, and a couple of guys low on the totem pole leaped onto the pier and tied off the boat. Movement on the dim deck.

"That settles that," said Darby. "They didn't use any knots to tie the boat off. Just wrapped the rope a bunch of times around the cleats."

"What's that mean?"

"These are no legitimate shrimpers."

Kenny smiled. "The eyes of the dock see all."

They watched a minivan pull up. No dead drop this time. Shipment must be too large. Cooler after cooler came off the boat.

From behind them: "Enjoying yourselves tonight?"

*How did one of the police officers sneak up like that? I must be getting old.* Darby turned around. No police officer. Instead, tank top, shorts, non-skid boat shoes. Bushy hair and mustache, almost a gray complexion. He stooped and set down a leather satchel, boxy on the bottom, tapering to the latch and handle. He straightened back up.

"Not doing too bad," said Darby, looking by the man's side. "What's the sawed-off shotgun for?"

"What? This?" He waved it offhand toward the water. "Comes in handy. Kind of a universal tool in my line of work."

"Why don't you have a seat?" said Darby. "It's a pleasant evening."

"*Was* pleasant."

*Okay, we're definitely drifting in the wrong direction.* Darby knew interpersonal dynamics. An escalation like that meant the man wasn't trying to arrive at a decision. One had already been made. Darby needed to undo it.

The man lit a cigarette. "We've been noticing that you're frequent visitors down here at night."

"We like the water." He turned to Kenny. "Isn't that right?"

Kenny was about to stroke out. His eyes responded: *How can you even function, let alone talk so calmly?*

A drag on the cigarette. "Your friend's the quiet type . . . And nice touch with your cane. Nobody would ever suspect."

"Suspect what?"

"That you're DEA." He waved the shotgun toward them. "Get up, both of you."

"Just stop," said Darby. "Listen, whatever it is you're thinking, I'm only a guy who used to weld in that shop behind you before I went on disability. I'm not a narc."

The cigarette was flicked into the water with a sizzle. "Get up!"

"You're making a huge mistake," said Darby.

"Don't act like you don't know what's going on."

"Of course I know what's going on," said Darby. "The whole dock does. You're too obvious. But I don't go talking about what's none of my business. Ask around." Darby pointed. "Heck, ask those cops over there."

"Oh, I'll be having a nice, long discussion with those gentlemen about letting a couple of feds in here after all we've paid them."

Before that point, it was just drifting the wrong way, but now they had crossed the Rubicon. Admitting to bribing cops. Not the sort of thing you tell people that you let go.

The end of the twelve-gauge poked Darby's ribs. "Up!"

*Chapter 19*

**S**illy Putty."

"I remember Silly Putty," said Coleman. "It came in a little plastic egg."

"Forget what the experts say, Silly Putty was the great generational divide." Serge raced south on Dixie Highway out of Miami. "Today it's all flashy game boxes, but back then kids were hands-on."

"Remember pressing Silly Putty on comic strips in newspapers, and then you'd peel it off and the comic strip would be on the putty?"

"I took it to the next level," said Serge. "My folks wouldn't buy me a Xerox machine no matter how many times I asked. I even put it on my Christmas list, which is supposed to go unquestioned, like a papal decree. 'Serge, why on earth do you need a Xerox machine?' 'We're living in important times. That's all I can say.' So I had to improvise, and Silly Putty became my copy machine that I'd use to make duplicates of newspaper articles on Nixon."

"I ate Silly Putty," said Coleman. "Didn't taste bad unless it was after comic strips and full of ink, and then my kindergarten teachers asked why my tongue was black again."

"Did you used to put everything in your mouth?"

"Pretty much." Coleman put a hardcover book to his mouth and sucked. "Where to now?"

"Coleman, what on earth?"

He exhaled a cloud of pot smoke. "Oh, this?" He opened the book to chapter three. "I hollowed out some pages, used a liquid-soap pump bottle for the chamber, made the stem from a metal pen, the carburetor is on the back end of the pages, and I suck right here in the middle of the title."

"You made a bong from a novel?"

"Figured since we're on your literary tour." Another hit.

"No, you're missing my meaning," said Serge. "*Why* would you make a bong from a book in the first place?"

Coleman exhaled more smoke. "So people will think I'm smart."

Serge blinked hard to reset his brain. "I lost my place."

"Where are we going?"

"Right, the next literary-tour stop." Serge took his hands from the wheel and rubbed them with high friction. "When you mention Florida authors, people always blurt out Hemingway and Tennessee Williams, but they weren't full-time Floridians. Interestingly enough, our biggest lifelong literary lions were women, and we had a bumper crop. Marjorie Kinnan Rawlings, Marjorie Stoneman Douglas, Zora Neale Hurston. For some reason they all had three names, like assassins."

The green Nova hung a right on Sunset Drive and entered the thriving subtropical jungle of a neighborhood called Coconut Grove.

"Banyan trees!" said Serge. "I can't get enough of banyans! I'm all about banyans!"

"Didn't a chick get stuck in one last year in Key West?" asked Coleman.

"Yes, and she was only three feet off the ground," said Serge. "Instead of a single trunk, many have complex support structures that you can climb inside and get stuck. That's the beauty of banyans."

Ten minutes later, neighbors gathered on the sidewalk. The homeowner stormed out his front door. "What in heaven's name is going on?"

"We're stuck," said Serge, only an arm exposed. "Isn't it great?"

"Help," said Coleman, wiggling a sneakered foot out the side of the trunk.

"Get the hell off my property!"

"Maybe you need to look up 'stuck' in the dictionary," said Serge. "Banyans are also in the fig family, another big selling point."

"I'm calling the police!"

"I'm also an escape artist," said Serge. He hoisted himself up by an aerial root, then pulled Coleman free. They hopped down. "You have this magnificent, century-old banyan on your property and you've never gotten stuck in it? You're living a lie."

"Leave! Now!"

"We have an appointment with history anyway." The Nova took off.

Coleman looked out the back window at the gawking crowd in the street. "What was their problem?"

"It's all political." Serge cut the wheel. "People *say* they want change, but whenever I show up . . ."

The Nova passed a street sign: STEWART AVENUE. Serge slowed as they navigated a winding, tree-canopied road just a spit from Biscayne Bay.

"Almost there. *Alllllll*most there . . ."

"Look at these big honkin' houses," said Coleman.

Serge checked street numbers. "There it is! Three-seven-four-four!"

"Where?"

"Back in all that vegetation."

Coleman hung out the passenger window. "What's that tiny little home doing in the middle of all these mansions?"

"Being preserved, thank God!" Serge eased up to the curb. "It's Marjorie Stoneman Douglas's old home, exactly the kind of place I'd expect her to live."

"It looks weird."

"Because it's tasteful," said Serge. "Like a modest English cottage, stucco, brick and cypress timber with curved wooden shingles, built 1926."

"Can we go inside?"

"It's not open to the public, but we can look in the windows," said Serge. "Actually, we're not supposed to, but there are certain things beyond our control."

Serge trotted across the yard with a thermos of coffee and pressed his face to glass. "You have to understand what this area was like back then. You say 'Miami' and everyone pictures a giant metropolis that's been here forever. But in those early days it was virtually nothing, the kind of place that you drive through today and all you'd notice is that the speed limit drops for a couple minutes. Some hearty souls, however, knew paradise when they discovered it, and settled here on the edge of the bay."

"Looks dusty inside."

"That's why you have to use your imagination engine," said Serge. "It was a rare intersection of a magic time and place. I'm going to take a look. Engine on!" He closed his eyes a few moments. They flew back open. "Whoa! That was intense!"

"Let me take a look," said Coleman. He closed his eyes. "It's just dark."

"That's because you're on the wrong channel," said Serge. "In your case, the whole cable service is probably down." His face returned to the window. "I'm getting chills. Right in there is where she wrote the opus, and I just conjured the image of Marjorie sitting at a desk typing away on her history-setting 1947 masterpiece *The Everglades: River of Grass.*"

Coleman's nose smudged the window. "Never heard of it."

Serge seized his pal by the front of his shirt. "What! It's just the most important Florida book ever published! Changed the course of the entire state!"

"Please let go."

"Sorry, I'm in a time flux right now, so the astral plane is unstable." He took a sip of coffee. "It's hard to conceive, but before Douglas, the common wisdom was that the Everglades were something that people needed to put a stop to."

"Why?"

"It was considered a worthless, water-clogged waste of land." Serge spread his arms expansively. "Plan after plan was floated to drain and fill the swamp so we could all stay in hotels and play golf. But Marjorie was the lone beacon. She stood in defiant opposition, beginning her book with a call to arms that this was the only Everglades we had in the whole world. I like books that tell everybody they're wrong."

"What happened?" asked Coleman.

"I'll show you!" He took off running. "Back to the car! . . ."

The Nova sped north into Little Havana and picked up Calle Ocho, the local designation of the Tamiami Trail.

"There's a pet store," said Coleman. "Can we stop?"

Ten minutes later, Serge turned west and drove along a canal. A cat toy was now suction-cupped to the windshield. It was plastic and pear-shaped, with numerous holes and a furry mouse inside. Jingle bells hung from the bottom. Coleman batted it around and drooled. The last landscaped neighborhoods dribbled off into the wildness of the Glades.

They came upon an anonymous dirt road.

"I love anonymous dirt roads! Anything can happen!"

The Chevy sat still a half mile later. Wind and birds and a flat panorama untouched by the hand of man.

"This is what I'm talking about!" said Serge. "The perfect place!"

"The perfect place to smoke dope," said Coleman. "Nobody messes with you."

"No," said Serge. "I'm talking about Douglas's legacy. Without her, we might be looking at outlet malls and laser-tag hippodromes. The cosmos rewarded Marjorie by letting her live to a ripe hundred and eight years."

"Wow," said Coleman. "That's older than being dead."

"You *are* an existentialist." Serge broke out his camera as the sun began to set on the western horizon. *Click, click, click.* "The most excellent part is after dark when a whole 'nother world blooms."

It got dark. And loud. Insects, frogs, more birds.

*Jingle, jingle.*

"Coleman, what are you doing?"

"Thinking like a cat." Coleman exhaled an extra-large hit of pot into the cat toy. Then he quickly moved his hands, covering one hole after another. "Smoke's coming out there . . . now there . . . now over here . . ." He put one of the holes to his mouth and sucked. "Now there . . . and there . . ." Sucking again. "Over there . . ."

"Coleman!"

"I got the mouse's tail!"

*Jingle, jingle.*

Serge stared. "Are you finished, Tinker Bell?"

"Look," said Coleman. "Here comes the moon."

"And here comes some headlights."

"Who do you think it is?" asked Coleman.

"Probably a fellow nature lover," said Serge. "There's no other reason to be out here."

The headlights turned off, and so did the engine. A moon-lit silhouette got out. The moon hit another silhouette: a naked woman on a *Playboy* bumper sticker.

"I don't think he saw us." Coleman held his joint down to conceal the glowing orange tip. "What's he doing?"

"Not sure," said Serge. "He's going around to the back of the pickup truck."

They watched for clues at a range of a hundred yards, but none arrived.

"Now he's getting back in the truck and leaving," said Coleman.

"When someone comes out to such a remote area and only stays a few minutes, it usually isn't a constructive activity." Serge started up the Nova and slung dirt as he sped to the spot where the other vehicle had parked. He leaped out with a flashlight, scanning the watery nests of reeds and bulrushes.

He seized his heart and jumped back. "Dear God and all the saints!"

"What is it?" asked Coleman.

Serge grabbed his friend for balance. He lowered his forehead onto Coleman's shoulder and began to cry.

"Easy there, buddy." Coleman patted the back of his head. "It can't be that bad."

Sniffles. "It is! Just look!" Serge raised his head and aimed the flashlight again. "Asbestos, biomedical waste, and—yikes, I didn't see that before!"

"What is it?"

"Computer and cell-phone batteries!" Serge bent down. "That means heavy metals! Cadmium, lead, mercury, chromium, manganese, zinc, all leaching into the delicate food chain!"

"A turtle just crawled on top of a battery," said Coleman.

"*Nooooooo!...*" Serge splashed down into the water and picked up the critter, tossing it a short distance. "Live long and prosper."

Then a boomerang mood swing. Serge jumped back in the Nova, and Coleman ran alongside until he could lunge in.

"What's the plan?" said an upside-down Coleman on the passenger side.

"He's got a head start, but there's only one route back to Miami and we've got miles of swamp to make up ground." The needle arced across the speedometer. "Keep your eyes peeled for a pickup."

"How will you know which one?"

"Oh, I'll know."

The Nova blazed east on the Tamiami. There was such a differential in velocity with the other cars in their lane that the approaching red taillights almost seemed like oncoming traffic. Serge whipped around each motorist in turn.

Coleman watched them go by. "Serge, you're freaking out every driver you're passing."

No answer. Eyes low, locked on the back end of the next vehicle.

A Ford pickup.

"Hey, Serge, there's the *Playboy* bumper sticker."

He never slowed, blowing by the truck. *Then* he slowed, and slowed some more. Checking the rearview.

"What are you doing?" asked Coleman.

"Making him go around. I need him on my driver's side."

The pickup pulled out into the oncoming lane. Its driver let off the gas as he passed, in order to let Serge know how he felt about matters.

"Look," said Coleman. "He's giving you the bird."

Serge simply aimed a pistol out the window and shot the front tire.

# Chapter 20

The sight of the shotgun spoke silent volumes.

Darby studied the man's dilated pupils, fidgetiness and sniffles. He clearly had been dipping into his own product. It's hard enough reasoning with a psychopath, but add chemicals and it's a fool's errand.

"Stand up, goddamn it!"

Darby raised his hand. "Okay, okay..."

...Back in the police car. Officers balled up wax paper from their sandwiches and poured the dregs of their coffee out the windows.

"Oh shit!...Roger, look!"

"Hector's got Darby and that other guy," said the officer in the passenger seat. "What the hell is he thinking?"

"They're being marched down to the end of that dock with a shotgun. This can't end well."

"What do we do?"

"What *can* we do? If we run out there we risk showing that we're involved."

"He just jabbed Darby in the back again with the gun."

The cops continued observing as the Pope and Kenny stood side by side at the very end of the pier with their heels hanging over the edge, hands in the air. Staring down the shotgun.

"There's one thing we can do." The officer leaned and hit a couple of switches. A rack of red-and-blue lights came on with a single whoop of the siren.

The man with the shotgun turned and gave the officers the finger.

"That is bad."

At the end of the dock, Darby watched his captor flip off the cops, then saw the shotgun swing back around.

Reckoning.

Some people freeze. Others kick in with magnified focus. Darby saw everything in slow motion. Tunnel vision. All sound dropped out in his ears except a high-pitched ringing.

As the thick barrel was almost back to him, Darby spun. His right hand swatted the barrel aside, then both hands shoved Kenny hard off the end of the pier.

*Blam!*

Kenny had just surfaced in the dark water when Darby's body splashed next to him. The Pope was facedown, the blast clear through him with a large red circle in the back of his shirt. Kenny's eyes almost popped out of his head. A brief yelp of a scream before he covered his mouth.

*"Get that other guy! We can't leave a witness!"*

A hail of bullets from a half-dozen guns raked the water without aim. Kenny dove back under. He didn't know the port anywhere near as well as Darby, but he'd been spending enough time there to know how the piers and docks met and curved and formed the best hiding spots for someone in his situation.

He held his breath until reaching the dark overhang of the next pier, cutting himself on barnacles as he clung to a piling.

*Bang, bang, bang, bang, bang, bang . . .*

"Stop it!" Their leader waved both arms in the air. "Knock it off!"

The guns went quiet and they all looked at Hector.

"Do you see him?"

They shook their heads.

"Then what are you shooting at?"

"Uh, the water."

The gang looked over the side of the pier into a light chop. A dead snook bobbed to the surface.

"Brilliant," said the leader. "You prevented a fish from testifying . . . No more shooting unless you see him. You're just making noise, and we need to be able to hear his splashing."

They stopped and listened. Kenny remained still.

Both cops were out of their car now, sprinting down the pier. "Fuck me! Hector, what have you done!"

The leader turned around. "Took care of something you should have. Do we not pay you enough? Do you not understand that letting a couple of DEA agents in here is not compatible with our business?"

"DEA agents? Are you insane?" The officer pointed at the body floating out into the channel. "That's the Pope."

"The Pope?"

"His nickname. Darby. Everyone knows him." The officer grabbed his head with both hands. "You've just brought the world down on all of us."

"Is he someone important? Politician? Connected businessman?"

"No, a retired welder who used to surf," said the officer. "But everyone liked him."

"You're telling us we should be scared because people *liked* him?"

"You don't know this town," said the other cop. "Why did you have to shoot him? He was just sitting out there minding his own business."

"Wait, back up. You *knew* he was sitting out here watching our whole operation?"

"He could be trusted. It was *Darby*."

Hector tightened his lips in frustration. "We'll continue this most enjoyable conversation later, but right now we have a more immediate problem. A witness got away, and your well-timed interruption is helping him escape."

It was. Kenny silently slid through the water, pylon to pylon, and dog-paddled along the seawall in the stretches where there was nothing to grip. Behind him, search beams swept the water, and someone hung over the side of the pier, shining a flashlight into the space where he'd first been. But now Kenny was so far away that not even the wind could carry the sound of their voices, and the distant flashlights were like fireflies.

"See anything?" asked Hector.

"Nothing."

"Spread out. Take the dinghy." Hector pointed. "He couldn't have gotten up past the marina or we would have seen him. Head south!"

Kenny reached a ladder on the seawall. He looked up and recognized the back of the welding shop where he and Darby had just been sitting in those plastic chairs. He *had* to get up that ladder. He would be exposed, but just an indistinguishable dark form. As long as he moved slowly enough so they couldn't detect human movement. He began slithering up the rings, water dripping off into the basin. One painstaking inch at a time.

The perfect plan. Except now there was a boat coming toward him, flashlights hitting the water and the seawall. Now Kenny was on deadline. The clock ticked down faster than he expected, and the high-powered search beams were just feet away on the seawall, about to hit him. No more time for stealth, exposed or not.

He scrambled over the last few rungs and threw himself flat onto the concrete dock next to the plastic chairs.

*"Did you hear something?"*

*"Kill the engine! . . ."*

Kenny controlled his breathing as the boat drifted below, flickers of errant light shafting up over the seawall and hitting the back of the welding shop.

*"Okay, keep going . . ."*

The boat started up again and motored away. Kenny rested his head on the dock in relief. He wasn't out of the woods yet, but the initial, full-force panic of evasion had dissipated enough to reveal a vortex of emotion. Kenny lay there, his head swirling downward into a dizzying whirlpool of sadness, confusion, guilt, self-doubt and then . . . rage. To this day, Kenny wouldn't be able to tell you why he did it, but a notion of revenge was probably in the mix. His eyes rose from the pavement, and they saw the leather satchel, the one Hector had set down when he first threatened them with the sawed-off. He wasn't sure what was in it, and it wasn't about greed. Didn't matter. Whatever the contents, it was important to Hector, and losing it would piss him off.

Kenny jumped up, grabbed the handle, and took off down the docks.

Back at the boat ramp, the police officers begged Hector to collect his men and clear out. Maybe Darby would float somewhere else and it would be off them.

"Are you brain-dead?" said Hector. "There's a witness out there to the murder, and in case you're behind on the law, they'll hang you along with us. Plus, we have to move all this coke into the van and . . ." He was forgetting something. Not for long. "The money! The satchel!" His head snapped toward those cheap plastic chairs a hundred yards up the port. "It's gone!" Then, raising his eyes, he saw the dark form of just such a bag sail over the chain-link fence at the dry docks, followed by the silhouette of Kenny hopping the top and running away with it.

Hector looked around to find he was alone with the cops—all his guys out on search patrol in the dinghy. He jumped down into the shrimp boat and grabbed the radio. "Get back here! He's on land! He has the satchel!"

"On our way."

But Hector was losing critical time waiting for the gang to return. He swung toward the cops: "Go kill him!"

"We're not killing anybody," said Roger. "We all need to calm down and clean up this mess and get out of here."

Hector pulled a bullet snorter from his shorts, and snorted.

"That's less than advisable," said Roger.

Hector sneered at the cops. "You worthless pieces of shit!"

"Now it's time to seriously calm down . . . And stop with the coke."

"You did this! You did *all* this," said Hector, gesturing into the tidal current taking away the Pope. "And my money! Millions!"

"Bullshit," said Roger. "This size load? There's no way that bag could hold that much cash."

"Bearer bonds." Those would be untraceable certificates, about the size and look of diplomas or stock documents with eagles and lions, payable to whoever showed up. They were known as the best way to skirt whatever someone wanted to skirt. Big in Switzerland.

Flashlights chaotically swung in all directions as the dinghy arrived back at the boat ramp. "You wanted us for something?"

"You morons! He got away!"

"Where?"

"Right where you were at the dry docks! With my money!"

"Want us to go back out after him?"

"Duh!"

They jumped in the minivan and screeched out.

A while later, they returned.

"Well?"

The driver got out and shook his head. "No sign of him anywhere. We followed his wet footprints until they dried up, then fanned out and checked every possible place he could hide. Even looked in spots if he backtracked."

"Son of a bitch!"

"Widen the search outside the port?"

"No, too much time has passed. He's gone for now," said Hector. "We'll wait until tomorrow and pick up his trail. Start loading the van from the boat."

One of the men lifted a cooler off the pier. "You yelled something on the marine radio about a satchel?"

Hector braced himself, holding the shotgun's cold steel barrel sideways against his forehead. He clenched his eyes shut. "I know, I know." He opened them and raised the twelve-gauge. "I would never have imagined that anyone could be so incompetent as to fuck up my load, lose a death-penalty witness, *and* my bearer bonds!" He took another bullet snort and raised his barrel.

"You can't be this stupid!" said Roger. "You can't shoot cops!"

*Blam! Blam! . . .*

The officers toppled backward.

"Holy shit," said one of the crew. "What do we do now?"

"Finish loading the truck."

# Chapter 21

**THE PRESENT**

A vulture circled. A turtle crossed the road. An alligator watched with two eye bumps that looked like knot holes on a log floating down a drainage canal.

Serge grunted with a lug wrench, tightening the final nut on the spare tire that replaced the shot-out one.

"Someone's pulling over," said Coleman. "And the tarp is moving."

Serge looked over into the bed of the pickup truck. Groaning from under the tarp as the hostage beneath it regained consciousness and attempted to stand. Serge whacked the rising spot with the wrench, and the tarp fell flat and quiet. Headlights lit up Serge and Coleman. Another truck parked behind them.

A man in a uniform got out and hitched up his pants like a southern sheriff. His vehicle had a winch and tool compartments. "You fellas need any help?"

"No, Mr. Road Ranger." Serge leaned casually against the side of the pickup and sipped a thermos. "But thank you for your service. Everyone takes the road ranger for granted, tirelessly driving up and down the highways and byways of America, looking for stranded motorists with families huddled in a ditch, watching steam pour out from under the hood and wondering how they will survive to see another sunrise, as if their plane had gone down in the Himalayas, until suddenly, 'Hooray! It's the road ranger! He's our hero!' You guys should wear capes and get all the girls. If you have a petition I can sign to that effect, because I remember the day long before road rangers when we all had to depend on each other, and small-town folks actually stopped to help neighbors in distress. Then those days passed and now drivers see broken-down motorists and immediately construct a belief system giving them a free pass not to stop and help: 'If you hadn't been lazy, you could have afforded a more dependable vehicle, and you're probably on welfare or drugs or both, not to mention in this country illegally. In fact now that I think about it, I'm *glad* you're broken down. Fuck you people.'" Serge's hand shot out. "They hit the pedal and zoom! Speeding right on by. But not the road ranger. You guys are policy-neutral. Thank you."

The man scratched his head.

A groaning from under the tarp.

Serge and Coleman began coughing.

"Are you sure everything's okay?" asked the ranger. "Did I hear something?"

Serge pointed over the man's shoulder. "Is that a broken-down car with small children and a pregnant woman in labor?"

The ranger spun around. "Where!"

Serge reached over and conked the tarp with the wrench again. "Sorry, it's just a tree. My eyes must have been playing tricks in this light." He knelt next to the truck, pumping a metal handle to lower the tire jack. "That just about does it. We'll be on our merry way." A muffled groan. He tossed the jack hard onto the tarp. "Thanks again for all you do! Go get the girls!"

Serge climbed in the pickup, and Coleman got in the Nova.

The ranger continued staring in puzzlement as both vehicles drove off into the dark swamp.

Twenty minutes later, two pairs of headlights swung down a previously anonymous dirt road. The pickup stopped at the location of the illegal dumping. Serge got out his flashlight and splashed down into the water again. He inspected the heavy-metal batteries, tossing them one by one onto the side of the road.

Coleman crouched at the edge of the dirt. "Are you going to clean all this up yourself?"

"No." Serge shined his light on the label of another battery, discarded it and picked up another. "I don't remotely have the proper disposal resources. I'll need to call in an anonymous tip and let the authorities handle it."

"Then what are you doing now?"

"Looking for the appropriate battery." Another hunk of plastic and metal landed at Coleman's feet. "My teaching seminar requires scientific precision."

"You're going to teach that guy under the tarp a lesson?"

"Whether he chooses to learn is up to him." The light hit another label.

"What exactly are you looking for?"

Serge plucked more rectangles from the water. "These lithium-ion batteries are both amazing and harrowing. It's a major advancement that such a small package can power a computer for hours. At the same time, the technology is hell on the environment when it's run the course. Not to mention that there have been more than forty recalls in the last decade and a half."

"Why?"

Toss. "They have a nasty habit of exploding. But most people think, 'Okay, it's just a little battery in my laptop. Big deal. How bad can an explosion be?'"

"Except it's serious?"

"Most definitely." Serge wiped hands on his shirt and pulled out his phone. He tapped buttons as he climbed the bank. "Check out this video. There are dozens of these on the Internet where special laboratories force a battery into a runaway state . . . See how it vented out the side of the computer."

"Doesn't look scary to me," said Coleman. "Only a little smoke."

"That was just the first cell. Ion batteries usually have between three and twelve. Each cell ignites the next, growing hotter and more violent. When the public heard about the recalls, they imagined a single bang, but it's a rolling fireworks show, building to a big climax."

"The second cell just went." Coleman squinted at the tiny screen. "That one sent fire out the keyboard . . . Wow, the third was like a Roman candle shooting up to the roof of the lab. Except it didn't look like a regular flame."

"That's because it was a shower of incandescent heavy metal burning at more than a thousand degrees."

"The fourth blew the whole cover off the computer, and there's fire everywhere . . . Now five. Ka-boom! . . . That rocks! Can you save this so I can watch again later when I'm more stoned?"

Serge jumped back in the water. "Knock yourself out." His quest continued. Eventually he had an array of batteries lined up on the hood of the pickup.

"What's special about those?" asked Coleman, still watching the phone screen.

"I need to select the batteries with the most cells."

"Why?"

Serge grinned big. "Longer life expectancy."

He went to the trunk of the Chevy and pulled out his own laptop. He removed the battery and began comparing it to those assembled on the pickup. "No good, no good, no good, not this one, not that . . ."

"What's the problem?" asked Coleman.

Serge picked up another battery, but negative results. "I need to find one of these he dumped to fit my computer."

"Why not just use the battery that came with your computer?"

"You're joking, right?" The next battery snapped perfectly in place. "If there's no irony, what's the point? The reason some of these explode is that the cells overcharge. That's why they all come with an overcharge-defeating circuitry. That's the key. And the batteries that go rogue usually have one of three bad things in common: the circuit was already defective leaving the factory, it got damaged by dropping a laptop, or there's deliberate sabotage. You'll notice that in all those Internet videos, scientists omitted showing us the critical yet utterly simple step that their labs use to set off the batteries, because you can't have the general public running around knowing how to detonate laptops, or life in Starbucks will suddenly become way too exciting. Suffice to say, all it takes is an ordinary screwdriver." Serge reached in his pocket. "Well, I'll be!"

"A screwdriver," said Coleman. "What are the odds?"

Serge leaned over the battery . . .

# Chapter 22

It was noon and it was dark.

The curtains were closed in the beach-style bungalow, and all the lights were off. Just little glowing slits from the blinds.

The slits created an eerie effect, lighting up the dust in the air at striped intervals, like a black-and-white pulp movie from the fifties. They made horizontal lines across Kenny's hot chest.

Kenny remained perfectly still in the old La-Z-Boy where Darby used to sit. He reclined with a Remington rifle across his chest and an open box of ammo on the adjacent table.

He had been there for hours. All his senses at battle stations. He heard a fly buzzing somewhere in the room. He hadn't eaten and wasn't hungry. He only slept minutes at a shot before startling himself awake and aiming the gun at nothing.

Kenny kept wondering why nobody was bursting in. He'd had so much luck the other night at the port that it would surely run out.

The whole horror show was a repeating loop in his head. He

nodded off again, and the nightmare became real: climbing out of the water, hopping the fence . . .

. . . Kenny sprinted past the dry docks at full gallop and made the corner between empty boat lifts. Subtlety had left town. A hundred yards ahead across an abandoned lot, sanctuary. He now fully appreciated the value of creating separation from your car. It sat on the edge of U.S. 1, parked at the port and away from it at the same time. But the final space between him and the vehicle was completely naked. No obstruction, with clean sight lines. And the car was fully lit up by the highway's jarring crime lights. Anyone would see him.

He never broke stride, alone in the middle of the wide-open, feeling more and more exposed. Nothing else around in the closed-down industrialness. No other movement to dilute noticing *his* movement. No pedestrians, birds, not even traffic on the road, because everyone knew this wasn't a place to be at this time of night. The racket of his feet slapping the pavement made what seemed like deafening echoes off the metal buildings.

The car was only feet away, and Kenny slowed to get his hand in a pocket for the keys. That's when he saw the headlights. A minivan. No time to reach the driver's seat. Just dive behind the back bumper.

He peeked under the car. The headlights came right toward him and lit up the pavement under the vehicle, forcing him to scoot around behind one of the tires. He sat on the ground, back against the fender, staring up at the stars and bracing for what surely would come next.

Then it didn't come. He looked under the car again. Unbelievable. The headlights had swung toward the fence at the dry docks. The fence's gate wasn't even locked, but the minivan smashed through it anyway. The van stopped. Sounds of frantic men running around. Shouts.

*"I found his footprints..."*

Kenny kept glancing at his driver's door handle. This was a dilemma with fangs. Go for the door and risk being found. Don't go for the door and risk being found. He took quick breaths, steeling himself to make the lunge. And every time he was about to spring, another shout in the distance that froze him.

*"I think he went that way..."*

The crew checked all the logical hiding places: between the cargo containers on the loading dock, all the train cars in the railroad yard, even climbed on top of the petroleum tanks.

*"Check under the semi-trailers..."*

It finally hit Kenny. They were locked in the mind-set that he'd never had time to clear the port and was sheltered in position somewhere in that haystack of metal. He hoped they didn't suddenly grow an IQ.

Kenny was looking under the car when the headlights came his way again, through the busted fence, and turned back in the direction of the shrimp boat. He waited and watched to make sure nobody was left behind on mop-up detail. Then he quietly stood, got in the car and pulled onto the road. They didn't know what his car looked like, so he took the quickest route to safety, back north past the municipal marina. As he approached the scene of the crime off to his right, he couldn't help but glance over.

Two more bright flashes from a shotgun, and two police officers fell over. "Jesus!"

He raced the rest of the way back to the bungalow...

... Where he now sat staring at an open leather satchel on the floor. All those bearer bonds with high denominations. He started thinking extra loud inside his head: *Why the hell did I grab that case? It just made me a magnet. For that matter, what am I doing sticking around Darby's pad? I don't know anything about smug-*

*glers, except from TV, but they're always tracking down witnesses or people who take their money, and I'm both. Then again, all they'd heard was Darby's first name. Maybe it isn't so bad after all. I'll simply go to the police. I didn't do anything wrong. Just an innocent bystander that the bad guys are after. The satchel will be a little awkward to explain but I'll convince them. All I need to do is calm down and be rational. I'll go to the police.* He nodded to himself and began to stand. *Shit, the police! After last night, I don't know which ones are honest. And the dirty ones know that I know too much! They're on the hook for murder! I definitely can't go to the police!* He dropped back down into the chair. "I'm so screwed!"

Hours of trembling and abject panic.

Kenny eventually coaxed himself back in from the emotional ledge. His right hand left the gun and pulled on his chin. *Hmm. The police just lost two of their own. So they have to be seriously pissed at the smugglers right about now. Maybe if I come forward and offer to testify to put them away—and play dumb about the rest . . . No, they're sure to figure it out . . . Or maybe they could . . . On the other hand . . . But then . . . But not . . . But . . . Wait! I've got it! There's no way the whole department is in on it. I just need to take the temperature of the situation and figure out my best move. There must be something about this on TV. And on the bright side, it can't get any worse.*

He grabbed the remote control and clicked on the midday report. A press conference at police headquarters. Behind the podium, a massive showing of the force—black mourning bands around their badges. The top brass and a vast majority of the department were on the up-and-up, and in the dark. Only a handful knew the real story. But they had been the first ones on the scene, and their initial reports were driving the narrative.

The chief stood at the microphone. ". . . As you know, this city has lost two of its finest, and none of our resources will be spared until we bring those responsible to justice. We are asking the public's help for any leads in solving this most heinous of crimes . . ." He turned the podium over to the head of the detective division.

". . . While it is still early in the investigation, we've developed a theory based on the discovery of a third victim, a civilian named Darby Pope, whose body washed ashore this morning at Phil Foster Park. Apparently the port and marina were being used in a major drug-smuggling operation. We have reason to believe that all three victims stumbled upon this activity. And although Mr. Pope was not involved, we've received information that an acquaintance of his was the gunman who ripped off the smugglers' money . . ." A photo of Darby in better times filled the screen. ". . . Anyone out there with information concerning who has recently been in Mr. Pope's company is asked to call this number . . ." Digits appeared over the bottom of the podium. ". . . A fifty-thousand-dollar reward is being offered by the Benevolent Association, and of course your identity will be kept strictly confidential . . ."

A rush of shit hit Kenny's heart. *They're pinning it on me? Holy fuck! Forget trusting anyone. The entire department is now ready to shoot first!*

He heard noise outside in the driveway and peeked through the blinds. Four police cars. Officers got out. *This is it,* thought Kenny. *They might not know I'm in here, but it's obvious procedure to check a victim's residence. Either way, it's probably not a good idea that I'm holding this rifle.*

He threw it across the room. He waited.

And waited. No knock at the door. Nobody crashing in.

Kenny went to the blinds again. The officers were getting back in their patrol cars and driving away.

He returned to his chair, clicked off the TV and began panicking again in the dark.

*What in the hell is going on?*

**W**hat was going on:

Just after the discovery of the slain officers, a frantic meeting had been set up in the wee hours. This time at a quarry west of West Palm, out in the swamp and cane fields near Twenty Mile Bend.

A minivan was waiting when the patrol car rolled into the gravel darkness with its headlights off.

The officers got out and didn't wait for hello. "How could you fuck this up so badly?" said a sergeant. "We should kill you right now!"

"Me? Are you serious?" said Hector. "Your boys screwed the pooch on this one. Letting outsiders watch the whole drop at the marina, then making a stupid excuse that these civilians could be trusted."

"So you shot them?"

"I was a little coked up, but I'm good now."

"Our friends are still dead, you cocksucker!"

A long stare. "Okay, I've tried being reasonable, but I'm getting tired real fast of taking that kind of mouth from a couple of peasants," said Hector. "How much do you make a week before what I kick in?"

"You know what happens to people who shoot cops?" said the sergeant. "You're just lucky that killing you would only increase the risk of our business arrangement coming to light."

"I'm lucky?" Hector snapped his fingers, and four men got out of the van with pistols and the sawed-off. "How would you enjoy ending up like your friends?"

"You forget," said the sergeant. "This is *our town*. Nobody comes here and pushes us around."

Hector hadn't seen the other patrol cars before, waiting in the dark at the quarry's entrance. A trio raced in, hitting their high beams. Hector raised a hand over his eyes. Officers jumped out with weapons drawn.

"Hector, our business deal has concluded," said the sergeant. "Consider your port privileges officially revoked."

"What about my money? I want that asshole brought to me on a platter!"

"You got your drugs. Consider it a bargain."

"Fuck you!" He headed back toward the van. "This isn't the end of it! We'll be back! And with more men and guns!"

"Well, why didn't you say so earlier? That changes everything."

"What's that supposed to mean—"

All the officers opened fire until their guns were empty.

The whole thing took less than ten seconds. That's what police training on the shooting range will do. The smugglers' eyes were still open in a permanent expression of shock, bodies perforated and limbs at weird angles. Smoke hung in the air with a heavy musk of cordite. One of the officers walked over and spit in Hector's vacant face. "That's for Roger and Pedro."

Another officer walked up—one who'd had a sick child visited in the hospital by a famous local surfer. He spit as well. "And Darby."

The patrol cars drove away.

# Chapter 23

THE PRESENT

**B**ungee cords snapped free. A tarp flew off the bed of a pickup truck. Serge slapped a cheek.

"Wake up! Wake up!" He dropped the pickup's tailgate down and dragged the man out by his ankles.

*Thud.*

"It's time for the games to begin!" He helped the woozy captive up and got him into the driver's seat. "There, that's more comfy."

Out came the duct tape. Tear, tear, rip, rip, until half the roll was gone. And the hostage was fully alert.

"Let me go! I'll scream!"

"Go ahead," said Serge.

*"Ahhhhhhh!"*

"I can scream louder," said Serge. *"Ahhhhhhh! . . .* The Everglades are the perfect place to scream. You're not bothering anybody."

The man stopped to review the confusion of his circumstance.

A laptop taped to his lap. Hands taped to the steering wheel. He struggled to free them, but no luck.

"And I taped your neck to the headrest of your seat, because there's no way to get your hands loose unless you think like me and chew through the tape. But I also made sure the neck tape wasn't too tight or it would be unsafe."

The captive took a deep breath. "What's going on? What have I done to you?"

"It's what you've done to all of us," said Serge. "Dumping the worst possible refuse in the most delicate of our ecosystems."

"Oh, a tree hugger."

"Literally," said Serge. "Have you ever tried it? You connect to the life force that flows through the entire universe, and sap."

"Fine, I'll clean it up." He wiggled his fingers. "Now cut me loose."

"Too late. You've violated the contract of existence." Serge gestured up and down the man's chest. "You think the cells in your body came without strings?"

"Then what do you want from me?"

"Be a happy contestant." Serge began clapping. "That's the audience applause. And here's the contest you're about to play . . ."

The man listened to a convoluted, tortuous explanation about the science of the new batteries, why they were bad for the environment and might soon be very bad for him.

"The only thing left is the bonus round. I always give my contestants a bonus, some better than others." Serge shrugged. "The home office makes the rules." He held up a thick cable with a familiar adapter on the end. "This is an emergency charger. It fits into the cigarette lighter, which is good for you, because unlike using a wall socket, this takes much longer to charge." Serge turned the key in the truck's ignition. The instrument panel came to life. "I see you have a quarter tank of gas. That's either good or bad for you, depending on gas mileage. Your engine runs the alternator, which charges your truck's battery, which in turn charges the laptop on your legs. Once the engine turns off, the big battery under the hood won't get any more juice and start to deplete. And there you have the bonus round: Will the gas run out and your pickup's battery die before the computer has a chance to overcharge? If so, you're free to go. My promise to you . . . Now here's the key part: If you're really limber and can get your toes up to the dashboard, you can turn on the headlights and wipers to speed the depletion." He saw the captive's eyes go to the side of the steering column. Serge grabbed the roll of duct tape again and secured the key in the ignition. "Sorry, no cheating."

Serge closed the pickup's door. He opened it again. "Almost forgot. I need to tax you for my research trip." He reached behind the man and extracted his wallet. "Driver's license here says your name's Diego. Nice knowing you . . . Ooo! And a company-issued credit card for travel expenses. I'm back in the workforce! . . . Well, cheerio!" The door slammed.

Serge headed back to the Nova, where Coleman was already seated with a joint and a beer, rewatching a video on a cell phone.

"What do you think?" said Serge. "Pretty cool contest?"

"He's thrashing around," said Coleman, "and his leg is out the window."

"He'll get the hang of it."

Coleman turned off the phone and took a hit. "Too bad we can't stay and watch."

"This time we can."

A big, round head swung sideways. "You're kidding! Whenever it's a long contest, you always make us leave."

"This time's different. I checked the battery level and charge rate," said Serge. "This could be a short contest."

The leg struggled to get back in the window, and the truck's headlights came on.

"Well, what do you know?" said Serge. "It looks like we have a game."

"Now the wipers are going," said Coleman.

"And the washer fluid, and the horn, and radio. Finally! Some-one who listens."

Coleman licked the back of a suction cup and re-attached his cat toy to the windshield. "How long before the fireworks start?"

"We've still got some time to kill." Serge turned on his phone to surf the Internet.

Coleman batted the toy. *Jingle, jingle.* "What are you looking for?"

"I'm honing tactics to bend people to my will." He called up another digital page. "You know my concept with clipboards, orange cones and safety vests? They're everyday items that anyone can buy, and yet when you put them into play in society, people just assume you're official and don't question."

"You want something else official-looking?" *Jingle, jingle.*

"No, this definitely won't look remotely official. I'm going hard in the opposite direction this time." Serge scrolled down the tiny screen. "But what's the underlying principle of the other three things? They throw people off balance and tilt the interpersonal equation in your favor."

"So you're looking to buy something on there?"

"Already bought it. This is just further research." He rummaged under the driver's seat and handed Coleman a plain brown bag.

Coleman reached inside. "A giant dildo?"

Serge nodded. "I put a lot of thinking into that one. Everyone views dildos in the sexual context. We all know they're out there, except we never, ever see them in public. But what if some creative person introduced one into a non-sexual scenario? They'd auto-matically have the advantage."

"How so?"

Serge grabbed the flesh-colored column from Coleman. "Say you're at a customer-service desk trying to return something you purchased. They're giving you a hard time, and you start to lose it: 'What do you mean "thirty-day limit"?' 'What do you mean "all the original packaging"?' 'What do you mean "underwear is excluded"?' So you pull the dildo from your pocket as casually as if you were getting out a piece of gum. Then you start slapping it into your other hand for emphasis with each point you make: 'I'm one of your best customers!'" *Slap.* "'Do you know how much money I spend here?'" *Slap.* "'I demand an immediate refund!'" *Slap* . . . "Of course by now they're not hearing a single word you're saying. You may get the refund, or they may call the manager, and then you take the more subtle route, shaking his hand and saying it's a pleasure to meet him, while your other hand is sticking the dildo in your ear and twisting it like a big Q-tip. It's all about establishing home-field advantage."

Coleman grabbed it. "Or you could pretend to think really hard and tap your forehead with it, like this."

"Precisely," said Serge. "It's the element of the unexpected, like that famous Monty Python surreal skit about the Spanish Inquisition."

"I remember that one," said Coleman. *"Nooooooobody expects the Spanish Inquisition!"*

*"Nooooooobody expects the dildo!"* said Serge.

*Jingle, jingle.* "I enjoy talking to you like this. It makes me feel intelligent." Coleman pointed. "The bottom of your dildo has a suction cup. What's that for?"

Serge threw his arms up. "An utter mystery! Who knows what these people are doing? That's why I needed further information from my phone to explore the possibilities." He glanced at Coleman's cat toy, then licked the bottom of his sex device and stuck it to the windshield. He went back to typing on the small electronic screen. "As I said before, America is way over-sexed and under-laid. The first time I saw an adult superstore, I thought they must have made a mistake at the sign shop. But now the concept is so mainstream that they've gone online. Check out this website catalog: double strap-ons, O-rings, ball gags, latex cat-woman masks, stilettos, whips, remote-control ten-function panties, here's a full-scale rubber ass, bullet vibrators, 'hands-free' vibrators—I assume for the multi-tasker—pocket rockets, pocket pussies, indoor adult swing sets, simulated mouths from seventeen to eighty-nine dollars depending on your budget and quality needs. And here's a 'narrow your search' function where you select essential criteria: multi-speed, single-entry, pulsate, rotate, glow-in-the-dark, made in the USA. This is so embarrassing! I'd be mortified to get caught with this stuff!"

Coleman looked up at the windshield. "I didn't know your dildo had flashing lights."

"In case I'm arguing with someone when it's dim." Serge clicked to a new page. "And here's another product section for people with allergies and dry skin. Don't they realize nothing's private anymore? That just by visiting sites like this, their identity is passed all over the place on marketing lists? And those lists are always getting hacked and posted publicly. Think of the shame!"

"How could you possibly explain it?" asked Coleman.

"I guess I'd just say I'm an author doing research for a book."

The dildo began chirping.

"There's even a pop-up box on this site for 'live chat with a service representative.' Can you imagine having *that* job? Not to mention the training class and PowerPoint presentation."

Other lights began flashing outside in the swamp. Coleman poked Serge's shoulder. "I think the show's starting."

Serge looked up. "You're right. The first battery cell just vented."

The pair sat back and watched as the interior of the pickup truck produced a light show of flame and smoke. Multicolored streams of sparks sent flecks of metal ricocheting around the driver. Then the illumination died down before the next, bigger eruption. The sixth battery cell cut loose, then the seventh, eighth, ninth . . .

Coleman gestured with a beer: "I think the inside of his roof just caught fire."

Serge took a deep breath and rested his head back. "I love this place."

The pair continued sitting in a muscle car with a cat toy and a blinking, chirping dildo attached to the windshield, watching flaming geysers of molten heavy metals inside a pickup.

"That's the beauty of the Everglades," said Serge. "Everything's natural out here."

# Chapter 24

1989

Just after dawn, a phone rang in a bedroom in Riviera Beach. A woman in a nightgown rolled over on the far side of the bed and adjusted her sleeping mask. A man in skivvies fumbled for the receiver. He was bald, except for the sides.

"Hullo?"

His legs went quickly over the side of the bed, feet in blue socks.

"Are you crazy, calling me on this line? . . . No, I'll just be a minute. Call you right back."

The man jumped in his pants and raced down to a pay phone on Broadway near the pawnshop. Quarters went in the slot.

"It's me . . ." He quickly pulled the phone away from his ear. "You're screaming! I can't understand a word . . . Yes, I know what happened at the marina last night. That's why I was sleeping. I was working on the problem practically till it got light . . . What? No, I didn't know about that. What quarry? . . . You're screaming again . . . Listen, we're on top of it. Just keep watching the news . . . And don't call me again unless I call you."

The man hung up and drove back home in his police car.

Two hours later, more patrol cars arrived at the sergeant's home on Silver Beach Road. So many black-and-whites, you'd think it was a murder scene.

Inside, a very private meeting.

A very *jumpy* meeting. All the officers from last night's shootout at the OK Quarry. Most of them had a can of cheap beer in their hands. Not partying; steadying nerves.

"We just need to remember two things," said the sergeant. "Stick to our story, and everyone remain calm. I don't need to mention that this whole group depends on every single one of us hanging tough. No weak links."

Then the floodgates, talking fast over each other.

"It's too much . . ."

"I didn't sign up for this . . ."

"Last night at the quarry will be our undoing . . ."

"Stop! Everyone!" yelled the sergeant. "This is the opposite of remaining calm." The sergeant's name was Franklin, but everyone called him Duvall, because he bore an uncanny resemblance to actor Robert Duvall, and he received more respect than normal because of it. "To start with, that business out west is the least of our worries. A bunch of dead drug smugglers—guns in their hands, no less—in a remote quarry. Clearly a deal gone bad, and other drug guys waxed them. It couldn't have a more beautiful bow on it if we tried."

"He's right," said a corporal.

"Of course I'm right, so put that one out of your heads. Everything's sealed up. The only thing we have to fear is ourselves."

"One question?" asked a patrolman.

"What's that?"

"Hector."

"I just told you that ending couldn't have gone better," said Duvall. "Weren't you listening?"

"No, I'm not worried about being suspected for that blood-bath in the quarry. Hector was strictly middle management. I'm worried about the rest of his organization down in Miami. They're bound to notice him missing by now and start nosing around."

"They already have," said Duvall. "I talked to them a couple hours ago."

"What!"

"Called me first thing this morning, my *home* line no less. So I drove to a pay phone."

"What did they say?"

"Pretty much what you'd expect. Apparently they use that quarry for a lot of meetings and discovered the whole clusterfuck around dawn. Then there was a lot of profanity and threats to kill a bunch of people," said Duvall. "But I told him we were on the case. Just watch the noon news. We were about to announce a suspect."

"The reaction?"

"They wanted to come down here guns a-blazin' and whack the guy we're going to pin it on. Jesus, we're only blaming this stooge to divert our department's attention away from us. But now with all the dead guys west of town, Hector's people think that this innocent schmuck is part of some rival gang moving in on their territory."

"I may be sick," said a corporal, trying to sip beer with shaking hands. "If they come up here acting crazy with revenge and one of them gets caught, they could spill the beans on all of us."

"Relax," said the sarge. "That's why I told them it wasn't an especially good time for a turf war. The attorney general is already involved because of the dead officers, and the feds will be swarming everywhere because of the drugs and port angle. I suggested they indefinitely suspend their whole Palm Beach County operation because this would soon be the hottest spot in the whole state."

"Did it work?"

"They're businessmen. After settling down, they agreed it was best. But they said they would never forget about this, especially the money. I told them that's exactly what they needed to do. Write it off as a business expense. I explained that if we found any rival group working around here, it would be in our own interest to take them out ourselves. But they insisted this was personal, and would wait as long as it took to get even."

"How long do you think that is?"

"Quote: 'We'll die of old age before we forget about this,'" said the sergeant. "What's wrong with those people?"

"There is *one* loose end," said a corporal.

Duvall sighed. "What?"

"The guy we're pinning it on . . ."

"If he talks . . ."

"Life in prison for everyone . . ."

"I don't care," said a rookie named Wes. "Enough killing. I'm not taking him out."

"I'm not saying take him out," added the corporal. "Just that it warrants discussion."

"I'm with Wes on this," said another officer. "Coke is gushing through Florida, and all the lawyers and doctors creating the demand are making more each year than we'll ever see. So what if we took some bribes? So I'm a dirty cop. But I'm not a killer cop."

"What about the quarry?"

"That was different. But there's no way I'm killing some poor innocent clown who was at the wrong place at the wrong time. I'm Catholic."

"I'm not killing him for another reason," said a detective. "This Kenny fellow was Darby's friend. It's the least we can do for his memory."

Several nods from the couch and kitchen table.

"Darby was definitely okay . . ."

"It's always the best among us that we lose . . ."

"Did I mention when my kid was in the hospital? . . ."

The sergeant sighed with departing patience, tapping fingers on the arm of the sofa. "Before we get all misty, I'd like to point something out. Is that copacetic? Because if you still need to get in touch with your feelings . . ."

"No, we're okay. The floor is yours."

"Killing him will only increase the risk of a follow-up investigation determining he was a murdered patsy and exposing us," said Duvall. "The best result is he remains at large, keeping all the attention focused on the search."

"Why not just off him and take care of the body so it will never be found?"

"From earlier comments in this conversion, I'm not overly confident about the solidarity in this room if we do that," said the sarge. "We've always worked on consensus. And if taking the added risk out of deference to Darby is what's required for us to stick together, then so be it."

"This is bad no matter what," said a patrolman.

"Look at the upside," said Duvall. "In case you haven't noticed, our witness still has all that money."

"For God's sake!" explained the corporal. "Look where greed has gotten us! And you want more?"

A grin. "Do I need to state the obvious? This so-called loose end will take care of itself out of self-preservation. He may have started as an innocent bystander, but somehow he ended up with those bearer bonds. He saw the crime and knows they saw him. If he isn't afraid of the cops, he's probably shitting himself about now over Hector's crew."

"And?"

"Another perfect bow," said Duvall. "He couldn't have more incentive to flee to parts unknown, and he has plenty of money to do it with. We just need to step back and sit on our hands. The only way anything can go wrong is if he's actually stupid enough to stick around town."

"The sarge is right," said a corporal. "I'm sure this witness is three time zones away by now."

"Not exactly," said the rookie. "He's hiding out at Darby's place near Blue Heron."

"What! . . ."

"Why? . . ."

"How do you know? . . ."

"Seemed logical," he continued. "Or at least a logical place we needed to rule out from due diligence. So I went over this morning and was peeking in the blinds. The light through the slits lit up the dust in weird stripes—"

"Fast-forward! What was he doing?"

"Sitting there."

"Just sitting?"

"No, this was abnormal sitting. Lying back in a La-Z-Boy with a Remington bolt across his chest, dozing off every few minutes, then jumping awake and pointing the gun at ghosts."

"That's pretty much what I'd be doing about now," said a corporal. "Except I'd be a million miles away from Darby's place. It would almost be funny, if it weren't."

Someone raised a hand in the back.

"This ain't third grade. Just say it!"

"Several units are bound to visit Darby's house today, if they haven't already. It's routine to check the victim's domicile for a secondary crime scene."

"If they already had, we'd have heard about it," said Duvall, his procedural brain spinning. "This is not good. Him sitting there freaking out with that rifle; cops busting in all hot and trigger-happy from just losing their brothers. It can't end anywhere positive."

"What do we do?"

"Head it off at the pass," said the sarge. "Someone call head-quarters to let them know we're cruising to the victim's house."

"What if the other units are already on the way?"

"We say, 'Cancel that. We're pulling up in the driveway now.'"

"But he's got that rifle."

"So what?" said the sarge. "We're only doing a Hollywood response."

"What's that?" asked the rookie.

"We make a theatrical show of checking out the place, but we're actually doing nothing. Just fill the driveway with cars, walk around the house conspicuously in view of the neighbors. We report that we went inside and it was empty and undisturbed."

"But we don't go inside?"

"Exactly. After that, we keep tabs at the office to make sure we're assigned any follow-up visits. Nobody else ever goes back out there." The sergeant stood. "Let's get rolling."

An officer whistled. "I'd hate to be in Kenny's shoes with Hector's gang after him."

"There's nothing we can do about that," said Duvall.

"What if one of these nervous, honest cops accidentally stumbles over him and blows him away?"

"Can't control that, either."

"Damn, Hector's gang *and* the whole police department. That's some jam."

"And we're wasting way too much time talking about it." Duvall noticed the warm beers still in all their hands. "Drink up. We're on duty."

One of the officers raised his can in a toast. "To Kenny, take care of yourself."

# Chapter 25

A seafoam-green Chevy Nova left the Everglades behind and reached the outer limits of Miami just after midnight. Serge drained the jumbo coffee he had bought back at the Dade Corners truck and airboat stop.

"I better call in that anonymous environmental tip before the Glades suffer any more battery damage." He dialed his cell phone. "Hello? Is this the secret tip line that people call when they swear they didn't do anything wrong but want to tattle on others? Normally I hate tattletales, like Jenny McAllister, who I accidentally hit in the twat with a yo-yo. I didn't even know what a twat was yet, but they made me go sit in the corner anyway, and that's one recess I'll never get back. Nobody takes sexual inappropriateness more seriously than me, but honest mistakes can be made without having your yo-yo confiscated, if you know what I mean, and I think you do. So listen, I need to report these batteries and medical waste and hypothetically maybe one little burned-up body in a charred pickup truck that you can't trace back to me . . . What?

This is Domino's Pizza? Shit." *Click.* He dialed again. "Hello? Is this the secret tip line that people call when they don't want a pizza but need to tell on someone? . . . It is? Great! Do you have a pen handy? . . . Okay, it was really stormy out, and the wind caught my yo-yo, I swear! . . ."

. . . Five minutes later. "Yes, four-point-seven miles, then turn south and the dump site is on the left, a bunch of crap still sticking out of the water. You can't miss it. And I really appreciate you understanding about me getting a little off track there . . . No, I *do* need to mention it. I *do* need to apologize. So in your official report if you could please leave out that one embarrassing part about my early years, because children are naturally curious about their bodies . . ." *Click.*

Serge stared at his phone.

"What happened?" asked Coleman.

"The tip line hung up on me. And I thought they wanted people to talk to them. Oh well . . ."

The Nova pulled up to a red light. A thumping beat arrived in the next lane.

Serge looked over at four gangsta thugs in a pimped-out Camaro. Lime-green neon lights glowed under the chassis, and more colored lights in fiber-optic tubes framed each window. The thugs turned to Serge with prison-yard glares.

Serge glared back, pointing at the blinking dildo in his windshield. Both sides nodded in mutual respect. The traffic light changed and they drove off.

The next afternoon a desk phone rang in a warehouse full of ringing phones.

"Salenca here . . . Which government agency? . . . I see. How may I help you? . . . Illegal dumping of hazardous waste in the Everglades?" Salenca slowly closed his eyes: *I'm going to kill that idiot.* He opened them. "I don't know anything about any illegal dumping . . . Excuse me? . . . Oh, you're not saying *we* did it? . . . You're looking to hire my company to clean it up?" His eyes briefly closed again: *Thank you, God.* "Yes, definitely, that's our specialty. We have all the resources to handle it. We'll head out there immediately . . . Excuse me? We'll have to wait because it's still a crime scene? Oh right, because of the illegal dumping? . . . What? A body in a burning truck? . . ."

Salenca hung up, thinking, *So that's why that idiot hasn't been answering his phone all day.* He urgently summoned the dumping crew into his office. They formed a respectful line as he paced in front of them. "We have a serious problem. Diego's dead. Murdered last night in the Everglades. And if my hunch is correct, this was no random crime. Someone's sending a message. They're trying to move in on our turf."

A hand went up. "What can we do to help?"

Pacing continued. "We caught a break. The authorities haven't been able to identify his body, or else they already would have connected him back to us, plus they never would have requested our help with the cleanup." He reached a wall and turned to pace the other way. "And if they can't ID him, it means that whoever did this probably took his wallet. I watch forensics shows, and they can pull ID from melted billfolds in the most involved car fires. So if the killers got his wallet, they also have the company-issued credit card I gave each of you for expenses."

Another hand. "Then we should report the card stolen?"

"Absolutely not," said Salenca. "If someone is trying to muscle in, I doubt they'd be dumb enough to use it, but who knows? We'll leave the account open and hope for a hit. In the meantime, you'll do all dumps in pairs. And keep your ears open on the street for any talk . . . Now back to work!"

A half hour away, a Chevy Nova rolled up U.S. 1 as the sun went down in Boynton Beach.

Other traffic slowed around it. Drivers checking to make sure their eyes were working properly. Yep, a blinking dildo. They sped up.

"I'm so excited!" said Serge. "The literary tour of Florida will reach my hometown tomorrow! But which motel should we pick for our staging area? I always love picking the motel because it determines the entertainment value! Forget how many channels they have on cable; it's the episodes in the lives of other guests that are priceless. Let's see . . . No, that one's too nice . . . That one's too nice . . . That one's *way* too nice—all the lights in the sign are working . . . Here we go. This baby looks comfy and lax on registration . . ." He loosened the suction cup on the windshield. Winos parted on the sidewalk as the Chevy rolled into the parking lot.

Serge approached the front desk. "One room, please, two beds, two adults, no pets even though we have cat toys, but they're for personal use, so don't get suspicious."

The desk clerk yawned and painted her nails. "How will you be paying?"

"Credit card! . . . Hold on." He stepped back from the desk and huddled with Coleman. "Which card should I use? The ones from Sterling Hanover are probably flagged by now, so we should only try them at gas stations and fast-food drive-throughs where we'll be on the move in case they try to annoy us . . . This one looks lucky. Diego Carbone."

"The guy from the pickup truck?" asked Coleman. "I don't know about that. They're probably tracking his cards, too."

"And normally you'd be right," said Serge. "You never want to use a purloined credit card for a motel you're staying at because you'll be sitting ducks. Except Diego was up to no good, which means he was concealing his movements, and the time it will take to connect the dots gives us extra hours of high jinks."

He went back to the desk. "Here you go!"

The clerk never looked up. "Swipe it through the machine when the light turns blue . . ."

The Chevy Nova drove over to room 108. Serge went inside, slapped the key card on the dresser and threw the receipt in the trash.

Coleman looked back out the door. "What about our luggage?"

"I thought you'd learn by now." Serge bent down next to the bed. "Because of the brutal Florida heat, the very first thing you always do upon arriving at a motel room is check the air conditioner. It could have a weak motor, freeze up from crud in the coils, be low on coolant, or simply have the wrong BTUs for the cubic feet, and then you've just checked into a sweat lodge and your whole stay is fucked . . . Wow, glad I checked. Take a look at the digital display."

"It says seventy-two degrees." Coleman stood back up. "I feel fine."

"For now," said Serge. "But the temperature is stuck on seventy-two and won't go any lower. In this state, that's a recipe for disaster."

They returned to the front desk.

A monotone from the employee side: "Is everything okay with one-oh-eight?"

"How did you know it was us?" asked Serge. "You've never looked up from your nails. Which gave me the advantage of not being properly vetted during registration, but now we're into customer service, that requires looking up."

She looked up. "What's the matter?"

"The air-conditioning doesn't work."

"It's not turning on?"

"No, it's turning on. It just doesn't go below seventy-two."

"So it's working?" said the clerk. "We can't fix what's not broken."

"Seventy-two is bad." Serge took out a sex toy and slapped his other hand. "Seventy-two is a crisis!" *Slap*. "I have night sweats!" *Slap*.

The clerk rolled her eyes and looked back at her nails. "I can put you in another room if you haven't messed up the first."

"Just like we found it. Nothing weird yet because I always check the A/C as soon as I arrive."

She ran two more card keys through her machine. "One-twenty-three, just around the corner."

Serge ran back to the new room and bent down. "Son of a bitch! Seventy-two again! It's a pandemic! I must isolate the variable." He ran out of the room.

Next door, a family was just returning from a restaurant with children and Happy Meals.

"Excuse me," said Serge. "Can you tell me how low you can set your air conditioner?"

"What?"

"I know the little tykes need to eat and find the surprise treasure at the bottom, but I have night sweats. Please check."

The father stared and thought, *If I just tell him, he'll leave us alone.* "Wait here." He went in and out. "Seventy-two."

Serge ran away.

The desk clerk looked up. *What now?* "How can I help you?"

"It's not the room! It's the A/C units!" *Slap*. "They're all set wrong!" *Slap*. "I need a maintenance man!" *Slap*.

Her eyes: *If it gets you out of my life* . . . She reached for the phone. "He'll meet you back there."

Serge sat perched on the edge of the bed, rocking anxiously and staring at the open door.

The maintenance man arrived. Grungy, two-day stubble, leathery skin from a de-moisturized lifestyle.

Serge sprang up. "Thank God you're here!"

The man preemptively placed his hand over the unit. "It's working fine. What's the problem?"

"It doesn't go below seventy-two."

"It's not supposed to."

"What are you talking about?" Serge pointed frantically at the temperature gauge. "I travel full-time and intimately know all the most popular brands of air conditioners. And at every other location in your chain, this type goes down to sixty-five."

"Yeah, they're all doing it wrong."

Serge paused. "What?"

"Seventy-two degrees is the optimum temperature for this unit to run at peak efficiency," he said in an increasing tone of authority. "It's set where you'll be the most comfortable."

*Uh-oh,* thought Serge, *another guy who wears a uniform to work and thinks he's king. But an oily maintenance shirt with* CHUCK *stitched over the pocket is the big tip-off that you don't go home to a castle. He knows this is not the kind of motel where I can call the home office and appeal, so I'm completely at his mercy. How best to handle him? If I mention the night sweats, he'll sense weakness. And the dildo could produce the first air-conditioning disagreement escalating into a hate crime. I'll start by playing to his ego . . .* "You speak the wisdom that befits your king uniform, and I would be a fool to question it. So seventy-two will be my first choice. But what if it unexpectedly gets hotter later? I would just like to have the *option* of lowering it."

"King uniform? Are you being a smart-ass?"

"Not as smart as you."

The man grew indignant. "Okay! I'm not supposed to do this . . ." He removed the unit's cover and pressed unseen buttons that were blocked by his body. "I'll give you control of the unit. But you really should keep it on seventy-two. Otherwise you'll burn out my compressor, and it'll cost me three thousand dollars."

"You got it!" said Serge. "Thank you!"

The maintenance man replaced the cover, stood up and gestured. "There. It's on seventy. Satisfied?"

"Uh, no," said Serge. "What would satisfy me is the temperature at the other places."

This time a sigh of terminal irritation. The maintenance man yanked the cover off the unit again, pressed buttons, and snapped the lid back on. "It's on sixty-nine now." The man sliced a hand through the air. "But that's as *low* as I go!" He briskly left the room.

Serge sat with his jaw hanging. "What just happened?"

"Sixty-nine." Coleman giggled.

"He was just making that shit up!" yelled Serge. "It's not his compressor!" *Slap.* "No motel unit costs three thousand!" *Slap.* "And even if it did, he wouldn't have to pay!" *Slap.* He tossed the dildo on the bed, activating the lights and chirping. "I respect everybody, and I don't judge. There's pride in being a maintenance man. We all have our roles to play. But when you're a maintenance man, you do maintenance. That guy was setting policy. You saw him: He looked like he'd just dropped his cardboard sign at the intersection and thrown on that maintenance shirt. And I'll bet the motel chain doesn't even know that he's on this power trip. He's probably another one of those bitterness-farmers because life didn't automatically send a special delivery truck with wealth and fame. 'I'm always at the bottom of the food chain. Something unfair must have happened while I wasn't charting my life's course. I've got to figure out a way to boss others around. I know! I'll set all the air conditioners to seventy-two, and then when they get the night sweats, who do they have to come begging to? Me!'" Serge stood and placed his hand on his hips. "This aggression will not stand."

Coleman looked at the bed and an artificial penis making birdcalls. "But what can you do?"

"Wage a battle of wits." Serge tapped the side of his head and pulled the cover off the unit. "He was doing something he wouldn't let me see. I just have to crack the code . . . Okay, here's a secret maintenance button you can only access by removing the lid. And here's a tiny schematic label. Jesus, the lettering is about a third the size of newspaper font. A child with new eyes couldn't read something this small." He grabbed his cell phone, took a picture and enlarged it. "There we go."

Coleman looked over his shoulder. "Instructions?"

"No, hieroglyphics. But it's the key to unlocking the code." Serge ran his finger down the screen. "There are two columns with various symbols and at first blush it looks like roughly a hundred and forty-four permutations. I'll just have to use trial and error until I gain control of the unit." He began slowly pressing buttons, each time glancing at his phone's display. Negative result after negative result. He kept going . . .

Coleman watched TV. Birds began gathering outside the window, chirping back at the dildo. After three episodes of *Gilligan's Island,* Serge snapped his fingers. "Dude, come take a look."

Coleman waddled over and checked the temperature gauge. "Holy cow, you did it! And you were even able to set it lower than the A/C at those other places."

Serge stood triumphantly and gazed out the window. "Yeah, Mr. Maintenance Man, how about a nice big cup of *sixty* degrees, motherfucker!"

He grabbed a roll of tape and ran outside to the end of the motel. He knocked on the first door.

A woman in curlers answered. "Yes?"

"We're here to fix your air conditioner."

"It's not broken."

"The temperature was inadvertently restricted to seventy-two degrees through inadequate psychological screening."

"Are you with the motel?"

"Of course," said Serge. "We're wearing uniforms."

"You just taped your room's magnetic key with the name of the motel to your shirts." The woman pointed down. "The roll of tape is still in your hand."

"We're behind on laundry," said Serge. "Thermal emancipation is only seconds away."

"I guess . . ."

Moments later, Serge snapped the cover back on and it was off to the next room, and the next, then around the corner and down the next row, until he came to a room on the far side and replaced the cover. He smiled at the occupant. "If this ever happens again, and I'm not around—as well as for those playing along at home—here's a cheat sheet to Fight the Power: Turn the unit off, remove the cover, locate and press the hidden *aux set* button, press the *mode* button several times until the numeral five is the first symbol in the display, press the down-temperature arrow until zero is the second character in the display, press *aux set* again, replace the cover, press the power button, and you've just successfully raged against the machine, passive-aggressively, that is."

"Thank you, I guess."

"Say no more! Your liberty is my reward!" He slapped Coleman on the back. "Come on, buddy. Enough good deeds for now. We'll reset the rest of the rooms after I watch some Science Channel about how if a magnetic burst from a neutron star is aimed precisely at Earth, it can pull the iron in our blood right though our skin."

Coleman looked at his arm. "Do I have time for a pizza?"

"Great idea! We'll pay with a credit card, and if the magnetic burst hits, our payment is wiped out and the pizza is free." He led Coleman back into their room and clutched himself. "It's fucking freezing in here."

# Chapter 26

1989

It was a mystery.

Driving Kenny nuts.

Police cruisers had filled the driveway. Officers all over the yard.

Kenny went from window to window, circling the inside of the house. They were everywhere, in the backyard, the bushes, checking his mailbox. They took photos and made dogs sniff stuff. More uniforms were next door and across the street, knocking.

They did everything but knock on *his* door. Then they all backed out of the driveway and just left. It made no sense.

Kenny sat back in his chair, convinced it was only a temporary stay of execution. He gripped the rifle and tried to stay awake. Adrenaline worked for a while.

Kenny dozed off. He awoke with a start.

The house was silent. What time was it? The slits in the blinds were dim and ambiguous. He peeked out the curtains at a gray sky. Was it dawn or dusk? His wristwatch was no help: 6:30. He turned on the TV. What? He was so exhausted that he'd slept clear through to the next morning. *How could I have been so careless? Anything might have happened!*

But then: *Hey, nothing did happen.* He went back to his chair. Up all day and night. Sensation finally returned in his stomach, and it was on empty. He went to the kitchen. Cupboards opened, the refrigerator door. It was a bachelor's pad. And it had been the end of the shopping week. Just condiments, cocktail onions and a jar of peanut butter.

The sun rose, and another countdown to fate. But nothing happened again except he ran out of peanut butter. The sun went down and it was miniature onions for dinner.

Then a few days of an involuntary hunger strike. But it was balanced out by budding hope that he just might get out of this.

*Knock, knock, knock!*

Kenny sprang out of his chair like it was an ejection seat. He ran to the window with the rifle and peeked outside.

A mail carrier. Whew, thank God.

*Knock, knock, knock!*

But why was she knocking? Why didn't she just leave the stuff in the mailbox like always? He snuck another glimpse. What was she doing? It looked like taping something to the door. What could it be?

Now his imagination took him down dark alleys. *This can't be good. Nothing has ever been taped to the door until now. That's no coincidence.* He was dying to know. But it was still light out, so he chose to speculate in panic until it got dark and the neighbors went to bed.

Near midnight, Kenny checked out the blinds a final time. He opened the front door only wide enough to slip his arm through, quickly snatching the notice, and closing up again.

Certified mail?

His mind juggled balls of bad outcomes. Who? What? The notice said he hadn't been home when the carrier came by, but he was welcome to sign the back of the form and leave it on the door. He grabbed a pen and scribbled. His plan was to avoid suspicion. Neighbors watched suspiciously as a disembodied arm swiftly shot out of the house again, slapped the notice on the door and slammed it shut. Great plan.

He counted the minutes until the mail truck arrived the next afternoon. Then more minutes until cover of darkness. Arm out, arm in. Door slammed.

The envelope was from an attorney's office. Kenny tore it open and read the letter from the lawyer. Darby's will had left him the house and a couple of modest bank accounts. Hmm, lawyer. He got to thinking.

The next morning at precisely nine o'clock, he dialed the phone number on the letterhead. A secretary put him through. "Hanley Dunn, how can I help?"

"I received your letter about the estate of Darby Pope."

"Oh, Darby was a dear friend. It's a tragedy," said the attorney. "I'm sorry for your loss, but if it's any consolation, he always spoke very highly of you."

"You're an attorney, right?"

"Uh, yes?"

"So anything I tell you will remain confidential?"

"That's how it works."

"I'd like to retain you," said Kenny. "I have some urgent matters."

"What kind of matters?"

"I'm really desperate," said Kenny. "I don't know where to turn."

"That's usually when you need a lawyer the most," Dunn said in a reassuring voice he had rehearsed for just such phone calls. "Now, what can I do for you?"

"I need food."

A young man rushed into the office of a Miami warehouse. "Sir, we've got a hit."

Salenca looked up from a balance sheet. "A hit? What are you talking about?"

"On Diego's credit card. I've been monitoring it like you told me."

"You're actually serious?" Salenca removed his reading glasses. "Please tell me it's some kind of off-brand convenience store where we can bribe the clerk for the security tape."

"Even better," said the messenger. "A motel."

"They can't be that ignorant. It makes them sitting ducks." Salenca stood and grabbed a pistol from a desk drawer. "Tell everyone to drop what they're doing. We're leaving as of five minutes ago . . ."

A half hour later, a Mercedes led a squadron of pickup trucks north on U.S. 1. They pulled into the parking lot of a discount motel.

Salenca and company entered the office. "Excuse me, can you tell me which room Diego Carbone is staying in?"

Another monotone as the clerk read a celebrity magazine. "We . . . are . . . not . . . allowed . . . to . . . disclose . . . the . . . room . . . numbers . . . of . . . guests."

"But we're supposed to be staying with him," said Salenca. "I can even give you the credit-card number he used because it's a company card and I'm his boss."

Still looking at the magazine. "We . . . are . . . not . . . allowed . . . to . . . disclose . . . the . . . room . . . numbers . . . of . . . guests." The clerk thinking: *I didn't know Taylor Swift had moved on with her life.*

"Listen," said Salenca. "This is a matter of life and death. Isn't there anything you can do?"

"I can call his room for you."

Salenca leaned over the counter and looked at her push-button phone. "Great. I'd really appreciate it."

She pressed three buttons, and handed the receiver over the counter.

*"Hello? . . ."*

"On second thought, hang up." He gave the phone back. "I'll just call him on his cell."

*"Is someone there? . . ."*

*Click.*

Salenca regrouped with his men outside the office. "They're in room one-oh-eight. I saw her dial it."

"How do you want us to handle this?"

A Datsun with a lighted yellow sign on the roof pulled up the driveway. A teenager in a baseball cap got out with a rectangular cardboard box in an insulated sleeve. Apparently silver was the best color inside a sleeve to deliver warmth.

"What room is the pizza for?"

"Three-twelve."

"That's us," said Salenca.

"Uh, I don't know why, but people are now intercepting other people's pizzas. Maybe they don't want to wait," said the pimply youth. "I've been instructed only to deliver to the room."

"You'll be delivering it to an empty room," said Salenca. "Then driving back with that pizza and no tip. Here's two twenties. Keep the change."

The young man flipped up the receipt stapled to the box. "But the pizza only costs— . . . Here you go."

Someone on a third-floor balcony recognized the lighted sign for Jack Rabbit Pizza on the departing delivery vehicle.

*"Hey, that's our pie."*

Six men stared upward with silent menace.

"Enjoy . . ." A door slammed.

The gang strolled along the front of the motel, 102, 104, 106 . . . "Hang back until they open up," said Salenca.

He was approaching the room to knock when the door surprised him.

Serge stepped out and bumped into Salenca. "Whoa. You scared me! . . . Ooo! Pizza! Somebody's lucky tonight!"

Salenca reached under the box for his pistol. "You staying in that room?"

"No, just fixing the air conditioner," said Serge. "Wish I was. I can smell the pepperoni!"

Salenca's entire face twisted into a violent countenance that said, *Get out of here! We have business!*

"Well, we'll just get out of here," said Serge. "We have business. Come on, Coleman!"

Salenca watched intently until they were around the corner and couldn't be witnesses. He knocked.

Footsteps came toward the door from the other side.

*Knock, knock, knock.*

Salenca felt the presence of someone looking through the peephole.

"Who's there?"

"Pizza."

"We didn't order pizza."

"Room one-oh-eight, right?"

"Yeah?"

"That's the number on the pizza box."

"Look . . ." The dead bolt unlatched and the door started to open. "We didn't order any—"

The door violently crashed open the rest of the way, pizza flying one direction into a mirror, the box sailing another way onto a bed. Guns in faces, men pouring into the room.

*Slam, lock.*

Two construction workers raised their hands and crapped their pants. "W-w-w-what do you want?"

"To know who you're working for!"

"M-M-M-Maloney Contractors."

"I mean who are you *really* working for."

"N-n-n-no, seriously, that's it. We've been troweling cinder blocks all day."

One of the lieutenants whispered, "His hands and fingernails. I worked masonry."

"Shut up." Salenca marched in a circle. "So you deny killing Diego Carbone out in the Everglades and setting his truck on fire?"

"Who's that?"

Something caught Salenca's eye in the trash basket. He pulled out the small piece of paper and uncrumpled it. "Well, well, well, what do we have here?"

"What is it?" asked one of the workers with hands still aloft.

"Just a receipt for this room with the last four digits of a credit card I recognize, in the name of one Diego Carbone . . . What a coincidence! . . ."

. . . Serge and Coleman returned to their room, and Serge slapped his cheeks to increase circulation. "It's like the damn North Pole in here!"

"You said that last time." Coleman grabbed a beer he'd been cooling by the A/C vent. "Why don't you turn the temperature up?"

"No way!" Serge put on five T-shirts. His breath was visible as he blew into his hands. "I'm savoring this victory!"

"I'm hungry."

"Me, too." Serge got out his wallet. "We got distracted and forgot to order that pizza."

"No avocados or cranberries like last time," said Coleman.

"I never would have gone in that kind of pizza place had I known. What's wrong with California?" Serge explored various fabric compartments. "I'm still pissed they tried to horn in on our citrus."

"What are you looking for?"

Serge held the wallet by his side and stared at the ceiling. "Where did I put that credit card? . . . Okay, let me walk it back. I came in the room . . ." He turned to a piece of furniture. ". . . And I could have sworn I put it on the dresser next to the room keys like I always do. Coleman, your thoughts?"

"You're asking *me*? I don't know where my beer is . . . Oh, my hand."

Serge smacked himself. "I'm a stooge! It's in the first room we checked into! I must have left it on the dresser . . ." He closed his eyes for the photographic memory technique he always used to find lost stuff. ". . . I unlocked the door, then I crumpled the receipt and threw it in the wastebasket, then . . ."—he turned around in the new room to aid the mnemonic process—". . . checked the A/C and discovered the heartbreak of seventy-two . . . Hmm, no visuals of putting the credit card on the dresser. But it has to be there." He opened his eyes. "We need to go back to room one-oh-eight, even though they'll be cranky because we're interrupting a hot pizza that just arrived."

They headed out the door and rounded the corner, reading descending room numbers: 124, 122, 120 . . .

"I feel terrible about this," said Serge. "It flies in the face of my personal ethics, but it's an emergency."

Coleman chugged Coors. "What are you talking about?"

"The Pizza Principle." Room 116, 114, 112. "It's a guy thing. Forget not boning each other's wives: If there's one code all men respect, it's don't fuck with a just-arrived, steaming-hot pizza . . ."

. . . A steaming-hot pizza was pressed into a screaming face and the victim flung upside down into a full-length mirror. "Don't lie to me again! Where did you get Diego's credit card!"

"I never saw that receipt before you picked it out of the trash can!" Wiping blood from eyes. "I swear!"

The others picked him up and flung him again, into a shattering headboard.

"I will only ask you one last time." Salenca bent over with a nickel-plated Colt .45. "Who is trying to muscle in on my business?"

"I don't know." Spitting out a reddish mixture. "I just got back from the job site—"

*Bash.*

*Slump.*

The gun swung toward the second construction worker on the other bed, where four henchmen were delivering a cringe-worthy beatdown, grabbing broken-off bedposts and chair legs. *Wham, wham, wham . . .*

. . . Serge stopped on the sidewalk outside room 108. "Do you hear all the racket?"

"Sounds like someone's being murdered," said Coleman.

"Can it get any worse?" said Serge. "They're enjoying hot pizza at the beginning of an action movie! The guilt is overwhelming! . . ."

. . . "Step back," said Salenca, pressing the pistol with a silencer to the first worker's nose. "God is next. Who sent you?"

"Please! I just work construction!"

*Pffft.*

He spun toward the other worker.

"Nooooo!"

*Pffft.*

Salenca ejected his clip. "Check their wallets."

Billfolds were retrieved and rifled. "I have their IDs, but Diego's credit card isn't in here."

"Keep looking!"

They ripped apart luggage and went through drawers . . .

. . . Outside on the sidewalk: "I feel awful about this but . . ." Serge raised his hand to knock on the door. "I'll just beg for forgiveness."

Coleman upended a Coors. "Maybe start by telling them you're not boning their wives. Get on their good side."

"Coleman." Serge lowered his knuckles from the door and looked at a rigid shape in his pal's pocket. "Where's your room key?"

"Right here." He patted his side.

"Let me see it."

"Sure thing." He shifted the beer to his other hand and dug a plastic rectangle out of his pocket. "Here you go— . . . Wait, it's that guy's credit card."

"You blockhead! I didn't leave it in the other room after all. That's why I couldn't remember." He turned and headed back toward their room.

"You're mad at me?"

"Nothing a hot pizza won't fix." Serge pulled out his phone and stared at the number on the credit card.

. . . Inside room 108, one of the goons stepped over the bodies. "Mr. Salenca? I always want to learn from you. May I ask a question?"

"You want a lesson now?"

"It's just that you shot those guys," said the aide. "Now we won't be able to find out who's moving in on us."

"That's the nature of someone moving in on you. You can't *help* but find out," said the honcho. "In the meantime, it was more important to send a message. They killed one of ours, we killed two of theirs." Salenca looked down into his aide's hands. "Now, *I* have something I'm wondering about. That pizza's been on the floor."

"I'm hungry."

Another goon reached down for a slice. "And it's still hot. Can we turn on the TV?"

"No!"

Something in the room began to beep. The first goon pulled out his cell phone. "I got an alert notification. Another hit."

"Hit on what?" asked Salenca.

"Diego's credit card."

"But—" Salenca looked over at the recently deceased. "That's not possible."

"All I know is what my phone says. Someone just ordered a large pepperoni."

"What company?" asked the boss.

"Jack Rabbit Pizza."

Salenca looked down at the cardboard box with a running bunny on the cover. He rubbed his eyes with both fists and looked again. "That's weird."

# Chapter 27

Hanley Dunn, attorney-at-law, was not new to the legal racket. He'd seen just about everything in his sixty years.

What struck him as new was sitting in an ultra-dark room in the middle of the day while Kenny Reese devoured a bucket of Kentucky Fried Chicken.

A bone flew back over the lounge chair as teeth sank into a wing. "This is the best meal I've had in my entire life!"

The attorney sat on the edge of his chair, patiently smiling to conceal his puzzlement. Kenny finally finished the last piece, along with the mashed potatoes and baked beans. He fell back in his chair, patted his stomach and burped. "I needed that."

Dunn continued smiling for a polite duration before: "You mentioned some other business? Besides the food?"

"Can you get everything out of my name?" said Kenny. "The house, utilities, banking, and I'd like all my mail sent to your office. Then I'm getting an answering machine, but I won't answer, and the recorded greeting will be in someone else's name, so just start talking and when I recognize your voice, I'll pick up. I guarantee I'll be here."

Hanley wasn't expecting this. Client strangeness was the norm, but this had turned into a fire-breathing unicorn with the face of Buddy Hackett. "Uh, may I ask what this is about?"

"Hold on," said Kenny. "And from now on, I'd like all communication from my agent and publisher to go through you."

"Wait a second," said the lawyer. "I thought your name sounded familiar. You're that *author*. I've always admired people who could write. It seems so difficult."

"Then you'll take me on as a client?"

"It's actually quite simple," said Dunn. "I'll set up a few things, power of attorney, some accounts, a shell corporation— that last part sounds shady. And usually it is, but not in your case . . . Sorry if I seemed a little thrown at first, but now I understand your situation. I'm a fan."

"You are?"

Hanley nodded. "You've reached a certain level of fame, and I'm sure you need to avoid some people who don't understand personal space and would bother you."

"I can say for a fact that you're absolutely correct."

The attorney stood. "I'll get the necessary paperwork drawn up, and we can meet at my office on, say, Wednesday?"

"No!" yelled Kenny. "I mean, I'm kind of on deadline. I can't leave the house."

"Understood again. I'll have my assistant drop it all by."

"Great! Leave it on the back steps, after midnight if possible."

"I'm sure that writing is a solitary process, and you want to minimize interruptions."

"Correct again." Kenny stood and handed the lawyer a slip of paper.

"What's this?"

"A grocery list."

Hanley Dunn maintained poise with that smile. "My assistant will take care of that, too."

## THE PRESENT

A green Chevy Nova crossed the steep arch of the Blue Heron Bridge on the way to Singer Island.

"Can't tell you how great it feels to be back in my hometown!" Serge slapped the steering wheel with zest. "I used to ride my banana bike over here all the time when it was just a flat little drawbridge."

"I remember this beach," said Coleman. "I popped jellyfish with my feet and screamed."

"I dropped a jellyfish on my mom's feet and *she* screamed," said Serge. "That was a bad week. Okay, so she had trouble walking for a few days. So keep a better eye on your kid . . . But in general, a great childhood. Regular tropical Huck Finn, barefoot and outdoors all day. They don't make childhoods like that anymore, with all the electronic gizmos now spawning whole generations of sickly, pale dumpling children who've never climbed trees or played in the mud. The only upside is they can type fast on small surfaces, which is an evolutionary dead end. When overpopulation turns the whole planet into a refugee scrum, the typists will be trampled. You can quote me."

"I remember climbing trees," said Coleman. "My parents got a new washing machine and threw out the cardboard box. I dragged it into the backyard and jammed it between a tree and the fence, then climbed the tree and dropped down into it. I was trapped. Couldn't get out. The box was wedged too good to tip over, and I was still too little to punch my way out. I fell asleep, and my parents went frantic for hours because the next thing I knew, the police were pulling me out of the box. For some reason, they were always calling the police."

Serge stared at Coleman a moment, then finished his coffee. "Why did you want to drop yourself into a tall box?"

"It was different." Coleman swatted at the windshield. *Jingle, jingle.* "I'm a cat."

Serge feverishly chugged his coffee. "Coleman, look at my knees! Look at them! Are you looking? Look!"

"*Meow* . . . I'm looking . . . What am I looking for?"

"Last night in the motel, I knew my childhood stomping grounds were coming up today, and for some reason I got the stray thought that I hadn't looked at my knees for a while. The key to life is not to ignore stray thoughts, so I looked." Serge glanced down. "And suddenly warm waves of boyhood bliss washed over me. Unlike the aforementioned youth of today, my knees are covered with so many overlapped scars that you can't even begin to count how many times I skinned them. You can always tell the quality and era of a childhood by the knees."

"I remember skinning my knees all the time," said Coleman.

"So does everyone our age." Serge hammered his travel mug of coffee. "My school alone probably kept the Mercurochrome people in business."

"Wasn't that the red stuff our parents painted on our scrapes?"

"What a scam! And my folks were always asking how I could skin my knees so often, and I'd just say, 'Hurry up with the Mercurochrome. I have to get back to the football game in the parking lot.'"

"You played football in a parking lot?"

"We're way too supervised now," said Serge, conjuring fond memories. "Football every day in the parking lot next to Saint Francis. *Tackle* football. In parochial school uniforms. And we'd all go home in shredded clothes that looked like we'd been attacked by wolverines."

"What about breaking your arm?" asked Coleman.

"Goes without saying." Serge grabbed his left wrist in nostalgia. "It's a kid's job to break his arm, and not just for fun. Broken bones are a critical element in cementing the playground hierarchy. It's like the first day in prison when you're forced to find the biggest, baddest dude and punch him in the nose, just so everyone thinks, 'That motherfucker's crazy! Let's butt-fuck someone else.' Similarly, out on the vicious jungle plains of childhood, you have to break your arm, the sooner the better. And the adults are in the windows saying, 'Oh, look how cute! They're all signing his cast!' But in reality it's about establishing that you're nobody's bitch on the teeter-totters."

"What if someone else breaks their arm first?" asked Coleman.

"You have to break yours worse. Then you tell the other kid, 'Unlike your cast last spring, mine goes up *past* the elbow, cocksucker!' That one gave me reign over the monkey bars."

"Did we really swear like that back then?" asked Coleman.

"'Poop-head' carried the same weight, like 'I am rubber, you are glue.'"

"Remember if you and another kid said the same word at the same time, the one who called 'jinx' first got to punch the other in the arm? And if you lost, you *had* to submit?"

"That's when the country still had honor." Serge wiped caffeine dribble off his lips. "Coleman, what's that on your shirt?"

Coleman looked down. "Where?"

Serge timed it perfectly like an echo: "Where? . . . Jinx!"

"Shit." Coleman offered his arm. *"Go ahead."*

Punch.

"Ow." Rubbing his shoulder.

"We live by a proud code, you and me."

The Nova cruised up Singer Island a short distance on A1A, then found a sandy patch and pulled off the road. Mangroves and water all around the thin ribbon of land.

John D. MacArthur State Park.

"This is the spot! This is the spot!" said Serge. "I narrowed it down with satellite photos until there was only one possible location that fit the description."

"Description of what?"

"The next stop on our Florida literary pilgrimage!" said Serge. "And I was astonished how many places were in my hometown of Riviera Beach! Like this one! Immortalized in the Elmore Leonard novel *Rum Punch*! You could literally draw a map of the crime routes from geographic details in the book so specific they could only come from Leonard driving around here himself and standing on spots like here. This is where he had Ordell—played by Samuel Jackson in the Quentin Tarantino adaptation, *Jackie Brown*—pop the trunk of an Oldsmobile and blow away Beaumont Livingston. Leonard even used the actual name of this park and described the turnoff."

Serge hit the gas, slinging sand as he headed back south.

"But how did Leonard know so much about your hometown?"

"At the time, he was spending a lot of winters in Palm Beach Gardens, and he did his homework . . . Then Ordell slams the trunk and races south on A1A just like we are, until he reaches the public beach and dumps the car with the body still in it behind the Ocean Mall—also mentioned by name." Serge pulled around the back side of a long retail building. "Can you dig it? Old Dutch was right there!"

"Where that dude is smoking and taking out the trash?"

"I just received a notification alert that this is the correct location."

"From your phone?" asked Coleman.

"No, my penis. Somehow it's now GPS-enabled . . . Come on!" Serge patched out again.

"Where to now?"

"An excellent confluence of literature." Serge swung west out of the parking lot and onto Blue Heron before taking a quick cutoff. "If Leonard wasn't enough, there was another future literary giant working around here who would become a mainstay of the Florida genre. Charles Willeford authored dozens of books but in my opinion none better than his four-volume Hoke Moseley series. Tarantino praised him in the trades, and Leonard even gave blurbs for his back covers! These are no coincidences. And in the third installment, *Sideswipe,* the burned-out Miami detective takes a sabbatical to manage his father's tiny beach apartment. Where? Singer Island! . . . And I can tell by how you're chewing the catnip sock that you're just itching to know how Charles found such an obscure location to set his book. Our next stop!"

Serge pulled into another parking lot, in front of another long building. "It's anchored on the end by the ancient 1940s-era Sands Hotel, and next is a nouveau cuisine bistro—which in the old days was the only strip club for miles, called the Island Room, where the dancers wore grass skirts and I wandered in as a bug-eyed eighteen-year-old. What a place to grow up! But that's a whole 'nother story, because the reason we're here is the place just to your right, 2441 Beach Court . . ."

Serge stopped. Coleman turned and took the sock out of his mouth. "You're just going to leave me hanging?"

"Letting the moment build."

"GPS alert?"

"Like a hummingbird. Back to live action: I got so into Willeford that I researched his formative years and learned he made his writing chops working as an editor for *Alfred Hitchcock's Mystery Magazine.* While employed there, the younger Charles aspired to see his own name in print, and in August of 1966, on pages seventy-eight to eighty-four of that internationally famous periodical, an unknown writer published a short story called 'Citizen's Arrest.' But wait, there's more! After additional Internet searches, a total surprise popped up with the name of the Hitchcock publication and my hometown. I'm thinking I must have typed in something wrong. To complicate matters, it's only a whiff of a reference with no context because it was just a sentence fragment in those bullshit search-engine results pages. So I repeatedly click on the listing to read the rest, but it keeps popping up that the page doesn't exist anymore!"

"Serge, you're hitting your forehead on the steering wheel again. You asked me to tell you."

"Wait! Wait! Wait! It was driving me insane! What was the connection? I knew the magazine was headquartered in Manhattan, so it made no sense. I'm on the hunt! I pressed on through the night and into sunrise, no food or sleep. Then I tripped over another oblique reference in another sentence fragment: HSD Publications. I charge down that digital side trail and find another shard of unconnected data, this time an address. I collect all my fragments and begin a round robin of cross-referenced searches until finally around noon I hit the jackpot: In 1960, the Hitchcock magazine relocated from New York City to Florida, and of all places picked Riviera Beach, specifically 2441 Beach Court." Serge pointed out the windshield. "Willeford got his start banging typewriter keys right in there! And people think I just waste my time."

He started the car and raced back over the bridge to the mainland.

"Where to now?"

"Remember that other big author from around here named Kenneth Reese?"

*Jingle, jingle.*

## Chapter 28

The house was dark.

No lights ever on, inside or out, as long as the neighbors could remember.

But someone still had to be living there. Always a car in the driveway. Except it never moved. And they often saw mail in the box by the door. Never anyone coming out to retrieve it, but the box was always empty by morning. And once in a while someone would drive up after midnight and leave brown paper bags somewhere around back.

It was extremely suspicious and the neighbors had a nosy curiosity because they're neighbors.

On the other hand, whatever was going on inside that house was keeping to itself, and why open a mystery door that you might regret?

The only sign of life was an occasional parting of the blinds about a half inch, just enough for an eyeball.

Like now. The person inside scanned the street for any hint of unwelcomeness, as he did every hour. Then he let the blinds snap shut and replaced the thick towel like the ones that now covered all the other blinds and made the house a bat cave at all hours.

A candle flickered on a small table next to a lounge chair in the middle of the living room. There was a telephone that was never answered. It was connected to an answering machine that greeted callers with a fake name.

A flashlight beam swept through the room until it reached the back wall, which consisted entirely of a built-in wooden bookcase. The beam ran along the spines of the dusty titles. The flashlight stopped on a volume. A hand grabbed it, and the resident settled into the lounge chair with a glass of merlot.

It was the other side of midnight. He opened the book to page one and read the first sentence. He stopped and checked his glow-in-the-dark wristwatch. He set the book down and waited. Practically to the second, he heard the sound. Someone coming up the driveway. He could hear it because microphones had been installed all around the house and amplified through a stereo. The loud sound of tires gave way to loud footsteps. They arrived at the side porch, then faded away and the car left.

The resident went through the house to the side door by the kitchen. A baseball bat that sent royalties to Wade Boggs leaned against the wall. The door itself had a three-foot-tall steel plate along the edge that housed the regular knob, then three additional dead bolts and a chain. He checked through a peephole before unfastening them. He opened up, took a quick glance around. The neighbors couldn't see the door unless they trespassed because that part of the property was concealed by overgrown sea grapes and birds of paradise. He looked down. Three large brown paper bags, neatly folded and stapled across the top as instructed. He gathered them inside and locked up.

The bags were ripped open on the kitchen table. The first had mail, mainly junk, some bank statements and invoices and subscription magazines addressed to a shell corporation: the *Econ-*

*omist, Foreign Affairs, New Republic, Popular Science, Rolling Stone, Mad, Cracked, Model Railroad Monthly* and *Alfred Hitchcock's Mystery Magazine.*

The next bag was heavier. Cans of soup, tuna, Spam, Vienna sausages, cling peaches; bags of noodles, nuts, dehydrated apricots; and three packs of baseball cards. The cupboards were opened and the cans meticulously stacked and arranged according to color. The canned goods were the home's "bomb shelter" food in case society was interrupted. The baseball cards came with a type of dusty pink gum that would outlast the highway system.

The last bag was the wild card. Its contents spread across the table. Bic pens, cinnamon dental floss, a box of ammo, mousetraps, the board game Mousetrap, shoelaces, a plastic castle for an aquarium and a bag of green army men.

After storing everything with obsessive precision, the resident grabbed a rectangular container and headed into the living room, where he tapped flakes of food into a goldfish bowl. "Here you go. Eat in good health. You are my only friend. You're the only one who understands, and you can be trusted. We're a lot alike, you and me. We define our own space. You have the bowl, I have the house. And I got you a present. You're easy to shop for." He held the plastic castle up to the outside of the glass. "I remember hearing that a castle is all a goldfish needs for entertainment. Anything else is overkill. Because you have a memory span of only a few seconds, the castle is like twenty televisions. Here you go." He placed it in the back of the bowl and bent down for a closer look. "Like it? The look on your face says, 'A new castle. Cool.' Now you're circling the bowl and coming back—'What? A castle?'—circling again—'Holy fuck! A castle!'"

The man stood up. "I heard that the breed of goldfish we use as pets have developed short attention spans to prevent insanity from the boredom of a confined space. Lucky you."

He abruptly lost interest and meandered down the hall toward a converted bedroom, talking now to *himself*: "You are my only friend. You're the only one who understands, and you can be trusted. We're a lot alike, you and me . . ."

There was a large square table filling much of the room. He flicked a switch and turned a dial. A tiny dot of white light came on and began moving as the model train emerged from the mountain. The resident opened his bag of army men and placed them on the track. The train approached.

"Halt! Ve vant to see your papers!"

The train scattered the green men off the track.

"*Aaaaahhhhh!*' . . . The French Resistance wins again."

He switched off the train and returned to his lounge chair in the living room. He picked up the book he had left on the table. A novel about old Florida. He opened to page one again and reread the first sentence before his mind began jumping thought rails: He had never come close to riding a horse, wax museums were overrated, there might be ants in the kitchen, *ketchup* or *catsup*?

He set down the book and rubbed his eyes.

Suddenly, a throaty roar filled the house.

The man frantically grabbed the rifle next to his chair and pointed it at a stereo.

A bullfrog had hopped onto one of the outdoor microphones. It jumped down. The man set his rifle next to the chair and walked over to the goldfish bowl. "Where the hell did that castle come from?"

He went into the kitchen and lit a kerosene lantern. He set it on the table and took a seat. He inserted a sheet of paper into the spool of a manual Underwood typewriter.

*Clack, clack, clack, clack . . .*

Twenty-three minutes later, he pulled the page out of the spool and replaced it.

*Clack, clack, clack, clack . . .*

The process was repeated until dawn.

The man finally stretched and yawned. He removed the final

page and neatly aligned it atop all the others from the night's efforts. He grabbed the stack and walked over to a freestanding antique cabinet. He opened a long drawer, placed the pages next to several other similar stacks, and shut the drawer.

He went back to the comfort of his lounge chair, where he dozed off with the Remington rifle resting across his chest.

## THE PRESENT

A Chevy Nova arrived outside the Riviera Beach Public Library, next to the train tracks along Old Dixie Highway.

Signs beside the road indicated that some vote had been taken to change the name of Old Dixie to President Barack Obama Highway.

"The train tracks had literally been the *proverbial* tracks, an invisible apartheid force field rigidly separating the two peoples." Serge clenched a fist. "It was an incorporated town of less than nineteen thousand, but race riots were sufficiently ambitious to garner national TV time in 1967. Brave souls moved across the tracks in 1968 to bring down the color barrier, and Riviera Beach High School integrated to become Suncoast High. The TV crews returned to cover the larger 1971 riot. We lived only eight houses away and could see the network helicopters and tear gas. What a childhood!"

Coleman gave a thumbs-up with a sweat sock in his mouth.

Serge hopped out of the car with his camera set on macro. "Earlier that summer, I was wearing flip-flops because of all the sand-stickers, and riding my bike all alone at age nine down to the school's football field to launch my model rockets. So I packed the little parachutes again and plugged in the nose cones and was about to head out the door. My folks said I couldn't launch my rockets at the high school that day. I said, no problem, I'll launch them somewhere else, but they said I couldn't even go outside. I look out the window, and *nobody* was outside, like a science-fiction movie about a nuclear winter, except with all the whapping of helicopters."

"Wow," said Coleman. "Grounded by a race riot."

"Which I couldn't understand because by then the neighborhood was fully mixed, and we all got along," said Serge. "I should know because I was the paper boy, and the black dads were the best tippers, always real nice and paternal to me: 'Here, son, buy yourself a Frosty.'"

"Frosties!" said Coleman.

"Down, boy," said Serge. "The point is every kid should grow up that way. Instead of being imprinted with anecdotal bullshit, I got a great boots-on-the-ground cultural experience. Then some of the old white guys who were a bit chippy about the changing complexion of the neighborhood—and non-tippers, by the way— would give me grief about the newspaper not being exactly on their doormat. The next day their paper went right on the roof."

They climbed out of the Nova and entered the library. Straight to the reference desk. Serge had a question.

"No beverages in the library."

"Right!" Serge drained his coffee and repeated the request.

The librarian directed them to special collections. Serge took off.

"No running!"

"Sorry. Just happy to be alive." He continued on.

"No skipping, either."

Serge slowed to a walk. "Who put the bee in her bonnet?"

They arrived at a row of old phone books. Serge pulled out the tattered volume from 1965. He flipped to a page under the letter *T*. "Coleman, check it out! Check it out!"

"What?"

"This listing: *Time of Day!* That was the coolest when I was a really little kid, because who else could I call at that age without blowback? So I'd sit at the table and dial. And I mean actually dial a real dial back then. This reassuring voice would come on the line, 'First Marine Bank of Riviera Beach . . . The time is . . . three- . . . oh-two.' I'd hang up and dial again. '. . . The time is three- . . . oh-three.' Click, dial. '. . . The time is . . .'"

"Let me guess," said Coleman. "Three- . . . oh-four."

"No, still three-oh-three," said Serge. "Endless fun! . . . And back then there were no answering machines or little beeps on the line that said you had an incoming call. And that night some relative would phone us with a family emergency. 'I've been trying to get through for hours, but the line was busy!' And my mom would tell Aunt Rita, 'We've been home all day and I haven't made any calls. I don't know how— . . . Hold on . . . Serge? You wouldn't happen to have been on the phone?' . . . 'Mom, did you know all the clocks in the house are wrong?'"

"Another spanking?" asked Coleman.

"Every pioneer gets a little dusted up." Serge pulled out his cell phone and pressed buttons, then put it to his ear as it began to ring.

*"Hello?"*

"What time is it?"

*"What?"*

"The time. What is it? You must have a clock or something. Did you know your number used to be Time of Day? I'm sure you're thrilled to learn that chestnut, and who else would have the courtesy to brighten your life? But along with that vaunted honor comes an obligation to assist the rest of us in reliving our childhoods. What time is it?"

*"Wait. Are you the same guy who calls me every year asking for the time?"*

"Uh . . . maybe."

*"What is your problem?"*

"Listen, I can't tell you how tickled I'd be if you could just tell me the time. Then I'll be out of your life . . . for a year."

*"Get lost, kook!"*

*Click.*

Coleman scratched between his legs. "What time is it?"

"Definitely not the Age of Aquarius." Serge flipped through the phone book again. The letter *R*. His finger ran down the page. ". . . Rangoon, Ratchet . . ." The finger stopped. "Here it is." He scribbled an address on a scrap of paper.

Minutes later, a green Nova pulled up in front of a house on Thirty-Fourth Street across from the high school.

"What's this place?" asked Coleman.

"Just the childhood residence of one of my all-time favorite Florida authors, Kenneth Reese."

"You talked about him before," said Coleman. "The guy who stopped writing and disappeared?"

"Such a shame. His books became instant classics." Serge walked up to the front door and rang the bell. "Everyone gobbled them up back then because they nailed the state."

"Does he still live here?" asked Coleman.

"Doubt it," said Serge. "The people inside now probably don't even know the literary significance of their property. Will they be thrilled! On the other hand, the author hasn't been seen in years. He's rumored to have turned into an eccentric hermit like Salinger or Pynchon or Sean Connery in *Finding Forrester*. So for all I know, maybe he does still live here."

"Nobody's answering," said Coleman.

Serge rang the bell again.

They waited.

"I don't think anyone's home," said Coleman.

"There's a car in the driveway." This time Serge rang the bell *and* knocked.

Nothing.

"Let's try around back." Serge led Coleman to the side door. He knocked hard and pressed his face to the jalousie glass to see inside. He quickly stepped back. "I hear someone coming."

The door opened.

*"Yes? How can I help you?"*

"What time is it?"

# Chapter 29

Midnight approached at the house with no lights.

The outdoor microphones now had chicken-wire enclosures to prevent any more bullfrog scares. The last one resulted in a rifle bullet through a goldfish tank. Which isn't really a hole. The entire thing just breaks. The goldfish had to live awhile in a bathroom sink, with no memory that there had ever been a bowl.

The man in the lounge chair checked his wrist. The stereo played the amplified sound of tires rolling up the driveway. A woman grabbed three paper bags off the passenger seat. She headed around the house again, taking care to avoid all the mouse-traps now guarding the back steps. She left the bags and returned to her car's trunk. This would be a two-trip stop. She removed a heavy box and started back again. She wasn't paid enough not to ask questions. "What the hell does he need a bear trap for?" She assumed she would soon be receiving instructions to avoid that as well.

Once the stereo was silent again, the resident retrieved his delivery off the stoop. He opened a bag and took out a new goldfish bowl, then collected his pet from the bathroom. It splashed into the water. "There you go." Then another splash. "And there's your stupid fucking castle." The man had lost faith in the fish. "Don't think I don't know what's going on."

Finally, he opened the box. "Excellent." He got down on his knees. The bear trap was so strong that it required a special wrench to crank its jaws open into the ready position. He stretched its chain across the floor and padlocked it to an old steel radiator.

The resident settled into his lounge chair with a book, a rifle, and a slightly elevated sense of safety.

It took almost a whole day . . .

*Snap.*

He fell to the floor with a throbbing ankle. "Shit."

He tried opening the jaws. "They're too strong." He spotted the wrench on the counter, but the chain wouldn't reach. He tried the radiator, but it wouldn't budge. The only bright side was that this was one of the newer "humane" traps with dull teeth. Deep bruising, but no risk of death from blood loss in case it caught the wrong thing.

The resident tested the reach of the chain and found that the kitchen table was in range. He dragged the trap over to a chair and sat down to assess the situation. He looked in direction after direction. The back door was too far away. The phone too far away. The canned food in the cupboards even worse.

He opened a pack of baseball cards, stuck the gum in his mouth and began hitting the keys of a typewriter.

*Clack, clack, clack . . .*

## THE PRESENT

The Nova raced away from a house on Thirty-Fourth Street in Riviera Beach.

"What the hell is *wrong* with people?" said Serge. "I'm only delivering heritage surprises. That should be happy news."

"You're like the history fairy."

"Exactly," said Serge. "If someone comes to their door with a singing telegram, do they shit on them, too?"

"Maybe you need a costume."

"And what was that crazy reaction back there when I asked to come in for only a few minutes and lie down in Kenny's bedroom?" said Serge. "I clearly explained I knew it was no longer Kenny's authentic bed, but whoever's it was now would be more than sufficient. I even promised to make the bed back up after I got under the covers. Didn't I bend over backward not to be imposing?"

"You just can't please some people."

*Jingle, jingle.*

Serge reached under his driver's seat and handed a book to Coleman.

"What's this?"

"Our next stop."

Coleman read the title. "*Conch Town USA?*"

"Finally released in 1991 by Charles Foster," said Serge. "Based upon his 1939 photography portfolio, along with the groundbreaking Works Progress Administration research performed by Veronica Huss and the eminent Floridaphile Stetson Kennedy. It lay unpublished and forgotten for more than half a century—the final word on the Bahamian fishermen who founded Riviera."

"Cool." Coleman tried handing it back.

"No, I need your help as navigator. Flip to the map in the middle . . ."

Fifteen minutes later, Coleman held the book a few inches from his face. "Okay, turn left at the next corner. I think."

Serge cut the wheel at Twenty-First Street and Avenue C, camera out the window. *Click, click, click.*

"Now make a right, and another right." Back down Twentieth. *Click, click, click.* Then Fifteenth, crossing Broadway.

Coleman looked up. "They're all empty lots, except for the boat storage yard."

"It's where the first settlers built their houses. Roberts, Sands, Moree. Often clapboard and simple wood frame, much less sturdy than the shipbuilders' homes of the other Conchs in Key West. But the vegetation is still here."

"Okay, trees. Big whoop."

"Coleman, much of our state's visual strikingness has been throttled by the shadow of tall, exotic nuisance trees. Not here: See how everything is low, dominated by palms." Serge began honking the horn. "It's a living canvas of what those early Conchs saw every day."

"Why are you honking?"

"You're allowed to honk after your team wins the championship," said Serge. "This is bigger. I was just privileged to follow in the footsteps of the giant Stetson, renowned author and earlier chronicler of Florida folklore, who studied under Marjorie Kinnan Rawlings of *The Yearling* fame, and traveled the state extensively with Zora Neale Hurston of *Their Eyes Were Watching God* fame. That's a rarefied club, Florida's version of expatriate Paris."

*Honk! Honk! Honk!* . . .

"Serge, you're just attracting drug dealers. They're starting to block the street."

"Don't be so quick to judge." Serge rolled down his window. "They could simply be history buffs with lots of underwear showing. I'll have a little chat to share the special word . . ."

. . . The Nova's passengers ducked as they screeched away from the mob in the street.

"Told you," said Coleman, licking the suction cup and sticking it back on the windshield. "They tried to take my cat toy."

"At least now I know that drug dealers aren't down with the

history fairy." He cut the wheel as they approached a stucco structure painted a sweet-potato shade of orange. "The House of Meats is still here! Our family's old butcher shop! This was still in the sentimental, small-town America era before supermarkets! Nothing says 'land of the free and home of the brave' like having to go to a separate building to buy liver."

"Now a Jamaican place," Coleman said as it went by. "There's a handwritten sign in the window for whole pig."

Serge uncrumpled a scrap of paper from his pocket.

"What's that?" asked Coleman.

"I wrote down a second address from another old phone book in the library, this one 1986." Serge smoothed it out in the middle of the steering wheel. "I told you how much I dug Kenneth Reese's books. He had this recurring character who was an actual person in real life, a legendary local surfer called the Pope of Palm Beach."

"The Pope?" said Coleman. "Jesus!"

"His full name was Darby Pope." Serge crossed over to the east side of U.S. 1. "Tragically killed under hazy circumstances at the port in the late eighties."

The Nova turned onto a quiet street south of Blue Heron near the bridge. Royal palms and bottle palms and fishtail palms grew wild among the low-slung row of ranch houses with bright white tile roofs. The sore thumb in the middle was an older wooden home that had survived the demolition of the fifties. Its dark brown planks were unpainted, lightly sealed with varnish. The front yard had become a feral pasture of grass and weeds.

The Nova rolled up in the driveway. "I called the number from the phone book, but only got an answering machine message from Guido Lopez."

"Who's Guido Lopez?" asked Coleman.

"The person whose lucky day this is." Serge hopped out of the car. "Let's rock!"

"Give me another second." *Jingle, jingle.* He snatched the cat toy off the windshield. "I'm ready."

They headed up the stone path to the front door.

"I'll give it one last try for the day," said Serge. "If these folks aren't totally blown away to hear they're living in the former home of Darby Pope, then they're dead people with a pulse."

He stepped up to the door.

*Knock, knock, knock . . .*

# PART
# Two

# Chapter 30

**K**enneth Reese awoke from a light nap in his lounge chair.

*Knock, knock, knock...*

He sprang up and grabbed the rifle. "What the hell was that?"

Harder knocking. *Bang, bang, bang...*

What the heck? Nobody had come knocking at his door in years. Well, not *nobody*. There were the occasional solicitors and urban missionaries who left literature for discount carpet cleaning and the kingdom of God. Except it wasn't unique to his home; those people were hitting all the houses on the street.

*Bang! Bang! Bang!...*

But this kind of prolonged knocking was specific. Kenny crept slowly to the door and pressed his eye to the peephole. He saw a giant eyeball staring back.

*"Aaahhh!"* He tumbled backward with his rifle.

Serge looked at Coleman. "I just heard someone inside. They're deliberately not answering and rejecting the Good News. They're not getting off that easily!" He moved sideways from the door.

*Bang! Bang! Bang!* . . .

Kenny tiptoed to a window, lifted the towel and parted the blinds. Serge was staring directly back. "Shit!" He let the blinds snap shut. "What do I do now?"

Serge pointed at the window. "Someone was just peeking at us."

"What do we do now?" asked Coleman.

"Follow me."

They walked around the side of the house. Serge loped like a ballerina and sliced the air with karate hands.

"Why are you doing that?" asked Coleman.

Serge gestured along the edge of the crawl space. "Look at all those surveillance microphones," he whispered, pirouetting and high-stepping. *Chop, chop.* "Something weird is going on."

"Microphones?" Coleman bent down. *Burrrrrrrp.* "Sorry."

They heard the belch amplified through a stereo from inside the house, then a paranoid shriek.

"This is more urgent than I thought," said Serge. "Someone in there might need the Good News *and* my professional lifestyle assistance."

They reached the back steps. Coleman bent down again. "Hey, Serge, look what I almost stepped on."

*Snap.*

"Owwwww!"

"Hold still." Serge pried off the mousetrap.

"My thumb's bleeding."

"Just wipe it on your shirt. It'll blend with the other blood." Serge climbed the steps and inspected the doorframe. "Reinforced steel to house the dead bolts. No entry here. Let's find a window that doesn't have bars . . ."

Inside, Kenny followed the sounds around the perimeter of the house, tiptoeing with the gun. It had been a brief glimpse out the front blinds, and he had expected assassins to look different, especially the chubby one.

He heard a snap. That would be a screen popping loose. He ran to the window over the kitchen sink. Shoot, it was so small and high off the ground that he'd never considered installing burglar bars. He opened the cabinet doors under the sink.

"Serge, my back is getting tired," Coleman said on his hands and knees. "You're heavy."

"Stop whining. I'm almost in." He worked diligently with a thin metal shim.

Another pop.

"It's open." He raised the window and squirmed through the tight opening, grappling over the sink and falling headfirst in a tucked roll on the floor. "Hello? Anyone home? I know you're in here!"

"What about me?" Coleman yelled from the backyard.

"You'll never fit. Go back to the side porch and don't pick up anything." Serge went to the door and undid all the locks, turning the knob. "Welcome! Watch your step. It's dark and the light switches don't work."

Coleman entered with his cat toy.

*Snap.*

"*Aaahhh!* My leg!"

"What now?"

"A better mousetrap."

Serge pulled down a towel and opened the blinds. "More like a bear trap. I have to find whoever's in the house. Stay right here."

"That was my plan." *Jingle, jingle.*

Serge wandered room to room. "*Helllllooooo?* Guido Lopez? There's nothing to fear. Everything's normal. It's just the history fairy . . ."

"Serge . . ."

"Not now, I'm busy." Another room. Opening closet doors, checking the shower. "Guido? Are you there? This isn't healthy."

"Serge . . ."

He came back into the kitchen. "What's so important?"

Coleman nodded toward the stove. A rifle leaned against the counter. Serge's eyes lowered. He quickly opened the cabinet doors under the sink and jumped back.

Hands shot up to shield a face. Someone curled in a ball around the gooseneck plumbing. "Don't hurt me."

"Nobody's going to hurt you, Guido." Serge offered a hand. "We're pacifists. We only fight people who claim they're bigger pacifists."

Serge carefully helped the trembling resident out from under the sink. "Guido, what were you doing under there?"

"Who's Guido?"

"You are," said Serge. He walked over to the phone and pressed a button on the answering machine.

*"You've reached Guido Lopez. Please leave a message after the beep." Beep.*

"Oh yeah." The resident nodded. "I get a lot of nuisance calls."

"Well, all that's behind you because this is about to become the luckiest day of your life! Are you ready? Hold on to your hat!" Serge had a painfully wide grin as he hopped up and down. "You're living in the home of real-life literary character Darby Pope! Isn't that super?"

The homeowner's eyes practically popped out of his head.

"What?" said Serge. "Not super?"

"Darby Pope!" exclaimed the resident. "You knew Darby? He was my best friend!"

"No, I didn't know Darby. Just read about him in these books, but— . . . wait a minute. You said he was your best friend?" Serge stepped forward to study the man's face, mentally comparing it to book-jacket photos. "This actually might be the luckiest day of *my* life. You wouldn't by any chance happen to be . . . Kenneth Reese?"

"Okay, you found me," said Kenny, dropping down into a chair at the table. "But I didn't do anything! And I swear I never told anyone!"

"Stop! Slow down! Back up, and don't be a spaz." Serge grabbed the chair across from him. "Now what exactly are you talking about?"

Kenny sniffled. "You're not here to kill me?"

"Hell no! Besides the pacifist thing, you're one of my favorite authors!"

"You aren't pulling my leg?" Kenny uncoiled and momentarily set his head on the table. "That's a relief."

"Kenny! Why did you ever stop writing?" Serge looked around the home's interior. "More important: What's happened to you? You're living like a nut."

"Serge," said Coleman, "can you help get the bear trap off me so I can enjoy my cat toy more?"

"Not now! We're in the presence of greatness." He faced Kenny again. "What's the deal?"

"This is on the level? You really are just a reader?"

"Only your number one fan!"

A heaving sigh of resignation. "Why not? After all these years, I've kept it in so long . . ." And Kenny began giving Serge the short version, which became the long version.

The Greek tragicomedy wrapped up after dark, and Serge whistled. "That's some story! But don't you worry another moment. Serge and Coleman are on the case now."

"What case?"

"Fixing your life."

"But I don't need my life fixed."

Serge laughed heartily. "No offense, but ask yourself: 'What's wrong with this picture?'"

*Jingle, jingle.*

"Kenny, first we have to get you writing again."

"I've been writing."

"When?"

"This whole time."

"But I haven't seen any new books at the store since *Hang Ten*."

"Oh, I don't get them published," said Kenny. "I just write. If you write, it's what you do."

"Holy moly!" said Serge. "You've got unpublished manuscripts lying around?"

"A few."

"How many is a few?"

"Maybe a dozen."

A gasp as Serge's head rolled back toward the ceiling. He sprang to his feet. "You have to show me! Right now!"

Kenny shrugged and walked over to a cabinet, pulling out three full drawers in succession and leaving them open. Serge grabbed his own head, then seized one of the piles of pages and ran back to the table.

"I need light."

Kenny lit the kerosene lantern as Serge began flipping through the pile of loose typed pages, his jaw falling lower and lower. Hours passed. Midnight came and went. Serge stopped and stretched. "This is fantastic stuff! Even better than the old books! You have to get this published as soon as possible!"

"No way."

"But the public is hungry!" Serge grabbed the manuscript. "Be right back. I'm getting this out to the masses . . ."

# Chapter 31

**PUBLISH OR PERISH**

Kenny barred the door.

"Stand aside," said Serge. "This is for your own good."

"Weren't you listening to that story I just told you?" said Kenny. "Somehow I skated out of that whole mess, and nobody has bothered me for almost three decades. Only bad things can come of attracting any attention to myself. And publishing a book about smuggling at the port couldn't be any more attention."

"We'll table that topic for later, but don't think I'm done." Serge got up and looked around at the towel-covered windows. "I have to get you back in proper mental health. I'm a professional."

"Sort of like a psychiatrist?"

"Emphasis on *sort of*." Serge picked up the lantern and walked around like a railroad engineer. "So you mean to tell me you've stayed inside all these years?"

"I used to put on a big floppy hat and sunglasses in the middle of the night if I really needed something from the convenience store. But too many police are out at that hour, and I haven't renewed my license in forever, so I knocked that off as too risky. My nerves."

"But how does the whole thing work?" asked Serge. "It doesn't seem possible."

"I still get royalties from the books that pay for everything," said Kenny. "My lawyer takes care of the rest: banking, taxes, lawn service once in a while. He had a dentist sign a confidentiality agreement, and I pay a lot extra for house calls to get my teeth cleaned. And a doctor for physicals, but those are the only people I see. I didn't realize how much equipment they have to bring."

"What about everyday needs, like groceries and mail and the all-important new underwear when it's time?"

"The lawyer has an assistant who brings things by. After all these years, I'm on my twelfth deliverer . . ."

Serge jumped up as he heard amplified footsteps from the microphones outside. "What's that?"

"Just the assistant," said Kenny. "Leaves brown bags on the steps."

Serge ran to the door and swiftly flung it open. "Hello, assistant!"

A woman was leaning down with paper bags. She leaped back and grabbed her heart. "You scared the shit out of me! . . . Who *are* you?"

"Kenny's new life coach." He waved urgently. "Come on in!"

She shook her head. "I'm not supposed to. Just drop the bags and avoid contact. Strict instructions."

"Kenny," said Serge. "Tell her it's okay."

*"It's okay,"* called an unseen voice.

The woman tentatively crossed the threshold. "Actually, I've been making these deliveries for so long that I was dying to know what was going on inside."

*Jingle, jingle.*

She looked down. "Then again . . ."

Serge had entered a rare laconic moment.

"What are you staring at?" asked the assistant.

"You," said Serge. "You're a mature woman."

"What's *that* supposed to mean?"

"Most guys are only interested in giggling young twits. But you're the full course: intelligent, poised, self-assured enough to wear hospital scrubs and a ponytail and not dye that coal-black hair blond. Kind of a Zeta-Jones thing going on. Right in the wheelhouse of any thinking man."

"You don't even know me."

"And unfortunately I won't get the chance," said Serge. "If I didn't have this zany travel schedule, I'd ask you out right now! Spare no expense! Because the women who don't carry themselves like they deserve to be pampered are the ones who deserve it most. We'd form deep emotional connections by visiting state parks, landmarks, galleries, reading the same books together. You're not the first woman a guy would pick out in a nightclub, but you have the kind of disarming cuteness and substance of thought that lives on long after the first night of sex and the clumsy morning that follows with fuzzy teeth. But as I said, I'm a ramblin' kind of guy, so you'll have to wait for the next man just like me to come along. Sorry."

"Do you always talk like this?"

"Life's short. What's your name?"

"Chris."

"Chris, I have some publishing business to discuss with Kenny." He took the bags from her arms. "So you'd better be going before you torture me further with beguilement."

"Hey, no problem."

She walked briskly out the door and back to her car. "I thought it might be a *little* strange in there . . ." But as she drove from traffic light to traffic light in the loneliness of two A.M., she found herself thinking more and more about the impromptu visit.

Back inside, Serge called out from the living room. "Are these Darby's boards up there in the rafters?"

Kenny came around the corner. "Most of them. The last one's mine. You would have liked him."

"I said I didn't *know* him, but we actually did meet once."

"You did? When?"

"At Trapper Nelson's," said Serge, moving on to inspect the classic titles in the bookcase. "I was just a little kid and stole a canoe at Jonathan Dickinson, then paddled upriver to see what everyone was talking about. Turned into a big commotion because my parents reported a lost kid at the park, which wasn't accurate because I knew exactly where I was the whole time . . . Anyway, Darby came along—"

"Wait," said Kenny. "*You* were that little kid? I was with Darby that day."

"You were?"

"Yeah, and Darby called the rangers on the radio to say he was bringing you back. But you took off first and we had a devil of a time rounding you up. You were a slippery little sucker."

"It's on my résumé," said Serge, removing a book from a shelf and holding it toward Kenny. "Your first novel. I love the almost photographic details, right down to the makeshift water tower and hurricane log, just like the day we met."

"Small world," said Kenny, easing himself down into his lounge chair. "Okay, now I definitely know you're on the level. You're a real local who's read my books. But seriously, what are you doing breaking into my house? What do you want from me?"

"It wasn't in my plans at the beginning of the day," said Serge. "But now that we've had this uncanny introduction, you absolutely have to get your new books published!"

"I told you, that's never going to happen," said Kenny. "Just put it out of your head."

"But you won't mind if I finish reading this manuscript, and the others?"

Kenny made himself comfortable in the lounger and closed his eyes. "Go crazy."

Serge grabbed the pile of pages and settled into the other lounger next to the author. He flipped a page, and another, and another . . .

. . . A half hour later. "Pssst! Kenny, are you awake?" Serge waved a hand in front of his face with no response.

He slipped into the kitchen and roused Coleman from a snoring blackout.

"Huh, what? Where am I? I was having a wild dream. These giant house cats—"

"Not now!" Serge grabbed a tool and cranked the bear trap open. "We have to work fast, before he wakes up."

Serge methodically moved through the house, opening drawer after drawer.

Coleman yawned and rubbed his stomach. "What are you doing?"

Another drawer opened. "Invading his privacy."

"Isn't that wrong?"

A drawer closed and another opened. "Used to be, but now it's the coin of the realm. And forget Big Brother. The NSA has nothing on Google and Amazon. If you want to function at all in today's society, you're constantly checking off 'Agree to Terms' boxes at the bottom of documents longer than *War and Peace* that nobody can understand but grant corporations the right to track your roaming habits by satellite, archive your Internet search terms, and sell your consumer patterns to boiler rooms in Jakarta. Then you buy *one* dildo, and a United Nations assembly of sex workers paralyzes your in-box . . . Here we go . . ."

Coleman looked over his shoulder. "What is it?"

"Address books, business cards." Another drawer. "Unopened mail."

Serge stuffed it all in an empty shopping bag. "We're on the move . . ."

. . . A green Chevy Nova sat in front of the plate-glass fluorescence of a twenty-four-hour copy shop.

*Ka-chung, ka-chung, ka-chung, ka-chung . . .*

Pages fed high-speed in one side of a machine, and copies spit out the other.

Serge stood at a nearby table, the contents of a paper bag dumped out, sifting through addresses and phone numbers. When he had what he needed, he gathered up the copies and made himself comfy at one of the computer stations. *Clack, clack, clack.*

"What are you doing?" asked Coleman.

"Writing a letter," said Serge. "The key to letter writing is an opening that won't send your letter directly into the wastebasket. That's what happened when the apostle Paul first wrote to the Ephesians: 'Open immediately! You may already be a winner!'"

Serge finished his missive, printed it out and signed with flair. In another person's name. He pulled a padded mailer off a shelf and addressed it. He approached the customer-service counter.

Someone studying calculus looked up from a textbook. "Can I help you?"

Serge licked the mailer and sealed it. "Any of those private mailboxes over there still available for rent?"

"Yes."

"I want one," said Serge. "You also mail stuff?"

"Yes again."

Serge set the packaged manuscript on the counter. "Mail this."

# Chapter 32

## THE NEXT MORNING

**U**pbeat humming from the kitchen.

Serge awoke to the aroma of eggs frying in a skillet. He usually arose before dawn "to get a jump on the others," but it had been a late night at the copy shop. "What time is it?" He grabbed his watch off the nightstand in a back bedroom of the bungalow. "Seven o'clock! The others have the jump!"

He jumped.

Practically landing in his sneakers next to the bed. Serge quickly tied the laces and rushed down the hall. Something stopped him when he reached the living room. "What's going on?"

Warm, healthy sunlight streamed through all the windows. Blinds open wide. He slowly turned to appreciate the full impact of the space: the array of vintage surfboards hanging from the rafters, that stunning library in the sprawling bookcase, hard-pine walls, a painting of a royal poinciana, and finally—in the centerpiece spot over the mantel—the framed black-and-white enlargement of Darby Pope catching a wave in his prime at Singer Island.

The smell of bacon.

"Who's humming?" Serge's head swung around. "Coleman?"

"Down here." He crawled out from behind a lounge chair. "Didn't make it to a bed again."

"What's going on?"

Coleman yawned and smacked his lips. "I just tuned in."

The humming grew louder. Then lyrics.

"*. . . I can see clearly now . . .*"

Serge followed the voice into the kitchen. He stopped again.

Kenny was dancing a merry jig as he squeezed juice oranges into a ceramic pitcher. Wearing sandals, swim trunks, an old Riviera Beach Surf Club T-shirt.

Serge's brain didn't know where to start. Kenny had told him he usually slept well past noon. Depression and skewed circadian rhythms from all the blacked-out windows in the house. And his appetite had been down to nothing. Something was going on.

"Kenny, what time did you get up?"

He stuck his hands in oven mitts. "Before dawn."

Serge inventoried the breakfast menu. "Where'd you get all the fresh meat and eggs?"

"And citrus." Kenny tossed Serge an Indian River grapefruit.

"But you only have cabinets full of all that canned survival food for hydrogen-bomb attacks."

Kenny opened the oven and removed a tray of southern buttermilk biscuits. "I went to the store."

"You mean in the middle of the night? In a disguise?"

"No, this morning right after my swim." He set out three plates. "Help yourself."

Serge noticed Kenny's still-moist spiked hair. "Where'd you go swimming?"

"In the ocean." Kenny unfolded the *Post*'s sports section and scooped hash browns with a fork.

Coleman poured OJ from the pitcher and added an equal amount of Smirnoff. He grabbed a chair next to Kenny.

Serge remained standing. "Sorry if I'm having trouble processing all this . . ."

"Oh, and I know you like coffee," said Kenny, munching a biscuit crammed with bacon. "I just brewed that pot over there."

"What? Coffee?" Serge loped across the room and grabbed a mug. Then they were all seated together like family.

Serge rapidly alternated between the grapefruit in one hand and cup of joe in the other. "Kenny, man, you were a wreck yesterday, and now this. It's such a startling transformation. What . . . *happened*?"

"I have you to thank." A big fork of scrambled eggs. "What was I doing with my life? What a serious rut!"

"I've heard of fast rebounds," said Serge. "But this is like giving a heroin overdose a shot of Narcan."

"You guys were just the kick I needed." Kenny continued chewing like someone who had been rescued at sea. "You had so many questions, and once I started talking, the floodgate of memories opened wide, like the Peanut Man."

"The Peanut Man?" said Coleman.

"Serge and I were jumping from topic to topic . . ."

Serge finished off his coffee. "I said, 'Remember that old black guy who sat on the northwest corner of Old Dixie and Blue Heron, selling peanuts out of a baby carriage?'"

"He was an institution, planted there with that stroller for years as if he had taken root on that sidewalk," said Kenny. "He was like the unofficial mayor. *Everyone* knew the Peanut Man."

"The midnight blowing of the horn on the SEC railroad," Serge continued. "The blinking stacks at the power plant, the Trylon tourist tower, Captain Jack's fishing report, nude 'Air Force Beach'—the kids never stopped talking about that one."

Kenny wiped up his plate with one last bite of biscuit and took it to the sink. "What a great life I had growing up here! And then I looked around this dank house of despair and thought to myself, 'What the hell are you doing, Kenny?' . . . To think it all started with you breaking in through the window over the sink. I'd been hunkered down terrified of someone coming after me. And when you broke in and nothing bad happened, it was an epiphany. What are your plans for the day—"

*Knock, knock, knock.*

Serge jumped up in alarm—"Who the hell is that?"—instinctively reaching for his waistband.

Kenny remained calm. "Talk about role reversal." He headed for the side door.

"But Kenny," said Serge, "why didn't we hear any footsteps through the stereo?"

"Because I turned off those stupid microphones." He reached for the locks.

"Wait!" said Serge. "Are you expecting a delivery?"

"Not until Friday. And she only comes at night." Kenny undid the bolts.

"No!" said Serge. "Don't—"

Too late. The door opened.

"Oh, hi, Chris," said Kenny. "What are you doing here? It's not Friday."

Chris smiled and lifted the single brown bag in her arms. "It's my day off, and I thought I'd bring a few extra things by." She angled her head to see around Kenny into the house. "Are your friends still here?"

He swung an arm. "Right at that table . . . Join us for breakfast."

"Already ate." She came inside. "Hi, Serge."

"Chris!" He jumped up and relinquished his chair. Serge was about to say something, but momentarily lost his vocal cords.

"What's the matter?" asked Chris. "Cat got your tongue?"

Coleman pointed with a piece of toast. "You're wearing plaid." He dipped it in yolk.

"Plaid?" She chuckled. "What's that got to do with anything?"

Serge blushed and adjusted his waistband. A forced grin. "I didn't think I'd see you again. Or at least not this soon."

"Was in the neighborhood."

Coleman raised his hand. "I'm Coleman."

"Chris," said Kenny, "what's in the bag?"

She began unloading cheese and bread and salads from the deli.

Serge looked accusingly at her. "Don't lie. You were planning a picnic, weren't you?"

Her turn to blush. She pulled out two bottles. "I got both red and white. Didn't know which you liked."

"I don't drink," said Serge.

Coleman lunged with outstretched claws. "Mine!"

"Everyone stand back," said Serge, grabbing his wristwatch. "It's a marvel of nature."

Coleman chewed the seal off one bottle, then grabbed car keys from the table and began excavating the cork.

"I do actually have a corkscrew," said Kenny, but Serge waved him off.

Coleman finally plunged the last broken chunk down into the bottle, where it bobbed as he upended it for a long slug. He slammed the bottle down. "Time!"

Serge pressed a button on his watch. "Twenty-three-point-four seconds."

But Chris was still gazing at Serge. "So what are you up to today?"

"Depends on Kenny. He's made a remarkable breakthrough... Kenny, what's on the slate?"

"I'm going surfing."

"I surf, too," said Serge. "Great memories of carrying my board through the Colonnades and seeing John D. MacArthur in the coffee shop all the time."

"It's amazing he managed his vast empire from that table," said Kenny. "So where do you want to catch waves?"

"The Pump House?"

"You do know the area," said Kenny.

"I surf, too," said Chris.

"*You're* a surfer chick?" said Serge. "Oops, I didn't mean anything by 'chick.' Grew up in a different era. But I have total respect. Like Eleanor Roosevelt, Susan B. Anthony and Mother Teresa. Incredible chicks."

Coleman raised his hand. "I surf."

"You do not!" said Serge.

"Do too!"

"When?"

"All the time," said Coleman. "When you're not around."

"You lie—"

Kenny clapped his hands hard. "Guys, are we surfing or not?"

"Just one second." Serge faced Chris. "This is a test, like in the movie *Diner*. The Peanut Man?"

"Corner of Blue Heron and Dixie."

"You're in." Serge turned to Kenny. "Surf's up."

Kenny grabbed a step stool, and they got the boards down for the first time in ages.

"We'll only need three of them," said Serge.

"I do too surf!" said Coleman.

"What's the harm?" Kenny asked Serge.

"Trust me when I say the possibilities are endless."

None of the vehicles had racks, so they used beach towels and rope to lash the boards to the roofs.

Kenny was up first at the Pump House, riding a strong wave off the sandbar like he'd never left the place.

Then it was Chris's turn, timing the next wave and standing up in a one-piece black-and-turquoise bodysuit. Even Kenny was impressed by the agility of her cutback.

"It's been a while," said Serge. "Nobody laugh." He stood up on his board in front of a small wave. No moves or anything, just maintaining balance, which was no small feat.

Then, from the other side of a swell: "Okay, here I come!" yelled Coleman.

It was a larger wave than usual, and Coleman suddenly appeared bobbing in the water with an inflatable swim ring around his stomach. The ring had the head of a sea horse, and a built-in beverage holder. *"Yabba-dabba-doo!"* He expertly crested the wave drinking a beer mixed with salt water.

The foursome swam back out again. And they rode the next wave back in again, then the next wave and the next, each member of the gang pretty much executing the same respective styles, except Coleman was now drinking pure salt water.

An hour later, they all hit the sand hard, wiped.

"Man, I forgot how much the water and sun take it out of you," said Kenny, lying back with his head on a rolled-up towel, smiling like the kid he used to be.

Serge opened a beach umbrella and rammed it in the sand. Coleman opened a beer cooler and shotgunned. Chris opened a paperback and found a dog-eared page.

"What are you reading?" asked Serge.

She turned the book over to show. "MacDonald. *The Long Lavender Look.*"

"Johnny D.!" said Serge. "I've read that whole series. Twice. Forward and back."

Chris turned a page. "I'm ten books in. Eleven to go."

"Allow me." Serge unrolled a beach towel. "You shouldn't have to lie in the sand."

She brushed herself off and was about to lie down again. "Where'd you get that thing?"

"What? It's my favorite towel."

"It's ancient. One of those old maps of Florida with little symbols illustrating what each area is known for." She got on her hands and knees. "This is so cool! There's a mermaid, water skier, Bok Tower in the middle, oranges and alligators naturally, lighthouse in Key West, deco hotel in Miami, race car in Daytona—you can tell how old it is because there isn't a rocket yet at Cape Canaveral."

Serge became awkwardly coy. "I . . . could show you my View-Masters."

"That's the worst line I've ever heard to get me in bed."

"Me? . . . I? . . . What?"

She laughed and lightly touched his arm. Sparks. "I love old View-Masters."

Kenny hopped up. "This is too great a day! I'm going back in!"

"Me too!" said Coleman, grabbing a beer and blow-up sea horse.

"Grab the end of my board!" said Kenny. "I'll tow you out!"

Serge watched the waves. "Now that's a pairing I didn't see coming."

"You used to live around here?" asked Chris.

"This very town." Serge pointed north. "I remember first coming to that beach when I was in diapers and a playpen. I mean, I remember the photos."

She began unconsciously twirling her hair with a finger. "So, uh, tell me about this big literary tour of yours."

"Okay!" Serge plopped down next to her cross-legged. "It's really cool! . . ."

The sun began to fade, and so did the surfers.

They packed it all in and secured the boards back on the roofs.

"Meet you at the house?" said Kenny. "We can shower, and I just read about this fantastic locals bar with the coldest beer for miles! They put bags of ice in the pitchers."

Coleman dove into Kenny's vehicle.

"See you in a while," said Serge. "I'm going to give Chris the hometown tour."

They crossed back over the big bridge and parted ways.

". . . There's Saint Francis, where I was an altar boy . . . there's my Little League field . . . there's where I launched rockets . . . here's my house, where I climbed on the roof when I was six by shimmying up the old TV antenna . . . here's the storm-drain access point where I explored under the city . . . that used to be Jack's Coin

Shop, where I got a little carried away about pennies . . . that Walgreens used to be the town theater where the nuns took us to see *The Sound of Music* because it's the only movie where nuns defeat Nazis . . ."

The Nova arrived back at the bungalow as Kenny was slipping into a golf shirt. "What a great day! Coleman's hilarious! We're heading out for dinner. Want to join us?"

The couple glanced at each other. "Both of you are going out for a while?" asked Serge.

"Hell, yes!" Coleman hoisted a beer. "This town rocks!"

Chris stretched. "We're a little tired from the day."

"Yeah," said Serge. "Probably watch TV and order something."

"Suit yourself." Kenny grabbed his wallet. "If you change your minds, we'll be at the Brass Ring. Come on, Coleman!"

"Surf's up!"

The door closed.

Five minutes later: "*. . . Yes! Yes! Yes! Yes! Yes! . . .*"

"I take it you're happy?"

"*. . . Don't stop! Don't stop! Don't stop! . . . Stop! Switch places! . . .*"

"What?"

"*. . . Switch! Now! Hurry! . . .*"

The headboard banged.

"*. . . On the floor! . . .*"

"What?"

"*. . . Yes! Yes! Yes! . . .*" She hopped up and turned around. "*. . . Against the dresser! . . .*"

"What?"

"*. . . Yes! Yes! . . . I hope I'm not throwing too much at you . . .*"

"Consider me your golden-glove shortstop."

"*. . . Good.*" She ran out of the room, her voice echoing back. "*The kitchen table! . . .*"

Dishes broke. A woman shrieked in rhythm and arched her back, then collapsed. She hugged him with wet matted hair. "That was unbelievable."

"Oh, but we're not done," said Serge. "My turn to call the offense."

"What?"

"Where's your plaid shirt?"

"Right here."

"Back to the bedroom! . . ."

". . . *Yes! Yes! Yes!* . . ."

Serge leaped off her and ran into the living room. "Help me get down the surfboards . . ."

". . . *Yes! Yes! Yes!* . . ."

Serge jumped up and ran to the bookshelf. "This is one of my favorite positions." He got back on top of her and opened a novel next to her head.

"You're going to *read*?"

"If you haven't tried it, you have no idea what you're missing! . . ."

". . . *Yes! Yes! Yes!* . . ."

"'*The first time Yossarian saw the chaplain*' . . ."

A half hour later, the front door opened.

"We're back!" yelled Kenny. "Hope you kids behaved yourselves."

The pair were reclined in respective lounge chairs, eating popcorn and watching a black-and-white movie. "Just having a nice boring evening," said Serge.

Kenny laughed. "We didn't."

"I'm really sorry," said Coleman.

"I told you not to worry about it," said Kenny.

"What happened *this time*?" asked Serge.

Kenny was still chuckling. "We hopped over to the Polo Lounge, and Coleman climbed up on the bar and started doing the tequila dance."

"I've seen that in a bunch of bars," said Serge. "The patrons love it."

"Except it's not that kind of bar, and they weren't playing 'Tequila,'" said Kenny. "In fact, everyone was staring in silence."

"Until I broke some stuff," said Coleman. "Sorry."

"It's all good," said Kenny. "I greased the bartender and said he was a Kennedy. For some reason I'm not tired at all . . . Coleman, nightcap back at the Ring?"

"We rock tonight!"

They ran out the door.

Serge and Chris both looked at the plaid shirt sitting on the table between them, then raced each other down the hall . . .

And that's how it went, the next day and the next. The bonding of the odd quartet.

# Chapter 33

## THE NEXT MORNING

**C**ars honked. Cops rode horses. Cabdrivers cursed. Corner vendors tonged hot dogs into buns. All in a New York minute.

Just below Central Park near the Carnegie Deli, a fifty-story office tower rose in midtown Manhattan. A double-decker sight-seeing bus drove by. A statue of Marilyn Monroe with a blowing dress stood over a sidewalk grate. A delivery truck parked, and a large rolling bin took the elevator to the third floor.

The bin arrived in a spacious open room where everyone was on their feet and on the move. Someone upended the bin, dumping its contents onto a long steel table surrounded by employees efficiently sorting the pile of letters, large envelopes and boxes of all shapes. As they say, many successful people get their start in the mail room. Many more just become unpleasant.

A young man named Lupes had a cheap apartment across the river in Jersey and dreams of producing a one-man off-Broadway show on the Helsinki Accords. He wheeled a smaller bin out of the mail room and up to the forty-ninth floor, making the rounds down corridors of busy window offices. People on the phone, on the computer, holding meetings. They all briefly looked up from their tasks and smiled as the day's mail arrived, and if they were asked a moment later if they had smiled at Lupes, they wouldn't be able to tell you.

The bin arrived at a corner office and a regular stack landed on a desk. Neal Toth was a respected senior editor who specialized in nonfiction naval history and southern lit. It was a half hour before he got around to opening the mail.

Toth was as hard-nosed as they came, and he turned into a little kid. Running out into the hallway and calling to everyone in earshot, "You have to see this!"

A major publishing house is not known for hallway screaming, and a curious group collected in his doorway.

"What is it?"

Toth held a stack of pages over his head in triumph. "Kenny's back!"

"Who?"

"Kenneth Reese."

The older editors knew, and the younger ones were filled in.

"Oh, *that* Kenny," said a celebrity-cookbook editor. "But I thought he was dead."

Toth shrugged. "Who knew what happened to him?"

Indeed.

Toth had been a young editor when he began working on Kenny's series of Florida books, and now he was one of the oldest. Back then, everything was fine until the fourth book came due. They had already started designing the dust jacket. Kenny wasn't answering his phone. At first, nothing seemed off. When authors were writing, they were notoriously hard to reach, often checking into motels with typewriters to avoid disruption. Happened all the time. But then a few days of no contact became a month. They tried his agent, who reported the same difficulty. Time went on and the deadline was long past.

Urgent phone calls and mail went into a black hole. They were just about to call the police when a certified letter arrived from an attorney informing them Kenny would not be writing anymore and that all further communication should be directed to his law office.

Writers were strange cats. Complaining about the color of their name on the cover, shouting about the size of their author photo on the back flap, or simply unexplained crying when an editor picked up the phone. But this was another league. Kenny had been at the height of his popularity, and never a disagreement. An editor's dream. Who stops then?

The publisher and agent had tried everything to bring Kenny back into the fold, even flying down to meet with the attorney, but he was resolute. They didn't lose hope, continuing the overtures every month or so for the next three years. Then the attempts became less and less frequent. Until they lost hope. Lives had to move on. Good-bye, Kenny, wherever you are.

The eighties became the nineties, then the new millennium. Rumors, myths, mystery. A ghost.

"He's back!" Toth repeated.

"But how do you know it's really him?" asked a book-tour scheduler. "It could be a hoax. Remember the Howard Hughes thing?"

"I was skeptical, too," said Toth, looking down and flipping pages. "You can try to mimic a writer's style, but this is spot-on. If anyone should be able to tell the difference, it's me."

"Any reason for the turn of events?"

"Just this odd cover letter." Toth held it to his face. "Says he's sorry he hasn't called except he was out of communication on an eastern journey to find himself, and he discovered the key to life: 'You will never really find yourself, but never stop trying.'"

"Sound like Kenny?"

"No, but neither does pulling a Jimmy Hoffa." The editor set the page down gently on his desk calendar. "He ends by saying he's ready to jump back into the game, and gave me a phone number to use day or night."

"You haven't called it?"

"Not yet. I'm still dazed. What do you say after all these years? After— ... whatever the hell happened to him?" Toth picked up the phone. "Could I have the room, please? And close the door."

Everyone left, and the editor stood there so long just holding the un-dialed phone that it started that obnoxious beeping when you don't dial in time. He hung up and grabbed it again. He began dialing...

A green Nova cruised along the beach on Highway A1A. "And here's another way to fight back against The Man," said Serge. "Say you have a reservation at a motel, and something comes up that's not your fault, like remembering there's an eclipse in the Keys, or having to sanitize a crime scene, especially if it's yours. You can't just go through life leaving DNA material for the next person."

"It's not how we were raised."

"And you have to cancel the room, but it's past cancellation time and you're going to lose your money."

"But Serge," said Coleman. "What can one person do?"

"This is why you always stay at national chains," said Serge. "They won't let you cancel, but they will let you reschedule. So you call the eight-hundred reservation number to say your business itinerary has changed because you landed the huge Mongolian zinc-mine account, and need to move your reservation from Monday to Thursday. They happily agree, which also moves your cancellation time, and you just call again the next day and ditch the room without penalty."

"That's pretty clever," said Coleman. "Only one thing. You agreed to the cancellation rule when you first booked the room, so isn't that dishonest?"

"Doesn't matter," said Serge. "The whole reservation process is adversarial. They have all these *rules* that you're forced to accept or sleep in the woods. Does that sound right? Yet they can break their own rules anytime they want with two simple words. I once tried to use a perfectly valid coupon. 'Sorry, we don't honor those. We're *independently owned*.' They wave the phrase around like a magic wand. Another time: 'I'd like the late checkout that's a benefit of my platinum status.' 'Sorry, *independently owned*.' And there's no mention about any of this on the website when you commit. How did that start? That's why I always wait until the staff is watching to abuse ice-machine protocol. 'Hey, the sign says not to fill coolers.' 'Sorry, I'm *independently owned*—'"

A cell phone rang, and Serge grabbed it.

"Hello?"

"Is this Kenny Reese?"

"Who's asking?"

"Your old editor, Neal Toth."

"Oh, hi, Neal. I've been expecting your call. How's it shaking?"

"Good grief, you're acting like we just talked the other day," said the editor. "I'm still in shock that I received your package."

"Better late than never."

A pause. "Your voice sounds different."

"What do you expect after all these years?" said Serge. "Your voice sounds different, too, Ned."

"It's Neal."

"Right, Neal. So what did you think of the manuscript?"

"I was floored! Your best yet!" said Toth. "We going to rush this right out in time for the holidays."

"Sounds great," said Serge.

From the passenger seat. *"Noooobody expects the dildo."*

"Shut up, you idiot!" Serge pointed importantly at the phone. "It's New York."

"What was that?" asked the editor. "Is everything all right?"

"Couldn't be better."

"Glad to hear," said Toth. "Because I have something big to ask. Hope this isn't too much all at once, but would you, uh, say, be up to doing a book tour?"

"A book tour?" said Serge. "Can't think of anything I'd like more! Sign me up! My only request is that I reserve my own motels. I have special tricks."

"No problem," said the editor. "And forgive me if I'm still a little off here, but this is all so out of the blue."

"Ain't that life?"

"Okay, then, it's set. I'll have someone from promotions call to set up your schedule." A huge smile practically came through the phone. "It's so wonderful to finally be talking to you again!"

"Same here, Ned."

"Neal."

"Right. Later." Serge hung up.

"What's going on?" asked Coleman.

Serge floored the gas. "Is Kenny going to be surprised!"

# Chapter 34

**THE BUNGALOW**

Y ou did what!" screamed Kenny.

"For your own good," said Serge.

Kenny seized him by the collar. "Which manuscript did you give them?"

"I think the first. Figured that would be the logical place to start your comeback."

"You *think*? What did it say?" demanded Kenny. "What was the plot about?"

"You know, all the smuggling at the Port of Palm Beach, police corruption, your big escape," said Serge. "Personally I was a little surprised that you included the death of Darby Pope. But that's what makes you so great. You had the courage to explore your most intimate emotions."

"Oh my God!" Kenny grabbed the sides of his head. "This is a disaster!"

"I did you a big favor."

"Favor!" Kenny paced feverishly. "You just killed me!"

"I guess that's the same as 'thank you,'" said Serge.

Kenny clutched his collar again. "You have to stop them."

"That train's already left the station," said Serge, fiddling with his cell phone. "They're rushing it into print as we speak. And even if I could stop it, I wouldn't. It's a critical element of my biggest project ever!"

"What project?"

"To fix your life."

"It doesn't need fixing! And my judgment is far better than yours!"

"You wouldn't say that if you saw yourself the other day when I tumbled through your kitchen window." Serge raised his cell phone. "Hold still."

"What for?"

"Your updated author photo."

"Get that thing away from me!"

*Click.*

Serge checked the screen. "Kenny, I'm going to have to take another. Your hand was in front of your face."

"No, you're not!" The writer ran around the room, quickly checking out all the blinds before closing them.

"But your publisher said you needed a new photo for your book tour."

"What book tour?"

"The one I agreed to. They're scheduling it right now. The next critical step in my project to restore normalcy."

*"Aaaauuuuuuu!"* Kenny ran down the hall to a closet and returned with an armload of towels, which he began hanging back on all the windows to darken the room. He switched on the stereo and cranked up the volume from the outdoor microphones. Bolted the dead bolts. Reset the bear trap. Ran back and jumped in his lounge chair, trembling with a rifle across his chest.

"Kenny, we're going backward now."

No answer.

Coleman stumbled into the room with a chilled can of Pabst. "Why is it so dark in here? Did I miss sunset again?"

"No." Serge nodded toward the lounge chair.

*Belch.* "What's up with him?"

"This is technically what they call a setback." Serge approached the chair with his phone. "Kenny, think of what you said the other day about having been afraid of nothing all this time . . ." He snapped fingers in front of the writer's face. "Kenny, you in there?" *Snap, snap.* "Shoot, he's catatonic." He raised the phone again. *Click.*

"Coleman." Serge held out the screen. "What do you think about this author photo?"

"His eyes." Coleman leaned closer. "He looks like a madman."

"You're right. I'll just take another one later when he's in an appreciation frenzy. We still have plenty of time before the book launch." Serge was sticking the phone back in his pocket when it rang.

"Who is it?" asked Coleman.

Serge checked the display. "New York." He put it to his ear. "Hello? . . . Yes, I'm still as thrilled as you are . . . Could you repeat that part again? . . . No, it's good news . . . Of course I'll be ready . . . I'll get it to you as soon as possible. Peace out."

"What did he say?" asked Coleman.

"Turns out we don't have plenty of time. They moved up the release date." He snatched keys off the kitchen table. "And they need the new publicity shot immediately to print the dust jackets."

"What are you going to do?"

"To the Party Store."

"I love the Party Store!"

The Nova arrived back at the bungalow after dark.

They ran inside and checked on Kenny, still in his chair, transfixed.

"Damn," said Serge. "I was hoping he'd rebounded. I guess it's plan B."

He dumped a shopping bag out onto the kitchen table, then reclined in a chair. "Coleman, I'm going to need your help."

"But I don't know how this works."

"I'll walk you through it. Start with the glue . . ."

A half hour later:

*Knock, knock, knock . . .*

Serge got up and opened the door. "Chris!"

She startled and jumped backward off the steps, just like the first time. "Shit, you scared me again!"

"Why? It's just little ol' Serge."

She climbed the steps and touched his face. "You going to a party or something?"

"No, what gives you that idea?"

"The fake beard, makeup, eyebrows . . ." said Chris. "Where'd you get all that?"

Coleman poured beer into a funnel. "The Party Store has everything!"

"Ignore him," said Serge, leading her into the living room.

"Good lord," said Chris. "What happened to Kenny?"

"He's just excited about going back into print."

"He looks absolutely terrified."

Coleman drained the funnel. "There's been a setback."

"He's a little freaked out. Okay, a *lot* . . . But there's a silver lining." Serge broke into a grin. "I've always wanted to go on a book tour."

"You're going to impersonate Kenny?"

"Look at the guy," said Serge, picking up a new remote control from the Party Store. "He's not exactly audience-ready."

"That's fraudulent," said Chris.

"Only if I'm stealing from him." Serge worked levers on the control box. "But in this case I'm helping boost his circulation—"

The phone rang, and it went through to the answering machine: *"You've reached Guido Lopez. Please leave a message after the beep." Beep.*

"Kenny, this is your attorney. Pick up. It's urgent!"

Serge grabbed the receiver. "Hello?"

"Who's this?"

"Kenny."

"You don't sound like Kenny."

"I have a cold. Who else would be answering this phone?" said Serge. "What's up?"

"'What's up?' What the hell's *going on?*"

"What do you mean?"

"I just got a call from your old publisher," said the lawyer. "He told me you submitted a new manuscript, and they're overnighting me the contract."

"So sign it," said Serge. "You have power of attorney. And put the money in the regular account."

"They said you're going on a book tour?"

"That's right. I can't wait! Getting my autographing hand limber now."

A long pause.

"Hello?" said Serge. "You still there?"

"We've worked together a long time, so may I be frank?"

"Cool. Get your frank on."

"Our business is the strangest in my entire practice. And any practice I've ever heard of, for that matter. So over the years, I've kind of developed a picture. I get it. You're a writer, but you're not a public person. A lot of people aren't. The sudden fame kind of blindsided you, and you became a recluse."

"Pretty much on the money," said Serge. "What's the problem?"

"You do realize what this book tour will be like? Especially after you've been gone for so long," said the lawyer. "I'm just surprised that you'd— ... I'm just surprised. Thought I'd call to make sure everything's all right over there."

"A-OK," said Serge. "I've had an awakening. Anything else?"

"Just that I can't wait to read the new book," said the attorney. "I'll send over a signed copy. Later." *Click.*

"But Serge—" said Chris.

"Hold that thought." Serge ran outside, flicked open a pocket-knife, and sliced the phone line. He dashed back in. "What is it?"

"You don't know anything about a book tour."

"Even better," said Serge, pressing a button on his remote control that produced a whirring sound. "It'll be a book tour like nobody's ever seen before. Kenny is going to be so happy with his press coverage!"

Chris pointed as something lifted off from the kitchen table. "What's the drone for?"

"Book signings." Serge maneuvered the small craft around the corner and into the living room. "Weren't you paying attention?"

Chris raised her eyebrows. "I've only been to one book event before, but I think—"

"Just a sec." Serge's tongue stuck out the corner of his mouth in concentration as he hovered his new toy over a lounge chair. "Kenny, check out your newest gimmick!"

*Bang.*

"Kenny shot down the book-tour drone."

# *Chapter 35*

A green Chevy Nova sat in front of the twenty-four-hour copy shop.

Serge approached a wall of private mailboxes. He stopped in front of them and stared at a little brass door, number 127. He clasped his hands. "Please, please, please . . ."

Private mailboxes had a legitimate use: Some parcel companies won't deliver to a regular U.S. postal box. The rest of the time these boxes fell in the same category as offshore accounts and safety deposits, when people needed to keep their private affairs *private*. Certain things weren't meant to be delivered to a home with the wife and kids and especially search warrants.

A middle-aged man stepped up to Serge's left. He quickly looked around before inserting a key and removing several Social Security checks for people he wasn't. He quickly left the store. Another man stepped up on Serge's right. He glanced around and opened a box containing a plain brown package of DVDs titled

*The Golden Shower Girls, Vols. 16 and 17.* He ran away. Serge kept his eyes on 127. "Please, please . . ."

His hand inserted the key.

"Crap."

"What's the matter?" asked Coleman.

"Only more junk mail." He tore open envelopes in succession. "An advance copy of Kenny's new book is supposed to arrive. I've been counting down the hours every day, but instead I just get offers for life insurance, credit-card balance transfers and gift baskets from Vermont."

Serge sorted the unwanted matter on a table.

"What are you doing now?"

"The same thing I always do." He licked a flap. "Junk mail is a scourge on our nation with an astronomical opportunity cost because everyone has to waste time going through it all since there could be an actual bill in there somewhere. And if you simply toss the whole pile in the shit can, you're in trouble. Most people just accept the oppression, but I'm fighting back!"

"How?" asked Coleman.

"Notice all this paper nonsense that's clogging up my life right now?" He folded pages. "Most of it comes with prepaid return envelopes, so I just cram it all back in and off it goes. See how *they* like it. Now they have to waste time opening *my* envelope until they realize they've been had."

"And they also paid the postage?"

"Ain't irony grand?" He licked another flap. "The problem is so bad that it reaches out and fucks with my life when I'm not even getting junk mail. I'll go to a bookstore and be reading a magazine at the racks, and I'm trying to quickly flip to critical knowledge not available elsewhere, but I can't quickly flip because my progress is impeded by those subscription postcards that are stuck loose in the pages."

"There's like five in every magazine," said Coleman.

"They all fall to the floor," said Serge. "And now more time is sucked out of my existence having to pick them all up, because my personal contract with society requires me not to leave a trail of subscription cards. By then, I'm steaming under the collar."

"What do you do about it?"

"I start going through all the magazines, even ones I would never read with articles like 'You Ate a Cupcake? Burn It Off with These Sex Tips!' Until I've collected a hundred prepaid cards, and right in the mail they go. Then my inner child is centered again."

Serge grabbed all the newly sealed envelopes and headed to the counter.

"You missed one back there," said Coleman. "The gift baskets."

Serge shook his head. "Vermont is good people. They get a pass . . ."

The next night, Serge stood at the wall of mailboxes. A man ran off with a letter from his mistress. Serge inserted the key.

"Son of a bitch!"

"Junk mail?" said Coleman.

"A double whammy," said Serge. "No novel *and* this garbage. That's a hypergolic combustion of my demons. But I'm taking my game to the next level!" He began tearing open the flaps as before. "It was staring me in the face the whole time. The prepaid envelopes are not weight specific. They're just prepaid, so the senders have to cough up the dough for whatever comes winging back at them."

"What are you putting in the envelopes?"

"Large galvanized washers and flat pieces of scrap metal," said Serge. "They think they're playing with children?"

The next night. A hand turned a key on door number 127.

"Motherfu—!"

"Junk mail again?" said Coleman.

"The gloves are off," said Serge. "Until now I've been playing nice under Queensberry rules, just wasting a little of their time and postage fees. Not anymore."

"What are you putting in the envelopes today?"

"I'm not. I'm taping the postage label to this big box of rocks. Then they'll have to reevaluate their entire belief system."

They came back to the mailboxes night after night. Only more disappointment and cursing. Until . . .

Serge gleefully thrust a package in the air. "I can't believe it finally arrived!" He opened the padded mailer and removed a book with a bright, Day-Glo cover of orange and green. *Tropical Warning*. He flipped it over.

"Hey," said Coleman. "That's a picture of you in a fake beard."

"Let's get moving." Serge stuck the book under his arm. "I can't wait to show this to Kenny. Is he going to be happy! . . ."

. . . Eight hundred miles away, an employee sat perfectly still, staring into a cardboard mailer.

"Rocks?"


Serge was full of vinegar when he practically crashed through the side door of the bungalow. "Kenny! Kenny! You've got to see this!" He sprinted into the living room to find the author as usual in the lounge chair with a rifle. No reaction or movement.

"Check out the cover!" shouted Serge. "You'll be famous again!"

Kenny had the million-mile stare. He slowly lowered his eyes and shortened their focus.

"Pretty snazzy, eh?" said Serge. "And look at the dashingly handsome gent on the back cover!"

Kenny looked. Then with equal slowness, he set the rifle down next to the chair and stood up.

"You're walking!" said Serge. "Good for you! That's a great sign! All it took was seeing your name on a novel again!"

Serge followed the author as he deliberately rounded the corner into the kitchen. "Remember when you didn't want me to do this and went batty? But I said it was for your own well-being?

Aren't you happy now that you listened to me? Well, not really listened because you didn't have a choice—but happy that I forged ahead? Isn't this super! . . . Kenny? Kenny? . . ."

Kenny calmly and quietly got down on his hands and knees. He opened the cabinet doors under the sink, crawled inside and closed them.

"What's he doing?" asked Coleman.

"Probably so happy that he needs privacy in case he becomes emotional . . . Come on, Coleman!" Serge led him outside to the car and opened the trunk. "We need to make the advance preparations. The next big step is Publication Day! All authors love Publication Day. If you think Kenny is emotional now . . ."

# Chapter 36

PUBLICATION DAY

W hen Serge awoke each morning, there was never any middle ground. No period of grogginess or covering his head with a pillow or hitting a snooze button. His eyes opened once, big, full—*Hooray! A new day!*—and his feet were on the ground in full gear.

This particular morning, even more so. *It's Publication Day!* He ran through the house. "Kenny? Kenny, where are you? It's Publication Day!"

He found Coleman sprawled in front of the bookcase. "Get up!"

"Huh?"

Serge jerked him to his feet and grabbed his hands so they could dance in a circle, ring-around-the-rosie. "It's Publication Day! It's Publication Day!"

Coleman: "Wooo."

Serge dropped his friend's hands. He fished an empty toilet-paper tube out of the trash and used it as a small megaphone. "It's

Publication Day! It's Publication Day!" He lowered the tube. "I have to find Kenny! This is all about him!" He sprinted from room to room, closet to closet, until he wound up kneeling in front of the sink cabinets. He opened the doors. "Kenny, there you are!" He leaned closer and put the cardboard tube to his mouth: *"It's Publication Dayyyyyyyyyy!"*

Kenny reached out and closed the doors.

Serge grabbed his keys. "Coleman, we're on the move!"

The Chevy Nova raced south on U.S. 1 as Serge hit the news-stands, collecting local papers from Miami to Palm Beach. He knew from experience as a reader that papers like to time their book reviews with the date of publication.

"Coleman, check it out!" Serge's fingertips became ink-stained as he savagely tore through the pages. "Kenny made most of them! That's an omen."

"Made what?"

"Book reviews! You know, like when a newspaper says a book is 'amazingly horrible,' and the publisher puts out a press release with excerpts: 'The *New York Times* calls it 'amazing.' Except these are all genuinely positive."

Back in the car, racing to a bookstore that wasn't open yet. The employee in charge of unlocking the front doors saw Serge outside bouncing up and down.

A key turned, and Serge flung the door open. *"It's Publication Dayyyyyyyyyyyyyy!"*

The employee was practically trampled. Coleman stumbled in behind.

"Is that a beer?" asked the man with the keys.

"No," said Coleman. *Glug, glug.*

"It's here! It's here!" Serge's excitement echoed through the empty store. "And right on top of the new-release pyramid facing the door." He snatched a copy and caressed the dust jacket. "It's beautiful."

Coleman stuck the empty beer can on top of an autobiography. "I thought you already got a copy."

"It's different in a store."

"Are you buying it?"

"No, let's rock! More stores! . . ."

. . . Serge burst into the bungalow and ran for the living room. "Kenny, it's Publication Day! You should see your book in all the stores! Aren't you excited?"

Kenny sat still in the lounger with his unfocused stare.

"Okay, you've been around this block before, so the excitement is a little diluted. But I'm seriously stoked!" Serge began singing Foreigner. "*Feels like the first time*' . . . I have to start rehearsing my speech for your first book signing tonight. You sure you don't want to come see yourself? . . . All right, there'll be other events." He grabbed pages off a table and ran from the room. "Esteemed customers . . ."

## MEANWHILE . . .

The warehouse was empty, because it was Sunday.

Some people like to go in to the office when no one else is around. Easy to think.

Salenca propped his feet up and opened the pages of *El Nuevo Herald,* the Spanish-language version of the Miami paper. He always started with the comics, then whatever was going on with the Dolphins, in season or out. After that: Surprise me. Today's paper would not disappoint.

He read about unrest in the Middle East, unemployment in the Midwest, and the undead at a zombie convention in Fort Myers. He flipped to the lifestyle section, and found a bright orange-and-green image in the middle of the books page. He read the review. He was about to turn the page when he went back and read it again. Specifically the description of the plot that didn't reveal any spoilers. He set the paper down and stared out the window of his office at an empty floor where people made fake credit cards the rest of the week. He picked up the paper again.

Salenca was confident his hunch was wrong, but also certain he had to check. Back in 1989, he was just a seventeen-year-old kid getting paid more than he dreamed to unload whatever he was instructed to from dark boats on the Miami River. He hadn't personally been involved with what had gone down up at the Port of Palm Beach, but he'd heard the stories. Everyone had.

A manicured hand with a gold watch snatched car keys off the desk, and Salenca drove across town to the nearest chain bookstore. He and his toupee went inside and found the orange-and-green book in the new-release display. He went home and opened the cover. Salenca didn't actually have to *read* the book, just skim the main points of the plot and details at the port. His hunch continued gaining credence until he read enough to seal its certainty. He grabbed his keys again.

A fternoon came in Little Havana. Which meant four old men in straw hats sat around a table in a public park playing dominoes. Salenca arrived and pulled a chair up next to the one with the oxygen tank. He whispered in his ear. The old man turned with a curious look. Salenca just set the book down in front of him. The author's bio said he currently resided in Riviera Beach.

The oxygen man may have been frail, but even after all these years he crisply recalled telling that cop that he would die of old age before he ever forgot. And now, thanks to Salenca, he had beaten the clock. He gave Salenca a slight nod, all that was needed.

Permission.

## THAT EVENING

Serge and Coleman and Chris arrived at the Delray Beach bookstore ahead of time. Early birds were already waiting.

"Can I take a selfie?"

"Sure! Just let me finish my coffee!" *Glug, glug, glug.* He pressed the corner of his beard back in place and smiled.

Twenty more selfies, and then someone with two heavy shopping bags. "I brought all of your old books, several copies. Didn't know how many you would sign, because some of the other authors . . ."

"Are fuck-sticks!" said Serge, helping unload the bags. "I'll sign them all! Obsessive behavior is underrated!"

The next person glanced around. "This is for you." He furtively placed something in Serge's hand.

"What's this?"

"A couple joints, for all the reading pleasure you've given me."

Serge handed them back and pointed. "They go to Coleman."

"Oh, right. I didn't know how it worked."

Someone else: "Everyone says I have a fascinating life story. Will you write it for me?"

"That's an easy one!" said Serge. "No . . . Who's next?"

"I just got out of prison. Your books helped me get through."

"That's fantastic!" said Serge. "Don't do it again."

"I just recovered from a long illness and your books got me through."

"Fantastic! Don't do it again."

The next reader leaned and whispered, "I got a couple joints for you."

Serge pointed at Coleman.

A woman gave Serge a business card. "I'm on a business trip. My hotel and room number are on the back."

"Super!" Serge pocketed the card. "Don't wait up."

The next person had a phone out. "Can you talk to someone for me? He's in prison."

"Definitely!" said Serge. "Hello? How are things in the Gray-Bar Hotel? . . ."

A blond businesswoman came around the counter. "I'm Joanne, the owner. Thanks for putting us on your tour."

"I have to go to the bathroom," said Serge.

"Back there," she said. "Through that door to the storeroom."

Serge trotted off as readers continued filling the store.

Books were rung up at the registers, seats taken.

Serge ran back to the owner. "I hate to tell you this, but people are vandalizing your bathroom."

"What!"

Serge nodded sadly. "There's a bunch of graffiti."

"Oh, that." A light laugh. "Some of our authors write insults to each other."

"The monster of envy is so bad in the publishing world that they deface your store?"

Another laugh. "No, actually it's all in fun. They like each other."

"Really?" Serge clapped. "Can I play?"

"Here's a Magic Marker."

Serge took off.

More patrons entered the store. The cash register spit out receipts.

Back in the bathroom, Serge read the scribbling of some of his favorite writers. He found one in particular and uncapped his marker, leaning against the wall as he wrote:

"*Remember your novel* Twelve Mile Limit? *Should have been* Twelve *Word* Limit."

He returned the marker. Bookshelves had been rolled aside to create the seating area. Serge waited in back as the store owner walked to the front of the room.

"Coleman," said Serge, "this is really exciting! What do you think?"

Coleman patted the new contents of his pants pocket. "I love book signings!"

The owner stood behind the podium and bent the microphone holder closer to her mouth.

"I was going to give a long introduction because there's so much we're all excited about tonight. But you didn't come here to listen to me. So without further delay, the writer who needs no introduction, Kenneth Reese!"

Applause broke out as Serge warmly shook the owner's hand. The clapping finally subsided, and Serge cleared his throat.

"Anyone here watch *Law and Order* or *CSI* or one of the other police shows?"

The majority nodded.

"Ever notice how whenever anyone gets a phone call on those programs, it's exactly on point with whatever they're talking about at the time: 'We'll know a lot more if ballistics gets a match.' A phone rings. 'Hello? . . . Okay, I'll tell them . . .' *Click.* 'Ballistics just got a match.' Or 'This jerk is going to walk on three murders and make fools of the whole department! If only they could link his DNA!' Ring. 'Hello? . . . They linked his DNA.' How often does that happen in real life? For the sake of credibility, I would just once like to see: 'We've got a serial rapist on the loose and the whole city is in lockdown, but we just might have caught a break with a security camera at a tollbooth to the Lincoln Tunnel. Forensics could call us any minute now!' Ring. 'Hello? . . . No, you idiot, this isn't the prop department! You've called the set again while we're filming! Fuck off!'"

A hand in the audience went up.

Serge pointed. "Yes?"

"Is this in your book?"

"No, I just thought about it on the drive over and it started bugging me . . . And another thing! You know how a phrase is repeated so often that it just becomes accepted without question? 'God helps those who help themselves.' And everyone automatically thinks, 'Yeah, sounds good to me.' Phooey! Where is that in the Bible? In fact, it's the opposite of what the Bible teaches. Someone just made that shit up as an excuse to throw unfortunate people under the bus. Show me one gospel where the apostles are walking along the Sea of Galilee. 'Hey, Christ, that old man over there is pinned under a really big rock and could use some help.' 'Don't look at me. He's not even trying' . . ."

Another hand went up.

"Wait, wait, wait," said Serge. "I got another. Tax collectors who add a charge if you pay with your credit card and call it a 'convenience fee.' Yeah, convenient for your lard-ass office to continue munching Kit Kat bars . . . And television commercials that mock the Amish as they never would any other religion, probably because they don't have TVs . . ."

A half hour later. "Check it out! Check it out! I just bought a new and improved one!"

The audience ducked as a drone swooped over their heads.

# Chapter 37

**THE NEXT MORNING**

An hour's drive north of Miami, a black Mercedes took the exit off Interstate 95, followed by several pickup trucks.

Salenca had a private detective look into the matter, but he'd rolled snake eyes the night before. Most investigative success these days comes from computers, but the detective couldn't locate anything. No tax records, nor liens, nor court filings, unlisted numbers, utility hookups. Nothing. Not even old stuff in the Internet databases that went back almost twenty-five years. The investigator had never seen anything like it. The author's bio must be wrong.

Salenca thought otherwise.

Time for old-fashioned field research. The vehicles entered a municipal parking lot, and five men entered the Riviera Beach Public Library.

"May I help you?" asked the research desk.

"Phone books."

All business, no expressions or extra words. The librarian got the same nervous vibe that most did.

"Uh, that way, special collections."

They headed off with the same lack of ceremony, and soon began pulling down thick volumes with tattered paper covers. Salenca stood back and let the others flip pages, jotting down every address for anyone named Reese. All of them thinking: *This is going to take forever.* But they'd heard the rumors about why they were there, and they all knew better than to question.

"How far back do you want us to go?"

The others momentarily froze. *You asked a question.*

Salenca firmed his mouth in irritation. "All the way back till he was born."

More books came down from the shelves, 1977, '76, '75 . . . They gathered around a table and compared addresses. Most were duplications of the same people appearing in multiple phone books years after year. Salenca's senior lieutenant compiled a master list, newest to oldest. Forty-three total.

They hit the streets, knocking on doors. Some opened up. "Are you cops?" Others shouted through closed doors, "We're not buying anything," which bought louder knocking until they opened up. But none had any relatives named Kenneth, at least none who wrote novels or looked remotely like the photo from the book jacket. Salenca and his crew never needed lie detectors. Their direct glares sufficed. These people were genuinely clueless.

They kept going down the list, back in time, until the residents were no longer named Reese. *Knock, knock, knock.* "Kenneth who?" "I don't know anything about the previous owners." "Probably three different families have lived here since then." "You've got the wrong house."

Only three addresses left on the list when they turned onto Thirty-Fourth Street. They rang the bell.

The door opened. An older woman still in bedclothes in the afternoon, smoking a Pall Mall. She was immune to their glares. The TV was up loud on a game show.

"... *Let's play* ... *Family Feud!* ..."

She took a long drag. "What the heck's wrong with you people? Don't you talk to each other?"

"How do you mean?" asked Salenca.

"You're the second guys who've come around looking for this Kenneth whatever."

Salenca and the others exchanged glances.

"... *Name a musical instrument that people try to take on airplanes but is too big for the overhead bins* ..."

"Who exactly came by asking about Kenneth?" said Salenca.

"Abbott and Costello, one tall and thin, the other not."

"What did they say?"

"Are you cops?"

"Detectives," said Salenca.

"... *A tuba* ..."

She shrugged. "The tall one wanted to lie down in a bed, but I told him to get his lazy-bum ass out of here."

Salenca showed her the back of a book. "Have you ever seen anyone who looks like this?"

She put on glasses that were hanging from her neck by a decorative chain. "Maybe, yeah . . ."—tapping the photo with a finger—". . . but he looked younger and didn't have a beard."

That got the whole crew's attention.

"... *A grand piano* ..."

"Where did you see him?"

Another Pall Mall drag. "You're not very good detectives, are you?"

"What do you mean?"

"He was one of the two guys I just told you about. Weren't you listening?"

"... *Those big harps that stand on the floor* ..."

"But ..." Salenca turned the book around and pointed at the author's name. "It's a photo of the writer. Kenneth Reese."

"That doesn't make any sense," said the woman. "The guy in the picture was asking about Kenneth. Why would he be looking for himself?"

Another round of glances.

Salenca abruptly led his group back to the car.

From behind them: "You're welcome, you assholes!"

"... *A Chinese gong* ..."

The door slammed.

The crew huddled by their vehicles and decided to dismiss the woman as a confused old coot.

They drove. Two addresses left. Two more dry holes. Salenca stopped to ponder, and nobody interrupted. He began nodding to himself. "We need to come at this from another direction." He handed the book to his top lieutenant. "Call the publisher. Find out where he is."

"What do I say?"

"Who cares? You're doing a documentary. You need a keynote speaker. Make something up."

He called and made something up.

"I'm sorry, but our policy is not to give out information on our authors," said Kenneth's publicist, typing on her computer as she talked. "But I'd be happy to pass along your information."

"It's actually pretty time-sensitive," said the lieutenant. "We're down here in Palm Beach now—last-second kind of thing. Otherwise, we'll have to cancel. Any way at all to reach him?"

The publicist looked up and smiled as a guy from the mail room dropped the usual pile on her desk. Then into the phone: "Hold on a second." She pulled up a page with Kenneth's contact profile, and virtually everything was in the name of a lawyer. No harm in giving out that info; he was paid to represent Kenneth, after all. And it would get this annoyance off her plate. "You have something to write with? . . ."

The Mercedes drove south into downtown West Palm Beach, and found a modest yellow-brick legal office on Banyan Street next to a bail bondsman.

The lawyer was packing up his briefcase at the end of the day when the bell rang. He'd already let his secretary go home and had to answer it himself. "Can I help you?"

"Hanley Dunn?"

"Yes?"

"We would like to discuss some business," said Salenca.

"I'm actually closing for the day, and I work by appointments," said the lawyer. He stood blocking the partially open doorway in a manner that indicated anything they had to discuss would be from the sidewalk. "But if you leave your card, I'll have my secretary call you tomorrow to set something up."

"It's an emergency." Salenca reached in his pocket. "What's your hourly fee?"

Dunn quickly calibrated upward. "Three hundred."

Salenca peeled off large bills from a wad with a gold-horseshoe money clip. "Here's four hundred." He stuffed the bills in Dunn's shirt pocket. "You're on retainer."

The crew barged past him and marched toward his office.

"Wait." Dunn caught up. "This isn't how I operate."

"Then give me my money back," said Salenca.

Dunn took a pensive breath and found his desk chair. "Okay, let's all sit down and start over."

They chose to stand. "Where's Kenneth Reese?"

"Who?"

"We know you represent him."

"I'm not at liberty—"

"Cancel liberty." Five automatic pistols were suddenly in his face. "Where can we find him?"

Panic, but the kind that brings clarity in some people. "If you kill me, you'll never find out."

"You're right." Salenca turned around so his back was toward the attorney.

The others rushed the desk, seizing him by the arms. They always started by breaking the nose, to set the theme. What followed was rapid and effective.

Salenca didn't need to watch. He knew the lawyer's type—the kind without street experience who fold rather quickly. Salenca listened to the screams and begging until he was sure the jar lid had been sufficiently loosened. He turned back around. "Where's Kenneth?"

The attorney spit out some blood, a tooth, and an address.

"Blanco, stay with him while we check this out."

Serge opened the cabinet doors under the sink. "Kenny, we're leaving now for tonight's book signing. Sure you don't want to come?"

No response.

"Okay, maybe next time." Serge closed the doors.

Salenca's crew bolted from the legal office, leaving just Blanco to watch the attorney. Blanco considered it easy lifting. White-collar types like Dunn were too traumatized to try anything. He took a seat on the far side of the office to create enough separation, just in case the lawyer *did* try something. He picked up a magazine and turned the pages with his pistol held casually in his right hand.

Dunn's mind reeled. He'd always thought Kenny was just eccentric, but now he got it. He watched the gunman guarding him, who wasn't really watching back. Dunn waited to see how attentive Blanco was, except he didn't have time to wait. It wasn't that long of a drive over to Kenny's house. The lawyer jacked forward, pretended to hack up more blood, but it wasn't much of an acting stretch. Blanco smirked and turned a page. Dunn reached into his pocket and pulled a cell phone out under his desk.

He turned the volume off and dialed. And dialed again, over and over, but the screen kept indicating the number was out of service, as if someone had cut the line . . .

. . . The Mercedes screeched up the driveway of a wood-frame house south of Blue Heron. They didn't even mess with the front door because of nosy neighbors. Four ran around the side of the house, leaving one in front, in case Kenny made a break that way.

Kenny had crawled out from under the sink to stretch in his lounge chair, when the stereo blared heavy footsteps. Kenny sprang up. He grabbed the rifle and ran to the windows to peek. Four bad dudes with guns already drawn.

Violent banging on the back door.

Kenny shrieked and flung the gun without realizing it.

The banging stopped. Through the stereo: "It's got a steel plate. Get the battering ram."

That did the trick. The steel plate held, but the doorframe was splinters. The four men fanned out. All rooms and closets checked. The crew regrouped in the kitchen.

"I know he's here!" said Salenca. "I heard a shriek . . ." His eyes slowly lowered. He got down on his knees and opened the cabinet doors under the sink.

A quivering ball.

"Jesus!" said Salenca. "None of you fools looked down here? Get him out!"

They threw Kenny into one of the kitchen chairs, and Kenny threw up.

Salenca got in his face. "Are you Kenneth Reese?"

Urine puddled under the chair.

One of the crew stepped forward. "We'll get him to talk."

Another yanked Kenny to his feet and seized him from behind by the arms.

"Stop!" yelled Salenca. "Let him go!"

"But he hasn't said anything yet."

"And he's not going to!" said their boss. "Just look at him. He's more unnerved than most of the other guys at the *end* of a beating."

"That means he's guilty!"

"No, it means he's acting like half the innocent people in this town would if we knocked down a door and barged in with weapons," said Salenca. "We want the truth, not something he makes up out of fear."

"Then what do we do?"

"It's more than simple," said Salenca. "Just find something in here that says who this guy is."

"Like what?"

"Do I have to do all your thinking for you?" Salenca thrust out an arm. "You're standing right next to the goddamn answering machine, for heaven's sake! Just press the button to play the fucking greeting!"

He did.

*"You've reached Guido Lopez. Please leave a message after the beep."* Beep.

Salenca grabbed a drinking glass off the counter and smashed it against the refrigerator. "That cocksucking attorney! He deliberately gave us the wrong address!"

"I wouldn't be so sure," said one of the crew, sneering and gripping Kenny by the arm. "I think he's trying to trick us!"

"Are you seriously stupid?" asked Salenca. "This poor fool just decides out of the blue to anticipate us showing up here today, and he records a fake greeting?" Salenca charged toward the door. "Let's get out of here before the cops arrive."

The Mercedes raced south toward Banyan Street. Salenca led the way storming back into the law office.

Blanco stood quickly when he heard them, tossing the magazine aside like he wasn't goofing off. "He hasn't moved an inch since you left—"

Salenca ignored him, taking three quick strides toward the front of the desk. Dunn began to open his mouth. Salenca swiftly pulled a nine-millimeter with a silencer.

*Pfft! Pfft! Pfft!*

A tight grouping of three bullets in the middle of the forehead. The wall behind the desk became modern art. The leather chair toppled over backward with only a polished black dress shoe still showing.

# Chapter 38

A folded-over newspaper shook in front of Kenny's face as he lay back in his lounge chair.

"Look!" said Serge, tapping the paper. "You're climbing up the *New York Times* bestseller list. Isn't that great?"

A whimper.

"Okay, you're modest." Serge set the paper aside. "Are you sure you don't want to come to your next book signing tonight? I never realized how busy the publishers schedule you guys."

Another pitiful sound.

"You'll snap out of it. You should see your crowds."

"They give me drugs," said Coleman. "I love books!"

"Serge," said Chris. "Kenny looks worse than usual. He hasn't said a word since we got home last night."

"He'll come around."

"I don't know," said Chris. "Do you think something happened yesterday while we were at the signing?"

"His normal brain patterns have been altered by years in solitary. He just needs some interaction." Serge worked a remote control. *Bzzzzzz.* "Kenny? Want to try shooting down my new drone? But I'll have to warn you, I've been working on evasive maneuvers."

Kenny just stared.

"Okay, not into the drone right now." Serge walked to the front of the room. "How about some TV?" He clicked it on.

"*. . . Police continue to investigate the gruesome, execution-style murder of West Palm Beach lawyer Hanley Dunn . . .*"

Piercing shrieks as Kenny thrashed in his chair.

"I understand," said Serge. "Crime today can be a downer." He changed the channel. "How about *Family Feud*?"

"*. . . Name something you might find under a motel bed . . .*"

"*. . . A body . . .*"

Kenny shrieked.

"*. . . A body is the number one answer! . . .*"

Serge turned the set off. "Maybe peace and quiet is the best thing right now . . ." He faced the others. "Chris, Coleman. Ready to head out?"


## MIAMI

A man in an odd-looking beard smiled.

Just as he had been doing all morning.

The smiling man was in the photo on the back cover of a novel, and the novel sat in Salenca's lap. "I *know* this guy from somewhere."

Tito entered the warehouse office. "Sir, we still haven't been able to find anything."

"Keep looking. And call our private eye back."

"Yes, sir," said Tito. "But word is that this author's a hermit. Nobody's been able to find him for years."

"There's got to be some— . . ." Salenca suddenly hung his head with an angry exhale. "I am such an idiot!" He quickly tapped his computer's keyboard.

"What is it, sir?"

"Right in front of us the whole time!" Salenca pushed his chair back and extended a palm. "Look for yourself."

Tito came around the desk and squinted. "A book tour?"

"I don't read much, so it's not part of my world." Salenca scribbled an address and stood. "But it still should have been obvious."

"What do you want us to do?" asked Tito.

"What else?" Salenca grabbed the pistol out of his desk. "Get autographs."

## BOCA RATON

A lighted marquee outside the library: KENNETH REESE, 7 P.M.

The parking lot was already at overflow, and the pickup trucks had to park in the street. Salenca called a huddle at the curb. "Have any of you been to a book signing before? Does anyone know what goes on at these things?"

A hand went up. "I went to one as a kid, a book about a lonely panda. I got a balloon."

"Okay, shut up. Anyone else?"

Heads looked at each other.

"Then we need to play it careful because of all the civilians," said Salenca. "We watch and observe and nobody does anything during the event, unless he tries to pull something. And then you only do something if I do it first. As soon as this foolishness starts breaking up at the end of the night, we'll pick our move . . ."

A cell phone rang. Tito took the call.

". . . Is everyone clear on their roles? On how delicate this is? There are way too many bystanders."

A round of nodding.

"Good—"

"Sir . . ."

"What is it, Tito?"

"That was our private eye."

"Doesn't matter." Salenca jerked a thumb toward the library. "We've got him in our cross hairs. He can't escape."

"No," Tito replied. "Our detective says it's not him."

"Come again?"

"He did a facial-recognition scan on his computer that he adds to our bill—"

Salenca pounded the hood of the Mercedes. "Dammit, I know what we're paying him! Get it out of your mouth!"

"It's not him."

"You said that." Salenca held up a book. "Of course it's him! Bestseller! Author photo! National book tour! His name's on the cover, for heaven's sake."

Tito shook his head. "The detective kept working on the case like you told him. He compared the photo on the newest cover with the older books, and they don't match."

"Of course they don't match," said Salenca. "He's older and has a beard."

Tito shook his head again. "He said age wouldn't have changed the distance between key points on the face—nose, eyes, ratio of forehead to chin—unless the guy had plastic surgery."

Salenca stared quietly at the ground, then slowly began to nod. "Okay, it's starting to make sense now. I've had this weird feeling that I've seen the guy in the photo before, and I know I've never met this author." He faced the group urgently. "Scrap plan A. No hot-and-heavy response at the end of the night. We don't have any idea what we're dealing with, so until we do, I need to collect intelligence. Put him under surveillance, and he might even lead us back to the real author. He's clearly involved some way, but we can't spook him or he'll have home-field advantage before we even know what game this is . . . Tito?"

"Yes?"

"To avoid attracting attention, the rest of us will wait nearby while you attend the book signing alone. Observe, gather what information you can, and loosely tail him," said Salenca. "Once he's a safe distance away from all these people at the library, give us a call and we'll join the surveillance."

"You got it," said Tito. "One question: What do I do at a book signing?"

"How should I know? I've never been to one. Just do what everyone else is doing."

Tito nodded respectfully and ran across the street.

"The rest of you," said Salenca, "move out. The Waffle House, on me."

The trucks drove away as Tito joined the readers funneling through the doors. He entered the rear of a well-lighted community room. He stopped to watch. People were loading up on punch and cookies from a back table. Tito loaded up. They took seats. Tito sat down.

A bearded man stood at the front of the room, talking with some readers ahead of time. A handful of people seated around Tito got up and headed that direction. Tito followed. They took selfies. Tito got out his own phone.

Serge chatted amiably with the group before excusing himself for the restroom. Several followed Serge, and Tito followed them.

Serge faced a urinal and unzipped his pants. Someone approached the next urinal and unzipped as well. "I can't believe I'm peeing next to you!"

Serge smiled. "I feel the same way."

Someone else walked up behind Serge. "I love your stuff! Hey, dude, if you haven't gotten started yet, can I shake your hand?"

Serge reached back over his shoulder and shook.

The next person. "Can I take a selfie?"

Serge leaned his head back and grinned. *Click.*

"Thanks, man!"

Serge zipped up and went to the sink. Someone else was waiting with a cell phone. "Can you talk to my father? He couldn't make it."

Serge took the phone with dripping hands. "How's it going? . . ."

He left the restroom, and a woman waiting in the hall handed him another phone. "Could you talk to my daughter at college? . . ."

"Study hard and don't do drugs, but it's okay to be curious about the lesbian thing—"

The mother snatched the phone back.

. . . In a nearby Waffle House, the crew dug into omelets, burgers, grilled cheese, BLTs and slices of lemon meringue. A cell phone rang. "Salenca here."

"It's me, Tito. I have someone here to talk to you . . ." A shuffling sound with voices in the background. "Hello? Mr. Salenca? This is Kenneth Reese."

"Uh . . . okay . . ."

"Tito says you like my books. Really appreciate it. I have to go. Here's Tito again . . ."

A fumbling sound. "That was him, Mr. Salenca."

"Tito, what in the fuck are you doing?"

"What you told me to do. Acting like everyone else. Who knew this was going on?"

"Jesus! Get off the phone! No more calls! Just watch and don't talk to him anymore!" Salenca slammed the phone down, sloshing coffee around the table. "Unbelievable! . . ."

. . . Back in the library, Serge chugged coffee as he listened to the introduction from the library director. She handed him the microphone.

"Hello out there! Is everyone ready for a good time?"

"Yeah!"

"Thanks for coming! Just a couple of housekeeping items before we begin. I'll sign as many books as you want, but I'm not writing anyone's life story right now, and any drugs go to

Coleman . . . You know what's bugging me? Quite a few things, actually, like when a company delivers a package that you have to sign for, and you discover a note on your door and now must drive across town to pick it up. Except you were home the whole time! They're ninjas! . . . Or you're checking out at a register, and the clerk puts the bills and receipt in my hand first, and *then* the coins on top of it, and now that ordeal is on me . . . Another thing: A checkout clerk is not the person you're supposed to talk to about your latest flare-up. And if you're a clerk, don't act interested! 'Yeah, it flared up again.' 'Oh, that's terrible. What happened?' 'I spent most of the night in the bathroom but got some knitting done.' At this point I just reach all the way over and start scanning my own items myself, and then they both look at me like *I'm* the problem . . ." He grabbed a thermos. ". . . And these big-box stores that barely have any employees anymore. Try finding one when you need help. Here's my new motto: 'No customer service? No problem!' And then the manager goes to lock up at the end of the day. 'What the heck happened to our sidewalk?' . . . Coleman!"

Coleman wheeled out a large library media cart with a television and video machine. He hit play. A bone-rattling industrial sound filled the room.

*Ching-ching-ching-ching-ching-ching-ching!* . . .

"As you can see . . ." Serge pointed at the screen. "If you're wearing an orange vest and a hard hat, and you have a couple of those wooden barricade things with round amber lights on top, you can use a jackhammer just about anywhere you want without questions . . . Any questions? You, over there."

"Are you going to read something?"

"No! You're going to read the book anyway, so let's not waste time! Ever watch a book event on C-SPAN? Some guy with leather elbow pads on his jacket, reading the biography of a vice president from 1809 who made his mark as a ruthless haberdasher and had his wife committed to the sanatorium for compulsively licking people and then quacking. That's not what you want! We're here to celebrate life! . . . Coleman, the karaoke machine!"

Coleman wheeled away the TV, and wheeled back a rented contraption from the Party Store.

"Who'll break the ice and go first?" asked Serge. He pointed in the back row. "Tito, get up here, you maniac!"

"Me?"

Serge waved frantically.

Tito walked stiffly to the front of the room. "What do I do?"

"Just sing from the prompter. Here's your mike."

Tito cleared his throat. ". . . *Like a virgin . . .*"

Ten volunteers later. ". . . *Everybody was kung fu fighting . . .*"

Serge turned off the machine. "Remember when you were kids? Remember all the great stuff we had to play with? Kaleidoscopes, kites, kazoos?" He reached into a gym bag on the floor next to the podium and began shaking an aerosol can. "Hope nobody just came from the beauty shop."

The talk soon ended, and a long line of people formed with books in their arms and Silly String in their hair.

The library director pulled Serge aside. "Just thought I'd give you a heads-up. You've got admirers. I overheard those two women over there say they were going to try to follow you back to your hotel."

"They're pretty young." Serge grabbed his thermos. "This requires coffee."

Serge was collecting his pens after signing the last book when Chris came up. "Wow . . . a different show every night."

"Listen, you and Coleman go on ahead without me." He clandestinely gestured to the side of the room. "I have to ditch some people."

"Well, look at you. Groupies."

"This shouldn't take long . . ."

Tito was waiting for the crowd to thin so he could begin his tail. Finally, the room was down to the staff, the author, himself and two women whispering and giggling.

Suddenly, Serge ran over to the wall and poked the two women on their arms. "You're it! Can't catch me!"

A piercing alarm sounded as he bolted out the emergency door. The women were right behind. And Tito was behind them . . .

**F**ingers impatiently tapped a table in a Waffle House. Empty plates with syrup and crumpled napkins. A waitress refilled coffee.

The boss checked his watch. The door to the restaurant opened.

"There you are! Where have you been?" He paused to look Tito over. "What's in your hair?"

"Silly String."

"How did you get all scraped up?"

"Running through the woods with two women."

"What for?"

"It was a book signing." Tito set a novel on the table. "I got you an autographed copy."

"Didn't you tail him?"

"Yes."

"And? Where did he go?"

"I lost him in the woods."

"Why didn't you call me?"

"You told me not to call anymore after I let you talk to him. Remember?"

Salenca rubbed his forehead hard. "So what took you so long to get back?"

"After the women and I lost him, *we* were lost. But one of the women was smart and could use the position of the moon."

Salenca calmly took off his glasses and squeezed drops in his eyes. "Anything else I should know that goes on at these book signings?"

"They also made me get up in front of everyone and sing," said Tito. "I didn't do well with Madonna, though I improved with the next song where this guy has never been to Spain, but he kind of likes the music."

"Stop! I don't need to hear any more. I don't *want* to." He turned toward the toughest case at the table. Prison stretches for aggravated assault and attempted murder. "Lars, you're up. Next book signing tomorrow night. Think you can handle it? No phone calls, no signing, no losing him in the woods."

"No problem."

# Chapter 39

## LARS

A group of intimidating men sipped Chardonnay at a sidewalk bistro as the sun went down.

Salenca checked his watch. "Lars, you're on."

Broad shoulders silently rose from the table.

A few blocks away, Serge and friends entered the library. He went to the bathroom, followed by readers.

More patrons arrived, including a pair of broad shoulders that filled the doorframe. Punch and cookies were especially big tonight. Lars remained in his chair like stone.

Another introduction and round of applause. Serge placed a coffee thermos on the podium and yanked the microphone out of its stand.

"*Helllllllllo,* Palm Beach Gardens! Everyone wants me to read from my book even though I hate to, so let's get that out of the way. 'Chapter One. My day had been exceedingly normal—which extended the streak to 9,632 normal days in a row—when the shotgun blast sent my life in an entirely new direction . . .'"

... Three minutes later: "*Blah, blah, blah* ... Hey, did anyone hear about the zombie stampede in Fort Myers? Totally true, look it up! They had a zombie convention at the popular tourist area by the yacht club. Everyone was in costume, and some guy got in a fight and started shooting a gun. Naturally all the zombies began screaming and running for their lives. But it gets better! All these other regular tourists with no awareness of the convention were out strolling the sidewalk cafés and galleries and martini bars, and suddenly they see all these zombies completely out of their minds, yelling and sprinting full speed toward them, so the tourists start screaming and running from the zombies! ... Coleman!"

Coleman wheeled out a TV and began replaying a newscast of the chase along the waterfront. A Latin hunk named Johnny Vegas ran past one of the news cameras. *"Baby, come back. It's just a few zombies ..."*

Coleman turned the set off as Serge wiped tears. "Sorry, I shouldn't be laughing. A few quick points: I just found out that the skinny-dipping chick who gets eaten at the beginning of *Jaws* was a Weeki Wachee mermaid. Children laugh an average of seventy-five times a day, but adults only twelve. A common critical error is an uneven distribution of salad dressing. Next item of business: the book tour. Everyone thinks it's all sex, drugs and rock and roll. But you know what authors really do back in their motel rooms? We hack the air-conditioning. Get out your pens and write down this procedure because it could come in handy with a certain maintenance fringe element ..."

The evening wore on more or less as usual.

"Coleman, the karaoke machine! ... I'll get us started." Serge jumped and flapped with the microphone. "... *Superfreak! Superfreak! She's super freaky! ...*"

... Coleman rolled the machine away.

"The drone! ..." *Bzzzzz.*

"Silly String! ..." *Pssssst.*

"Everyone up!" said Serge. "Jumping jacks . . . One, two, three, four . . ."

They all joined in with perplexed amusement. Except one hulking figure who remained grim in the back row. He caught Serge's eye.

The evening eventually wound down as Serge scrawled Kenny's name and handed novels back. "Thanks for reading my books!"

Coleman stuffed his pockets. "Thanks for the joints!"

The audience dissipated as Serge snuck a glance toward the back of the room. "Uh, Chris, Coleman, why don't you two head on back without me and we'll meet up at the bungalow."

"Groupies again?" asked Chris.

"Yes," said Serge. "That's exactly what it is."

The last customer waved good-bye, and Serge thanked the library director. "Listen, do you think I could slip out the back? I noticed a door to the alley next to the bathroom."

"Enthusiastic fan?"

"Occupational hazard."

"Be my guest. Go through the staff room and out to the alley by the loading dock."

Serge departed, and Lars followed.

"Hey," yelled the director. "What are you doing? You can't go back there!"

Serge pushed the steel door open into the darkness of Dumpsters and skinny cats. He waited leaning against a tree, hands casually behind him.

Lars stepped out into the alley and looked both ways.

"Over here," said Serge.

"What?"

"You wanted to see me?"

"No, I was just out for some fresh air." Lars feigned nonchalance as he lit a cigarette. "Pleasant evening."

"Until now," said Serge. "What do you want with Kenneth Reese?"

"What do you mean? *You're* Kenneth Reese."

"We both know the truth about that," said Serge. "Or you would have come in bigger force. You want to find out what my connection is, or maybe hope to follow me and I'll lead you to Kenny."

"I don't have any idea what you're talking about." Lars took a drag, hoping to draw Serge's attention away from his other hand reaching for the bulge under his coat. "But I guess writers have great imaginations."

Serge began to nod wistfully. "I guess you're right. My mind's running away with me. You wouldn't believe some of the people I get at these things."

"I can guess."

"Could you spare a light?" asked Serge.

"Sure." He stopped reaching for his pistol and began fishing through a pocket inside his jacket. "There you go . . ."

"Thanks." Serge flicked it.

"Where's your cigarette?"

"Oh, I don't smoke."

"Then why do you need a lighter?"

"For this . . ."

Serge pulled out a can of Silly String and began spraying the bulky man up and down his shirt.

Lars was more confused than anything else, holding his arms out and staring down at the insult on his chest. "What the hell—"

Serge moved the lighter's flame in front of the can, and the stream ignited. A Silly String rope of fire raced to Lars's torso, and all the previously sprayed string that had stuck to the shirt now went ablaze like ribbons of napalm.

"*Aaaahhhh! Aaaahhhh!*" Swatting himself. "*Aaaahhhh! . . .*" Eyes crazed in shock: "*Mmmm!*"

"Oops, you moved and opened your mouth," said Serge. "Sorry, I got some in there."

In alarm, Lars inhaled the flame. Ask any doctor: It's never good. The yelling stopped. The outcome had been determined. All over but the shouting. Lars thrashed against the building and Dumpsters like a pinball, self-inflicted contusions and scrapes. He hit his neck on the sharp metal corner of the trash bin, cutting his jugular. He fell to his knees, spurting, then flat on the ground for the death rattle.

Serge stood over the smoldering body. "Damn, that was faster than I thought." He glanced around. "I need to get him out of sight and buy some time. But where?"

A waiter in a white uniform held a small faux-leather binder to his chest. It contained the bill. This was always awkward because his tip was at stake.

"I'm sorry, but we closed twenty minutes ago."

Salenca checked his watch. "Lars is even worse than Tito."

The waiter would not worry long about the gratuity as several hundred-dollar bills were dealt onto the table.

"Let's find out what happened to that stooge."

Several hours later, they regrouped in front of the darkened, closed library. *"We looked all over the place." "He's not answering his phone." "It's like he just vanished."*

"He has to be somewhere!" said Salenca. "Let's think!"

They made painful faces in case Salenca didn't think they were thinking.

A thud as someone crashed to the ground.

"Tito!" yelled Salenca. "Are you drunk?"

"I just had a couple glasses of wine. Something made me slip."

"You're bleeding."

"I am?" He got up, checking himself for wounds. "I don't see any cuts."

Salenca looked at the sidewalk. "There's way too much blood for that to have come from your fall . . . What on earth happened here?" He surveyed the black-red slick, eyes moving toward the source and a steady drip, drip, drip. His gaze rose up to a square metal case bolted to the sidewalk.

"Get a crowbar!"

The crew quickly popped open the book-deposit box and looked inside.

"That settles the mystery."

# Chapter 40

## THE LAST BOOK SIGNING

Just after dark, Serge slipped into one of his trademark tropical shirts.

"Hey, guys, why don't you all sit this one out tonight."

"What for?" said Chris.

"I want joints," said Coleman.

Serge shrugged. "If you've seen one book signing, you've seen them all. You must be getting bored by now."

"Are you kidding?" said Chris. "Every single one's an absolute hoot."

"How about this?" said Serge. "Just as a favor to me, can you stay home tonight? I promise I'll be right back afterward, and we'll all go out to a fancy dinner."

"Did something happen last night?" asked Chris.

"Why do you say that?"

"You took a lot more time ditching the groupies. And you seemed different when you got back, preoccupied."

"It's all good," said Serge. "Just do me this one favor and stay put."

Reluctantly: "If you insist."

"I do, and thanks."

They watched out the front door as Serge climbed into the Nova and sped away.

Chris spun around. "Where are my keys?"

"Why?" asked Coleman.

She snatched them off the kitchen table. "This is way too interesting. Now I *have* to go. Coming with me?"

"Joints!"

The pair ran outside and drove off.

The Miami warehouse was closed. A solemn line of men in the office. Salenca sat at his desk checking his pistol's magazine. "No more fucking around! No incremental half measures!"

"So we're going to another book signing?" asked Tito.

"Yes, except there isn't going to be a book signing."

"I don't understand."

Salenca stood. "To hell with the civilians. We're taking him at the beginning. The audience will be too shitless to come forward as witnesses. Pack!"

The crew filled duffel bags with ammo, clips, exotic pistols and sawed-offs. *Zip, zip, zip.* They hit the road . . .

. . . A half hour before the event, Serge made small talk with the library staff. He looked up at the door. "Oh my God!"

"Thought we'd surprise you," said Chris.

"Yo!" said Coleman.

"What are you doing here?" Serge grabbed Chris by the arms and glanced around. "I told you to stay put!"

"Wow! You're really weirding me out," said Chris. "So you're going to tell me right now exactly what's going on."

Serge's frustrated head rolled around on his neck. "Okay, okay. Kenny wasn't being paranoid. He really is in danger. All of us are." And he proceeded to give her the Twitter version of the Port of Palm Beach. "We have to get you out of here immediately."

"Now you're being as paranoid as Kenny," said Chris. "There's no way . . ."

Serge's eyes popped as he saw the door again. "Don't turn around. They're here."

"Who's here?" She turned around. "Who are all those guys?"

"I asked you not to do that. Run!"

They took off through a door at the back of the conference room, and Serge jammed a chair under the knob. Which bought them all of ten seconds as Salenca's men crashed through. But it was enough to reach their Nova parked behind the building, and the pursuing gang had to run around the front of the library to pile in the Mercedes.

Chris faced out the rear window. "Did I really hear gunshots when we were pulling away?"

"Afraid so."

"Here they come," said Coleman.

Serge checked the rearview as a Mercedes wove in and out of traffic.

"I don't get it," said Chris. "If you knew they were going to be at the library, then why did you go?"

"To draw them into the open." Serge hit the gas. "I didn't know who they were or where they hang. I had to find out to protect Kenny."

"You were just going to take out all those guys by yourself?"

Serge checked his mirrors again. "When this is all over, there are a few things I'll need to tell you about myself."

"I don't recognize this route," said Chris. "Where are you going?"

"Home-field advantage." The Nova whipped around a city bus. "You'll understand when we get there . . ."

. . . In the Mercedes, Salenca was up in the front passenger seat, staring at the back of a novel. "It's still bugging me but I can't— . . . Wait!" Fingers snapped. "From that motel! He was the guy fixing the air-conditioning when we went to that room. He killed Diego in the Everglades . . . But if the facial recognition didn't match, then who is the real author— . . . Quick, give me your phone!"

Someone in the backseat passed one forward, and Salenca rapidly surfed the Internet until the screen stopped on an old author photo from one of Kenny's first books. Salenca slapped himself in the head. "We had him all along!"

"Who?" asked the driver.

"The guy in the bungalow! I was comparing his face to the photo on the newest book," said the boss. "I didn't yet know they were two different guys . . . Turn here . . ."

. . . Chris trembled as she faced backward in her seat. "They're veering off. They're letting us go. Why would they do that?"

"Which way did they turn?"

"South on Prosperity Farms."

"Shit, they figured it out."

"Figured what out?"

"They're going for Kenny." Serge made a skidding right through a yellow light. "I know a shortcut. Hold on!"

The Nova zigged and zagged south through the county, passing city-limit signs of towns that were quite wide, but not very tall on the map. PALM BEACH GARDENS, NORTH PALM BEACH, LAKE PARK, RIVIERA BEACH.

Serge skidded left onto Blue Heron. "This is gonna be a close one. No time to explain to Kenny in his state. Just snatch him . . . Coleman, stay here or you'll slow us down."

"Right-o."

The Nova hopped the curb and tore up the lawn before parking diagonally in the middle of the front yard. Serge and Chris were a crack team. Kenny's feet barely touched the ground as they whisked him out the front door, leaving it open behind them. The Nova peeled away.

"So far, so good," said Serge.

Chris turned around. "Not so fast."

The Mercedes hopped the curb and landed roughly in the same spot as the Nova had. Someone in the car pointed at the house. "The door's open!" Another pointed up the street. "They're getting away!"

More sod flew as the Benz spun out backward and resumed pursuit.

"Where can they be going?" asked Tito.

"Just stay close!" said Salenca.

The chase was long and slow on the narrow, heavily trafficked coastal route of Alternate A1A, a veritable tour of the upper Gold Coast. Northlake Boulevard, RCA Boulevard, PGA Boulevard, Donald Ross Road, Indiantown Road, Frenchman's Creek, Admiral's Cove, Turtle Creek, Juno Beach, Jupiter, Tequesta.

"We're heading toward Hobe Sound. That's the dunes," said Chris. "I know where you're going now. But the gate's locked at this hour."

"I know another way," said Serge. "It'll be easy. We just need a navy."

"Oh, easy-peasy," said Chris.

"There's the lighthouse." Serge executed another hard turn and bounded down a road near the inlet, then left the road, crashing through landscape to park as close as possible to the private pier. He grabbed a gym bag. "Everyone out!"

They seized the catatonic Kenny again, this time his heels skipping across the boards of the dock. The dock's owner had two boats to steal, but it was a simple choice. Kenny was tossed into a center-console fishing skiff that was overpowered with a Mercury 350.

The homeowner blasted out the back door of his estate with a drink in his hand. "You ripped up my property! And what are you doing in my boat?"

Serge undid the mooring line and raised his shirt to show the butt of a gun. "It's an emergency."

"Bon voyage." The homeowner sipped his Bombay gin.

Serge tossed his gym bag in the boat and took off. The skiff raced inland, under the tall bridge at Old Dixie, then the exceedingly low railroad bridge alongside, disappearing around a bend and speeding past a line of private docks at a planned golf community.

Back at the inlet, the property owner didn't even speak as openly armed men poured out of the Mercedes, taking his bigger boat, the twenty-nine-foot Chris-Craft Catalina. One of the gang was left behind to watch the Benz and keep the owner on ice, away from the cops.

Twin Yamahas roared to life. The bow rider left a massive wake as it plowed west up the famous river.

# Chapter 41

## THE LOXAHATCHEE

An osprey with a majestic wingspan circled high overhead under the full moon. Snook and redfish fed along the reeds. A raccoon rummaged through snarls of brush. The waterway got its name from the Seminole tongue, "River of Turtles."

A flat-bottom fishing skiff raced by in a graceful banking turn, steered by someone who knew these waters by heart. Minutes later, a V-hull crashed through the shallows, steered by someone who didn't.

The wind whipped Chris's hair in her face as she looked back. Salenca's more powerful boat made its appearance at the last bend. "They're following us. They stole a boat, too."

"I expected that," said Serge, steering gently to port.

A couple more bends and they left civilization behind, crossing the county line and entering the brackish water in Jonathan Dickinson State Park.

"They're gaining," said Chris. "Why didn't we take the faster boat?"

"Everything's fine." The skiff tilted the other way. "It's all part of the plan."

"There's a plan?" She glanced back again. "They're even closer!" *Bang, bang, bang.* "And they're shooting!"

"Everyone get down," said Serge, remaining upright. He locked in on the river like a downhill skier. Hard to port, hard to starboard. He glanced at the watermarks on the spidery mangrove roots to gauge the falling tide. More gunfire. Another hard turn.

The moon may have been full, but it was less than needed to navigate this river at speed. For the ordinary boater, that is. As the snaking tributary wound inland, its bends came faster, sharper and narrower. Either boat could easily run aground or worse, end up jammed nose-high in the mangroves. A bullet grazed the side of the steering console. Chris, Coleman and Kenny huddled together near the bilge. The chase boat was so close now they could hear the shouts.

As adrenaline spiked, Serge's dim night view of the river began to strobe with bright flashbacks. Daytime memories as a child in a little yellow baseball cap, paddling around the same turns. Another bullet pinged off the engine and punctured a bait well. The next shot hit the stern at waterline.

Serge spotted a jutting outcrop of slash pines, then a bright flash in his brain stem from the eyes of a small boy, jamming a paddle into the water to push off from an unexpected shoal. Serge cut the wheel for the most jarring port turn yet, needing to stay on the far left of the river and avoid the wide, unseen shallows extending from the right bank.

Salenca's boat stayed center, and the men were thrown against each other. The boat shuddered and chugged through the sand. Salenca threw the throttle all the way forward, the propeller tearing up the bottom, until he finally pulled free like a slingshot. But they'd lost sight of Serge.

Chris sat up and looked back. "Are they gone?"

"Not for long."

"But you lost them." The rumble of the engine suddenly dropped in pitch and volume. "Why are you slowing down?"

"Have to," said Serge. Overhanging vegetation closed in on both sides of the boat. "Drafting's touchy from here on."

Two consecutive hairpin bends in the river.

"Now you're stopping and coasting."

Serge pointed ahead at the dark forms of water plants and a grassy flat in the middle of the river. "It's unnavigable beyond there."

"You deliberately took us up a dead end?"

"I took *them* up a dead end."

The skiff drifted toward the left bank as Chris strained to see. "Is that some kind of falling-down dock?"

"Trapper's old place."

"You mean the myth I heard about as a kid?"

"Everyone ashore." Serge helped her by the hand. "We don't have much time."

"But why'd you bring us here?"

"Home-field advantage."

A V-hull slowly idled through the branches. A search beam swept the water.

"Why are we stopping?"

"We didn't stop," said Salenca. "It's too shallow. We just hit bottom." The searchlight found something in the distance. "There's their boat!"

"But we're stuck. What do we do?"

"It's also shallow enough to walk," said Salenca. "Afraid of a little water?"

They all hopped over the side with a series of splashes. Single file, trudging through the muck toward a decrepit landing.

"*Aaaahhhh!*" Tito screamed from the back of the line.

They spun around. "Where'd he go?"

Tito's face popped out of the water for another scream. Then he was pulled away and under.

"What happened to Tito?"

"Alligator," said Salenca. "Can't help that now. Keep moving."

The rest of them took off in a motivated dash through the river until they made it up the bank at Trapper's . . .

. . . Chris raised her head. "I just heard something."

"They're coming," said Serge. "You're all concealed in the woods behind the old animal cages, the best hiding spot on the whole property. Just remain still and quiet until I come back. Take this."

"I can't take your gun."

"Sure you can," said Serge. "I have a spare."

"No, I mean I could never shoot anyone."

Serge wrapped her fingers around the pistol's grip. "From my experience, if you have to, you will. Now, whatever else happens, do not leave this spot."

"Wait," said Chris.

But Serge was gone.

Salenca led the remnants of his crew into the murky compound of primitive shelters and wildlife pens, crisscrossed with trapping trails through the hostile Florida brush.

He stopped in a clearing and faced a pair of his men. *We're really down to three?* He did the math. They'd started with five, but left one back to watch the Mercedes, and then Tito. Salenca was getting seriously pissed off. "Victor! Pablo! Spread out! Kill them all!"

They crept in various directions with guns drawn, jumping at every noise—insects, frogs, owls. Serge sprinted silently at his fleet-footed best up one of the trails, barely making a sound. "If I remember Trapper correctly . . ." He stood at the edge of another clearing and threw a rock. Vague movement. "There they are."

Serge retraced his path fifty yards and stopped. There were only so many trails for them to check. He waited patiently. Soon, clumsy footsteps and a shadow. Serge picked up a thick twig and snapped it.

"*What was that?*"

Serge watched the shadow walk off in the wrong direction.

"You've got to be kidding me." He snapped another twig.

The shadow came back and veered off another errant way.

"It can't be this difficult," Serge said to himself, cupping hands around his mouth. "Hey! Over here!"

He took off sprinting down the trail, bullets hitting trees on both sides. *Good,* Serge thought, *he's shooting. That'll do the trick.*

It did. Everyone and everything at Trapper's perked up at the sound of the gunfire.

Serge reached the edge of the previous clearing and shinnied up the nearest tree.

Victor stopped and stared ahead at something coming toward him. "What the hell is that?"

"Wild boar," Serge yelled down from the tree. "Four hundred pounds and charging. Might want to avoid those tusks."

"*Aaaahhhh!*"

"Nobody listens to me." Serge dropped back down to the ground and vanished . . .

. . . Salenca and Pablo converged from different directions. "The gunshots came from over here!" *Thud.* "What the—"

Pablo looked down. "You tripped over Victor?"

Salenca pushed himself up from the ground. "I'm really getting mad at this guy! Go! . . ."

. . . Serge was on his belly, alone with more flashbacks. *Trapper: "It's all about scent."* He was on another trail, but not human, much smaller. That's why he had to crawl, just like he had as a child on the rabbit trail. He easily could have trapped a rabbit for bait using a vine snare, but that would be time-consuming and cruel. He continued slithering until he found a pile of scat. A sneaker came off a foot and was smeared with the scent. Then he tied a vine to one of the laces and tossed it down the trail. He waited a short while before tugging it to simulate a small mammal in distress. He waited. Voices and footsteps coming within yards and passing. It took a half hour, but it worked. Serge scrambled on hands and knees and rescued the sneaker, grabbing his prey by the throat. "Got you! . . ."

. . . Pablo crept forward in the blind. One silent step at a time. "Where can he be—"

Serge pounced from the brush behind him, wrapping the four-foot python around Pablo's neck before disappearing again.

Pablo quickly learned that once a constrictor snake is coiled around the airway, a human isn't strong enough for the task. He couldn't breathe, couldn't speak, could barely stagger. But he still had his gun.

He began shooting the snake, which released him and slunk away with flesh wounds.

Pablo stood still a moment, comprehending the folly of shooting multiple times into anything that's around your neck. He toppled over.

Serge circled back toward the river landing. Only one adversary left. Serge decided to hunker down where he could keep the animal pens—and his friends' hiding spot—under watch. Just in case. He picked up a vine and fashioned a larger-than-usual loop, then a slipknot . . . when he felt cold metal against the back of his head.

"Don't move or you're dead!" said Salenca. "Now stand up!"

"Which is it?" asked Serge. "Don't move or stand up?"

"I've grown tired of you! On your feet!" Salenca marched him into open ground by the main cabin. "You'd already be dead if I didn't also want to kill your friends. Now call them!"

"They're all gone."

"I understand. Loyalty." He paraded Serge at gunpoint along the front of the animal cages. "Then I'll call them! *Come out, come out wherever you are, or I'll blow your friend's head off!*"

"Okay, don't shoot, don't shoot!"

Coleman crawled from behind the last pen.

Salenca motioned him over with the gun. "Where's the girl?"

"Coming out! Don't shoot!" Hands raised.

"That's more like it," said Salenca, untensing with the chaos brought to order. "Now, finally, where's that author? Probably curled up in a sniveling ball back there. Pretty please, where are you?"

"Right here." A gun to the back of Salenca's head. "Drop it."

Serge stood inches from Kenny's ear. "Don't do it. Listen to me. You'll regret this forever."

"I don't care anymore." The gun barrel pushed Salenca's head forward, and Kenny's finger was halfway through the trigger's pull. "This whole trip up the river, lying back there by the pens. All I could think of was Darby. More and more. It started coming back." Tears rolled down cheeks. "I owe it to him to stop cowering and wimping out. He gave me the strength."

"What a time to snap out of it," said Serge.

"And now this fucker's going to pay!" Squeezing . . .

"Don't move! Don't flinch!" said Serge. "Just give me a second. This isn't you. And this isn't a bell you can un-ring . . . Hand me the gun and go back to the boat with the others. I give you my word I'll do right by Darby."

Kenny shook his head. "*I* need to kill him. This ends here!"

"Okay, then forget it's my voice you're hearing," Serge whispered. "What would Darby tell you right now? You claim you're doing this for him? What you really owe him is to listen to what he'd say, and in your heart you know what that is."

It was a minute that lasted a year.

A finger began to relax.

"That's better," said Serge, gently taking the pistol.

Kenny hung his head. "I failed him."

"Just the opposite." Serge stuck the gun in Salenca's back. "You've done him proud."

Chris took Kenny's arm. "Come on . . ."

The others went back to the boat.

**A** strap tightened around a wrist.

Serge was singing. "*. . . Alone again, naturally . . .*"

"*Mmmmm! Mmmmm!*"

"What is it, Lassie? You want to sing, too, but the duct tape won't let you?"

"*Mmmmm! Mmmmm!*"

Serge finished with the last ankle strap, leaving Salenca suspended upright in an X shape. "I might as well just tell you. This handmade wooden rack is where Trapper used to stretch out his animal pelts while preparing them for sale."

"*Mmmmmmmmmmmmm!*"

"I'm not going to stretch you out or skin you alive, so don't get a bowel syndrome . . . Okay, too late. Anyway . . ." Serge reached down into his gym bag, pulling out a half-dozen stuffed sweat socks that he tied to various parts of Salenca's body.

"You know how you can always learn something from even the most unlikely person? Coleman taught me about catnip. I did further research and learned that house cats aren't the only ones who go bonkers over this stuff. Because of genetics, a lot of the bigger felines are crazy about it, too. And something else: Catnip has the same effect on felines as pot does on Coleman. After they're done wigging out, they're really hungry." He patted Salenca on top of the head. "Have to get going now. But I wouldn't worry, there are no lions or tigers in these parts."

Salenca's head snapped toward the sound of growling in the dark brush. Then it snapped the other way at another growl.

"I'm guessing you're curious what made that noise." Serge pointed. "Can you read the sign that Trapper painted on that last animal pen?"

Salenca's eyes strained in the moonlight.

BOBCATS.

# *Epilogue*

The fishing skiff made its way back down the Loxahatchee to the inlet by the Jupiter lighthouse, where the river dumped into the Atlantic.

A nosy neighbor had called in the tip, and police lights flashed onshore by the docks where they had stolen the boat. The last member of Salenca's crew was arrested and vehicles impounded, including a seafoam-green Chevy Nova.

Flat-bottom skiffs weren't meant for the ocean, but it was calm enough for Serge to navigate down the coast a few miles. Then it wasn't calm, and a wicked chop caused the boat to take on water. Serge was able to fight the waves and make landfall on the beach where the *Amaryllis* had grounded during Hurricane Betsy.

They walked to the Ocean Mall and caught a cab back to the bungalow. Serge told the driver to leave the meter running.

"Listen, Chris, for reasons that have now become all too obvious . . ."

"I get it." She gave him an extended, tearful hug. Then, "Wait here. I need to give you something . . ."

Moments later, the cab drove away, and Serge and Coleman and a plaid shirt disappeared into the night.

Thanks to an anonymous satchel of bearer bonds left at city hall, Darby Pope became the largest single benefactor in the history of Riviera Beach.

According to the simple instructions, massive donations were made in his name to school improvements, college scholarships, health care, the police department's benevolent fund, and a public park with a bronze surfing sculpture of uncanny resemblance.

When the "Pope Endowment" was initially announced, everyone said they knew him.

A maintenance man entered the office at the Deep-Discount Motel. "You wanted to see me?"

"You set all the air conditioners to sixty and burned out the compressors!" said the owner. "You're fired!"

Two men in dark suits entered a Fort Lauderdale bookstore and approached the author's table.

"You have a couple more customers," said the writer's assistant named Chris.

Kenny looked up and smiled. "Would you like me to sign something?"

Badges flashed. "We'd like to talk to you about your book."

*Oh no.* After all these years, just when Kenny thought he was in the clear and breathing easy. He tried to maintain his smile at the agents, but the trembling had already begun. He decided that this was no way to continue living. Might as well come clean.

"What do you want to know about the port?"

"What port?" asked the first agent.

Kenny glanced at the stack of hardcovers on his table. "The port in those books."

"Not that book," said the second agent. "Your next one."

"But . . . it's not out yet."

"You posted a blog about it on your website," said the first agent. "What can you tell us about this character of yours named Serge?"


A royal-blue '78 Ford Cobra sat parked outside the Contemporary Hotel at Walt Disney World.

Up in room 317, Serge stomped his feet in a tantrum. "But it's no fun doing it alone!"

Coleman lay in bed on the verge of consciousness, sipping a bottle of Mad Dog. "Give me a few more minutes."

"You said that hours ago!" Serge frantically pointed out the window. "Space Mountain is right there!"

"Let's just visit a little longer."

# ABOUT THE AUTHOR

Tim Dorsey was a reporter and editor for the *Tampa Tribune* from 1987 to 1999, and is the author of twenty other novels: *Clownfish Blues, Coconut Cowboy, Shark Skin Suite, Tiger Shrimp Tango, The Riptide Ultra-Glide, Pineapple Grenade, When Elves Attack, Electric Barracuda, Gator A-Go-Go, Nuclear Jellyfish, Atomic Lobster, Hurricane Punch, The Big Bamboo, Torpedo Juice, Cadillac Beach, The Stingray Shuffle, Triggerfish Twist, Orange Crush, Hammerhead Ranch Motel,* and *Florida Roadkill.* He lives in Tampa, Florida.